OVER
THEY CO ... **F**
LAB

Grady grabbed ... hone. "Palmer, I want you to report! What's going on up there? Over."

"Weird ... really weird ..."

"*What's* weird? Report, Palmer! What is happening?"

"Report ... re ... ort ... -e-ort ..."

"What the hell's the matter with him?"

"I—I don't know, sir, but he's playing with his radio," Berry said, pointing toward the console. "Look at how his broadcast light is flashing on and off."

"... -ey're dead ... all ... -ead. Ever- ... ody ..."

"Repeat that, Palmer. You're breaking up. Please repeat. Did you say that all the survivors are now dead? Over."

This time there was no answer from the summit except for the distant howl of the wind.

KOTA

By the same author:

Bishop's Landing
Fangs

RICHARD FORSYTHE

KOTA

W🌐RLDWIDE.

TORONTO • NEW YORK • LONDON • PARIS
AMSTERDAM • STOCKHOLM • HAMBURG
ATHENS • MILAN • TOKYO • SYDNEY

KOTA

A Worldwide Library Book/April 1988

ISBN 0-373-97065-X

Copyright © 1988 by Richard Forsythe. All rights reserved.
Philippine copyright 1988. Australian copyright 1988.
Except for use in any review, the reproduction or utilization of
this work in whole or in part in any form by any electronic,
mechanical or other means, now known or hereafter invented,
including xerography, photocopying and recording, or in any
information storage or retrieval system, is forbidden without
the permission of the publisher, Worldwide Library,
225 Duncan Mill Road, Don Mills, Ontario, Canada M3B 3K9.

All the characters in this book have no existence outside the
imagination of the author and have no relation whatsoever to
anyone bearing the same name or names. They are not even
distantly inspired by any individual known or unknown to the
author, and all incidents are pure invention.

® are Trademarks registered in the United States Patent and
Trademark Office and in other countries.

Printed in U.S.A.

For Connie Bump Pruitt, and my dad, Gene Forsythe. They would have liked it.

I've always believed in giving credit where it is due, so please bear with me as I offer it to those who helped me with this story:

Mr. Robert W. Smith of Florissant, Missouri, who is a fine writer himself and whose knowledge of aircraft and aviation helped both the C-181 Transport and XM-221 helicopter to fly;

Mr. Thomas Knight of Webster Groves, Missouri, an experienced climber whose knowledge and practical suggestions about rock and alpine climbing provided many of the technical climbing details.

Any errors about either of the above subjects are mine alone.

And once again, my thanks and love to Peggy. Her contributions to my work are invaluable; her contributions to my life, priceless.

Kota is a work of fiction, and to construe it as anything else would be a mistake. The only factual things in the story are certain towns, cities, states and a few military installations, all of which are easily recognizable. I should mention, however, that Fort Endicott, Fort Stanton, the Blackstone Arsenal and Wheeler Barracks do not exist. The 332nd Airlift Wing, the 191st Light Infantry Brigade, the 2nd Search and Rescue Battalion, and the 5th Army Central Intelligence Division are all fictitious, as well. There is, of course, a 5th U.S. Army, and the Army itself maintains a Criminal Investigation Division. But this division and its officers, agents and operatives should in no way be mistaken for the organization, characters, and events invented for this novel. All names, characters and events are used fictitiously, and any resemblance to actual people—living or dead—events or locales is entirely coincidental and unintended.

RF
Staunton, Illinois
September, 1985

PART ONE

★

Flight J-440

"I still don't know how it happened. All of a
sudden the whole ridge collapsed under us. We were
lucky not to fall with it."

"They were a hundred feet ahead of us, in good
shape. The next minute, they were gone. They'd
just disappeared ... vanished...."

"Maybe the rope broke. Maybe he slipped. I
don't know. I heard him yelling something, and then
he fell ... flying down right past me. He was
screaming...."

—Assorted comments from
some of those who tried it

Everything put together falls apart sooner or later.
—Simon's Law

You can't tell how deep a puddle is until you step in it.
—Miller's Law

CHAPTER ONE

September, 1968

TO THOSE WHO KNEW SOMETHING about airplanes the sight of a C-181 Transport conjured up something they couldn't quite place. People would stare curiously at one, tap their foreheads, snap their fingers and mumble, "Yeah...it's a...a, uhh...a C...a C...oh, what the hell, don't tell me...." and so on. 141 feet long and with a wingspan of 165 feet, the four engine plane looked like an overstuffed sausage, and appeared slightly less airworthy than one. It was thirty feet high at the fuselage, fifty feet high at the top of its flukelike tail section, and its Westinghouse J-555 Turbofan jet engines hung from the bottom of the wings like so many amputated forearms. Despite its appearance, it could fly reasonably well. It could take off or land on twelve hundred feet of runway, and boasted a fifty-percent payload. It was maneuverable, responsive and fairly inexpensive—as airplanes go—and it required fewer training hours than any existing transport in the Air Force.

For the time being, eight were in the air, being considered and tested on a step-by-step basis by the Military Airlift Command. They were being kept within the boundaries of the continental United States until fully approved and qualified, and that was one of the wisest decisions that the Air Force had ever made; a rash of peculiar and unnerving problems had surfaced, causing some pilots to swear off C-181s for good. Bugs and glitches were expected with every prototype, but those cropping up in the C-181 could be frightening. Most had been traced to the on-board computer system, and the most common were radar and altimeter malfunctions. At times the radar would display unknown blips; twice this had caused near-collisions. Six of the eight prototypes had experienced false altimeter readings; local radar would spot a C-181 at a certain altitude, and when the pilot reset his altimeter it might give him an impossible reading moments later, or sometimes it failed entirely.

Hence, Major Kennedy and Captain Waddell, the pilot and copilot on Flight J-440 bound from Fort Bragg, North Carolina to the Oakland, California Army Terminal, had orders to confirm their altimeter setting every fifteen minutes—more often if they thought it necessary.

It was a run-of-the-mill flight even if they had spent the day hedgehopping across the country on a route that would have pleased Wrongway Corrigan himself. They had done this once a week for the past eight months—grunts going west, cargo going east. And this week's passengers—Company C, Second Battalion, 191st Light Infantry Brigade—were exactly like all the others bound for Southeast Asia.

The upper deck of the transport looked like an unkempt barracks. Most of the 122 officers, NCOs and enlisted men were either playing poker or gin rummy, or trying to sleep. A few played chess; others read newspapers, paperback novels or *Playboy* magazines. Several tried to write letters, and a few talked about their destination, a place called Quohong Tau Province. They complained about the tasteless freeze-dried food, about not having anything stronger than coffee to drink, and whenever someone had to climb over two or three people to get to the can.

The crew chief knocked and entered the flight deck.

"How're they doing back there, chief?" Captain Waddell called over his shoulder.

"About like usual, sir. Most of 'em told me that I was the ugliest goddamn stewardess they ever laid eyes on." He shrugged. "They're all bitchin' about something. Anybody want some coffee up here?"

"Yeah, sure thing. Thanks, chief."

The huge airplane rolled gently to the left, setting its course for the west coast.

BECAUSE CHARLIE COMPANY was light infantry they carried nothing that couldn't be packed on foot. They were issued rifles, pistols, light machine guns, rocket launchers and assorted hand grenades. They were authorized 3 two-and-a-half-ton trucks, 3 three-quarter-ton trucks and 4 jeeps. They also carried four- and eight-man tents, collapsible furniture, cots and bedding, medical supplies, mess hall equipment and piles of personal belongings.

Rooting around through all of it was Private First Class Ron Malachi. "Where the fuck is all my stuff?" he said for the fifth time, standing in the center of a pile of duffel bags. He had run out of cigarettes a while ago, so he came down to the lower cargo deck to get more, but he couldn't find his bag anywhere in the mess.

The removeable slide-in plates that served as the upper deck creaked above his head. Everything in the lower deck was illuminated by an eerie glow from the red lights installed every twenty feet on the bulkheads. With each movement of the plane all the cargo groaned, squeaked and creaked, or bumped together as if trying to get comfortable. As well, all the structural ribbing in the cargo area had been left exposed, giving Malachi a peculiar feeling of being inside the belly of some huge mechanical monster. After ten minutes he thought, The hell with it. All of his shit must be on the bottom of the pile. He'd just have to bum smokes until they got to California.

"Fuckin' Army...!"

"Hey, whatsa matter, Malachi, no Commies down there? We didn't hear no gunfire."

"That's because ol' Malachi likes to sneak up behind 'em and poke 'em with his dick!"

"I got a chick stashed down there." Malachi grinned, deciding to join in. "One of those honeys from the Bottoms Up— Bambi. Remember Bambi, Newton?"

Of course he remembered, and each man hooted, priming himself to retell another in the ongoing series of Bottoms Up stories. Each was more outrageous than the last.

"Which one was Bambi?"

"She was the little blonde...about five feet tall, and a hundred pounds. Fifty pounds of tits."

"Yeah, she was the one with the hots for Newton."

"Except that dumb shit didn't know what to do with her...!"

"Well, get this: the last night we were there, Bambi came dancin' over to our table, shakin' everything, slappin' them big, bouncy tits all over ol' Newton, here. Man, he got so shook that all he could do was just sit there like a piece of wood or something. But little Bambi, naked as a fuckin' bowling ball, just kept on dancin' all around ol' Newton, here, rubbin' his pecker, lickin' his ear and stickin' them big tits in his mouth, so pretty soon ol' Newton, here, decides that he's gotta do something, so—"

"I was drunk, you asshole—"

"So he gets up, whips out his billfold—"

"*I'd* whip out my crank if she'd done that to me."

"Wait a minute, this is better. Ol' Newton, here, whips out his billfold, pulls out a fiver, then starts rollin' it up like a little green cigarette. And there's Bambi, still dancin' all around him, goin' through all those fuck motions, but she's beginnin' to wonder just what the hell ol' Newton, here, is doing with that five dollar bill. The crowd's all laughin' at 'im, so ol' Newton, here, with his usual cool, takes the fiver and tries to stick it right up her snatch—"

"Shit, man, there wasn't anyplace else to put it," Newton groaned. "All she had on was her hair, and that was all the money I had left anyway. All she wanted was a big tip."

"All she wanted was a big dick!"

"She could've had mine."

"That's your trouble, Miller, you're too easy."

"Yeah, but I ain't cheap."

"Your sister is."

"Fuck you. . . ."

2

"OKAY, THANK YOU, CONTROL," Major Kennedy said, reaching toward the instrument panel. "22,500 feet and holding. Resetting altimeter now. Four-forty out."

"This is unreal," Captain Waddell said. "I thought they solved altimeter problems back in the barnstorming days."

"They didn't have on-board computers back then. Or radar. You flew by your ass."

"Yeah, that's progress for you. Back in World War Two my ol' man flew Corsairs. One time he met up with a Jap Zero that was trying to shoot him down, and you know what he did?"

"I'm going to hear it anyway. . . ." Kennedy smiled.

"He was almost out of ammo, so he ran right up on that Zeke's tail and straight into his rudder. No shit, right into the rudder. Chewed the goddamn thing right off. He said that that Jap pilot couldn't believe it. Here was this crazy American going after his plane like he was flying a lawn mower. But he did it . . . put that Zeke right into the Pacific, and that Jap was screaming at 'im all the way down. Didn't even scratch the paint on the Corsair."

"Yeah, I heard that some of those old fighter planes were built like anvils. But some of them flew like that, too."

"That's my point. One of those planes could be shot to shit, parts falling off everywhere, and maybe even on fire. But they'd still fly." He gestured at the control panel. "Hell, you can disable this thing with a piece of lint."

"Gimme a smoke, Johnson."

"Smoke your own, Malachi."

"I would, but I ran out. That's why I went downstairs a while ago, but I couldn't find my shit anywhere. Come on, I'll pay you back when we get to Oakland."

"Watch it, Johnson, he still owes me ten bucks from last month."

"Yeah, and he owes *me* four beers from the last time we were at the Bottoms Up. Stay away, Johnson, or Malachi'll bleed you like a fuckin' vampire."

"Yeah, he's pretty good at suckin' things anyway . . . !"

"Fuck you, Armstead!"

"You should be so lucky. I'd be the closest thing to pussy you'll ever get. Your only friend is your hand."

"My hand and your mouth, Armst—"

That was as far as it got. Everything came to a halt with a sudden, violent lurching of the airplane. Men were thrown from their seats; others fell all over one another in tangles of arms and legs and grunts of pain and surprise. Books, magazines, cards, coins and papers flew through the air and on the deck as the plane rolled to the left and was jerked nose-up. Outside, both wings groaned from the strain, and the turbine whine from the four engines rose to a painful, violent scream.

MAJOR KENNEDY WAS FROZEN in his seat, staring out the windshield in complete disbelief. He had been looking at the altimeter; it had been reading a comfortable and reasonable 22,500 feet when the Ground Obstruction light began flashing crazily, followed by the piercing warning alarm. When he looked up all he could see was an immense white-capped rock speeding straight at them.

"Oh, shit!" he bellowed, pulling the control yoke back toward his chest, and jamming the throttle levers as far forward as they would go. Lazily, dreamily, almost like a movie film slowing down, the next two seconds passed like hours as he fought the plane, trying desperately to bring it up. His mind raced as he tried to think of something that would bring them up just a few more feet, a few inches—anything to clear this big bastard of a rock that had suddenly materialized out of the clouds. The huge plane trembled and moaned under the stress, trying to perform as it was told; the rest of the crew sat motionless, prayers flying through their minds, eyes fearfully wide, staring helplessly at the great mountain growing larger and larger in front of them.

No good. A tremendous boom jolted the airplane and hurled them from their seats in a din of explosions and shrieking metallic bedlam. The transport plowed through the snowy summit, hurling shreds of steel and aluminum, smoking debris and splashing burning fuel against the rocks like molten lava. Junk and cargo flew everywhere; twisted wings and pieces of the engines sailed lazily over the side of the mountain like torches; the flight deck was ripped from the fuselage, and slid into a rock outcropping that marked the western boundary of the summit; the tail blew itself to pieces against the rocks on the eastern boundary; and the center section of the fuselage crushed itself almost flat before halting near the center of the mountain's top, its cargo of human life strewn and scattered through the snow like so much trash.

Only a minute had gone by. The only sounds to be heard amid the cries and groans were the eternal winds, and the stinging of blowing ice and snow.

3

BRIGADIER GENERAL Charles Streetor leaned across the table, staring at the maps and photos. He was the 191st Light Infantry Brigade commander; upon learning of the accident he had taken the first plane out of Fort Bragg. He still didn't have his necktie fastened. "Jesus Christ!" he muttered. "I can't believe it," and he turned to his host. "How high did you say that damned thing was?"

His friend and former West Point classmate, Major General Thomas Grady, replied: "19,163 feet, Charlie. Kota is the third tallest mountain in North America, and the tallest in the States . . . not that that does us any good."

"What do you mean?"

"Well, crashing on the summit of Mount Kota is kind of like crashing on another planet. We don't practice on Kota, so I don't think we can get to the wreck. Or any survivors, if there are any." They would learn that answer shortly, when the recon photos were delivered. In the meantime, all they could do was wait and watch as General Grady's communications center hummed with its usual quiet efficiency. Everyone there was trained for emergencies such as this one, and they had set into motion everything at their disposal.

Both generals envied their subordinates; at least they were busy. And if the impossible happened—survivors—they wouldn't be the ones issuing the life-or-death decisions following.

Grady put a hand on his friend's shoulder. "I can't guarantee anything, Charlie," he said quietly. "If this had happened anywhere but Kota there'd be no problem. But at least we're equipped to give it a better shot than most...if you can call that a bright side to this."

Fort Endicott, Montana, located in the southwest end of the state and next to some of the roughest country in the northern Rockies, had been put there just for that reason. Endicott was where all the Army mountain climbers were trained for their primary missions of Alpine Search, Rescue and Recovery, and High Altitude Survival. They maintained twenty fully trained and equipped climbing teams, which stood ready to go after anything from stranded climbers to enemy planes to the President's plane, Air Force One. To a man they were more highly trained than many Special Forces units; some of them, in fact, had helped train a few Green Berets. For all of this they practiced and drilled on most of the nearby peaks. Two of the teams were always out practicing.

Except on Mount Kota. Kota was an alpine pariah.

Although the lesser mountains surrounding it were in many ways as rugged as Kota, they had all been climbed repeatedly. They were difficult, but not impossible. An attempt on Kota, however, especially by a team unfamiliar with it—and no team was familiar—seemed akin to attempted suicide. It sat square in the center of a large national park, but the rangers never bothered patrolling it because no one entertained the notion of trying it; no one except a handful of seasoned professionals had ever tried it. In fifty-six years of attempts, Kota had been bested only once. And until that night, nobody had ever crashed an airplane on it.

Now that Grady had had time to appraise the whole situation he realized that any rescue attempt—should one be considered—might be out of the question. He personally knew almost nothing about the mountain, but the information from his climbers was enough; odds for success on Kota were practically nonexistent. He was trying to think of a delicate way to say that when one of his communications men came into the room with that I've-got-some-good-news-and-some-bad-news look on his face. He had just gotten a call from the photo analysis lab about the pictures taken over the summit less than half an hour earlier.

Grady braced himself. "What do they show?" he said after taking a deep breath.

"Clear evidence of survivors, sir."

Oh, Christ! "How many?"

"They're not certain, but it's at least ten. Probably more."

Everything quieted in the room. Grady stared at the floor, and Streetor stared into space.

"You are going to try, aren't you, Tom?" Streetor finally whispered. "I know what you said about that mountain, but you can't just abandon those men."

Grady looked up from the floor. "Alert the rescue team on duty tonight," he said to the communications man. "Tell them to stand by. Send the team leader over here." When the man had left the room, he added, "We're not climbing yet, Charlie. Not until I know all the options," and he thought, Assuming there are any.

FIVE MEN LEANED ACROSS the conference room table as the recon pilot explained his flight. An officer from the photo analysis section assisted, pointing out certain details about the mountain, and the wreck.

"Kota has an unusual summit," he began. "It's not sharply peaked like many mountains, but it isn't flat either. As you see, it's quite wide east-to-west and narrow north-to-south. The plane hit it going due west. If they had struck it going any other direction they would have slammed into one of the sheer walls or skidded off over the side like a rock skipping on water. The bottom rear of the fuselage hit the eastern edge first; then it bellied in, flying to pieces on impact."

The entire summit and some of the lower elevations were littered with broken pieces, the snow black with burned debris and bodies.

"The starbound wing and engines broke off and went to pieces here in these rocks around and below the summit," the pilot said. "The port wing was torn loose and fell in this area below the South Face...except for part of the port inboard engine here." He lined up three more photos. "This is part of the aft cargo section and door, and what's left of the tail assembly, the central cargo bay doors, two of the landing gear, and this is the forward section and flight deck. It broke loose and crushed itself against these rocks." He pulled up another photo. "But this is our main concern. It's part of the central fuselage section, about forty feet of it, and the only part of the plane to come through reasonably intact. And there are some of the survivors.''

Perhaps twenty-five men could be seen in the picture. The analysis officer explained which of them were alive and moving, and a similar photo taken during the second pass over the mountain showed three of them to be looking up. None of the summit photos was that good because of all the smoke and blowing snow, but there could be no doubt about survivors; at least ten men were still alive.

''Another couple of feet, and they would have made it,'' the pilot said to himself with a sad shrug.

But they hadn't. The question was still as big as ever: how was anyone supposed to get to them? They began discussing different ways, from airdrops to helicopters, and five minutes' consideration of each was enough to kick out those ideas. Paratroopers were completely out of the question; and no known helicopter could reach a nineteen-thousand-foot altitude or maneuver in any kind of high wind. The Army had been helping to develop a high-altitude search-and-rescue helicopter, but a flying prototype was still months away. Besides, someone added, they had no idea of where on Kota a helicopter could even set down, or where the climbing routes were located.

The fifth man at the table said, ''The only way I can see any chance is for someone to climb to them.''

''You're Lieutenant . . . ?''

''Palmer, sir,'' he said to Grady. ''First Lieutenant Gary Palmer, Team A-2-1 leader. The team on standby tonight.''

''Do you know something about Kota that we don't?''

''Not a whole lot, sir. But enough to know that it's the last mountain I'd want to try. In fact, I think my suggestion sucks— if I may be blunt. But I said it because there's no other way. And that's no good, sir, because nobody on this base is even remotely qualified to try Kota.''

Streetor shook his head. ''I don't get this. All right, the damned thing is a little bigger than most mountains, but what makes it so tough? Why is everyone so scared of it?''

Palmer tried to explain. It was a combination of things that a non-climber wouldn't understand, and professional climbers had been trying since 1912. Only five years ago had it been climbed to the summit, and the men who succeeded took eleven years to do so. "And even then, sir, one of them got killed up close to the top. Fourteen people have died on that thing. There are places where the features change almost daily, and other places that are simply impossible for any climber to negotiate, so it's—"

Grady put up a hand. "I think we understand, Lieutenant. Thank you."

Streetor slammed a fist on the table. "Dammit! We're orbiting men around the moon. You'd think we could get to the top of a second-rate mountain."

"We'll do everything we can, Charlie," Grady said with a sigh, knowing that it was not enough. But since Palmer had made the only logical suggestion, they discussed the assembly of a climbing team. They had to do something, at least the motions of an attempt, or they were no good as a search-and-rescue operation. They decided first of all to try air-dropping supplies, and Grady ordered that done immediately, along with additional reconnaissance flights over the summit at one-hour intervals to check on the survivors' progress. In the meantime, they would put together a team and begin setting up a base camp at the bottom of the mountain in preparation of a climb. Palmer was ordered to work on a list of their best climbers.

Which has to mean you, too, Palmer thought with a sigh. Of all nights to be on standby duty; it wasn't even his turn. He had traded with a buddy so he could have tomorrow night free to spend with his girlfriend. So he considered names for the list, thinking that the root of the problem was really the mountain and how little they knew about it. If only they had a starting point or a route; but nobody had the slightest idea of where to go. For that matter, it had taken the only successful team eleven years to learn exactly where to go up there....

That was it. He jumped up. "May I use your phone, sir?"

"Who are you calling?"

CHAPTER TWO

DOUG GORHAM, JOHN KARBER and Steve Woodhull had spent more time on Mount Kota than anybody. It had taken them eleven years to find the top; they were the only ones who had ever reached it, who had even come near it. In the process they not only found the best route to the top—such as it was—but also marked two alternates—such as they were. Gorham's advice to other climbers was to find themselves another mountain.

They had found many of the mountain's peculiarities during those years; they photographed and named most of them, and while doing so they left behind pieces of themselves on the hazards. Through eleven years they scraped off yards of their skin on sharp, frozen rocks; they suffered frostbite a dozen times; they experienced hypothermia, cerebral edema and snow blindness. Their blood stained the snow in scores of places. They had cussed, cried, shivered, sweated, laughed in triumph and screamed in rage while trying to make their way to the top. Steve Woodhull came within a hair of death on their third attempt when he was nearly stranded high atop the murderous South Face; Doug Gorham lost his way in a whiteout and almost stepped off a seven-hundred-foot ridge; and on their final climb, John Karber lost his life in a fall above the pass that now bore his name. The summit was almost in sight.

So would the two surviving members ever try it again?

Not on your life, Steve Woodhull was quoted as saying (and what he really said was for the interviewer to go fuck himself). He had other things to do with his life. He never wanted to see Kota again.

And Doug Gorham, the man who had brought them there eleven years earlier? In his own words: "There isn't that much to tell about our first few climbs up Kota. We tried different routes, different techniques, and we got into trouble a lot of the time because they didn't work. You try. You're on a learning curve.

"And we learned fast on Kota. What to do... what not to do... where to go... what to stay away from. That sounds simple, and kind of corny, but it was true. We didn't dare forget anything up there because it would jump up and bite our asses if we forgot the next time. That's true on any mountain, but it was doubly true on Kota because it was a completely different mountain every time we tried it.

"But we still had some good climbs. All three of us had been up our share of tough mountains, so when we got together and decided to take a run at Kota we figured we were ready for it. I'd studied the mountain. I dug up all the information I could find about it, and I even located a few of the older guys who'd tried it years earlier. They all thought we were nuts but they helped wherever they could, and they gave us a lot of good information. When we were finished with all the talking and studying, we thought that if anyone could make it to the top, we could. We thought we knew where some of the earlier attempts had gone wrong. We thought we could get around them, do things a little better, and use some of the newer and more sophisticated techniques and equipment. In those days, Kota was a little taller, a little meaner in spots, and it had a reputation. But it was still another mountain to us. It was just shaped differently. So, there we went.

"And right off the bat we were in trouble. After the third climb we began to see what those old guys had been talking about. That rock beat the holy hell out of us. We couldn't even get halfway up, not even as far as some of the earlier attempts. We'd never seen anything like it. It was as if we were learning all over again, and people were laughing at us. You just never knew what you'd find up there. About the time you'd get over a bad spot and were feeling like you'd really accomplished something, just ahead was a place even worse. You'd get yourself all pumped up, give it a go, and boom. It would beat you again. You'd try everything you knew, and it'd still beat you. And I know we must have been in a dozen tight spots I thought sure would kill us, and I'm still not sure how we got out of some of them. And all of this was after three or four climbs. At that point we were wondering what the hell we were doing, and that maybe we'd better quit before we killed ourselves. I swore five or six times that if I ever got back down I'd never look that big bastard in the face again.

"But somehow we always got down. We'd come down dragging ass, all busted up, bleeding, frostbitten, sore and mad as hell. And then we'd turn around for a last look before crawling back home. That always seemed to do it. That was the magic, for lack of a better word, about Mount Kota. When you stepped back for a long look, it showed you another face, another side of itself. And it never failed that after we'd had a chance to sit and think awhile, and to lick our wounds, that we'd start talking about it. Before long we'd be talking about this place or that place or how to get around something else, and there we'd be—planning the next climb. Beat ourselves to death, swear never to come back, and within a year or less we'd be on our way up again, sure we could lick it this time.

"A shrink probably would have had a field day with us. But, then, maybe not; not if he'd never tried anything like that for himself. It's the feeling you get, and maybe that's what they call obsessive behavior. You know—that deep-down gut feeling that just keeps pushing you on and on in spite of yourself. It must be the way a hungry fighter gets when he knows he can stomp the champion, when he can almost taste the victory, and feel that championship belt being tied around his waist. But instead he keeps getting his teeth knocked out and his head busted. I know the feeling. You keep going until you win, or get yourself carried out in a rubber sack. I guess that's what we were doing up there; I was, anyway. And we did everything short of strapping on wax wings and trying to fly up there.

"Like I said, though, we had some good climbs. There were sports equipment manufacturers who helped finance five or six climbs, and they gave us a lot of their stuff to try out. By the ninth or tenth climb we had more stuff than we could ever use. Three guys can carry only so much, and we would have needed Mack trucks to pack all of it. A few of them actually paid us to test their stuff, and Woodhull *never* got over that one. He got to the point where he'd use only the equipment we were being paid for. He'd sit and calculate until he came up with the highest dollar amount, then start packing. He worried more about that than he did the climb, or if he'd forgotten anything.

"I think it was the ninth climb that we almost made the Northeast Plateau, which is only eleven hundred feet below the summit. I thought we were going to make it, and we should have if it hadn't been for the weather. We were held up longer by bad weather than on any other ascent. When it lifted we took advantage and went back down because our supplies were getting low. But by that time we'd learned that any final assault had to be made from somewhere along that route. We were sure of the routes by then, and there are only three, all of which converge about a thousand feet below the plateau. And two of them are no good at all unless the weather's perfect—which it rarely is.

"So, we didn't see the Northeast Plateau until the tenth trip, and damned if the weather didn't stop us again. We made that climb later in the season than ever before, and the weather was threatening most of the way. We spent exactly one hour on the plateau. There was a storm on the way, and we had to turn and run or we would have been trapped. So...scratch number ten.

"And then came eleven—the best and the worst. It started out fine, the only one where everything seemed to go right for a change. The weather was with us all the way, we stuck to the main route, and our climbing time was less than ever. Everything was perfect when we got to the plateau. We set up camp, got a good night's rest and were all set to go the next morning. It was almost spooky if you're superstitious. Maybe we were at that point because a climb up Kota just didn't seem natural without the usual shitpot load of problems. In fact, it seemed too easy...to me, at least. And then Karber found that pass to the top—Karber's Pass. Was *that* something! It turned out to be a walk. No shit. A walk. No tougher than walking up a hill. We couldn't believe it. After eleven years of hell, up we go through this pass like three little kids skipping and whistling on their way to school. The final assault. And it was the easiest part of the whole damned mountain.

"Then Karber fell. He just went up into the rocks above the pass as if he'd lost something there on an earlier trip. I yelled and went up after him, but he'd already fallen by the time I got there. Woodhull was bringing up the rear about a hundred feet or so behind us and didn't see anything until he heard all the shouting. But John had fallen, and I came back down in shock. I told Steve what had happened and that we had to go get his body, and we both went a little crazy there for a few minutes. We were yelling at each other, throwing punches, each blaming the other for something neither of us saw... and after we settled down I guess we went into shock again. I can't remember much after that, not even much about the summit. We just collected our stuff, and plodded back down. We found John's body about two thousand feet down the north side... and I barely remember helping carry him back down. We answered questions from the authorities, and we made a full statement to the chief park ranger that I can't even remember doing. Nothing focused until we were in the trucks, driving away. That was the last time I saw Kota. I've never even looked at a picture of it since.''

2

"...AND SO THAT'S THE SITUATION, Mr. Gorham. Will you help us?''

There was no response from Seattle, Washington except a sigh.

Lieutenant Palmer waited. "Mr. Gorham?''

Another weary sigh came through the line. "They sure picked one hell of a mountain to crash a plane on.''

"Yes, sir, we know that. But any assistance you could offer would be a great help. We don't know anything about Kota, and if you could just come to Fort Endicott and fill us in on some of the hazards or a route to take, we'd certainly appreciate it. We have to try to get to those men.''

"You have survivors now. But you probably won't by the time anybody could get there... which is damned unlikely. My advice is to forget it. I know how that sounds, but there's nothing you can do for those guys. You'd only get more people killed or injured.''

"How about you leading us up?''

"Lieutenant, I haven't seen Kota for five years. I haven't done any climbing at all in more than a year. Besides, even if I did lead a party I'd have inexperienced men with me. The climb would still be useless. Just forget it, okay?"

"We can't, Mr. Gorham. We have no choice. So...thank you for your time. Sorry to have bothered you so late in the evening."

"Hold on, Lieutenant. Don't hang up yet. I don't think you understand just how difficult that mountain really is. It isn't a matter of climbing certain obstacles in a certain way. Sure, you'll run into a lot of them that you've seen and climbed before, but they're just not the same up there. There's a thousand little tricks along the route that took the three of us eleven years to learn. You might even be able to pick your way along if you're good enough, but it would take days. Your climb would still be just for the hell of it. You wouldn't have any survivors by the time you got up there...assuming you got there at all. You have a noble cause, but no reasonable way to go after it."

Palmer sighed. "This is getting us nowhere, Mr. Gorham. We have to try, and I'm wasting time arguing. I have more people to call. So again, thank you for—"

"Who?"

"What?"

"Who are you calling?"

"Well, Steve Woodhull for one. And I saw in a magazine where Rudi Gurdler is on a lecture tour in the States right now...in Denver, I think. He might be interested in helping us."

"Gurdler's pretty good," Gorham said, almost as if reminding himself. "He'll probably help. But forget Woodhull. You'll never get him near Kota again. He'll spit in your ear, and hang up. So, I still don't—"

"Now *you* don't understand, Mr. Gorham. We need the best help we can get. But even if we get no outside assistance, we'll still be ordered up the mountain. We have survivors, and we can't pretend we don't."

There was another long silence on the line. Palmer was losing patience; Gorham was sounding like a child.

"Okay," Gorham said at last. "I'll try to help you. How do I get to that base of yours?"

"We'll authorize a military flight for you right away. Should I still call Mr. Gurdler?"

"Yeah. You'll need all the experience you can get."

"All right. Thanks, Mr. Gorham. Thanks very much. I'll see you here in a little while."

"Don't thank me yet. I said I'd help. I didn't say I'd climb."

RUDI GURDLER HAD SCALED almost every major peak on the planet. People who followed his exploits had lost count of the times he and his expeditions had been featured in *National Geographic*. Gurdler had twice taken on Mount Everest and K2, numbers one and two respectively in height and difficulty.

He had been the first to scale Mount Cuzzoco, the giant of the Peruvian Andes, and he'd returned two years later to solo it. Over the past few years that had become his habit—an attempted solo of all his highest and most difficult mountains simply because there were few records left for him to break except his own. He had managed to put several out of anyone's reach.

Gurdler was self-confident, self-assured and, to a large extent, self-centered. He endeared himself to few people because he played the role of a famous personality to the hilt. He loved the accolades, the adulation and anything else his adoring public might offer on his behalf. But many insisted that his attitude explained why he had taken to soloing—that many climbers, some of whom were nearly as good as he, refused to climb with him anymore. A few made no secret of the fact that they couldn't stand him.

But there was always a certain amount of guardedness to their criticisms. Even Gurdler's most bitter critics had to admit, if to no one but themselves, that he was an extraordinary mountain climber. He frequently took fearful chances but he always seemed to know what the risks were. He got away with it. And all the chances and risks had made him world famous. They had to concede that Rudi Gurdler might be the best. Ever.

"THE CRASH OCCURRED about two hours ago, Mr. Gurdler," Gary was saying. "We've tried dropping supplies, but it didn't work because of strong winds at the summit. We know there are at least ten men alive up there. Maybe more. But we have no way of knowing their exact condition or how long they can hold out. All we can do is climb as soon as possible and hope for the best, and for that we're trying to organize the best rescue party we can assemble. We're asking if you'd like to help. It would be a great asset."

"Well," Rudi Gurdler said after a pause, "it is a very bad situation, Lieutenant Palmer. For men to be trapped on the summit of your country's most difficult mountain. Quite difficult in view of the fact that only one party has ever succeeded in climbing it. And circumstances such as these will only compound a difficult climb." He was quiet for a moment before asking, "Do you know yet who else would be climbing?"

"We're not sure, but at least one of our own men. Probably me. Mr. Gorham is on his way here but we don't know if he'll climb or not. All he has offered so far is technical assistance— information about the mountain itself."

"I, too, would like to help," he said without pause. "I will come to your army base to do so. But if I am to climb on an emergency mission I would prefer that Mr. Gorham lead the party. He knows the mountain best, and we would have to proceed with all possible speed and efficiency. But what about the third man in his party who climbed Mount Kota? Could you reach him, and perhaps persuade him to assist?"

"Steve Woodhull. I tried, but I couldn't get any answer. And we don't have time to locate him. Besides, Gorham said that Woodhull would refuse."

"I see. Well, then, we must make the best of what is available. Now, I must make arrangements to postpone my tour. And how do I get to your military base?"

"We'll make the arrangements for that right now, Mr. Gurdler."

GARY WAS THINKING that maybe a little good would come out of this after all. He might actually be climbing with two of the best mountaineers in the world.

His excitement lasted until he returned to the communications center with the news. There, the base meteorologist was explaining what all of his computer data and stratospheric charts meant. A massive low pressure system, which had developed over the northern Pacific a few days earlier, had moved inland and was now stalled over southern British Columbia. From all indications it could stay there for the next thirty-six to forty-eight hours; on the other hand, it could move again at any time. They didn't know. As the first major storm of the season in the high country, it was unpredictable. And big—an inch and a half of rain had already fallen at sea level, and snow of no less than twelve to fifteen inches in depth was being predicted for all of the higher elevations in the Canadian and Montana Rockies. "Which means us," he said. "It should pass through this area. But we don't know when."

General Streetor sagged in his chair. "Jesus!" he muttered. "What next? Those men wouldn't stand a chance against a storm; nearly as bad, anyone climbing to get them might be trapped in it as well."

"Okay, I want your section to monitor that thing starting now," Grady ordered the meteorologist. "Don't take your eyes or instruments off it. We'll have to watch it every minute until this thing is over, or until we have to call it off."

"Yes, sir. We'll have updates every hour. Sooner if it moves."

"Well..." Grady sighed, looking at Streetor. "Maybe they can hang on. We won't give up on them yet."

"Maybe you're right, Tom. Maybe it's hopeless, and all you'd do is endanger more men needlessly. Hell, they can't have any food or water left, or medical supplies...no shelter...no cold weather survival gear. How any of them survived the crash is a mystery."

"We'll keep trying, Charlie. We'll get everything ready, and— Yes, what is it?" he said to another man who came into the room.

"Excuse me, sir, but a local radio station called. They're asking for the latest information about the crash. And any possible rescue attempt. What should we tell them?"

"The truth. That we're organizing a rescue. That we've got survivors."

3

At 1:45 a.m., Doug Gorham unfolded his maps, records and photographs across the conference room table. "Since you've got a storm on the way, you're left with one route. It's the toughest." Two easier routes wound their way up the northern and northwestern slopes, but neither could be trusted this late in the year. Even a minor storm could leave them impassable. The southern flank appeared deceptively easy, he added, and so it was until the south face had been traversed. There, it ended. No route existed except to go back down, which was what had once happened to Woodhull. As for the western side, no known route was there, either. That left only the northeast route, and Gorham began explaining what it was.

The first major obstacles were mazes of boulders below the eastern face, which had fallen off over aeons of runoff and erosion. He had marked a path with a red pencil, warning that any deviation could leave them lost for hours. The real climbing began at the top of the southeastern base—a rock. As in *rock*, an ascent up a stone slab featuring angles that varied from twenty to forty-five degrees. From a distance it looked like an immense broken tombstone, and this was its name—the Tombstone, a 985-foot climb intended to offer one his mountain legs for the next traverse.

Gorham pulled out another photo from a yellowed stack of black-and-white glossies. It was a distant shot of Mount Kota's best known and most feared feature, the Lunatic Wall. The stair-stepping ascent up the Lunatic, he said, would cover the upper 1800 feet starting at the top of the Tombstone. The distance from the base to the top of the wall was a heart-stuttering 3250 feet, with nothing except wild blue yonder in between. "Every move across the Lunatic has to be right," he added. "It's slow and dangerous, and the way you cross an obstacle will depend on how you took the one before it. Screw up down here, and you'll pay for it up there. Too much of that will cost you twice as much time crossing it.'' Still another photo showed the wall's worst feature, a bulging outcropping of rock that ran horizontally across the widest area. They would have to cross under, then over it, and they would be upside down part of the way—''Sort of like dangling from the bottom of an airplane wing.'' He smiled. ''The route is marked, and it's critical. If you get off it you might have to traverse a section twice. You'll have to end up...here.'' And another picture came out.

''Good Lord!'' Gary mumbled.

It was the Devil's Finger, a fifty-foot column of rock pointing straight up at the sky, as if making a blasphemous gesture at the heavens; viewed from a distance, the spire with the lumpy piles of rock surrounding it looked exactly like a closed fist with a protruding middle finger.

''You'd better be good at climbing trees or telephone poles because the Finger is your next ascent. The easiest way to get to the slopes above is to shinny up the finger and climb across to this,'' and he produced another picture. It was of a slippery incline angling upward at about twenty-five degrees. ''I've always thought that this place was one of the most dangerous areas on the whole mountain,'' he said. ''You've got to crawl about 450 feet. And you can never tell what condition it'll be in, what the surface will be like. Sometimes it's hard and icy; other times it'll be slushy. We've been on it when it was snow over ice, snow over slush, and sometimes other combinations. It freezes in the wind, melts in the sun and might even be dry in spots. Its condition changes almost daily.''

Once they cleared the Finger, Gorham continued, the slope would level off slightly, and only there could they get a breather—assuming there would be time enough to take one. From there on up they would be in ice and snow most of the way, and the amounts of either were dependent upon fickle Mother Nature.

''From here on you're fully exposed to the north, and everything depends on when that storm lands on you. If you're ahead of it, this area—the Razorback Ridge—will be partly snow- and ice-covered, and partly exposed rocks. It will be a long climb up the Razorback, but it's actually easier if it's covered. But it's also one of the worst places to be in a storm, because you're out in the open with no protection anywhere. When you're on the Razorback you want to be way ahead of the storm . . . or else way behind it.''

Their first bivouac would be somewhere on the northeastern slopes, and he warned that they couldn't stop anywhere along the Razorback or North Buttress; they could be buried in the snow if the high winds didn't blow them over the side. Fumbling through the stack, he produced a photo of the best—and the only, really—place to spend the night. It was a picture of himself and John Karber standing in front of what appeared to be a small cave. ''We found this little inset in the rocks on our seventh climb. Four people can sleep comfortably inside, and you can cover the entrance with a tarp.''

The remaining 3100 feet were mostly a series of steep slopes and switchbacks that wound through deep snow, up ice-covered walls and over a score of obstacles. The climbers would also experience the same hazards found on any mountain—low oxygen, intense cold, high winds, lack of moisture and quick exhaustion—all of which could produce a dozen different physical and mental problems, any one of which was potentially lethal.

''What's the highest you've ever climbed?'' Gorham asked Palmer.

''A little over fifteen thousand feet.''

''Then you're fairly well acclimatized, but not so much that you won't have trouble. You'll end up four thousand feet above that—assuming you make it. But it'll feel like four thousand miles.'' To the group he added, ''That's what I'm talking about when I say that you guys should forget it. Of all the climbers around here, only Mr. Gurdler and I are experienced above fifteen or sixteen thousand feet. Without that experience, the higher you go, the harder it gets, and the slower you go. The last three or four thousand feet would take an inexperienced climber two, maybe three times as long. He might not be able to do it at all, and even if he does, there won't be any rescue left to perform . . . except maybe for *you* getting *him* off the mountain.'' He stopped himself. He was surprised that he should be telling these facts to these people; they should already know all the risks as well as he.

"I think we understand, Mr. Gorham," General Streetor said. "Please go on with your information."

Gurdler, who had remained silent since his arrival, now spoke directly to Streetor. "I must disagree with you, General Streetor. I do not feel that every person here fully understands the situation. You should listen carefully to Mr. Gorham because he speaks the truth. I must agree with him on all points. Your rescue might do nothing more than put three or four more men in danger. The very least it will do is to waste time and energy. I do not like to say this because I came here to help, but I do not think you should proceed with any rescue. I do not think it can succeed."

"Je-sus!" Streetor grunted in disgust. "I don't believe I'm hearing this. We were told that you guys are two of the best climbers in the world, and now you say there's no chance? That we should forget the whole thing? Just say 'The hell with those men'? What kind of people *are* you? Tom, I'm fed up to here with this shit. Let's get something moving right now. Hell, you've got an army post full of climbers and equipment; get some of them moving. That's what they're here for, for Christ's sake."

Gurdler offered him a quizzically astonished look. Clearly, the man had no idea of what he was talking about. With military leaders like this one, raving about taking the high ground at any cost, it was no wonder their country was involved in something as insane as Vietnam. But he remained quiet; he was a guest here, and it was best that he stay clear of any arguments. He was just grateful that they couldn't order him to climb as they could the poor lieutenant across the table, who now looked as though he was trying to blend into the woodwork.

The man in the middle—Grady—turned to the meteorologist. "Is there anything else you can tell us about that storm?"

"No, sir. About fifteen inches of snow have fallen in the mountains so far, and two inches of rain down at sea level. It's still stalled over British Columbia."

Grimacing, Grady muttered, "Is there any way at all of telling when it might start moving?" His voice held a slight pleading; his expression was pained.

"No accurate way, sir. I'm sorry. Ordinarily, another front would come in behind it and push it along, or it would be moved by the prevailing winds. But the seasons are changing right now, faster in the mountains, and during these seasonal transitions there are periods when all the traditional weather patterns go a little haywire. This is one of those times. I wouldn't want to get anybody's hopes up, but it could disperse, too. But we don't think so. We're sure it'll move through here. We just don't know exactly when."

"Speaking of the weather, let's talk about the weather at the summit," Gorham said. "The all-time high was fifteen below zero, recorded in the middle of July. It averages about thirty or thirty-five below. The wind is usually blowing, so you've got the chill factor, which brings us to the lowest temperature—minus 102 with a wind chill of a negative 176. It will be a lot like that when the storm hits. Those guys up there have no protection from it: no shelter, no clothing, no food, no water, no medical care. They can't possibly survive. We can't possibly get to them in time. Do you understand all of that?"

With a heavy sigh, Grady said, "All right, here's what we'll do. We'll get the base camp assembled at the foot of the mountain, and we'll get a team ready to go at first light. If that storm begins moving, we call it off. If it hasn't moved by daybreak, we go ahead. We'll proceed with everything right up to the minute we hear that the storm's on the way; if we get no word, we keep right on going." He turned to Palmer. "Lieutenant, who do you recommend to go with you? We can't order either of our guests up the mountain, so we'll have to try it ourselves...unless, of course, they volunteer." And he left the question open.

Gorham began putting all his papers and photos back into his case. "I've been up there. It was always under better conditions than this. Since you people don't want to listen to what I'm saying, count me out. I don't have a death wish."

To everybody's surprise, Gurdler agreed. He got up from the table and addressed them. "Under the circumstances, I would not wish to climb, either. If this were a personal climb, it would be one thing. Since this is intended as a swift and efficient rescue attempt, that makes it quite another. Without Mr. Gorham leading the party, I think the attempt would be useless."

"Okay," said Grady. "Now, Lieutenant, do you have any feel at all for how long it would take you and two other men? It doesn't have to be accurate."

Palmer sighed and ran his fingers through his hair. He had no idea. "Oh, boy!" he said, staring at the table. "Two days . . . maybe three. I really can't say, sir."

"That's all right. It's a start. If you could make that plateau, or whatever it is, and set up your high-altitude base camp in thirty-six hours or less, it would give those men a fighting chance, I think. We'll just have to hope that the weather holds long enough for you to get to the top and to get whoever you can down to the high-altitude camp. We'll give you all the backup we have. If we can't outrun the storm, then we'll call it off, and you'll have to hold wherever you are until it blows over."

Doug Gorham and Rudi Gurdler looked at each other in disbelief. Rudi shook his head sadly; he also appeared on the verge of laughing out loud. Doug couldn't help but say, "You people really are crazy. This is amazing. You haven't the foggiest goddamn notion of what you're saying. All you're going to do is get three more men killed, and you're going about it as if you're ordering them to take out the trash."

"Look, Gorham, if you don't want to help, that's fine," Streetor said, pointing a finger. "But you have no right to complain now, so don't say anything. We'll handle this."

"You'll handle *shit*! Those guys will never make the Northeast Plateau in under a week, probably not at all. The weather won't hold long enough for them to get halfway . . . if they get halfway. And they won't be able to curl up and snooze peacefully while the storm blows over because they'll be buried under eight or ten feet of drifted snow and ice—if the wind doesn't blow them somewhere over Iowa. They *won't make it*." He turned away from the group for a moment. In a quieter voice, but one that quivered, he said, "Mr. Gurdler, I believe you said that you'd climb if I led the party?"

"Yes, Mr. Gorham. I came here to climb. As I have said, I thought it would be with you. I would not wish to try Mount Kota any other way under these circumstances."

Doug nodded. He said nothing else for a minute. "All right, then. Let's get to work gathering all the equipment we'll need." He shook his head, unable to believe that he had just volunteered for something doomed from the start. "I guess I'm crazy too," he whispered.

Both generals started to thank them; Rudi ignored them, and Doug put up a hand to stay any further comment. It was the last thing he needed to hear.

"Uh, sir, I have a quick errand to run before we get started— a phone call," Palmer said to Grady.

"A phone call?"

"Yes, sir. I have to tell her that I won't be able to make it to dinner tomor—tonight."

Grady smiled. "At this hour? Won't you wake her up?"

"Yes, sir. But she'd be damned mad if I didn't call."

"All right, Lieutenant, but make it fast. And don't tell her anything about the mission—only that you have to go on one."

"Yes, sir."

CHAPTER THREE

WIND GUSTED ACROSS the summit, fanning sandlike ice pellets against the twisted wreck. Small fires burned here and there from splashed fuel, ragged pieces of cloth and canvas and sizzling electrical wiring. Metal groaned, and hunks of shattered Plexiglas dangled from the portholes like wind chimes. Flame- and oil-streaked wreckage blackened the snow; a mountain of debris scattered around the site, carried on the wind. And amid all of it were green-clad bodies—some dismembered, some mangled, a few remarkably whole, almost unscathed. Or so they appeared. But they were dead. Scores of them lay dead.

Two hours had passed since the crash. The fourteen men who had somehow lived through it huddled together inside the wreck. Shivering, in great pain and still stunned at the sudden disaster, they tried to hang on. No one had been quite aware of what happened during those first moments as they pulled themselves from the wreckage. Screams of agony came from all around them. A few men had passed quickly and mercifully into oblivion; others died later before they could be located in the confusion. Fires crackled, and dull bumps and groans came from the wreck as it settled into its death throes.

The first man out alive was a quiet, good-natured private first class from Tempe, Arizona named Ross Stevenson. He dragged his buddy out with him, Private First Class Duane Hamilton, from Mason City, Iowa, and for long minutes they both were immobilized with shock; they couldn't believe it. They thought at first that they were the only ones who had lived through the crash.

So did Sergeant Randall Jackson from Paris, Kentucky, and his friend in the adjacent seat, Sergeant Todd Anderson from Ogden, Utah. Somehow, the deck section to which their seats were attached had remained in place. Even though everything and everyone else all around them had been hurled violently forward or out the sides, they had stayed belted in their seats. Both were badly injured; Anderson had suffered broken bones in one hand and arm plus serious cuts from sharp metal and flying glass, and Jackson had sustained, among other things, a broken leg, a shattered ankle and at least four broken ribs.

"Oh, shit! Mmm...! What...what the hell happened, anyway?" Jackson grunted as Anderson dragged him from the seat.

"I...I think we smacked a mountain."

"Any-umm! Anybody else make it? Goddamn, that hurts!"

"I don't know. If I can get out of here, I'll take a look."

One by one they pulled themselves from the wreck. They tried to help their buddies, and when they had pulled themselves together inside their only shelter, they silently wondered if it wouldn't have been better to die with their friends. They quietly tried to help one another, and they tried to think of what they should do next. They were trapped on top of a mountain; the weather was murderous; they had no food, no water, no medical supplies, and little shelter. They couldn't be sure if anyone knew where they had gone down, and even if someone did it probably would be long hours, perhaps days, before they could be reached. For that matter, they might already have been presumed dead. Who ever survives a plane crash? And who is likely to live through one occurring on some remote mountain?

"We're in deep shit, man," one of them said.

"No shit," another answered. "What does it matter? We'd be better off dead anyway."

"Bullshit. We ain't dead yet, not by a long shot. I don't want to hear no more of that kind of talk outa any of you." That order came from Sergeant First Class Marvin Daley of Ithaca, New York. A tall, carrot-shaped black, Daley had taken his thirteen years in the Army with the utmost seriousness. He might now be reduced to crawling like a lizard; he might have a ruined right leg and internal injuries he could only guess about and try manfully to hide; but he was now the boss here. And it wasn't because he was the only ranking man left alive.

"What were you doing back in this section of the plane, Sarge?" one of the men in his platoon asked as he tried rigging up a splint. "I thought you were up front with the rest of the senior NCOs, and officers."

Daley shifted his weight, and tried to smile. "Had to take a piss." He grinned. "Just my luck, I guess." He had been inside the aft toilet when the plane hit, and thrown through the rear into the rocks when the tail section ripped loose. He owed his life to the fact that the forward toilet had been occupied.

"Good thing you got done before this happened."

On the other hand, he was thinking, maybe not. Now that he knew their situation, it made no difference because there wasn't a damned thing he could do. He was now responsible for these men, and he could do almost nothing for them—they didn't teach this sort of thing in NCO school. Only fourteen of them were left, and without immediate medical attention that would be quickly reduced to eight or nine. They were on top of an unknown mountain with no way off the damned thing, so they would just try to hold out until help arrived—if help could get to them.

He addressed the men. "I ain't got no bright ideas about this. The only thing I can see is that we've gotta stay calm. We've gotta be cool, help each other out and not panic. We have to stay in here out of the weather, and we can get clothes from the dead men if we have to...stay bundled up and huddled together because we'll freeze if we don't. After daybreak we can have a look around, maybe start rummaging through everything and see if there's any food or water left. We can get us a fire going. We'll just have to try and hang on."

"What if no one knows where we're at, Sarge?"

"Somebody'll know. The pilot would've been in radio contact, and we would have been on someone's radar. Airports and air bases know where all their planes are at. That means they'll be out lookin' for us, and they're probably lookin' for us right now. I don't know anything about mountains, so I don't know how long it'll take for somebody to get to us. All we can do is take it easy...just hold on."

"I thought I heard a plane a while ago...a couple of 'em."

"They won't be landing up here, Young."

"No shit? Maybe it was a search plane, Richardson."

"Okay, knock it off. Let's try to do what we was trained to do. Let's straighten up and act like soldiers."

"What the fuck? That's all we need."

"Sit down, Richardson," Daley said. "I don't like the pep talk bullshit either, but if we don't pull together this time, there won't be a next time."

"Next time, my ass!"

"You heard what I said, Richardson."

"Well, I don't know about all of that, but I can't hardly breathe up here."

"Yeah, neither can I. Outside a while ago I couldn't catch my breath at all. How high are we?"

All of them had noticed it. Even the mildest exertion left them breathless.

Sergeant Anderson began recognizing the problem; he, too, found breathing difficult, and as he thought about it he seemed to be getting more easily confused, and disoriented. "Sit down," he told everybody. "Everybody sit down and save your strength. McDaniel's right. There isn't much oxygen up here. We're at a higher altitude than I thought."

"How high, Sarge?" Daley asked.

Anderson had spent time in the mountains when he was a kid, and he remembered running out of breath much more readily while trying to run and play. He didn't think it had been quite this bad, but he couldn't remember. He did recall something about a very tall mountain in this part of the country, but nothing else came to mind. He shook his head. "I'm not sure, but we have to be somewhere in the northern Rockies," he finally replied. "We might be sixteen, seventeen thousand feet up, maybe higher. I think I know where we're at, but I can't remember the exact name of the place. Anyway, just keep still. Don't try to overdo it."

"Okay. All of you do like Sergeant Anderson says. There's supposed to be some rations aboard, maybe some medical supplies. We'll need our strength to find 'em . . . and to do anything else."

They tallied up their injuries; those still able to move volunteered to take care of those who appeared critical. Specialist 4 Curt Beacher of Long Pond, Pennsylvania, and Specialist 4

Enrique Gomez of Los Angeles, California, looked to be the worst: Beacher had four serious punctures in his midsection and had lost a great deal of blood; Gomez had suffered at least two serious blows to the head, leaving the entire left side a purplish color, and his left arm had been mangled. Another man, Specialist 5 William Lyman from Macomb, Illinois, had been unconscious ever since being removed from his seat. His breathing was barely noticeable. Both legs had been broken. And not far behind them were Sergeant Jackson and Private First Class Hamilton; Jackson's injuries seemed to be getting worse by the hour, and Hamilton had succeeded in hurting himself worse when he tried helping the others earlier. But all any of them could do was sit. And wait.

"You light someplace, too, Eckrich," Daley said, sighing. "You're makin' me nervous jumpin' around like that."

Specialist 5 George Eckrich, the company clerk from Hutchinson, Kansas, was the least seriously injured of all. Miraculously, he had come through the crash with only a few cuts and scrapes and a bump on the head, and that was typical for him, they all thought. As the company clerk he always seemed unaffected by what happened to the company in general. He got out of all the shit details, never had to perform extra duty and had been promoted over many who had far more time in grade than he had. When brigade headquarters came down with the orders that they were all shipping out to Nam, Eckrich pitched the loudest bitch. He immediately typed and tried to process his own transfer papers, and howled even louder when Captain Hayden headed them off and threw them into the trash. You're going with the rest of us, he was told, and he'd been in a blue funk ever since.

But now, at this scene of disaster, the others had cause to wonder and worry. That goose egg on Eckrich's head might be worse than they thought because he seemed close to blind panic; the gasping and heaving of his chest had little to do with the altitude. Eckrich was flat scared shitless, and he had been scurrying here and there like a rat in a cage.

"Man!" Private John Young muttered as he watched the clerk. "He's double shook." He felt sorry for Eckrich, and thought somebody should try to calm him down. He would have done it himself if he hadn't hurt so much.

"He's gonna mess around and walk right offa the edge of this rock, man," Private First Class Edward Stacey said to Sergeant Daley.

"We take care of 'im," Daley answered quietly. "You just take it slow. You an' me, we the only niggers left up here. We gotta watch out," he added with a wink.

Stacey tried to laugh. "Equal opportunity!" He grinned. "Gotta have us token niggers ever'where...even at a plane crash."

But Eckrich had seen enough to shake anybody—far more than enough to rattle him. As the most mobile survivor he had already been over the entire crash site; every detail he came to was more gruesome than the last, and as all of it mounted and penetrated his terrified mind, he was threatening to crack. He was double shook all right. The thunderous impact had only been the beginning; over the past two hours he had seen more wreckage, more destruction and more tangled and twisted remains of men than he had known was possible in one place. Only a little while ago this had been a powerful, graceful machine filled with talking, laughing, breathing men, safely snug as it carried them through the night.

But now...

The great airplane was smashed, destroyed, blown into a million pieces. Nearly all of the laughing, talking men had been thrown into the snow and against the rocks, their bodies torn like cloth. In the forward section, which had slammed into the spires, he found Lieutenant Emory, who had been crushed between two accordioned bulkheads, his face smashed like a tomato against a structural rib, and his body skewered in a dozen places by knifelike metal spears. One arm dangled loosely in the wind, blood dripping from the fingers. The left eye was frozen open, staring balefully at whoever happened by. And ten feet away, next to a pile of broken metal and glass, was a combat boot with part of a leg protruding from the top; the leg was cut at an odd angle but sliced as neatly and cleanly as if a surgeon had amputated it. The boot was big, and Eckrich knew at once it belonged to First Sergeant Moro, a mountainous hulk of a man from Honolulu. There were other parts in the snow and a few laid across rocks as if deliberately placed there for later use. There were torn duffel bags, boots, pieces of dark green jungle fatigues, arms, legs, broken boxes and wooden crates, shreds of canvas, pieces of trucks, tires, three M-16 rifles—two broken and bent, the third intact—a jeep lying upside down, wadded like a pretzel, a box with a steel rod driven through it, parts, pieces, broken bits of metal . . . Nothing was whole anymore.

Tears came to Eckrich's eyes, and he hurried back to the flattened fuselage where the rest of them huddled, trying to keep warm and alive. He sat in a corner by himself, his legs drawn up against the world, his womb a tattered and oil-stained field jacket with the name Miller stitched over the right pocket. He shivered.

They all shivered. They sat and stared at the blackness and listened to the wind as it peppered the broken fuselage with snow and ice. One by one the small fires died out. Now and then someone would mumble something; he might, or might not, get a reply. They huddled close together, trying to keep warm, trying to catch a little sleep. Pain and fear went away when you were sleeping, and just maybe—if they were lucky— they might awaken to find that all of this had been a terrifying dream; that really they were still thousands of feet in the sky on board a mighty jet airplane that would deposit them safely at their destination. Or perhaps they would hear the drone of airplanes in the sky that had come to look for them; or the shouts of men coming up the mountain to take them down to safety. And everything would be fine then, just fine, and . . . well, you could always hope. You could go to sleep and dream. And that little poetic glimmer might be all it was lauded to be, the one little spark that could be their ticket out of here.

Two hours had passed. The airdrop of supplies had been attempted, and had failed. Doug Gorham was en route from Seattle to Fort Endicott, and in half an hour Rudi Gurdler would board a military plane in Denver. While these events were occurring, Sp5 William Lyman died without a whimper and without having regained consciousness; later, as Gorham and Gurdler argued against climbing, PFC Duane Hamilton drew a ragged breath, coughed once and died, too. His friend PFC

Stevenson, wept. Only minutes earlier they had been talking about going out and getting drunk when this was over.

"How you doin', Sergeant Anderson?" Daley asked.

"Not real bad...sore as hell, but I think the bleeding's stopped."

"Sergeant Jackson?"

"Oh Lord...umm...! Every time I bre...umm...breathe, my hair stands on end. Ohh...! My ribs are kicked around sideways."

"How about you, Sarge?" Anderson asked Daley.

"I'm okay...long as I don't try to get up and boogie." He was lying. The pain was unbearable. He was glad it was dark so his men couldn't see his agony.

Two men were watching over Specialists Gomez and Beacher. Gomez was awake but in shock, and trembling badly; PFC Damon had gotten Beacher's bleeding stopped but there was little else he could do.

"Let's all try to get some sleep. And don't be shy about snuggling up with a buddy or two—it'll keep you from freezing."

"Okay, Sarge."

"Hey, who's that? Who the fuck is singing?"

"Guess...Eckrich. He's humming to himself."

"Hey, Eckrich, willya knock that shit off?"

"Goddammit, that's all we need! Shut up, Eckrich... goddamn flake..."

"Pipe down, Richardson."

"Is that 'Amazing Grace' he's humming?"

"What the hell difference does it make? The fucker's flipped out, man. Come on, Eckrich, will you shut the hell up?"

2

THERE WAS NO CONVERSATION—only thinking.

Doug Gorham was thinking about helicopters, and that whoever nicknamed them coffee grinders and eggbeaters hadn't taken the description quite far enough. He didn't like flying anyway, and this thing was like some sort of berserk carnival ride. Whop-whop-whop-whop, like a frantic old woman beating the shit out of a rug. He pictured the inventor as a wild-eyed lunatic twirling a beanie on his head while straddling a broom.

He glanced over at Rudi Gurdler.

The Swiss climber was a picture of tranquillity, as calm as if on his way to a church social. Back against the bulkhead, legs straight out in front of him and crossed at the ankles, both hands folded, Rudi maintained a neutral sort of smile on his face, almost as though he had found "true peace" at last. It was difficult thinking of him as the premier daredevil mountaineer, the man who had conquered the worst of them, and who had made the Himalaya System and the Annapurna Chain his second home. But he was in form. Every picture ever published of him projected the same look of total relaxation, near boredom, in fact. His wiry frame didn't look big or strong enough to carry heavy packs up mountains; those long, slender fingers looked too delicate to be digging into rocks or wielding axes and hammers; and those unblemished features topped off with wispy blond hair and accented by pale blue eyes belonged on top of a body covered by a conservative three-piece suit.

Doug Gorham was rough-looking with that windblown and sunbaked complexion, big hands with thick fingers and an agile but solid-seeming body; he looked like a mountain climber. Rudi Gurdler looked like an accountant.

Rudi glanced over at Doug. The noncommittal smile widened for a moment, then returned to position, and he resumed his stare toward the front. With a sigh, he stretched both legs, then folded his arms as if about to fall asleep.

The pilot reached above his head and flipped a switch. The copilot adjusted something on the control panel, then leaned back to speak to the crew chief, who was sitting in the jump seat facing the three passengers. The chief was the classic illustration of military boredom, whose only conversation had been low grumbles and gripes.

Lieutenant Gary Palmer looked out the window; he shifted position for the tenth time, and he tried to relax. He was wishing that he was going anywhere except where he was going. He was beginning to wish that he had never taken up mountain climbing, that he'd forgotten all about ROTC at college as his friends had asked him to do, and that he'd never heard of Fort Endicott or Mount Kota or rescue teams.

But not really, not the climbing. He had been climbing since he was a kid. He had climbed through high school, and working as a guide had helped put him through college. When the mandatory four years of service came afterwards he was delighted to be assigned to an army search-and-rescue team. The duty wasn't that easy, but it kept him out of Vietnam.

He kept up with everything going on in the sport, subscribing to three monthly periodicals, and when duty permitted he got away with his girl and a few friends for camping and more climbing on weekends. Together, he and Janey had spent a sizable sum of money on camping and climbing equipment the way some couples save for houses and furniture. Neither of them regretted a penny of it.

On duty, he and his team had rescued only a handful of people, most of them tourists who had gotten themselves stranded while rock climbing. The team practiced once a week regardless of the weather, and every three months they made a practice run up one of the bigger mountains in the area—usually Mount Shawnee, Mount Grant or Shelby's Peak, all of them just over ten thousand feet high.

But they had never practiced on Kota; they'd never even considered it.

And there it was to the west, towering over the horizon like a great stone idol. Ahead of them now, it even blotted out the darkness. And they were about to tackle it.

"Where are you going this time? Another practice?"

"No. It's a real mission this time, Janey."

"Can't you say anything more about it?"

"No. Not now. But it'll probably make the news by morning. You'll hear about it soon enough."

"Sounds serious."

"Yeah . . . But don't worry, okay?"

"I'll worry, soldier boy. Count on it."

"Whatever suits you. I'll call you when we get back."

"Okay. I'll keep my chastity belt locked up!"

"What about your chastity muzzle?"

"Smartass."

"Look, I've gotta go now. They're waiting on me. I'll see you in a few days."

"Okay. Hey, be careful, huh? I want you back in one piece."

"Don't worry. I will. I'll be all right."

Which is bullshit, he thought. You're about to try Kota. Saying that you'll be careful and you'll be all right and not to worry is like saying you can stand naked in a blizzard because you're immune to pneumonia.

A static crackle came over the intercom. "Mount Kota dead ahead, gentlemen," the pilot announced.

They all leaned forward for a look—all except the crew chief, who appeared to be dozing. Gary smiled. It didn't matter who they were—troopers, airmen, marines or sailors—one of their universal talents was the ability to snooze absolutely anywhere, even at five thousand feet inside a shaking, tooth-rattling pile of plumbing.

Dead ahead, Gary was thinking. That was some way to refer to a direction. Who had thought of that? You had straight ahead, straight up, straight down—why not dead up or down? Why only ahead? Why dead? But it fit tonight because there was nothing but death ahead, lots of death on top of that rock. He thought about all those men. What had the transport pilot thought when he saw that big son of a bitch coming at them? What did he say? Probably it had been something direct and expressive such as "Holy shit!" or more likely, "Oh fuck!" You don't mince words with death ahead of you—dead ahead.

The expression on Gorham's face was undeterminable at that moment. He was staring at the mountain as if it might be alive; it almost looked as if it had grown over the past five years. And tonight it appeared to look more like some colossal sacrificial altar.

Gurdler, on the other hand, stared at the mountain with a sort of clinical curiosity, as if regarding a new species of animal. His look of confident relaxation had vanished, going to neutral, but the giveaway was in his eyes. The pale blue eyes now sparkled with an anxious fascination; had he been sitting closer, Gary would have noticed Rudi's sudden quickness of breath, and his tensed muscles. Gurdler looked as if he might leap from the helicopter and take off running toward the mountain.

The helicopter slowed, its tail boom easing around, and began settling to the ground, rocking like a Ferris wheel seat. The rotor blades hammered the cool night air, throwing dirt and debris out in a storm. Twenty-five or thirty men scurried here and there, moving equipment and setting up the base camp; a man wearing a luminescent orange vest and carrying a pair of orange-shielded flashlights guided them to the ground. The helicopter rocked, touched ground and settled, and the man with the flashlights crossed both arms above his head. The pilot began flipping switches off. "Here we are, gentlemen," he said as the turbine whine slowed. The crew chief managed at last to roust himself, and slid the doors open.

Yes. There they were.

SUNUP WAS FIFTEEN MINUTES AWAY when Gorham, Gurdler and Palmer were called into the command tent. They studied a topographical map of Mount Kota with the base camp commander, Major Evans, and his assistant, Captain Childs. Gorham explained briefly the route they would be taking.

It didn't take long—barely six minutes. When he was finished, he turned and walked out.

"Uh, Mr. Gorham?" the major said. "Is that all?"

"Yeah . . . that's about it, I think."

"What if you get into trouble somewhere? Shouldn't we know how to come after you? Or where?"

With a slight shrug, Gorham said, "If we get into trouble, there won't be a hell of a lot anybody can do about it." For that matter he didn't know why they were taking a radio with them. It was extra weight they didn't need, and they would be too busy to talk much among themselves, let alone to those at the base camp. Besides, there was little to talk about. "Once we're up there, Major, we're on our own. There won't be anything you can do for us."

"Couldn't we fly you up as far as possible?" Captain Childs asked. That was part of the plan for bringing survivors back down, getting helicopters as far up the northern or northeastern slopes as they could to airlift them out. Assuming, of course, that they brought survivors down, and that the standby climbing teams could get up to the slopes as well—there were a lot of untried ifs in the mission. But Doug had already rejected the idea. He could feel the north wind; it was getting stiffer, colder. Helicopters would be unable to land anywhere up there right now. And he knew in his gut that the storm would be moving again soon, long before they reached the summit.

The sun was beginning to show itself over the horizon, and Doug paused a minute to view it. He wondered if it might be one of his last sunrises. Then he turned to his climbing partners. "Well," he said, sighing, "if you gentlemen are ready, we'd better get saddled up and on our way." He almost added, What the hell, we can't live forever.

Rudi nodded.

"Yeah..." Gary muttered. "I'm ready." It was a lie, of course. His mind was suddenly alive with excuses, ways to beg off the whole thing. If a way had existed, any way, to catch a cold, fake a broken leg or, shit...even go blind, he might have done it. But he didn't. He followed Gorham and Gurdler to the supply tent and strapped on all the equipment he would be carrying. When it was lashed to his back and around his waist he followed them to the top of the foothills and on to the base of the mountain.

3

AT SEVEN-THIRTY THAT MORNING, Janey Burns found out where Gary Palmer had gone. The only thing she could manage to say was, "Oh dear god!"

The story of the crash took up most of the TV and radio all day long. She heard it everywhere she went. Just before she left for work she turned the TV on, and a camera was panning against Kota's eastern face. A newsman came on camera then with his latest story, but she turned him off, and when she walked outside, there was Mount Kota again, the white peak jutting up out of the southwestern sky. She tried not to look at it.

They talked about it at work; every customer coming into the bank was talking about it; on the streets, groups of people were everywhere, just standing and staring into the southern horizon at Kota. And when she went to lunch at the diner two blocks away, everybody had their ears cocked toward the radio.

"Hi, hon," Mary said. "You want the usual?"

"Yes."

"You heard the news, I guess."

"...crashed last night," the man on the radio was saying. "Army and Air Force officials are here at the campsite at Mount Kota's base, and I have with me the officer in charge of operations, Major Charles Evans. Will you tell us about the effort to reach the crash site, Major?"

"Yes. Leading the attempt is Mr. Doug Gorham of Seattle, Washington, who was part of the only group ever to reach Kota's summit five years ago, and who is the expert on this mountain. With him is Mr. Rudi Gurdler of Bern, Switzerland, a world-famous mountaineer who just happened to be in the United States on a lecture tour. Both of these men volunteered to help with the rescue and were flown here a few hours after the crash. The third man is one of our own search-and-rescue team leaders, First Lieutenant Gary Palmer of Yakima, Washington."

"How are these men proceeding so far?"

"So far, as well as can be expected. Kota is a very difficult mountain, even under ordinary conditions. They're going as fast as possible, but that isn't very fast. Time is our biggest enemy. The survivors have been trapped up there nearly fifteen hours, which is a very long time to be injured and unprotected at more than nineteen thousand feet. There's a storm approaching, and the weather experts say that it will be on top of us long before the climbers make the summit. So they're doing the best they can, and all we can do here is wait. And hope."

"Are there any high-altitude effects from the storm that could be slowing them down yet?"

"Probably not yet. They're having to carry a lot of extra equipment. They're packing extra tents, additional food and quite a few medical supplies along with their own equipment.

Because of the nature of the mountain, they are also carrying a lot of extra climbing gear.''

"Such as?''

"A lot of ropes,'' he went on. "Carabiners, or elongated clips with spring gates on one side.'' He explained what they were to the listeners. "They attach their ropes to them, and clip the carabiners to pitons.'' Once more he launched into an explanation of the device. "A piton is a metal stake driven with a piton hammer into cracks in the rocks. The carabiners clip into the eyelet holes on the outer ends. Mr. Gorham also explained that his former partners set in a number of contraction bolts at certain locations. A contraction bolt is about what its name implies. It's a heavy bolt driven into solid rock. It is left behind after use, and any climber may use it later by attaching nuts or other hardware to it. They also carry snow and ice equipment such as ice screws, which work something like pitons; ice axes; crampons, which are metal spikes strapped onto their boots; plus insulated clothing, bottles of oxygen, a small camp stove, lanterns…you name it. All three of them are packing more than one hundred pounds of gear apiece. The higher they go, the heavier the packs will become.''

"Why didn't they take two or three more men with them?''

"That was considered, but rejected by Mr. Gorham. More men, he felt, would slow their progress even further. I haven't done much climbing, but I could explain how they're having to do it for the benefit of those who know nothing about it.''

"Please do,'' and the newsman chuckled. "That includes me.''

"Well, the man in the lead—Mr. Gorham—has to set all of their climbing aids into position as he goes up, the aids being the pitons, carabiners, chocks and wedges, and tie onto all the bolts. He also works two ropes into place as he moves up, a primary and a safety rope. But he can go just so far, usually until his ropes or aids run out, then he stops, and the second man comes up. The second man acts as the relay man, passing equipment up to the one in the lead. When the third man climbs up, he has to remove all the equipment set by the lead man. This is called cleaning the pitch. When he has all the aids he passes them up to the relay man, who passes them to the top, and the whole process starts again. I should add also that the relay man usually acts as the main belay man for the team. A belay is simply holding the ropes tight and helping a man to climb up.

"As you can see, more men on the team would slow them down. Mr. Gorham also thought it foolhardy to put two or three extra men in such danger, especially when it was unnecessary."

"How many survivors are there?"

"Ten that we know of, but there could be more."

"What happens if the climbers become stalled or trapped by that storm?"

"No one is more aware of the weather than they are. We can order them to turn back if the attempt appears hopeless, but the decision of when and where to turn around is up to them. If they get stuck, they'll just have to ride out the storm. If they think they have a shot at a successful rescue, they'll keep going. If not, they'll turn around. They are the only ones who can make those judgments. As I said, all *we* can do is wait."

With most of her lunch uneaten, Janey grabbed her purse and rushed out.

"Hon?" Mary called after her. "Are you all right?"

"Thus far," continued the man on the radio, "Army and Air Force officials have kept secret the flight number, its origin and destination and the name of the Army unit on board. We have, however, learned that the flight originated somewhere on the east coast and was bound for California. There also has been no explanation yet about the cause of the crash except for a possible aircraft malfunction. These details will be reported as soon as they are released. We will also remain here at Mount Kota National Park and relay the information to our listeners as it becomes available.

"This is Dale McClain, KSCM Radio News, reporting."

"Thank you, Dale," said another man. "In Vietnam today, elements of the Army First Infantry Division engaged . . ."

DURING THE CONVERSATIONS they had had Gary noticed most of the talk directed at him. Subtle, but a definite pep talk. The others were worried about him. He needed more confidence about this climb, and he also recognized that any such lack could mean disaster farther up. They now had only one another and no one could back off an inch. You know how to do most of this, Doug was saying. You know the basics, the mechanics. All you need now are the details of this mountain, and I'll give them to you one at a time. There's nothing to worry about until we get to it.

When they arrived at the base of the Tombstone, Kota's flanks appeared to shoot straight up. Playtime was over. The walk through the rocks was a stroll, something to give you your wind, your mountain legs, and as they were preparing to work their way up the angular slab, Gary recognized it as a last chance to reconsider. Do you really want to try this? the great mountain seemed to say on the wind. If so... well, good luck, friend. You will be on your own. Trust in yourself and your friends. Not in me.

They were ready at last, roped up, equipment set, Doug leading. His last warning to Gary was not to forget to remove any pitons they'd be driving into the wall. When they got to the Lunatic they would need every last one.

Trouble came barely three hundred feet up, when a contraction bolt popped out; Doug slid on his belly for fifteen feet before Rudi's belay stopped him. No conversation followed, no questions; Rudi and Gary knew what had happened, and they hung on to their ropes, belaying for each other as Doug shifted himself around and readjusted his precarious hold. The spot he was in was almost perfectly smooth; no cracks existed for another one hundred feet. Rudi looked up only once, and a small shower of rocks peppered him.

Five minutes passed before they heard the familiar *tink-tink-tink* of a piton being hammered into the rock. Dust and a few more small rocks tumbled from above; snaps and clicks could be heard as Doug secured a carabiner, then his rope, and finally yelled for slack. He went up, drove in another piton, called for a belay and secured the rope again. He was moving, and now, so were Rudi and Gary. Rudi looked down with a smile, giving Gary the circular thumb and forefinger sign. Gary returned the gesture, but when he looked up at Gurdler he was amazed to find the Swiss climber another twenty feet above him. He had to pause for a moment and watch the incredible rock-climbing technique he had heard and read about; crab-like, almost like a spider on a wall, Rudi skittered up, treating the Tombstone almost as if it were flat. He was going twice as fast as Doug; Gary wished he could get out the camera and record it.

"Run the ropes out faster, Lieutenant!" Gurdler called. "And watch yourself when you approach this area!"

"Okay!" He was belaying for Rudi Gurdler, he thought. Amazing.

They continued, calling to one another only for belays or slack. Gary concentrated on his work, looking up every few minutes so that he wouldn't fall behind. They were trying to maintain about one hundred feet between them, close enough to help one another, but far enough apart to prevent one man from taking anybody else down if he fell.

Gary passed the spot where Doug's bolt had pulled loose. It had left a deep, jagged hole with cracks splintering out like broken plate glass. He only glanced at it; don't dwell on the bad places, he was telling himself. Just keep going. That's it, baby, you're doing great, looking good.

An hour passed. Gary checked again on Doug's and Rudi's progress. Doug appeared to be nearing the top of the Tombstone while Rudi was roughly a hundred feet below, hooking up to another bolt. He called for a belay, and Gary pulled against the ropes. Rudi went up; minutes later, so did Gary. Ten more minutes went by, and Doug called out that he was over the top and preparing to anchor himself in.

Rudi went up. Gary knocked the next piton loose, snapping it and its carabiner onto his belt, and pulled himself up to the next one. Rudi worked his way to the last piton and stirrup about fifteen feet below the crest of the Tombstone; he was belaying for Gary as he moved to the next one. Doug prepared to haul Rudi over the top, and Gary was already several feet past the last piton when he realized that he'd forgotten to clean that pitch; instinctively, he reached down for it.

"Oh, shit!" The move caught both Doug and Rudi off belay. Suddenly, the ropes slackened, and Gary fell, rolling over onto his back as he kicked and fought for a hold, one hand hanging on to the rope, the other trying to dig into the rock.

Rudi grabbed his ropes and pulled as did Doug above him. He abandoned his own holds, hanging instead to the rope above with one hand and the rope below with the other. If Palmer fell more than thirty feet he would be a goner; if his rope didn't break they would have to cut it loose or Rudi would fall, too.

"Find a hold!" Doug bellowed. "Anything! Find a hold!"

Oh, Jesus! Gary managed to turn himself around facing with the rock again, and he dug into the stone wall with both hands and feet, looking for any crack or protrusion. The ropes tightened, and his fall was halted; seconds later he had hold of something. He didn't look to see what it was. He just held on. Below him, the forests of Mount Kota National Park looked like a green carpet. The portion of the Tombstone below his feet looked a mile long. If he fell he wouldn't stop until he was somewhere in New Mexico.

"I've got a *hoooold*!" he cried, and he fumbled along his belt for a piton. He positioned the point into a crack, readied his hammer and started pounding. He hoped it would hold; no other spot here would accept a piton, and he would not get a chance to drive in another one.

Tink, tink, tink, tink ...

You stupid stupid son of a bitch what's the matter with you you dumb shit! You could've been killed and dragged one of those guys down with you!

He pulled himself up, snapping in a carabiner and his rope. "I've got it!" he yelled. "I'm in!"

"Hang on!" he heard Doug reply. "I'm gonna pull Rudi up! Then we'll get you!"

DOUG CALMLY ASKED HIM what had happened; Rudi was preparing himself for the next portion of the climb, as if nothing at all had happened. "Lose a hold or something?" Doug finished, handing Gary a chocolate bar.

It was an out, an opportunity to avoid telling them what had really happened. But it was, Gary happened to think, a test of character. They had to trust one another, so he should tell Doug the exact truth and accept whatever followed.

Gary sighed. He looked their leader straight in the eye and said, "I screwed up. I forgot to clean one of the pitches, and like a dumb ass I tried to reach down and grab the piton and stirrup. Dammit, I know better than that."

Doug took a drink of water, then nodded. "Okay. It could've been worse, so don't worry about it."

Palmer understood that, too; the less said about it, the better. And he knew that such an idiotic thing better not happen again. Better judgment was expected of him from now on.

"Uhh...maybe I'd better rope up between both of you," he said, trying to make it sound natural.

"Good idea. We'll do that." It seemed Doug thought it a good time to change the subject, for he stood up and suggested that Gary and Rudi take a look at their next obstacle. "Now would be a good time for you to take a piss, too, because it'll be quite a while before we're able to whip it out for another one."

None of the hazards on Kota could be gauged accurately from any distance. Judgment of how to negotiate any obstacle had to be reserved until you were on it, and this was doubly true for the Lunatic Wall. A few feet from where they were standing on the rock ledge was their first pitch of the monstrous wall. But no photograph, no distant gaze from the ground far below, could do it justice or inspire the sudden awe and jolt of fear one got from standing there next to it, about to cross it. What was only huge when seen from a distance was now gargantuan, looking as if it stretched up and away from them for several miles. And this was only the midsection. A look down was both thrilling and hair-raising, a straight drop of one-quarter mile before you would hit anything.

Gary began looking for their exit point far away at the diagonal corner, but it was too far away to be seen clearly and partially obscured by the roof two hundred feet above them. And, as Doug had said, there was no route around the roof—only over it. It stretched across nearly the full width of the Lunatic, an uneven horizontal scar across the eastern face. Fortunately, their ascent would traverse one of the least prominent points.

They picked up their packs and equipment, Doug readying himself for the first pitch. At that moment the thought of having a fully paid insurance policy suddenly struck Gary as a comfort. He didn't know why such a thing occurred to him just then, and even stranger, he had an urge to ask Doug and Rudi if they had one, or if any life insurance company had been crazy enough to insure them at all. He had to fight down the urge; he couldn't believe he was even thinking these things.

Doug gave both of them a few final instructions. Gary nodded, determined not to screw up anything this time. There would be no second chances up here. Rudi coughed. He was still studying the wall.

"The rock is in pretty good shape until we get up there near the northeast corner." Doug pointed. "But it's pretty flaky from there on, the last fifty feet or so. The main problem is that most of the time we won't be in too good a position to help one another. We'll be attached only to whatever aids we've got. If anybody gets into trouble he could be on his own unless the other two are anchored in pretty well. And if you're anchored in it's hard to help anybody else. So make sure every move is the right one."

They had named this ascent the Woodhull Route. Steve Woodhull, the best wall climber of the three of them, was the first one ever to cross it, marking the route himself. It was a repetitive stair-step traverse that had taken Woodhull fully two days to mark and negotiate.

He had also been the one who named it the Lunatic. For years the eastern face had been called simply that, or sometimes Scarface because of the horizontal roof. Woodhull's comment had been: "Only a fucking lunatic would do what I'm doing, so this is a lunatic wall." The name stuck.

It was a hell of a name, and the lunacy didn't stop there. In early summer of 1961, a group of California rock climbers decided to scale it from the base to the top. Such a feat might not have been impossible, even though nobody had tried it, but two things halted the attempt. First, the leader fell. Nobody learned exactly why, but he still fell, and his sudden stop was at the end of a 265-foot plunge. And secondly, the park rangers—leery of

the attempt anyway—refused further permission to scale the
entire Lunatic.

"Any questions?" Doug asked, pausing to study the overcast sky for a moment. He was certain that they would see the
storm before the day was out.

No questions.

"Okay. Let's do it."

4

MAJOR EVANS WALKED UP to Captain Childs, who stared at the
eastern face through a pair of binoculars. "Can you see them?"
he asked.

"Yes, sir. It's a little hazy up there, but I can see them," and
he handed the binoculars to the major.

"Damn weather's really turning to shit. What's the latest on
it?"

"Last I heard, it was about the same." The captain barely
said that when one of the communications men hurried up to
them. He had two messages.

"Yes?"

"The storm's moving, sir. Endicott Center was just notified
by the National Weather Service that it's on the move, and
they're estimating it'll pass through here in about six
hours . . . eight at the latest."

"Son of a *bitch*!"

"What's the second message?"

"General Grady is coming. He's bringing General Streetor
with him. They'll need a place to bunk because they're spending the night in camp."

Evans almost asked: Now what the hell for? That was all he
needed, a pair of generals breathing down his neck. There was
absolutely nothing else for them to do in camp except what
everyone else was doing—wait. And their presence would only
make everybody more uncomfortable and less efficient.

"Okay, Sarge." Evans sighed. "Have someone fix up one of
the tents for them. You'd better notify the field mess, too."

"Yes, sir."

"Has there been any word from Lieutenant Palmer?" Childs asked.

"Not a thing, sir. Not since they started this morning. I think they've turned their radio off. We tried contacting them a couple of times but got no answer."

"Well, you'd better keep trying. Keep your channel open, and you guys will have to take turns sitting up tonight."

"Yes, sir."

"Man, oh man..." Evans said, shaking his head as he handed the binoculars back to Childs. "I sure hope those bastards make it through this."

"Which ones?"

"Both." But he really meant the men trapped at the summit. If they could live through this, they could survive anything.

None of the photo reconnaissance flights launched since dawn returned with any usable information. Only the first mission, launched immediately after the crash the night before, had showed that men were moving around on Kota's summit. By noon when a fifth mission had been ordered, everything at the crash site was obscured by high winds and blowing snow. The flight returned to Fort Endicott with hazy, foggy-looking pictures that showed only one brief glimpse of part of the wreck. Everything above fifteen thousand feet was already feeling the effects of the approaching storm.

By midafternoon, all further missions were canceled. The base meteorologist notified the airfield that all aircraft be grounded until further notice. The prediction from the National Weather Service was for thirty-five-mile-an-hour winds with occasional gusts of fifty miles per hour; twenty-four inches of snow was being predicted at all elevations above seventeen thousand feet. All of this would come over an eight- to ten-hour period commencing at approximately 7:00 p.m.

At the base camp, attempts were made every fifteen minutes to contact the climbing team. The orders were for them to dig in anywhere they could after they were off the wall.

On the Lunatic Wall, they needed no predictions or verifications of what they could already see. And feel. All they could do was keep climbing. They were in no position to stop.

CHAPTER FOUR

AT DAYBREAK, ONLY Sergeant Anderson ventured outside the shelter. He thought he might get lucky and find some food or supplies lying around that they could use. He also thought he had prepared himself for the scene of destruction outside.

He was outside for perhaps ten minutes. During that time he collected a few extra jackets lying in the snow; he found, by accident, several bits of food, mostly candy bars and oddities some of the men preferred to store in their pockets to eat later. He had to smile. Soldiers were always pack rats, scroungers, even about their food. At the end of those ten minutes as he hurried back to the wadded hulk where the men huddled in the bitter cold, he was frowning. As he had heard one of the men say last night: We're in deep shit.

Sergeant Daley grunted painfully as Anderson sat down next to him. Daley, he noted, was getting worse by the minute.

"We're in trouble," he said quietly.

"Tell me somethin' I don't know." Daley sighed, trying to shift positions.

"Well...I think I know where we are. Not that it matters much."

"Where?"

"On top of Mount Kota. In southwestern Montana."

Daley shook his head. He'd never heard of Mount Kota; in fact, he joked, he had heard only passing rumors about the existence of Montana. "Hell, man, I'm from New York where things are civilized."

That might have been true enough. And they weren't likely to find a spot in the whole damned country any less civilized than this, Anderson told him, because it had to be the most remote place in the States. "I think Kota is the third or fourth highest mountain in North America, Sarge. Only McKinley and Logan are taller."

"How do you know we ain't on top of one of them?"

"They're in Alaska and the Yukon."

"Oh." Daley shifted his position again. It was impossible to find comfort. It was too cold, too miserable, and he hurt too much. "Well," he grunted, "you're damn straight about that. It don't matter at all."

"I don't know…maybe it does. I'm from Utah, and I've seen this rock before. And if I remember my geography it's more than nineteen thousand feet tall."

"What about it?"

"Well…I wouldn't tell anybody this, but I don't think this thing has ever been climbed before. Not all the way to the top, anyway."

"Oh, shit! Are you sure?"

Anderson shook his head. "No, not exactly. I remember stories about some men who tried for years to climb it, but I don't know if they ever made it. A lot of people have tried, and a lot of them got killed."

"Yeah, well, keep it to yourself."

"Sure thing. I hope to Christ I'm wrong."

By then, they knew that people had learned of the crash and were looking for them. They heard planes go over now and then; they couldn't see the planes because of the overcast conditions, and they probably couldn't be seen from the air because of the wind blowing all the snow around. But at least people were trying to help them, trying to get to them. Anderson and Daley also mentioned the possibility of an air rescue, but neither knew if any kind of helicopter could fly this high or set down in a high wind. They knew little about aircraft—except that they sometimes crash and kill a lot of people. To Anderson, it all added up to one conclusion: they were all dead men unless help could get to them in the next few hours. If not, all they could do was wait. If their injuries didn't kill them, then the weather, or starvation, would. All they could do was wait for death.

At that point, Sergeant Daley found himself not caring one way or another. He had already resigned himself. Right after sunup he had worked up the courage to examine his injuries, his shattered right leg and the two large and painful spots on his midsection. Seeing them was a shock, but not a surprise. His leg looked as if he had taken two or three grenades. Chunks of blood-smeared flesh hung from it like blubber hacked from a whale, and most of it had gone completely numb. That had cinched it. No question. Even if by some miracle they got out of this, it was all over for him, his Army career, everything. You didn't have to be a doctor to see there was no possible way to save a leg that badly damaged, not even if a medical team arrived in the next five minutes. Even if he lived, the leg was a former part of him, and if it didn't kill him, his internal injuries would. His normal skin shade was a dark chocolate-brown, but the two bad spots were shiny purple with reddish patches all over them. That is serious internal bleeding, my man, he told himself. It meant that something—probably several vital organs—had been heavily damaged, quite possibly beyond repair. Or repair coming in time to help. Every movement caused the pain to worsen, and both of the places seemed to be growing steadily larger. He wasn't too worried about the cold, the snow, where they had crashed, or much of anything else, because he was sure he'd be dead long before any of those things got to him. You just keep your ass parked right here, he told himself, and make your peace because you ain't goin' nowhere, no way, no how.

"I just hope I don't gotta wait too long," he whispered.

"What was that, Sarge?" Anderson asked.

"Nothing'... nothin'. Just talkin' to myself...."

They had lost no one else during the night, but it wouldn't last. If Daley looked bad, Stacey and Jackson looked nearly dead, especially Stacey. The black private was just barely breathing. Short, desperate gasps wheezed and rattled in his chest, and each time he coughed he brought up bright red oxygenated blood along with small chunks of brownish tissue. He was shaking with the cold, and trembling in agony. Jackson, on the other side of the plane, had gone completely pale, holloweyed, and seemed unable to move at all. He had doubled up, shivering under two torn field jackets, and when Anderson asked him how he was doing, he couldn't reply. He grunted, spit up something, then closed both eyes. All three of them,

Anderson concluded, were down to their final hours, maybe minutes.

Not that any of them was becoming any better off. They were huddled together, shivering, injured, fearful. SP4 Beacher was still in shock, and SP4 Gomez was still unconscious—nobody knew whether he had come to in the night or not, and it didn't matter. They could do no more for him than anyone else. There were more serious lacerations, burns, fractures and contusions than Anderson had ever seen in one place; more lumps, bumps and bruises than he could count; more injuries than he could have invented. They all should have been killed outright. That was what happened in every other crash he'd ever heard about—no survivors. It should have happened here. It would have been a hell of a lot better for everybody involved if they'd all been killed. Some of them could still move—Private Young, Private First Class Damon, Corporal McDaniel, Corporal Richardson and maybe Private First Class Stevenson—and they would be able to find what food was available, get a fire going and help to make things livable for a while. SP5 Eckrich was a question mark, as he had always been. He was still sitting alone in a corner staring at nothing; the only good sign was that he had finally stopped humming to himself. Maybe they could make use of him—maybe not. Maybe everything they would do in the next few hours would be like jerking off, pretending to hang on, making believe that they would get out of this. Maybe the best thing for all of them was to jump off the top and get it over with. He didn't know.

But he said, "Let's try to find some food . . . some more clothing. We'll try to get a fire going, too. Stevenson, you stay in here and look after everyone. The rest of us will go outside for a look around, and—"

"You ain't gotta worry about Stacey no more," Daley said quietly. He pulled a jacket over the private's head. "A minute ago, that was it . . . he just sighed . . . and it stopped. . . ."

"Sarge, I'm sorry," Anderson muttered. He waited a moment before going on. "Uh . . . like I was saying, we'll get a fire going, make something where we can melt snow so we can have a little water. There was supposed to be one or two cases of C-rations on board. Maybe some of it can be found. And we'll grab anything else we can use…clothes, blankets, anything we can find.''

A drawled, laconic word came from one of them: "Why?"

"Because, Richardson," Sergeant Anderson said, sighing wearily, "we might just be able to live through this if we try. I'd appreciate everyone's cooperation. If we do get out of this, a lot of brass will expect a full report of everything that's happened, and if somebody doesn't help out or follow orders, then he's gonna get his ass in a wringer. Understand?"

"Yeah," Richardson answered with a cold smile. "I understand that that's a lot of goddamn ifs, Sarge. And I understand that you ain't got any answers—you, or that big nigger over in the corner. I understand that with you leading us, we'll never—"

"You'd best cool it, Richardson," McDaniel said, starting to get up from where he sat.

"Fuck you, McDaniel! I've got more than eight months time-in-grade over you, so sit down."

Private First Class Damon was starting to get up, too. "You might outrank me, too, Richardson, but I'll take your fuckin' head off if you don't shut up right now."

"All *right*!" Anderson cried. "That's enough! *I'm* giving the orders, Richardson, so get used to it! And if you don't like it, we'll settle it here and now. Understand *that*."

Richardson got up, but it was slowly. He glared at Anderson and the others, then stormed outside. "Stupid assholes…" he muttered.

Anderson started to go after him, but Daley halted him with a weak wave. "Let 'im go." He sighed. "Let 'im cool down." He wanted to give the younger NCO a lesson on how to handle his men under extremes, but he could not. For one thing, his arm seemed to be all he could move right now, and it felt as if it was wrapped with lead weights. For another, he felt as if he was losing everything—vision, concentration, hard consciousness, even rationality. He seemed to be drifting away into the distance, away from this crash site, away from his men. He couldn't stop it, and he didn't really want to. Most of his thoughts and worries had been replaced with a fearful sort of curiosity, and surprisingly, much of the pain had ceased. He actually felt warm all over, and he wanted to tell everybody that he was fine, just great, but even the slightest effort of movement or speech was now impossible. It ain't bad, he thought. It ain't bad at all...nothin' to worry about. Somebody—Anderson, he supposed—knelt next to him. He couldn't quite see whose face it was, and the words were faraway, foreign...no meaning...unimportant. Not bad at all....

"Sarge? Sergeant Daley?"

The tall black man from Ithaca, New York, slumped over where he sat, his head lolling to one side.

Richardson might be right, Anderson thought. Hell, he didn't have any answers; he really didn't know what he was doing. And if everybody began dying off like this, there was no point in wasting any effort trying to stay alive.

Even Eckrich, still mired in whatever delirium had caught him, seemed to know. As Anderson stood there, trying to think of what he should do next, Eckrich began laughing. It was only a chuckle at first, followed by silly-sounding giggles. He soon broke out in deep, maniacal belly laughter, and he looked as though he might double up and roll around on the floor. Laughter filled the inside of the shattered fuselage and rang above the steadily increasing howling of the wind.

2

THERE WERE PROBLEMS almost from the first traverse up the Lunatic Wall. Doug remembered nearly every foot of the Woodhull Route, but he found places that had deteriorated badly over the past five years. They had set in contraction bolts all across the wall along the route, but the first two he tried to use had loosened and were ready to pull out. He was forced to alter the route and drive pitons instead, using almost twice as much time as he'd intended. It occurred to him that if whole sections of their previous route had eroded this badly and they were forced to take alternate traverses, they might not get off the rocks and onto the snow for an extra day.

He began his vertical ascent early, then had to traverse horizontally some hundred feet farther than usual. It put him on sections of the wall he had never before used, but he reached the second traverse point in good shape, and he prepared to attach to the third bolt. This one felt solid, and he quickly twisted on a nut, then snapped his carabiner into place. Testing it again after his rope was attached, he called for a belay, and hoisted himself up.

Gary was on the wall below; Rudi was at an angle below him. Both of them heard the loud pop when Doug's bolt pulled out; both instantly tightened their ropes. Doug fell, but it was only three or four feet before he found a tiny ledge with his toes, and his hands dug into a crack just above his head.

"Doug!" Gary yelled. "Are you okay?" He happened to look down. He felt like a cockroach hanging on to the side of an airplane.

Panting, shaking a bit, Doug closed both eyes for a moment. It was his first slip of any sort on the Lunatic. "Yes," he muttered under his breath. "Just fine." *Except that I think I just pissed my pants.*

"Doug!"

"Yeah!" he called hoarsely. "I'm okay." Now, he thought, how many more of their bolts would pop out? After Woodhull marked the route across the Lunatic, all three of them had spent days setting in dozens of bolts at exactly the right locations, into good, solid rock. Surely five years hadn't deteriorated them this much. At any rate, there was only one good route across the Lunatic, and they were on it.

Pebbles fell as he readjusted his position, getting out another piton and his hammer. One foot dangled in the air as he set the piton into the crack above, and he called for a belay.

"One *belaaay*!" Gary yelled from below. The ropes creaked. More pebbles fell, bouncing against the wall.

Whack—pliinng . . .

"Shit!" He hit the piton in wrong, and it bounced from the crack, fluttering like a leaf to the ground far below. "One hell of a carpenter you'd make," he mumbled, then positioned another piton into the crack. When it was driven in he tested it twice; it was solid.

He took a deep breath, thinking, One more time. *"Slaaaack!"*

"Offff belaaay!" Gary yelled, and the ropes loosened. Doug grabbed another carabiner, pulled the rope through it, then pulled himself back up. Five minutes passed before he worked his way past the jagged, spiderwebbed hole. It looked as if someone had hit it with a high-powered rifle shot. But he ignored it; he was nearing the underside of the roof. The worst was just ahead.

Gary and Rudi worked their way up to a point just below the roof buttress, where they anchored in and took another breather. Doug called more instructions down to them. "I don't know if we can trust any of these old bolts, so get out all the pitons, chocks and carabiners. Get ready to relay." They were already more than an hour behind what they expected—not a considerable amount of time until they looked at the sky. It was getting darker and windier by the minute. The storm would be on them soon, and they had to get off the Lunatic and high above it, fast. Doug shook his head. If this climb was with Woodhull and Karber, they'd have been long gone by now. Crossing the whole damned wall wouldn't have taken more than four or five hours, and that would have been loafing.

He repositioned himself and called that he was ready to move. "If anything pulls loose while I'm trying to go over the edge, and I fall...well, don't get sentimental. Cut the goddamn rope and let me go. Don't stop to think about it, just do it. Understand? Or you'll go down with me." And with another deep breath he started up again. "Hail Mary, full of grace," he grunted, remembering Steve Woodhull's Lunatic prayer, "get me outa this fuckin' place...."

3

JANEY BURNS WENT HOME early on the advice of the bank manager. She couldn't concentrate on anything. After miscounting three deposits in a row she dropped two hundred dollars in nickels all over the floor. They were still chasing them when he told her to try it again tomorrow. "We all have our days, Janey."

Indeed. And when she got home, the radio was on. "...And officials at Fort Endicott have expressed concern about the weather as well. The National Weather Service has issued a severe storm warning, and we at the lower elevations can expect about two inches of rain over the next twenty-four to forty-eight hours. This will mean high winds at all elevations above fifteen thousand feet and at least a foot and a half to two feet of snow. Conditions for the men trapped on Mount Kota's summit will be critical, and quite dangerous for the three rescue climbers on the mountain right now...."

Mrs. Burns looked at her daughter, who was still frozen in the chair. She wanted to say something, just a word, anything, to assure Janey that everything would be all right, just as she had always done. Even during the worst times she always managed to find something that would comfort her children, to make their pain a little easier. It had always been more difficult with Janey, though; like the time when she was nine. They had had an old horse, a mare that got so old she could barely stand and couldn't even eat. They'd been forced to call out the vet to destroy the animal. It almost destroyed Janey. Any death around their farm left her grief stricken for days, and when her grandfather died, followed only a few short years later by her dad, Mrs. Burns wondered if her oldest daughter might need professional help. Whenever Janey took something into her heart its loss always seemed to amputate a piece of her. Death was a cold-handed, faceless thief. She had never come to terms with it.

But what could you say or do about something like this? she wondered, moving to another chair.

"...that the progress of the climbers, according to their last radio communication, has been excellent. They will not be able to make the summit by nightfall, but they expect to be in a good place in which they can bivouac. And since the storm is expected to be out of the area by morning, the climbers believe their progress tomorrow should be good as well...."

She took Janey's hand, and still wondered what to say to her. What comfort was there this time? I *think* it will be all right? Gary will *probably* get off that mountain okay? All of the wind and snow and ice and a million other hazards and obstacles *shouldn't* hurt them?

"Would you like a cup of tea, Janey?" she asked softly, stroking her girl's dark hair.

Janey sniffled once, and nodded. "Could you turn off that radio, too?"

4

So FAR, SO GOOD. Doug had pulled himself over the outer edge of the roof. All the bolts he came to had been in good shape. Now Gary and Rudi could hear the scrambling of boots above them and the familiar *tink-tink-tink* of pitons being driven in. They would send their packs up along one of the traverse ropes; Doug would anchor them to the top of the roof, and belay for Gary as he made his traverse.

Fifteen minutes later, the packs were up and tied down. Doug called for Gary to begin his ascent.

"Slow and easy, Lieutenant," Rudi said with a smile. "Take your time."

Gary tried to smile back. He reminded himself that he had the easiest job of the three of them. Right now all he had to do was get his ass up there. They were doing most of the work.

He roped up, then called for the belay. The lines snapped as taut as guitar strings, and he went out, hand over hand, each movement slow and careful. It was roughly eighteen feet out to the edge of the roof, and he watched only the edge and each advance he made. Slowly, he passed under the first bolt, then the second. The third was near the edge. The wind was gusting a little, and he felt a few icy drops of water hit his cheeks; one by one he collected his carabiners and snapped them to his belt. At last he came to the third bolt, and he paused for a moment to catch his breath. The edge of the roof was within reach; Mother Earth was a long way down. If he lost it now, regardless of whether or not it was his fault, nobody would be able to do a damned thing to help him. He would have to cut his own rope to keep from pulling Gorham down with him. Don't think about that, he told himself, and he reached for the edge. The

ropes drooped before going over the top, the worst part of this
traverse. The rocks out there were like knives, and he would
drop three or four feet before pulling himself over.

"*Slaaaack!*" he yelled, unfastening the last carabiner.

Doug was lashed and anchored into place at the top of the
roof where it blended back into the rest of the wall, tied at the
waist by a separate line attached to a pair of bolts behind him,
and to the ropes going down—a triangular web of primary and
secondary ropes. He heard the call from Gary, and loosened his
belay. The ropes trembled and creaked, and after he pulled
again, he saw a gloved right hand fumble its way over the top
of the rocks, searching for the next hold.

"To your right, Gary!" Doug called. "Okay, straight
ahead...keep coming...keep coming, that's it...another eight
inches... you're almost there, it's just ahead of—that's it!
You've got it!"

The left hand appeared, then the top of Gary's head. He
pulled, and Doug pulled against the rope. And Gary swung
himself over the edge.

"Good job, Gary. Just fine."

He was going to thank Doug for the help, but when he looked
up and saw the remainder of the wall still facing them, he
moaned instead. The Lunatic loomed above them like a colossal gray monolith reaching halfway to the moon.

"I'm beginning to see why Woodhull called this thing the
Lunatic."

"The rest of it isn't quite as bad as it looks. Now, get up here
and anchor yourself in so you can belay for Gurdler. I'm gonna
have to get my ass out to the next pitch and get things ready so
we can get going. I don't like the looks of that sky."

"You're not gonna free-climb this thing?"

"Not exactly. It's okay, I'll be anchored in. I know this pitch
pretty well." All of which was maybe half-true. Ordinarily,
Doug wouldn't consider going out there without being roped up
to somebody else. And any sort of free climb on the Lunatic
was out of the question, especially this high. Had he known of
that attempt back in 1961 by that bunch of dickheads from
California he would have taken himself and some of his larger
friends to stop it.

But there was no time for long or detailed explanations right now. The weather was rapidly turning to shit, so they had to get off the wall as soon as possible. With luck they might have six good hours of climbing time ahead of them, and he hoped it would be enough . . . or enough to get them to shelter.

Forty feet up and to the right of where Gary was anchored in, Doug attached hardware to another bolt, set the rope into place, then stopped for a minute to listen to his partners. Commands and responses were being shouted back and forth; he could hear faint snaps and clicks of aids being retrieved; everything seemed to be going well for a change, so he turned his attention back to the wall and what he had been doing.

Then he heard it—a loud *whap*, something like a whip snapping. And he heard Gary scream Rudi's name.

"Oh, Jesus!"

Gary had been watching for Rudi's hand to appear so that he could guide him up and over the edge. Rudi called for a belay; Gary tightened the ropes. The hand came up, then the top of Rudi's head. Gary was about to cry out that the handhold was just in front of him when Rudi coughed. In an eye blink he disappeared. The ropes trembled. One of them caught in the sharp rocks; the sudden strain cut it in half almost instantly, and it snapped like a rifle report, the upper end flying back toward Gary and almost hitting him.

It happened so fast that Gary had no time to take it in. He thought for a second that he was seeing things. He froze, seeing the unbelievable—Rudi Gurdler had fallen from the end of his rope, *his* belay.

Doug turned around to look. He was helpless forty feet above them on the wall. Whatever Gary did next would save or kill Rudi, and he would be entirely on his own.

Gary hung on to the only remaining rope. It was all he could do for the moment.

"Gary!" Doug yelled. "Don't answer me, just do what I tell you!"

Gary nodded once, afraid of looking up, terrified of saying anything.

"Get another rope down to 'im! *Fast!* Get that one secured to whatever's handy! *Anything!*"

Somehow, the belay rope had come out of the small pulley anchored near the edge, put there to keep the rope out of the rocks. Or maybe the pulley had come loose—Gary didn't know. And he didn't know what condition the rope was in now or how long Gurdler could hang there before it broke. All he could do was hold on and not make any sudden moves...such as sneezing or even breathing too hard.

Gary lashed the rope to every piton he could reach, frantically wrapping and double-knotting every remaining inch. He rechecked his own safety ropes, then grabbed the nearest one available from one of the packs.

"Swing yourself around, head down!" Doug yelled. "Set in another pulley! Then get that rope down to 'im."

The process took five minutes. Gary hammered in a new pulley as close to the edge as he dared, not sure that it was close enough, but the rock at the edge was too crumbly and weak. The new rope was threaded through, and he began running it down, hoping that it wouldn't get tangled in anything else—and that it would reach Rudi in time. He couldn't judge how far Gurdler had fallen; only that he was still down there somewhere. The rope strained and creaked like an old saddle.

Twenty feet below the roof, Rudi Gurdler dangled helplessly in the wind. He was afraid to breathe. The wind swung him gently back and forth; occasionally, he felt himself bounce slightly, and he cringed, closing both eyes.

After a time—it could have been seconds, perhaps hours—he heard Gary scrambling around on the sloped ledge above, and Doug's voice shouting commands that he could not understand. No doubt Gorham was telling the young lieutenant what to do; no doubt Palmer was frantic, probably thinking that the emergency was his fault.

Above, he could hear the faint whacking of steel against rock.

Gently, slowly, he dared a look up. Several pebbles from the roof's edge fell past him; several struck him, and he stiffened, frightened that they would cause the rope to break. When he blinked and looked again he saw—or imagined he saw—another line wiggling down toward him. Perhaps it was not, he thought. It didn't appear to be dropping to him at all as much as it merely blew about in the wind. But he watched anyway, squinting for a better look, and refusing to concentrate on anything else.

Minutes passed.

Gary thought, *Come on . . . come on. For Christ's sake, how far down did he drop, anyway?*

Doug was thinking the same thing.

Rudi watched the end of the rope. He was smiling. Its end was getting bigger, coming closer to him. It still appeared to be half a mile away, but it was getting closer.

Whipping around in the wind, the rope inched downward, seven feet above his head. He wanted to reach, maybe even make a leap for it, but he forced himself to remain perfectly calm and motionless. Only his pale blue eyes followed its erratic dance.

Four feet.

The breeze stiffened momentarily, then ceased. The end dropped, and Rudi saw that it was about two feet above him. It was all he could do to restrain himself.

Let it go past your head. Let it drop past your waist so there will be slack enough to tie it easily. Be patient . . . patient . . .

The rope danced past his head, then his chest. He refused to make a move toward it, watching it instead as if it were a poisonous snake that would go on its way if left alone.

Prudence . . . patience. Only a few more inches . . .

The rope danced past his waist, then down to his knees. He slowly extended his right arm. He would have to do everything in one motion, and he was certain he would get no second chance if he failed.

The rope around his waist belt creaked again. He bounced.

Gary slipped a little, knocking some gravel loose, and causing half of his nerve endings to short out. He thought for a moment that his own ropes had failed. "Je-sus!" he breathed, both hands trembling.

Doug grunted, then exhaled, closing both eyes. Only now did he remember that he should have told Gary to tie a weight at the end of the new rope. For all they knew, the wind might be blowing it out of Gurdler's reach. "Come on," he whispered. "Grab the damn rope, Gurdler . . . grab it!"

Holding his breath, Rudi reached, his arm moving only
inches at a time. His waist rope was now almost cut in two; he
could feel it. He could instinctively feel its vibrations as if they
were death throes. He kept reaching, touching the lifeline once
with his fingertips before the wind moved it; then it swung
back, tapping his wrist, and he brought his arm gently
back...back...slowly...and finally closed his fingers around
it.

And he had it. He wrapped it around his hand twice, and
gave the gold-braided rope a tug.

The movement was barely perceptible, but Gary felt it. He
knew he would; the way his nerves were on edge at that moment he thought he could have felt somebody walking up the
other side of the mountain. He snapped it into the nearest carabiner, not daring to move any other portion of it.

And now he held his breath.

Rudi was doing the same as he deftly threaded the line
through three of the carabiners clipped to his belt. He wanted
to wrap it around his waist at least twice, but there was no time.
His main rope was about to fail. He had to get this one secured as well as he could, and he let go of the main rope so he
could tie the new one. He pulled and wrapped and looped,
pulling tighter, trying to get it fastened, all delicacy and patience traded for speed and desperation.

And he started coughing again. Hard, chest-rattling hacks
like a severe case of whooping cough, he couldn't stop them.
They couldn't be forced back down. He tried holding his
breath, willing himself not to cough. But that only seemed to
make it worse. He was bouncing heavily on the frayed line; the
new line still wasn't quite tied. The coughing continued, and
Rudi worked, tying frantically, almost in a panic, praying that
he would get the new rope knotted and that this dreadful
hacking would stop because the main rope was...

grnnnnnk...grnnnnnk...waaaaap!

The top end snapped, flying back up at Gary; the bottom
sailed out into the wind and fell. Rudi bounced on the new
rope, the sudden jerk almost turning him upside down.

"We got 'im!" Gary cried.

Rudi heard that. Yes, he thought gratefully. You got me. I am safe, and I'm grateful, Lieutenant Palmer. I thank you. And at last I have stopped this damnable coughing...for the time being. Because I do not wish to fall from this place. No. For a man of my stature there can be only one place from which to fall...if one happens to fall.

"An excellent job, Lieutenant Palmer. Excellent," Rudi puffed after he was safely resting on the roof. "No one could have done better. You saved my life. I owe you a great debt."

Unable to do more than puff and pant himself, Gary waved the traditional oh-hell-it-was-nothing gesture with his free hand. Any more of this shit and he'd be in no shape to climb stairs.

As they lay there catching their breath, Gary found himself studying the Swiss master—particularly Gurdler's expressions, or rather, the lack of them. It was hard to believe, but he could see no trace of fear in the man, no evidence whatsoever that Gurdler had come within a split second of falling almost fifteen hundred feet to his death. There was no hint of nervousness—nothing at all. Hell, Gary was still shaking, probably chalk-white at the near-disaster. But not Rudi. He was acting as if it were nothing more serious than a stumble over his living room rug, and as he lay against the roof, perfectly calm and composed, he looked as if he might be lounging on a tropical beach. Either Rudi Gurdler had more guts than any human being alive, or he was crazier than a gooney bird.

The question sounded dumb, but Gary asked anyway. "Are you sure you're all right?"

Rudi smiled and turned his head. "Yes," he said, nodding. "I am fine, a bit winded, but fine. Thank you again." And as he said it, Gary noticed that all was not fine. A thread of crimson slid down from the corner of Rudi's mouth. He didn't seem to notice it.

"What's wrong with your mouth?" Gary pointed.

"My mouth?"

"Yes. Blood."

Now Gurdler's expression changed astonishingly fast, leaving behind a moment of pure, uncut fright that drained the color from his cheeks and widened the pale eyes into mirrors of terror. He wiped the back of his free hand across his mouth and stared briefly at the redness. There was fear in his eyes as if he had never seen his own blood before. Just as Gary was taking all of this in, another transformation occurred as fast as the first, and the face altered again. Now, however, it was a fabrication, a phony, almost sickly smile, thin as tissue paper. He looked at Gary and tried to laugh it off. "Oh...this. I...I don't know what it is. I must have struck myself when I slipped," and he shrugged. "Perhaps a rock struck me. I don't remember. But it is nothing."

Bullshit. "Are you sure?"

"Yes. It is nothing."

Now wasn't the time, and that ledge wasn't the place, for any third degree, so Gary dropped it.

"Hey!" Doug yelled down at them. "Is everything all right?"

"Yeah, we're okay! Just catching our wind!"

"Well good! Whenever you two are through socializing, I'd like to get the hell off this wall!"

5

MAJOR EVANS THOUGHT, Goddamn, I wish these two guys would go home and leave us alone. They're gonna drive me right out of my mind.

He wasn't the only one thinking that; generals Grady and Streetor were about to drive the whole camp crazy, especially Streetor. He couldn't stay out of the communications tent for more than five minutes. It was always the same question: *Have they radioed yet?*

No, sir, they told him every five minutes. *They're in a position where they can't use their radio.*

Well, haven't you tried contacting them?

Yes, sir, every fifteen minutes. But they don't respond. Their radio is shut off.

Shut off? Why the hell would they shut it off?

Because they can't talk right now, sir. They're hanging on to that wall. And right now there's nothing we can tell them anyway. There probably isn't much they could tell us, either.

Well, keep trying, goddammit. Keep trying.

Yes, sir.

"Sir," the communications sergeant had said a while ago when nobody was looking, "could you do us a big favor?"

Evans smiled sadly. He knew what was coming. "What's that?"

"Maybe I'm outa line, but would you speak to General Grady for us? General Streetor is driving us up a wall. We can't get anything done in there. He pesters my men every five minutes. Hell, sir, they can't even go out and take a leak with him around."

"I'll do what I can, Sarge."

"Thanks, sir. We'd appreciate it."

"He's been bugging me, too."

Grady had been staring at the wall; he came up to Major Evans to return the binoculars. "I think they're on the slopes now," he said. "I can't see them anymore."

"They seem to be making pretty good time, sir."

"Yeah, but they're gonna catch holy hell when that storm arrives. Sarge, what's the latest on it?"

"No change, sir. About six or six-thirty we can expect the start of two inches of rain down here. And two feet of snow up there."

That was when one of the sergeant's communications men came running up to them, out of breath. "Excuse me, sir," he said, panting. "We just heard from Lieutenant Palmer. They had a small problem, he said, but they're starting up the slopes now. They think they can make their bivouac point by dark, but they'll still get caught out in some of the storm."

6

THEY WERE OFF THE LUNATIC, and better, they had completed the last pitches above the roof in record time. There had been

no choice; the Lunatic was the last place they wanted to be in a
storm.

Whatever was wrong with Rudi seemed to have cleared up
during that portion of the climb. He coughed a couple of times,
and paused for two fast drinks of water; but, then, all three of
them paused for a drink. And from there until they exited the
wall at last, Gurdler appeared to be in top form, even gaining
ground on Gary despite having to clean each pitch as he came
up. Gary found himself watching Rudi from time to time because he hadn't bought the song-and-dance about being hit by
a rock, or cutting himself. But he soon forgot it, thinking that
maybe Rudi really had met with a minor accident during his
near-fatal plunge. Besides, he thought, it wasn't any of his
business, and now was not the time to badger anybody.

Gary did not see Rudi take a furtive glimpse at the back of
his hand after their stop for a drink.

And now they stood at the foot of the Devil's Finger. There
had been a brief rest, some regrouping, rearranging of their
equipment. Doug gave them a few last-minute pointers. It was
a crash course with no time to repeat anything—it was nearly
three-thirty, and the sky to the north looked dark gray, almost
black in places.

"Start here with your right foot," he explained, pulling
himself up onto the jagged column. "It'll feel a little awkward, but if you start off wrong you'll come out ass-backward
at the top." The climb was something like a utility lineman
going up a telephone pole, but without the ankle spikes. At the
top were more bolts set into the rock, and into the overhang-
ing ledge twelve feet away. Doug would have to string ropes
across the gap, something like a Tyrolean Traverse, or a move
across two unconnected points. But during this traverse they
wouldn't be transferring their packs across first because it
would be too awkward trying to get them back on while hanging on the opposite ledge. "This is the only place we could find
where we could cross," Doug added. "Every other pinnacle is
too short or too rotten."

It was John Karber who had found the right pinnacle, and
who had named it the Karber Ass-Pucker Traverse. It was a
good name. One wrong move, especially if the wind was blow-

ing fairly hard—as it was doing now, and as it usually did—and off the whole damn mountain you'd go. As Karber had also said: "You'll get to practice your half gainers and swan dives one last time on the way down."

And as Doug had said, what made this place especially dangerous was not the pinnacle or the steepness of the 450-foot slope beyond, but the unpredictable surface conditions. The slope was pitched at about the same angle as the roof down on the Lunatic, but it was rarely bare rock. It could be covered with anything from snow to ice to slush to any combination of things, and you usually couldn't judge what its condition was until you were on top of it. Doug hoped that because of the cold and wind, it would be frozen. "But I'll let you know when I get there. Just have everything ready... pitons, ice screws, crampons... everything. You don't know what you'll need."

He didn't have to remind them that they were now fully unprotected from the wind and anything coming with it. Or that, because it would be far more uncomfortable from now on, the likelihood of mistakes would double.

Doug started up. He looked as if he was climbing a smokestack jutting out from the corner of a building. Rocks fell from a couple of places, and he warned them about bad spots that had gone rotten over the past five years. It occurred to him, too, that if the Finger had deteriorated this much in only five years this might be the last time anybody could ever use this route. Future climbers would have to take the north slopes, or the treacherous northwest route that traversed the edge of Meataxe Ridge, which was like walking a tightrope. More climbers had been killed on Meataxe Ridge than on any other place on Kota. It was famous for avalanches, rock slides, and snow bridges and cornices that never collapsed until people were walking on them. In July of 1940, five Canadians had disappeared in one such collapse; their bodies were never recovered.

Not that the northeast route was much better than the other two. The only advantage was that they had been out of the wind for a while. And now, at the top of the Finger, Doug couldn't find any of the bolts he and Woodhull and Karber had installed. It was a moment before he realized that the rock they had been set into was gone—almost two feet of the Finger's top was gone, and what remained wasn't in any trustworthy sort of condition.

The wind blew a bit harder; now he could feel tiny ice particles stinging his face. There was no time for debate. Whatever he rigged would have to be done now and it would have to work. The quickest way was to loop a rope between one of the bolts and the top of the column.

He finally got it—after eight tries, throwing the rope like a lasso. And, he grumbled to himself, if he wasn't a carpenter, he'd never make it as a cowboy, either. He only hoped the loop would remain in place under his own weight and the sixty-five pounds of equipment he carried.

"How's it going?" Gary called.

"I'll let you know in a minute...." He held his breath and grabbed the rope.

It held. He made the traverse in good shape. The adjacent slope was mostly bare, wet rock spotted with patches of wet ice; they could still use their rock-climbing equipment. He secured the line, tightened the safety line and called for Gary to come across as he looked at the sky again. The storm was now on them. The summit was obscured in the clouds.

"Damn," he mumbled. Those guys up top didn't stand a chance. From the moment their plane hit the summit they were as good as dead. For that matter, it would have been better for everyone if they'd all been killed outright, and the few still alive probably felt the same way about now. By this time tomorrow, they'd all be dead anyway, so the climb was hopeless and the idea of a rescue was insane.

But here you are again, he thought. Right where you never thought you or anybody else would ever go again. In a few minutes you'll be crawling on your belly up this slope with the wind biting your ass, and you'll still have those two guys behind you. Maybe you'll get to shelter before the storm gets worse; maybe you won't. Either way it doesn't matter because you'll be going no higher today, and maybe not tomorrow, if the storm's bad enough. And that is fine. Just fucking fine. Because nobody belongs here anymore. Nobody.

Gary was on the slope now. Rudi was twenty feet behind him, almost across. They were making good progress—except that Gurdler seemed a little more winded than he should be.

Of course they were moving well, he thought, watching them. Otherwise they wouldn't be here. The only reason they were running behind was because they didn't know the mountain. A little more time on it and those two would end up as fast as *they'd* been a few years ago. Especially Palmer. That kid was good; a quick study in mountain climbing if he'd ever seen one.

Puffing, Gary pulled himself upright. "A little slick in spots, isn't it?" He grinned at Doug.

And Gorham knew at that moment: if Palmer climbed it once, he'd be back to do it again. He would return as many times as necessary to master this mountain.

And you brought him here.

"Take your time," Doug said. "We wouldn't want to run off and leave Gurdler." He noticed at once that Gary didn't take the comment as lightly as it was meant. The grin vanished, and Palmer turned to help Rudi, who was coming up slowly. Doug called to Gurdler and asked how he was doing, but Rudi waved that he was fine and for them to get started on the next traverse.

"I guess he's all right," Gary said. He sounded as though he wasn't sure.

Doug wanted to ask if something was wrong but now he felt the snow and ice stinging him. The questions could wait. They had to get the hell off this slope and to shelter.

When they were on their way again, Gary was right behind him, matching him move for move. He looked as if he was gaining on him.

"Slow down," Doug called. "Let me get at least twenty feet ahead of you." Yes, he thought. Palmer would be back again. He could see it now. There would be an investigation of the crash, and recovery of all the bodies. Men would have to climb to the summit for that, and Palmer would lead them; this would be a military investigation with military men conducting it. The whole mountain would be forbidden to civilians. And Lieutenant Palmer would be the man bringing them up here because he'd have already been up here, knew the route and didn't

CHAPTER FIVE

US AR Y C-RA IONS
INDIVIDU L M AL PACK GES 60 EA

There *had* been food aboard. The piece of torn tan-colored cardboard with green letters stamped on it was all that remained. And somebody else had located similar evidence of the medical supplies—part of a shiny, dark green carton with a red cross on it.

Sergeant Anderson cursed softly to himself. They had been out here in the freezing cold going on an hour and a half, rummaging through everything they could find; they had dug their way through a ton of junk, rolled stiffened bodies of their comrades aside and succeeded in aggravating their own injuries. All for the sake—the hope—of finding something, just one small parcel of food or medical supplies. Even if they had found anything—even if the food had been unfit to eat, or the medical supplies unfit to use—it would have been a help. It would have helped them keep going until someone came to their rescue. But there was nothing left.

Private First Class Damon sagged in disappointment. He looked as if he might break into tears. "Now what do we do? We've got no food."

Hurling one of the pieces of cardboard aside, Richardson grumbled, "What the hell do you think, Damon? We fuckin' starve, that's what!"

"No, we won't," Anderson said.

"Okay, then we'll fuckin' freeze to death, Anderson. What's the difference, anyway? If one thing don't kill us, the other will."

"Look, Richardson, the human body can go for something like two or three weeks, maybe longer, with no food. Water is what we're gonna need, and we can get that by building a fire

and melting snow. With no water at this altitude we'll dehydrate.''

"We'll *shit*! Come on, Anderson, how long do you think
we'll last trying to drink thawed snow? We don't have anything to purify it with, so we'll get the drizzlin' shits, and *then*
we'll dehydrate!''

"Well, I don't have all the answers, goddammit! Why don't
you see if you can come up with a few instead of bellyachin'
about everything?''

"You want a bellyache, Anderson? I can arrange one for you
right now!'' The corporal squared off against him.

McDaniel stopped it. He came running from the rear of the
plane, out of breath but excited. He had found something in the
wreckage.

CRAAAAAAK-FTZZZZZZT...

"...Repeating our top story: Army and Air Force officials
have confirmed the identities of both the Air Force transport
plane that crashed at 10:45 p.m. last night on the summit of
Mount Kota, and the Army unit on board. Neither of them,
however, have been formally announced due to...''

...ftzzzzzzt-zzzzzzzt...

"...of kin. The aircraft was en route from Fort Bragg, North
Carolina to Oakland, California, and experienced what is believed to have been some kind of control malfunction, which
sent it out of control and plunging into the mountain.

"Of the 126 men supposedly aboard, which included a flight
crew of four and a passenger manifest of one hun...''

...zzzzzzt-ffzzzzzzt...

"...killed. But there are survivors still on the summit according to officials of nearby Fort Endicott, Montana, and
these men have been clearly spotted in a series of reconnaissance photographs taken by air immediately after the crash last
night. A rescue attempt was launched at dawn this morning,
sending three rescue climbers up the mountain.

"Leading the attempt is a man well-known to many local
residents, Mr. Douglas Gorham of Seattle, Washington, who
with two other partners had climbed Mount Kota eleven times,
and who led the only successful assault on the summit five years

ago. Climbing with Mr. Gorham is the world-famous mountaineer, Mr. Rudi Gurdler of Bern, Switzerland, who has led various expeditions up..."

"*Ya-haaaaaa!*" McDaniel cried, leaping into the air. "Didja hear that? They're comin' to get us! They're climbing up this motherfucker right now to get us!"

They all cheered, even Richardson. They even found strength enough to dance around.

"I told you I heard a plane last night!" Young said. "I told you!"

"Hey, hold it down!" Anderson waved, taking the radio from McDaniel. "All of you shut up a minute! There's more."

"...and that their progress up the mountain has been good so far. They expect to reach a spot known as the Northeast Plateau at the eighteen-thousand-foot level sometime tomorrow where a high-altitude base camp will be established. The survivors will be brought down to this camp where they will be..."

... *fffzzzzzzt-zzzzzz-zzzzzt*...

"...til additional teams can ascend to bring them down to a second camp from which they will be airlifted out.

"The big question to the operation is the weather. According to the National Weather Service, the first major storm of the winter season is moving this way from southwestern Canada, where nearly two feet of snow have already fallen at most of the higher elevations as well as two inches of rain at sea level. The storm is expected to arrive in this area within four to six hours, and we can expect identical snow and rain accumulations all over this region of the Montana Rockies. This means that the conditions at Kota's summit will be brutal for those men. When the storm..."

... *fzzzt-zzzzzzt-zzzzzz-fzzzzzzt*...

"...cluding snow, high winds and extremely cold temperatures. There is some doubt that they could survive such an environment. The rescue attempt, however, will proceed as planned, and if the storm behaves as predicted it should be out of this area early tomorrow morning, maybe sooner. With two to three feet of fresh snow and high winds at the higher elevations, the three climbers expect to be slowed down, but will continue their ascent as soon as the storm has passed. They hope to be on the summit by mid- to late-afternoon tomorrow at the latest.

"We will be standing by, bringing you up-to-the-minute developments as they occur. This is Dale McClain, KSCM Radio News, at Mount Kota."

Nobody said anything for several minutes. Sergeant Anderson turned the radio off—the batteries were already getting weak—and dropped it into a pocket. They stood there—red-eyed, scared, shivering in the cold, the snow whipping all around them, stinging their faces.

2

MOST OF THE PITCHES went well enough until they were onto the Meataxe Ridge. By then the wind was not only blowing the new precipitation but throwing most of the existing snow as well. The ridge wasn't a long traverse as it wound upward, doubling back on itself in six different places, but to cross it in a high wind carrying fresh snow was frightfully dangerous. Doug had never tried picking his way along the edge except in broad daylight; now, it was getting dark, and the ferocious winds out of the north threatened to blow them right off the mountain.

They stopped three times to rope up closer together—once to give Rudi one of their oxygen bottles. Doug was amazed. Rudi Gurdler needing oxygen at this altitude? He wanted to ask what was wrong but there was no time. They still had to negotiate the North Buttress before they would find shelter.

High winds and rain hammered the base camp at the foot of the mountain. The men battened all the tents down, and by five-thirty, with nightfall beginning to settle, everybody was holed up inside one of them. The communications men stayed on the radio, trying every ten minutes to raise the climbers. Grady and Streetor hovered around like two mother hens; Evans and Childs sat in a corner and tried to wait everything out patiently.

By 5:45, Gorham, Gurdler and Palmer cleared the Meataxe Ridge. Doug shouted to them above the wind that the day's remaining climb was straight ahead. It would be a long climb in the wind—more than three thousand feet long, and all upward at a forty-five degree angle to the shelter. The only good thing about it was that they wouldn't be walking along the edge of a ridge; the worst thing was that he had never tried any such climb in the dark. He hoped he would be able to pick his way along the right route; the shelter in the rocks above was the only place on the north side of the mountain where they could bivouac.

"Are you all right?" he yelled to Gurdler. The cold and high winds could cause breathing problems with most people, but a master climber like Gurdler should be used to it. Almost no climber with any alpine experience at all ever needed oxygen below twenty or twenty-one thousand feet. Only when they got to twenty-two thousand feet did everyone use it most of the time, because the human body couldn't adjust to anything above that height.

Rudi's head nodded, the hood moving, the rubber hose on the mask bobbing up and down. He gestured that they should keep moving, pointing to his wrist, then toward the sky.

Right, Doug thought. Time's a-wasting. We're probably already out of time. And *this* is complete insanity. Doug hoped Woodhull never found out that they were climbing the North Buttress at night, or Doug would be a laughing stock. And Karber was probably spinning like a lathe in his casket.

"Stay within twenty feet of me!" he said to Gary. "Don't let me get out of your sight! Do everything I do!"

Gary nodded, and tightened his ropes. He couldn't believe he was actually trying to climb Kota in the dark. Ordinarily, he felt good on snow and ice despite the special dangers they presented. He had taught ice-climbing to many of the men at Endicott, joking, "In some past life I must have been a yeti." Some people liked palm trees and sandy beaches; others felt at home only on flat prairies or green valleys. He had always thought of home as the mountains, preferably high up in the silent, white solitude, and he could almost understand how a hermit might make the psychological adjustment of living alone in a place like this.

Well, maybe not exactly like this. The wind was screaming, and he could barely see ten feet in front of him. His backpack weighed three thousand pounds, and he was already exhausted.

He felt a tug on his rope and saw Doug motion for them to start moving.

3

"I DON'T LIKE THIS SHIT at all, man."

"Nobody says you have to, Damon. But you'll freeze your ass off if you don't."

"I'm already freezin' my ass off."

"No, you're not. You just think you are."

"Yeah, Damon, wait'll that blizzard gets here. You'll think the temperature now is balmy."

"How many jackets do we have so far?"

"Nineteen or twenty, Sarge. The rest of 'em are in too bad a shape to use."

"All right. Use whatever clothing you can find. When we get that done we'll try to cover all the holes in the fuselage with pieces of canvas from the trucks and jeeps, duffel bags... anything we can find."

"Why don't you turn that transistor radio back on, Sarge? Maybe we'll—"

"The batteries are weak," Anderson said. "Besides, we don't need a radio to tell us about the weather."

"What about those three mountain climbers?"

"What about them? Whatever happens, they won't be here until sometime tomorrow, O'Brien. Somehow we've got to make it through the blizzard tonight."

And they were doing all they could to ensure that. Bodies lying in the snow and inside the rear of the wreck had already been stripped; duffel bags had been jammed into small cracks and breaks along the airplane's outer skin, and smaller pieces of clothing—everything from GI socks to underwear to baseball caps—were being stuffed into every porthole. They were now ripping what pieces of canvas they could find among the remains of the vehicles, in order to plug up the gaping holes at both ends of the fuselage. They hoped their efforts would be enough; at any rate, it was nearly all they could do.

"Sarge?"

"Yeah?"

"I found two more jackets...uh, from inside the plane." Richardson held them up; one of them had a name tag that said Jackson over the breast pocket.

"When?"

Richardson shrugged. "Maybe ten...fifteen minutes ago. And Gomez finally bought it, too. But I don't know when he died." He didn't say that it had to have been several hours ago. He'd found Gomez with his mouth filled with blood, which had also trickled down both sides of his face; the blood had frozen and was covered with a sparkling white frost.

"Sarge?"

"What?"

"I got an idea. Not a good one...but it might work."

"What is it?"

"Well...we could take some of the bodies and pile 'em up around the holes in the fuselage. It would help keep out some of the wind and snow."

He was right, the idea was not a good one at all. Except for the fact that it might work. The snow wasn't that bad; they might all have to have certain extremities amputated for frostbite, but it still wasn't that bad. Nor was the cold by itself; they had clothing with which to bundle up to keep out the cold. But the wind would be murderous. It was already blowing at a steady thirty-five or forty miles per hour, and by tonight it might be twice that velocity. The wind might kill them faster than anything.

Anderson nodded. "Do it. Get Eckrich to help you. Where is he, anyway?"

ECKRICH WAS SURROUNDED by death. He had never seen such death, never imagined it; he had never dreamed he would be part of it. Death was inside the plane, just inches away...right

over there . . . over there . . . and over there. Death was just outside, everywhere he looked. You couldn't take a step anywhere
outside without stepping over it, right into it. He couldn't get
away from it.

"Yes . . . yes, we'll gatherrr . . . at the riii-verrr . . ."

It was in here. Here. It was moving around like a ghost.
Death. He didn't have to see it; he could feel its presence, hear
its foul breathing. Only minutes ago it was right over there, just
a few feet away, and this time it had taken Jackson. Oh, Jackson had tried to cry out the warning, tried to tell him that death
was about to touch him. But all he could get out was a short
gag, and then death slipped away from the spot with another
soul clutched in its bony hand.

". . . the beauuu-tiful, the . . . beauuuteeeful riv-errr . . ."

Now it had everybody inside this plane. And it was hiding in
some cold corner; maybe it was behind that mass of fallen wires
over there; maybe it had slipped behind the twisted pile of seat
frames back there; or perhaps it had hidden itself under the
floor plates for the time being and was just waiting to catch him
off guard long enough to slip up on him and . . .

". . . gather with the saiiiints . . . at the riv-errr . . ."

But it was there. Not far away. It was waiting for him. He
was next. It wouldn't leave this desolate place until it had him
in its grip—until it had all of them in its grip. You couldn't
cheat death; oh, you might stall it for a while, play games with
it, maybe even fool it into turning its head for a moment while
you tried to get away and hide where it couldn't find you. But
it wouldn't last. It would get you.

". . . that flows by . . . the throne . . . of . . . Gaaahd . . ."

Sooner or later it would find you, give you that awful grin,
and back you into the corner. *Your time, boy. I've got you now.*

No. No. He would stay right here. He would stay alert,
watching every move, listening to every little sound. He would
give it no opportunity, no advantage. It would not sneak up on
him as it had on all the others. He wouldn't let it.

Eckrich smiled. Yes, that was it, that was how to beat it. Of
course. You just keep your eye on it, don't allow it to get any
closer. If it couldn't get in close to you, it couldn't get you.

"I know you're there." He nodded. "You might've fooled the rest of 'em, but you ain't fooling me. I know where you are."

Outside, Richardson paused when he heard the words. Jesus, he thought, what was that nutty bastard up to now? Who did he think he was talking to?

"You try to come over here...I'll be ready for you." Eckrich picked up a piece of structural ribbing from the fuselage. "See this? You get any closer, and I'll take that skull right off...right fuckin' off."

"OKAY...EVERYBODY," Anderson called, gulping and panting. He waved to the men to come toward him. "That's it. Let's take a break." It looked as though they had gathered up every usable shred of material they could find that might give shelter or protection. And they were exhausted; he had seen three or four of them drop to their knees. It was getting colder by the minute, steadily darker, windier, and they had to stop before they defeated their own purpose. "Let's rest a while...then get back inside the plane."

"We may have a problem with that, Sarge."

"What the hell does that mean?"

"Eckrich. He's in there talkin' to himself right now...picked up a big hunk of metal...using it like a ball bat. A few minutes ago he threatened to take my fuckin' head off if I came any closer to 'im. Son of a bitch has gone right off the high side."

"Shit! That's all we need. Well...we'll just have to take it away from him...rush 'im...take it away...and tie him up if we have to."

"I know what *I'd* like to do with that candy-ass son of a bitch."

"Well, forget it, Richardson. You're not gonna touch 'im. The poor fucker probably doesn't know what he's doing. If he's a candy ass then he won't be hard to handle. Come on, let's get back inside."

4

ACCORDING TO THE National Weather Service, the storm came officially to Mount Kota National Park at 6:46 p.m., September 29, 1968. It behaved very much as they had predicted, never stalling as it had while over British Columbia, but moving across the region for a period of seven hours and fifty-three minutes. During that time the park, Fort Endicott, the town of Sioux Creek and everything else in a seventy-five mile radius was drenched in 1-1/2 inches of rain. Everything above fifteen thousand feet—which for all practical purposes meant Mount Kota—was covered with seventeen inches of fresh, blowing snow, all of it drifted into steep banks, cornices and ridges most of the distance from the lower end of the North Buttress to the summit.

Doug Gorham, Rudi Gurdler and Gary Palmer finally found the shelter above the buttress at 7:21 p.m. The high winds and snow forced them to crawl the last three hundred feet, and by the time they dragged themselves into the shelter, Gary was pulling Rudi Gurdler. He thought for a while that Gurdler might have injured himself somehow, because he seemed barely able to move under his own power. Only after they had collapsed inside the protection of the rocks and put up a tarp over the entrance did he see Gurdler's actual problem. The Swiss climber was hardly able to breathe, even with an oxygen bottle. Several wheezing, gasping minutes passed before Rudi was able to remove the mask and settle himself down. And even in the dim light of their tiny campstove and lanterns they could tell that Gurdler was in serious trouble. He looked, as they say, like death warmed over; and he couldn't seem to stop coughing.

"What the hell's wrong with you?" Doug asked. "Are you sick?"

"You were coughing like that down on the Lunatic this morning," Gary added. He decided not to say that the spasm had nearly caused him to fall to his death; he wanted to see if Rudi would bring it up.

Gurdler shook his head. "It is all right. I'm fine," and he suppressed another cough as he said it. Gary noticed that he quickly wiped the back of a hand across his mouth, then stared at it as if he expected to find something—blood, perhaps.

"You don't look fine. And it's affecting your performance on this climb, and you know better than anybody what can happen if one member falls down on the job. Now, I want to know what the hell's wrong."

They were momentarily stunned when Rudi looked up at them. He was hollow-eyed and frighteningly pale, emaciated, as though he belonged in a hospital bed—or maybe a casket. And again came that tissue-paper smile Gary had seen that morning. Rudi coughed once more and sighed. The game was over. "I . . . I have a disease," he said quietly.

Gary's expression became one of astonishment, the look of a man whose hearing has just gone haywire. That couldn't have been right—hell, this was *Rudi Gurdler*, Mountaineer Supreme. He was the alpine specialist whom every climber aspired to become. "A disease?" he whispered.

Doug knelt in front of Rudi. "What kind of disease?"

Gurdler sighed with a cold, hollow chuckle and held out both hands as if telling about a fish that got away. "I cannot remember the name, but it is that long. The doctors have said that it is caused by having spent too much time at extreme altitudes with too little oxygen. But there are complicating factors . . . my lungs among the worst. They have always been weak. My respiratory system has always experienced trouble in adjusting to high altitudes. As I've gotten older the condition has worsened. All of these things have combined to deteriorate my respiratory system to the point where I can no longer recuperate from anything affecting it. I have had pneumonia four times, a case of pleurisy with blood clots in both lungs, and other problems . . . all in the past six years alone. My last time was less than nine months ago. I spent two months in a hospital in Kathmandu, Nepal." And he shrugged, trying to smile.

Doug and Gary looked at each other. Neither could say a word.

Rudi went on. "It is a situation of too many sicknesses in too short a time, plus the mistake of not allowing myself to recover fully from any of them . . . to build up the necessary resistance. It is said that the worst any climber can experience is the loss of a limb, but I am not so sure. Bad lungs are just as crippling, and mine have steadily been less reliable with each passing year. Now they are on the verge of failing completely." He didn't sound at all worried or frightened, or even overly concerned—only fatalistic. Since there was nothing he could do about it he had accepted his fate.

"Then you shouldn't even be here," Gary whispered. It was stupidly redundant but he didn't know what else to say. "You never should have—"

Doug wasn't so sympathetic. "One hell of a time to think of that!" he interrupted. "Why didn't you say something, Gurdler? You, of all people...pulling a stunt like this." He flopped back against his pack. "I can't fucking believe it. We're trapped on the worst mountain in the country, in a storm, trying to reach a handful of people who'll be dead long before we can ever get to them, and now we're dragging a sick man along with us." He gave Rudi a look of contempt. "I still can't believe it."

Well, that was it. This wonderful little revelation had just decided the fate of *this* expedition.

"I am sorry for this, Mr. Gorham, Lieutenant Palmer. There is no excuse for my actions. The only explanation I can offer is that...perhaps I had it in mind to complete one last climb before quitting for good. A dangerous, foolhardy act, I freely admit...something I have never done before. But I thought I would be able to complete this climb. I honestly thought that Mount Kota would not be this difficult."

"Now you know better," Doug snapped. "But...it doesn't matter because none of us will be completing this climb. First thing tomorrow morning, just as soon as this storm blows over, we go back down. That's it."

"Hey, wait a minute, there are at least ten guys up there who—"

"Who are *dead*. Or will be by the time we get to them. Get used to it, Gary. There is no possible way they could survive a storm like this. Hell, I doubt if we could survive it. Now, I'm truly sorry about that, and I wish there was something we could do about it. But we can't. Those men probably won't last the night, and our climbing all the way to the top won't change it."

"Doug, we've gotta keep going," Gary insisted.

"The hell we do. Forget it."

"Perhaps if I were to remain behind—" Rudi started to say, but Doug interrupted at once.

"No. Even if we left you, Gary and I couldn't carry all the equipment and supplies—and that's assuming the impossible . . . that we actually found somebody left alive. This little jaunt requires at least three men—three healthy, strong men. Nobody stays behind."

"I've got orders," Gary persisted, "and I'm supposed—"

"Screw your orders! Up here, I give the goddamn orders, and it's settled. We go back down in the morning."

5

NOW, ALL THEY COULD DO was bundle up as much as they could, crawl into the sack together and pull some of the canvas over them. With luck, their body heat would keep them from freezing. They had plugged every hole they could find with anything they could find; both jagged, exposed ends of the fuselage had been covered with shreds of canvas, and frozen corpses had been stacked like cords of wood across the openings. The wind had arisen to a banshee howl, strong enough to cause the plane to rock and groan. The snow and ice blowing had reached tornadic proportions. The temperature seemed as if no further drop was possible. Nothing was left except to huddle together and try to ride it out.

"What about Eckrich?" someone asked.

Good question. When they returned to the plane they had found him doubled up in a corner talking to himself. Slowly, they filed inside, nobody taking their eyes off him for fear that he might start swinging the piece of ribbing he held. But he hadn't. They had had no trouble getting it away from him; in fact, he didn't seem aware that they were there at all. His eyes flitted here and there, and he seemed to be listening for something that only he was apt to hear. And he had remained that way while they prepared their shelter for the storm; he was still that way.

"We'll try to take care of him," Anderson said. He took Eckrich's hand, pulled him to his feet and led him over to the rest of the group. "We're gonna lay down here, Eckrich," he said. "We're all gonna lay down right here and bundle up together to keep the cold out. Don't be scared. We'll help you. We're right here, and we'll be all right."

Surprisingly, there was no resistance. Eckrich lay down where Anderson put him.

Ten minutes later, they all lay under the canvas.

"Oh, man!" Damon grunted, teeth chattering. "I didn't think it *ever* got this cold."

"When I left Kirkwood, Missouri two weeks ago," Young said, "it was eighty degrees. My ol' man had a barbecue for me, and I was playin' softball with my kid brother. Sweatin' my ass off, and complainin' how hot it was."

"That'll teach you to bitch."

"What did your ol' man barbecue for you?"

"Steaks. Four of the biggest, fattest, juiciest T-bones you ever saw. My mom baked some potatoes that were about the size of watermelons...baked beans...and a fresh tossed salad that came right out of her garden. Dad and I killed a couple of six-packs. Oh, yeah, and two great big slices of hot apple pie with homemade ice cream on the top."

"Sounds good."

"Know what sounds good to me right now?"

"Knowing you, Damon, it'd probably be dog shit."

"Believe it or not, SOS. Good ol' U.S. Army Shit on a Shingle. I must be the only grunt in the whole goddamn army who actually likes that stuff. I've had it every morning they've served it ever since I've been in."

"Like I said, dog shit . . ."

"I eat it, too. It ain't so bad."

"Right now, I'd like a nice, hot TV dinner. Or some cooked cornflakes . . . or maybe some—"

"McDaniel, you don't cook cornflakes, you dipshit."

"Hey, my mother was the world's worst cook . . . couldn't even boil fuckin' water. We never had nothin' anyway. Except cornflakes. And if all you've got is cornflakes, you'd be surprised what you can think up to do with 'em."

"Sounds like she must've been an Army cook."

"Yeah, remember that banana cream pie they had at the mess hall the night before we left Bragg? That shit didn't taste like any banana I've ever had. But it just now dawned on me where I've had that same taste before."

"Okay, we'll bite: where?"

"When I was ten we repapered every room in our house. Damned if that banana cream pie didn't taste exactly like wallpaper paste. I'm not kiddin', it was the same thing exactly."

"Be glad it wasn't the chocolate cream. That shit tastes like axle grease. Smells a whole lot like it, too."

"Well, their SOS ain't bad, I'll give 'em that much—"

Bwwwoooooommmp-pssssss . . .

"What the fuck was that?"

"I dunno . . . but it sounded like it came from underneath us somewhere."

"Yeah, it sounded like that to me, too."

"Hear anything else?"

"No . . . no, I don't think so. Nothing but that hissing noise . . . like a tire leaking air or something."

"That's all I hear, too."

"Yeah, me too."

"It might *be* that . . . a tire leaking air."

"What do you mean, Sarge?"

"I mean, it might be one of the tires on the landing gear. The landing gear is directly underneath us. The low temperature might've caused some of the air in one of the tires to condense and freeze. Then it would expand, and blow the tire out."

"Are you sure?"

"No. But it's the only thing I can think of. What else would've made a noise like that?"

Eckrich knew exactly what it was. He knew it had been hiding somewhere, patiently awaiting the right moment to show itself, and now it had. It was sly, this death entity, very shrewd, very clever. It had slipped beneath the bent floor plates when he wasn't looking, and it had been waiting all this time for him. But he had heard it. It had made a mistake, and he'd heard it. Well, it wouldn't get him this time, either.

"Eckrich! Get back here! *Eckrich!*" But Anderson was too late. Eckrich had leaped from the floor, dived over the stacked bodies and through the canvas tarp and disappeared into the storm before the sergeant could get to his feet. He yelled and screamed, looking vainly into the furious blowing snow, but Eckrich had vanished. "Son of a bitch!" He started to go after him but fell to his face—someone had grabbed him.

"No! No, Anderson! Let 'im go!"

"Let me go, goddammit! I have to go after him!"

"No!" bellowed Richardson, his arms still wrapped around Anderson's legs. "He's gone nuts! Wacko! You'll never find 'im out there, and you'll get killed if you try! Let him go!"

Anderson felt other arms press against him. Other voices came from the cold darkness.

"Yeah, he's right, Sarge."

"Forget him. Let 'im go."

"Yeah, Sarge, it doesn't make any sense risking yourself. You'd never find him."

They were right. Anderson knew that. Gradually, he relaxed, then moved back under the tarp with the rest of the men. "Dammit! I didn't know he was that far gone, or I would've tied him up."

"None of us knew it, Sarge. How could we? We ain't shrinks. Besides, it's too late now. There's nothing you can do about it."

They pulled the tarp up over their heads, crawled in close to one another and listened to the shrieking of the wind and the bumps and groans coming from the wrecked airplane. No one talked for a long time.

Until: "I wonder what that noise really was," McDaniel said. "And I can still hear that hissing sound."

"Yeah, I hear it, too," Young agreed.

"Yeah, and I smell something. Do you smell that?"

"No. I don't smell anything...except your breath, O'Brien."

"Well, yours ain't no day at the beach either, Damon. But this is different...kind of sweet, something like soda pop bubbling in a glass. Are you sure you can't smell that?"

"No, goddammit! Now would you quit buggin' me? I'd like to get some sleep."

"Wait a minute . . . I think O'Brien's right," Young said. "I think I smell it too. Sweet . . . like soda pop. Just like he said."

"I *told* you, Damon."

"How about you, Sarge? Do you smell anything?"

"No. Nothing. Just relax. Try to rest, you guys. Whatever it is, it's probably nothing...probably a liquid or chemical from the control system of the plane. Or maybe, now that I think of it, that liquid disinfectant from one of the chemical toilets. One of the reservoirs must have ruptured in the cold. Don't worry about it."

"Just our luck. The only shelter in this whole goddamn place, and it's right on top of the shitter."

6

LITTLE WAS SAID while they unpacked their equipment, prepared their meal and bedded down for the night. Gary wanted to talk; he wanted to ask Rudi more about his ailment, particularly how he had kept it so well hidden for so long. And despite the idiocy of trying to make one last climb—perhaps the most important climb any of them would ever make—he still admired the man. Perhaps he admired Gurdler a little more now than before; climbing all of those mountains for so many years had been a monumental feat, but doing it in his physical condition seemed Herculean. And he thought he could understand why this climb might be so important. But Rudi didn't seem conversational. And Doug had turned coldly unfriendly, refusing to look at either of them.

Nothing was said until they were ready to crawl into their sleeping bags.

"You'd better turn on your radio," Doug mumbled to Gary. "Tell 'em we're coming back down in the morning."

"They're not gonna like it," he said, pulling the radio from the pack. "In fact, they might or—"

"I don't give a shit what they like. We've had it. We can't go any farther."

"They might *order* me to go on up. Or at least try."

"Then they're even dumber than I thought. And you'd be stupid to try."

"I'm just telling you what they might do, and what I might have to do."

"Look, Gary, I'm not gonna argue about this. We're going down."

"Yeah." He clicked the radio on. "Base camp, base camp, this is Palmer. Do you copy? Over?"

"Roger, Lieutenant, this is base camp reading you five-by-five. Go ahead. Over."

"Roger, base camp. This is to advise you that we'll be starting back down in the morning. Repeat: we will begin a descent from our present location in the morning, as soon as this storm has passed. Do you acknowledge? Over."

"Roger, we copy that. Descent will begin in the morning. We will have to know the reason for the early descent. Over."

"Roger. Reasons complex at this time, but due to unforeseen difficulties, continued ascent not possible. Over."

"Roger, Lieutenant. We copy; continued ascent not possible because of unforeseen difficulties. We'll convey that to command. Over."

"Thanks, base camp. See you tomorrow. Over."

"Roger, Lieutenant. And stay bundled up tonight. Base camp out."

"We'll do that. Palmer out." He put the radio away. "If you hear a loud scream above the wind, that'll probably be Streetor."

THEY WERE UP, FED AND PACKED before dawn. The entrance to their rocky niche had nearly been covered by drifted snow, but as Gary poked through it with an ice ax he saw that the day was dawning a brilliant, cloudless blue in the sky, the sun casting a blinding glare down the flanks of the mountain. Everything out there was a contrast of deep blue or brilliant white. The wind had died down as well; it would be a good day for climbing—or descending, as the case had become. It was too bad. He felt that they stood a good chance of making the summit, and now that he thought about it, somebody would have to climb up there sooner or later anyway. There would most certainly be a drawn-out investigation of the crash, a million questions to be answered, and whose answers would come only from the crash site. They would want personal identification of all the victims; they would want parts and pieces from the wreck; and they would have to have about 150 pounds of pictures and volumes of reports. They would not leave the site alone until they had extracted every recoverable scrap of information they could find—or a climbing team could find. And despite what Doug wanted, if they already had a team on the mountain, they would try to gather some of that information as soon as possible.

Gurdler was still coughing now and then, but he looked much better than he had last night. In fact, he looked just as fit as Gary and Doug. He said nothing, but smiled a lot at Gary, and Gary couldn't help but feel a little sorry for him. It was a hell of a way to end a fine career, being turned back only halfway up a second-rate mountain—the last mountain he would ever set foot upon. But even now he appeared cheerful, ready to go. As Doug finished packing his equipment, and Gary dug out the radio once again, Rudi took a look outside, then glanced around the shelter.

"An interesting rock formation, Mr. Gorham," he said, running a hand over the rocks at the rear of the shelter. "I don't believe I've ever seen a formation quite like this."

"Yeah, it's a good little shelter. Karber and Woodhull and I used it enough." He stopped what he was doing and was watching Rudi carefully.

"Quite unusual," Rudi continued as if he hadn't heard Doug. "You know...these rocks appear almost as if they were put here. Do you see how they are stacked? I have never seen rocks stacked like this before. A very methodical, systematic arrangement, wouldn't you say?" He put a hand up over an opening between two stones. "And look at this. I can feel air moving through here. Do you feel it?"

"Yes, Mr. Gurdler. I know there's air coming through there. And the three of us put up those rocks eight or nine years ago for the sole purpose of keeping it out. That's why they're stacked so neatly."

"No kidding?" Gary said, looking it over himself. "What's on the other side?"

"A short tunnel...goes back about sixty, seventy feet or so. I don't know for sure because we never explored it."

"Why not?"

"Because we didn't have time. We were trying to find a route up to the top of this son of a bitch, remember?"

"If wind comes through it, there has to be another opening somewhere. If you're exploring for a route anyway, you'd have a lot of time to check it out. Maybe it goes farther back than you think. Or maybe it goes up."

"That would be an interesting route." Gurdler laughed.

"Goddammit, will you get on that radio, Palmer?" Gorham exploded. "Come on, let's quit screwing around and get the hell out of here. Now, *move* it!"

The red receiver light on the radio was flashing, meaning that the base camp was trying to contact them.

"Base camp, base camp, this is Palmer. Do you copy? Over."

"Roger, Lieutenant, this is base camp reading you five-by-five. Good morning. We have an important message. Are you ready to copy? Over."

"Ready, base camp. Go ahead. Over."

"Roger, Lieutenant. Endicott Center advises that another photo recon mission was launched at first light. The photos have been analyzed and show clear evidence of activity on the summit as of thirty minutes ago. Repeat: there are crash survivors still alive and moving on the summit. Do you copy? Over."

Gary looked at Doug, whose mouth was moving, forming the words, That's impossible, and whose face registered only stunned disbelief. The base camp could have said that the survivors had got tired of waiting, flapped their arms and flown down, and it wouldn't have been any more amazing to Gorham. Gurdler, on the other hand, regarded the news in the same way he regarded everything else—with an interested, eyebrow-raising sort of curiosity.

"Uhh...roger, base camp, activity on the summit. We acknowledge. Over."

"The CO requests an immediate report of your status, Lieutenant. Specifically, will the problems you encountered last night affect any attempt today? If not, they would like an estimate of climbing time, accounting for any new difficulties caused by the storm, or anything else you feel is worth mentioning. If the ascent is to be terminated they need immediate reasons why. Over.''

The impossible had happened. Just as Doug announced that the game was over, the ball suddenly reappeared in his court. And the other team was waiting. It was up to him, and for the first time since the climb started, he didn't know what to do.

''Lieutenant Palmer, do you copy? Over.''

''Roger, base camp, we copy. Please stand by. Over.''

Doug was still shaking his head. ''That can't be,'' he muttered to himself. He looked at his partners and repeated it as if to see if they agreed. All of those men should have been buried by now, frozen as hard as steel bars.

But . . . maybe not. Apparently not, if pictures showed them still out there moving around. Maybe they had a shelter of sorts; maybe they managed to get it buttoned up well enough to keep the snow and wind out. For all they really knew, those guys might be nice and comfortable right now. Hell, nothing was impossible if you wanted it badly enough.

Doug tried to think. All the fresh snow would slow them down, and its existence could produce scores of new hazards. After a snow, Kota always became a different mountain. All the landmarks changed. He was stuck with two unfamiliar partners; one good, but still a rookie, and the other sick. The higher they went, the worse Gurdler would become. If they made it as far as the plateau, Gurdler might be of little or no use to them; another casualty.

Gorham wasn't anxious to go anywhere except down. He should never have come here in the first place.

''Lieutenant Palmer?'' the radio voice crackled again. ''Is there a problem? Please report. Over.''

''We'll report in a few minutes, base camp. Please stand by. Over.''

Gary and Rudi awaited an answer. The people swarming all over the base camp waited for an answer. The whole damn world was waiting for an answer.

Doug looked at Rudi. ''I want to know exactly how you're feeling. *Exactly*. No bullshit, no cover-ups.''

"I feel fit this morning, Mr. Gorham. I feel good. I am certain that I can climb and carry my share of the load." He smiled slightly. "And this is no . . . bullshit."

Doug thought, Christ Almighty, how do I get into these things? He said, "Gimme that radio."

Trying to suppress a grin, Gary handed it over.

"Hello, base camp? This is Gorham."

"Go ahead, Mr. Gorham, we read you. Over."

"Are you guys absolutely sure about activity on the summit? We find that pretty goddamn hard to believe."

"Mr. Gorham, this is Major Evans. The answer is yes, a definitive confirmation of survivor activity this morning. We found it hard to believe, too, but the photo analysis section at Endicott has confirmed it. Over."

Gorham sighed and stared for a moment at the rock wall.

"Are you still there, Mr. Gorham?"

"Yes, right here. We should be moving out in about ten minutes."

"Roger, ten minutes. Do you have a feel for any additional delays because of the storm? Over."

"No. Not really. We'll just have to take it one step at a time and see what we run into. It'll take longer, but I don't know how much longer. And I can't guarantee anything. We'll call you."

"Roger, Mr. Gorham. Understood. And good luck, you guys. Base camp out."

Doug looked outside as he pulled up his pack, adjusted it, then pulled up the hood on his parka. An unbroken vista of brilliant blue and white surrounded the shelter; small whirlwinds of snow kicked up here and there in the light breeze. He set his tinted goggles and face mask into place, strapped on the canvas belt that carried his axes and screws, then pulled on his insulated mittens. Gary handed him one of their coiled climbing ropes. He pushed aside the tarp, and stepped out into the clear, cold morning.

THE WINDS WERE A LITTLE STRONGER at the summit, 3800 feet above the climbers, and the gusts were harder, more frequent.

Seventeen inches of fresh powder covered much of the destruction; the constant turmoil of the wind pushed the snow across thousands of burned and twisted pieces from the plane, bits of broken cargo and scores of frozen, green-clad corpses lying in the rocks. Nearly all of the north-facing starboard side of the fuselage where the survivors of Flight J-440 had taken refuge lay under a drifted white blanket. Only parts of its port side were still exposed to the morning sun, casting dull glints and gleams from the black-streaked aluminum skin; the U.S. Air Force numbers and markings were barely visible.

Close to the eastern edge of the summit, one piece of the tail assembly, which was all of the entire tail section left intact, had landed vertically in the rocks. It had been the outer half of the starboard horizontal stabilizer, and about four feet of it poked up from the drifts. Its outer edge was rounded, and it could be seen immediately as one exited Karber's Pass. Because of its shape—and particularly its location, sticking up above everything else—it looked a little like an old-fashioned grave marker; a bent, shiny aluminum facsimile of a tombstone.

Which it might as well have been. A tombstone was needed because as of 3:40 that morning the crash site and the summit of Mount Kota had become little more than a mass grave.

CHAPTER SIX

JOHN KARBER, STEVE WOODHULL and Doug Gorham met one another in Colorado during the summer of 1951. Rock climbing was *the* local sport, and all three had developed reputations as being among the best. One day they got together and climbed Lone Eagle Peak, and from the beginning they knew they were a functioning, well-oiled unit; they knew at once that they would have to tackle one of the monsters.

They considered Yosemite Valley and its two awesome walls, El Capitan and Half Dome. Karber, the one with the most alpine experience at that time, suggested either Mount McKinley or Mount Logan. It was Gorham who mentioned Mount Kota.

It sounded like a good idea—to them, at least. Almost immediately, bets began circulating as to how long the three of them would remain alive, especially with Woodhull climbing with them.

Steve talked. He had always been the talker of the group, and his nonstop lexicon of off-color stories and observations irritated nearly everybody who had climbed with him. Doug, however, found it entertaining. He enjoyed having Woodhull around, and the stocky, red-haired Steve's rapid, clipped sentences and profane judgments of the world in general were what they needed to break any dull monotony that could become dangerous on a climb. Beyond this, Steve was a first-rate climber, prompting Doug to nickname him "The Demented Genius," after their first two or three walls and peaks. Steve took risks that scared the shit out of less experienced climbers, and many thought he would have killed himself if Gorham hadn't come along. And not a one ever seemed to notice how much they learned from him while he turned their hair white. Doug came to trust him implicitly on a climb, something he could say about only two or three other climbers in the world. Steve did not make stupid mistakes. He was unorthodox, but he knew exactly what he was doing.

John Karber, on the other hand, rounded out the trio. He became the third gear, the final meshing. He was their arbitrator. Where Woodhull would take frightening risks, depending upon what might or might not be gained, Gorham might or might not. Gorham's judgment was tempered by a slower and steadier hand, which at times caused him to be more reliable, yet an added burden because he tended to slow them down. John Karber had been a little of both. He sometimes talked Doug into taking chances, or using more dangerous routes and maneuvers when he was reasonably sure they would work—and he talked Steve out of things whenever there was doubt. When Doug and Steve argued—and they argued a lot—John usually settled it. Both of them had influence over Karber, and yet neither of them did. And as the quietest of the three John was never overshadowed by his partners because he soon proved to be the most imaginative and inventive. He was credited with inventing a new dynamic belaying technique, a two-man rappeling procedure for use if one man was injured, and he personally designed and patented two new types of ice screws. And because of his fine eye for detail, half of the existing route up the mountain had been his discovery, including the final route to the summit—the pass that now bore his name.

But John never saw its exit. Doug was thinking about that as they labored through the deep snows covering Kota above its North Buttress. Doug was thinking about a lot of things that morning.

Mostly, he was trying to identify what, exactly, he was feeling. Being on Kota again brought up more old emotions than he remembered, or wished to recall. It wasn't a homecoming by any means, and even though they were going to try to save a few lives he could not feel that there would be any real accomplishment—at least not for him. Saving lives was a noble cause and a sterling achievement when it worked, but noble causes had never been his line of work. And here, on Kota, those things had never been achieved. He still doubted that they would be now. No, he was here for alien reasons; because nobody else

could, or would, lead them up the mountain. He didn't actually have to be here, and he certainly didn't want to be. Yet
there seemed to be no choice. In a strange way he felt as if he
had been out of jail for the past five years only to find that the
authorities had misplaced two or three days that he had to go
back and serve.

But it was just the mountain.

He knew Kota almost as well as men know the bodies of their
lovers—a little better, perhaps, because he had never failed to
learn something valuable each time he had taken this mountain into his embrace. And that was exactly what he had done,
he realized—he had embraced Kota. Kota was a female. For a
long time she had been fickle and dangerous, but a wildly in-
toxicating virgin who had extracted premium prices for very few
favors. She had teased, tantalized and promised everything. She
had yielded only by slow, maddening degrees, and just when the
conquest was at hand she demanded—and got—a higher price.
They should have known that she was giving in too easily; they
should have approached her with the trepidation that eleven
years had taught them. They should have known that her final
price would be steeper than ever before because she had always been overpriced. Kota was a virgin with the habits of a
harlot.

Maybe that was what bothered him, Doug thought. Maybe
it was because all the magic and mystery that had once surrounded her was gone. She had lost her maidenhead, and the
beauty that had been behind the veil was now that of an aging
old whore, laughing coldly at them from a face that displayed
scars, a crooked nose and rotted teeth. From now on she would
give in easily to the techniques they had perfected on her. She
would yield to the highest bidder.

It was a confusing love-hate relationship for him. He didn't
want to be there; he didn't want anyone else to be there. He felt
pleased that they had to depend upon him to take them where
they wished to go, but they didn't belong there. It was a little
like instructing a pair of strangers on how to make love to your
wife—and as though they were merely trying to complete an
impersonal, calculated mission while she didn't care one way or
the other. And that bothered him, too. Because you don't spend

eleven long years trying to do something without a feeling for it, and he couldn't help but feel for her. Kota was a female, and she had been his female for eleven years as surely as if she had been flesh and blood.

RUDI GURDLER TRUDGED ALONG, telling himself, I can do this . . . I can do this. It is child's play. It is easy. Easy . . .

Except that it was not easy. He wondered with every gasping breath whether he might collapse when he next inhaled. His legs hurt, his back ached under the weight of his pack, and his lungs were aflame.

Use whatever oxygen you need, Doug had said. Don't try to be a hero. It had helped, but the higher they went, the worse the pain became. Now he had to force himself to keep moving, to summon every ounce of concentration he could muster to keep from falling on his face. Yet he was determined to go on, not to halt or even slow the climb. Gurdler. You . . . are . . . Rudi Gurdler, he said to himself. You . . . are . . . *Rudi . . . Gurdler.* You are the most versatile climber who has ever lived. You are able to tackle any mountain. You have been to the top of the world over and over again, nearly every major peak on the planet. You are world famous. You are celebrated, an honored man who has been sought by celebrities, received by heads of state and decorated by royalty. There will never be another mountain climber in your class. You are special, and you are . . .

You are dying.

"There is no cure, Mr. Gurdler. I'm afraid your condition will continue to worsen, and there is nothing we can do either to arrest or retard it."

"Then I have only a limited time to live."

"Yes. If you remain in a hot, dry climate, I should judge a year, perhaps a little longer. But we don't know. It's hard to tell."

"How . . . how difficult will things be before . . . before—"

"At its worst, you may require an artificial respirator. Shortly afterward, even that won't help."

"So I will eventually suffocate?"

"Yes. I'm afraid so. I am sorry."

Ahead and above him, Gorham and Palmer made their way along almost easily. Their movements were erect and fluid, performed with practiced grace and disciplined experience. And there he was, lagging behind, struggling with all the willpower at his command just to keep up. Rudi Gurdler... veteran of mountains half again this tall and twice as treacherous. His predicament was worse than torturous—it was a humiliating disgrace.

Not that Kota was easy. It was not. So far, the route was one of the trickiest he had ever seen, a confusing maze of criss-crosses and switchbacks that had to be negotiated almost perfectly to keep them away from the most dangerous places. And the route had been surrounded by spots that looked deceptively easy, leaving a more inexperienced climber wondering why they weren't going this way, or that. Too, the storm last night had left many of the more familiar pitches utterly foreign to Doug—he had never climbed Kota this late in the year, or after such a storm. Several times he had had to pause and relocate part of the route; three times they had been forced to alter their route, and only Doug seemed to know which way to go. Kota was not the most inhospitable mountain Rudi had ever climbed, but it was, he had to admit, one of the most challenging from a technical standpoint. It required full concentration all the time; there was little time and almost nowhere to rest and regroup; and it looked as though it forgave no mistake. Under different circumstances Rudi was sure he could have handled it alone. But not this time.

There were, however, one or two places to rest, and he saw Doug stop and signal for him and Gary to hold it up. It was time for a drink, some food and, literally, a breather.

"What...is...our altitude...now?" he said, panting, dropping his pack. He tried to appear casual, and pretended not to notice as Doug watched him. But he was relieved, almost glad, to see that Doug and Gary were experiencing breathing difficulties, too. They weren't gasping or having the trouble he was, but the altitude was making itself felt. Their bodily functions had changed, and the tone and pace of the conversation had become clipped, with pauses every few words.

Now, none of their movements were quite as fast or deliberate.

"About 16,900 feet . . . give or take a few inches," Doug replied. "How are you doing?" and as he asked he took a quick look at the oxygen bottle.

"More . . . more winded than usual," he said. "But not bad . . . not too bad. I am . . . keeping up."

It was incredible that he hadn't mentioned anything about being sick, and Doug was worried that Rudi would gulp all the oxygen they owned just to stay on his feet. They should have gone down this morning regardless of those photos. He unzipped a side pocket in his pack and pulled out his own bottle. "Here. Take mine. If I need any, I'll take a hit of Gary's."

Rudi nodded his thanks.

"Christ!" Doug mumbled under his breath to Gary. "Woodhull and Karber and I probably didn't use a whole bottle among us during all eleven of our climbs up here."

"What about those guys up at the crash?" Gary asked. "Shouldn't we save some oxygen for them?"

"Let's wait and see what we find."

Staring into the distance, Rudi badly wanted to reply to Doug's comment. His lungs might be failing, but his ears were still as good as ever. He wanted to say, And why do you suppose I did not wish to climb without you leading us, Mr. Gorham? Do you think I could not climb this pitiful mountain alone? That if there had been no emergency I would have needed you? Oh, your Mount Kota is difficult, but there is no comparison between it and Everest, or K2. And your storm, while brutal, cannot compare with others I have faced. I would invite you to try an open bivouac at 22,800 feet on Macchapuchare as I once did. I have had snow bridges fall from under me, axes break and aids pull out from the sides of walls; I have experienced snow blindness, whiteouts, and I would remind you that it was I who nearly fell from your Lunatic Wall only yesterday. It is years of these things and more that have put me in the condition I am in, and I know of no other climber who would try one last time if he were facing the same predicament—not you, or any other. For I am a climber. All I have ever sought was to be found only on the rooftop of the world. Like an eagle I have soared.

"All set, Gary?" Doug asked.

"All set."

Rudi nodded once again, then picked up his pack. He looked toward the steepening slopes beyond. They would arrive at the Northeast Plateau before long; then, the summit. He would make it now, he was certain.

Because, like an eagle, there was only one fitting way for a climber to die.

2

Lieutenant Roger Goodwin glanced over his shoulder as the door closed behind him.

"Got 'em, sir," the sergeant said from across the room. "And they're not worth a tinker's damn. Take a look."

"Dammit!"

"My comment exactly, sir. There's still so much wind and shit blowing around up there that we can't make out a thing." And that meant that their most up-to-date set of recon photos were hours old, the ones taken at dawn this morning. Anything could have happened between then and now, and those three climbers might be killing themselves for nothing.

Their best set of pictures came right after the crash. The detail and resolution had been frighteningly clear, illustrating a mountaintop that had become a scene of utter destruction and death scattered everywhere. But they had also shown survivors out of the wreck and moving around. The same stark clarity came out in succeeding photo passes; it was actually possible to track the movements of several of the men, to tell where they had gone and what they had done. Later, however, as the storm approached, summit conditions had deteriorated steadily; by early afternoon additional pictures had been useless. The last set taken yesterday had been a blur of blowing snow and ice from which no detail could be distinguished. While the storm was in progress, the crash site had remained a mystery. Everybody battened down and tried to ride it out, and it wasn't until six-thirty this morning that the recon pilot radioed that summit visibility had cleared partially, and that he was going to try a couple of passes. The first pass was borderline, but it was all they could get; two succeeding attempts produced nothing usable. Even though the storm was gone and the weather had cleared, the wind on top of Mount Kota still raged, blanketing the site. If anything, the new snow had only made things worse. Visibility from the air—or from anyplace besides the summit itself, really—was almost zero. It had been that way all day, and there were no signs of it letting up.

Since eight o'clock Goodwin had been studying the six-thirty set. It was now going on three in the afternoon and Sergeant Kensor asked him how long he was going to sit there staring at them.

"It's these pictures that sent those three guys on up that mountain," he said. "They were all ready to come down this morning. But *this* set of pictures is what kept them climbing...that, and our word that we still had survivors." He turned back to the eight-by-ten glossies spread all over the table. "So I'm going to sit here until I figure out what the hell's wrong with them."

Kensor bent over the table. "What do you mean, what's wrong with them?"

"I mean, something's wrong. Something here doesn't quite fit. It's like looking at the kids' section of the Sunday paper...one of those drawings where you pick out the hidden pirates in the picture. And I just can't seem to spot that last one." He didn't know if he was looking right through the last pirate, or if it was there at all. He arranged the first day's photos in sequence, then motioned to Kensor. "Here. You take a look."

There were different angles of the same thing—a smashed-up airplane, debris thrown all across the mountaintop with scores of dead bodies. A lot of it had been covered by the snow but you could still see shapes and outlines; as the snow moved with the wind, spots were covered, then laid bare, then covered again. Other sets of photos became worse as the day dragged on, until nothing could be distinguished except blowing white.

The only big difference between the first and last sets was all the snow.

Kensor studied various pictures for nearly ten minutes before he came up shrugging. There was nothing to be looking for, nothing that should not be there.

Goodwin spread out the six-thirty stack. "Now. Take a good look at these."

Same scene, slightly different angles. There were tracks around the central hulk of the plane; they disappeared in the wind, but there were tracks visible at six-thirty nonetheless. And standing next to the wreck in two of the photos was a man who hadn't been there earlier. His tracks stopped at the wreck; presumably, he had gone inside. And in their final photo of that pass he appeared to have gone back outside with another man. But because of the angle of the shot, the distance from there to the camera in the plane, and still more blowing snow, it was difficult to tell for sure. The final photo pass taken afterward produced no detail at all.

"Well..." Kensor sighed. "It looks like one guy stepped out of the plane for a look around, went in to get a buddy and then they both went out. I don't know exactly what they're doing besides looking around... maybe at the photo plane. It's hard to tell." Nothing appeared to be out of the ordinary. He shook his head. "What am I supposed to be looking for, sir?"

"I don't know, but there's something wrong about the first man out of the plane. Something about it just doesn't look right, and I can't pin it down." He picked up a magnifying glass to study again the photo where the man first appeared. "If I could just figure out what that man's doing," he muttered.

Another ten minutes passed while both men examined the photographs. Then Kensor suddenly grabbed one of the pictures out of Goodwin's hand. "Wait a minute... just a minute. Who said he came out of the plane?"

"You did."

"I was wrong. Look at that. Those tracks."

The lieutenant looked again. He saw it. "Well, I'll be damned! He didn't come *from* the wreck. He came—"

"*Toward* it," Kensor finished. "But from where? I mean, I can see them stepping outside for a quick look around, but they'd probably go right back inside. They wouldn't be out wandering all over the mountain . . . would they?''

"You wouldn't think so. Not in that kind of weather. It's hardly the place to go for a stroll.''

"And this last shot with the two men together, sir," Kensor added, his nose almost touching the magnifying glass. "I sure wish they could have got a closer shot, or it hadn't been taken at such a weird angle."

"We're stuck with long shots and weird angles. What about it?"

"If I didn't know better I'd swear that those two guys aren't outside just looking at the scenery. I don't know what they're doing, but *that's* what looks all wrong to me all of a sudden. If the first man strolling all over the site is odd, this picture is stranger." He shrugged. "But you can't tell anything for certain about it."

"But you would agree that we have at least two men alive and moving up there as of six-thirty this morning?"

"Yes, sir. It looks that way to me."

"It looks that way to me, too. But I still don't like working in the dark. So I'm gonna call the airfield and request some more photo recon flights. We might have a couple of survivors left, but I'd still like to know what the hell is going on up there."

3

AT THE UPPER EDGE of a sharp, rocky ridge that appeared to drop straight off the eastern face of the mountain, Doug stopped and motioned for his partners to come up.

They did; they wondered what he was looking at, or where he was about to go next. Besides the mile-long drop-off, the only other obstacle was a sheer wall to their right. It appeared that they had come to a dead end.

"Almost there," he called above the wind. Turning to the right he stepped back down the route a few yards, then motioned for them to follow him into a pile of rocks. Again, they did so, finding him some thirty feet above them when they got there. They watched for a minute as he pulled himself over one rock after another until he was near the western corner of the wall, and he waved a third time.

They went up—Gary first, then Rudi.

Doug disappeared over the top of the wall; they joined him minutes later, stepping onto a flat, open area they had seen only in photographs. They were at the Northeast Plateau at last.

"Well, hot damn!" Gary said, dropping his pack. "We made it."

"Almost." Doug smiled. "We still have eleven hundred feet to go yet, but the worst of it's over. The rest is easy."

"It isn't really a plateau at all, is it?" Gary asked, looking around. "It's a big nook...like somebody took a bite out of the mountain." It was shaped more or less like a thirty/sixty degree right triangle with the point broken off and the entrance to Karber's Pass near the inside corner, or heel. Nor was the surface flat, but rising near the center, and lumpy at the corner. Hundreds of rocks from ledges and walls on two sides had fallen all over most of the surface, and snow was drifted high in the corners.

"How are you doing, Mr. Gurdler?" Doug asked, helping Rudi with his backpack. He looked exhausted, ready to drop.

Nodding, Rudi removed the oxygen mask. "Fine, Mr. Gorham. I need some rest...but I am all right. It was a fine climb...all things considered. You are to be congratulated, Mr. Gorham." He extended his right hand.

"We're not at the top yet." And Doug extended his hand, too.

"We have made it this far. We shall go the distance." And he still could not help but think about the times when he had existed in places more than eleven thousand feet above this gouged-out little cranny—which was one of the best North America had to offer. Yet he had to consider it a victory, and one of the last he would know.

Doug smiled. "We shall indeed. But in the meantime we'd better get our base camp set up."

They had three lightweight nylon tents; one for themselves, the other two for any survivors they found. Only one of the survivor tents was erected, but everything else was readied to accept occupants. Food was set out, water in insulated containers, medical supplies and their gas camp stove. Down-filled insulated blankets were laid out along with clothing of the same material. For the final climb they would take only bare necessities—three elementary first-aid kits, three blankets, one aluminum litter constructed from two of the backpacks, Gary's radio and a 35 mm camera.

When they were ready, Doug motioned them toward the southwest corner of the plateau. He pointed toward what appeared to be nothing but a pile of fallen rocks. "Right through there," he said. "The pass goes up that way...then toward the south."

Gary asked whether anybody had tried scaling either the west or south walls bordering the plateau.

"No. Both walls go up seven or eight hundred feet before leveling off, and neither one of 'em is in good enough shape to climb. We never tried them." He glanced at his watch, then up to the pass. "We have about four hours' daylight left, gentlemen. Let's get going."

In the base camp at the foot of the mountain every man who wasn't busy with something else had gathered around the communications tent. Grady, Streetor, Evans and Childs clustered around the radio console, hanging on every word between Lieutenant Palmer and Sergeant Berry, the communications NCO. No one else uttered a sound.

"Please keep your channel open, Lieutenant."

"Roger, base camp," replied Palmer's static-filled voice from eighteen thousand feet. "You'll get a full account from here to the summit."

4

THEY BEGAN TO SEE DEBRIS from the wreck about four hundred feet into the pass, mostly small bits and pieces from the cargo aboard the plane—pieces from boxes and crates, and a few twisted metal remnants from vehicles.

Gary reported to the base camp, describing each item they saw. He paused now and then to take pictures. The running conversation between him and Sergeant Berry sounded almost dull.

Twenty minutes passed.

"We are...about halfway through Karber's Pass. A lot more debris here...scattered all around us, in the pass...and all over the rocks on either side. Parts from the plane are getting larger...personal belongings from the men lying around. Just ahead is part of an axle and wheel...looks like it's from a jeep. Badly burned...tire burned off...black hunks of rubber hanging down like melted cheese. About thirty-five yards beyond is a much larger piece from the airplane, a jet engine, I think. Yes. I can see turbine blades bent out, fuel lines and tubes. Uhh...just a moment..."

The next five minutes were filled with clinks, bumps and thuds.

"A lot more junk up ahead now...everywhere. More parts...broken cargo...there's a part of a wing...part of a bed and tailgate from a truck...."

"Lieutenant, has there been any sign of the survivors? Over."

"Ahh...negative, base camp. Nothing yet. But there are a few bodies up ahead...but no survivors yet. We're still some distance from the crash site."

"Roger. Please go on with your report, Lieutenant."

"Will do. Uhh...both Mr. Gorham and Mr. Gurdler are ahead of me, and both have paused to examine some of the pieces. Rudi is looking at a box...with colored wires attached. Hold on, I'm going to take a few more pictures...."

...click-whirrrkk...click-whirrrkk...click-whirrrkk...

"The pass levels off just slightly up ahead...turns to the right. I can see from here that we'll have to stop and move some junk out of our way. It looks like it's blocked by a number of large wing pieces...a couple of flaps or ailerons...structural ribbing jabbed through the skin. One of them looks like it's fifteen or sixteen feet long...looks pretty heavy. Uhh, Gorham's waving to me, wants me to help move it. Hold on...."

Another five minutes passed. General Grady grabbed a chair and sat down next to Sergeant Berry. They heard Doug Gorham say something.

"What's that?"

"Up there. There's where Karber went...up in those rocks."

"Lieutenant Palmer?" Berry asked. "Is something wrong? Over."

"Ahh...negative, base camp. We're moving out again. We just had to move some junk...a lot more of it now. Some of it's blocking the path. And now we can see bodies. Some are partly buried in the snow, others in various places in the rocks on both sides of the pass...fifteen, maybe twenty, that we can see from here. We're going past some of them right now...."

...*click-whirrrkk*...*click-whirrrkk*...*click-whirrrkk*...

"We...we are nearing the upper end of the pass now. More victims in front of us, covered by the snow. A lot of arms and legs sticking up, some unattached, I think. And now, pieces of the plane and cargo are all over the place...something underfoot no matter where you step...*Jesus!* You should see this."

"Palmer, this is General Grady. I want you to settle down. Take it slow and easy. I can only imagine how things must look up there, but try to concentrate on your job. Just report what you see. Do you understand?"

"Yes, sir..."

"God-*damn*!"

"What was that, Lieutenant? What's happened? Over."

"Uh...that was Mr. Gorham. He was moving a piece of wing skin out of his way and...uh, uncovered part of a badly mutilated body underneath...."

"It's a crash site, Lieutenant," Grady put in. "You'll be seeing a lot worse before it's over. You'll just have to stomach it. Try to look past it. Just do your job."

"We're trying, sir."

"Any sign of the survivors yet?"

"No, sir. Nothing yet."

"All right. Continue with your report."

"The end of the pass is just ahead. We can see the bottom end of the summit...and tons of debris everywhere. Papers blowing around...pieces of canvas flapping. I'm standing over a steno pad...water-warped...the ink runny and smeared. Looks like someone started a letter home. Rudi is looking at a ripped-up *Playboy* magazine...got the foldout opened. Nice blonde this month...big tits. And Doug is—"

"Dammit, Palmer, you don't have to be that descriptive! Just tell us about the site in general, and that's an order."

"Yes, sir . . ."

The officers heard muffled laughter in the background. The men inside the tent were trying not to laugh.

Palmer's camera clicked another four times; the base camp listeners heard more footfalls.

"Base camp?"

"Go ahead, Lieutenant."

"We've arrived. Just ahead is the wreck . . . near the crest of the summit. Uhh . . . Gorham and Gurdler are going on up. I'm taking some more pictures. God, what a mess!"

"Palmer, this is Grady again. The pictures can wait. Go and check out the center section of the fuselage. We think that's where the survivors may be, using it as a shelter. Over." As he was saying that, he heard an airplane; it sounded as if it was circling around the mountain, and he wondered who had ordered another recon flight. But he didn't ask; another photo recon flight was a good idea. He should have thought of it.

"On my way, sir. Uh, Doug is already there, and he's waving at me. I think he's found something. Hold on for a few minutes. . . ."

"We're standing by." They could hear footsteps hurrying through the snow, and Palmer's labored breathing.

"What'd you find?"

"Take a look."

"Lieutenant Palmer?"

"Holy Jesus! Did you *see* this?"

"I didn't go in. That's why I waved. I wanted you to do that. They're your people."

"Lieutenant Palmer, please come in. Over." All they could hear were the sounds of bumping and banging.

"What the hell do you suppose caused this?"

"Damned if I know. But it wasn't the wreck. This shit happened after the fact."

"Lieutenant, are you copying? Please respond. What have you found? Over."

"Where's Gurdler?"

"I don't know. I haven't seen him for five or ten minutes."

Grady grabbed the microphone. "Palmer, I want you to report! What's going on up there? Over."

"Kota Base, this is Endicott Center, monitoring your communication. We're requesting a report as to the situation of the crash site. Would you—"

"Endicott, this is Grady, and I don't know what the hell's going on up there! We request that you shut the hell up and just monitor!"

"Roger, Kota Base. Will monitor. Endicott Center out."

"Palmer! Report your situation at once. That is an order. Over."

"Weird . . . really weird . . ."

"*What's* weird? Report, Palmer! What is happening?"

"Report . . . re . . . ort . . . ee . . . ort . . ."

"What the hell's the matter with him?"

"I—I don't know, sir, but he's playing with his radio," Berry said, pointing toward the console. "Look at how his broadcast light is flashing on and off."

" . . . ey're dead . . . all . . . ead. Ever . . . ody in the . . . ane . . . dead . . ."

"Repeat that, Palmer. You're breaking up. Please repeat. Did you say that all the survivors are now dead? Over."

This time, there was no answer from the summit except for the distant howl of the wind.

"Palmer! Report!"

Nothing. Grady threw the microphone down. "Dammit!" he roared, then whirled around in his chair. "All right, this is for everybody. As of right now, everything transpiring—*every single detail*—is classified. If anyone breathes a word of this outside this camp, I'll have his ass sent to the arctic faster than shit through a goose!" He turned back to Sergeant Berry. "Tell Endicott what I just said, too. And tell them to get in contact with that plane up there. Order them to get pictures and anything else they can get as long as they have film to burn. I don't want to see a single unexposed negative when they get back to Endicott." He waited helplessly until Berry had finished.

"What could be causing such bizarre behavior?" General Streetor asked.

"Damned if I know. Could be the altitude, could be anything. If they're using oxygen, and somehow their tanks were contaminated, they could be in real trouble. That's happened before. We had a contaminated air compressor that pumped carbon monoxide into some of the respirators once. The men using them started acting like that."

"Your orders have been received and understood, sir," Berry said at last. "Endicott's contacting that plane right now."

"Okay. Keep trying to contact Palmer, and tell him that if anybody's using oxygen reservoirs to get rid of 'em...throw 'em away." He turned back to Streetor. "And just hope that he comprehends that order."

"Lieutenant Palmer, this is the base camp again. Please listen carefully: if you are using oxygen, get rid of the tanks. Repeat: get rid of your oxygen tanks. They may be contaminated. Do you understand? Over."

There was no reply.

Berry repeated the message.

Still, nothing.

"I don't know if he got it or not, sir. Maybe not because he's still playing with his broadcast button," and again he pointed to the green flashing light on his console.

"For God's sake—"

"Gurdler!" they heard someone cry.

"Report, Lieutenant! That's an order! What's going on up there?"

No answer—only noises.

"Palmer!"

"He fell ... Gurdler ... he fell...."

"What was that, Palmer? Repeat your message! Did you say that Gurdler just fell? Over."

"Fell ... fell right off ..."

"Report your situation, Palmer! Immediately! Do you understand? Report your situation! Over."

"Sit ... sit ... chew ... aaa ... shunnn ... Bad. Verrreee... bad ... All dead. All ... dead ..."

In the background they thought they could hear sounds of something moving in the snow. There were strained grunts, and one or two choked cries for help; and someone was calling Palmer's name.

"Lieutenant Palmer! Lieutenant! Answer! Respond!"

They heard a thunk in the snow.

"He's dropped the radio," Berry said.

Footsteps moved away from the radio, then sounded as if they returned. In the distance, somebody said, "You... you... you're *dead*."

And he was answered.

"Holy shit, what's *that*?" General Streetor muttered.

"It sounds like humming... someone humming a tune!" Berry said, mostly to himself. "I think..."

But the last sound was not a hum; just before the radio went dead, they all heard a final word from the summit: "Deeeathhh..." it whispered.

5

THE STORY FILLED both the public print and the airways, but two more days passed before the military made it all official. Releases were issued, names were named, and General Grady made the official statement to the press at noon that day in Endicott's Public Information Office.

"The flight in question was a U.S. Air Force transport, MAC Flight Number J-440, which left Fort Bragg, North Carolina, at 2:00 p.m. on September 28, and was bound for the Oakland Army Terminal in Oakland, California. At approximately ten-thirty that evening, however, the aircraft experienced some kind of mechanical difficulty that apparently sent it out of control, and it struck the summit of Mount Kota in Mount Kota National Park, Montana.

"Upon learning of the crash shortly afterward, we launched an immediate photographic reconnaissance flight to survey the damage and the crash site. Our first sets of photographs, to our surprise, illustrated unmistakable signs of activity around the wreck. We do not know exactly how many people survived the initial crash, but we estimated at least ten men; perhaps as many as fifteen. At this time we began considering different means to rescue them. We could not parachute rescue personnel because of the extreme danger and eminent failure of such an airdrop, but we did attempt air-dropping supplies to the stricken men. Unfortunately, this was unsuccessful because of high winds and inclement weather conditions at the summit. So, we were left with only one choice, and we began at once to assemble a climbing team for the rescue attempt.

"At dawn the following morning, after a field camp was established at the base of the mountain, a three-man team began an ascent to the crash site. Later that day we ran into some more bad luck in the form of a storm, which had moved into the region from southern Canada. The climbers were forced to bivouac earlier than planned, but they commenced the climb again the next morning, and they reached the summit late that afternoon. Unfortunately, and through no fault of theirs, the climbers were too late. All who had been aboard the aircraft were dead.

"There were 126 men aboard Flight J-440: a flight crew of four, and a passenger manifest of 122...plus cargo and numerous personal belongings. The flight crew was part of B Flight, 332nd Airlift Wing, the Military Airlift Command, stationed at Andrews Air Force Base, Maryland. The passengers were all the officers, noncommissioned officers and enlisted personnel of C Company, Second Battalion, 191st Light Infantry Brigade, which is presently being relocated and reassembled in Quohong Tau Province, the Republic of Vietnam.

"The three rescue climbers were Mr. Douglas Gorham of Seattle, Washington; Mr. Rudi Gurdler of Bern, Switzerland; and one of our own rescue team leaders, First Lieutenant Gary S. Palmer of Yakima, Washington. I believe you ladies and gentlemen already have full profiles on these men. But it is now, and with the deepest regret, that I must announce that all three of them lost their lives during the attempt. At this time we have no precise information about the deaths of Mr. Gorham or Lieutenant Palmer, but Mr. Gurdler somehow fell from the summit. His body was found by park rangers shortly afterward. The other two climbers' bodies are still at, or near, the summit of the mountain and unrecoverable at this time. The deaths of all three of these men, as well as the crash itself, will remain under full investigation until all questions are answered, at which time a full disclosure will be made. Mr. Gurdler's body has already been flown to Switzerland, accompanied by an honor guard, and our Swiss ambassador has made official condolences to the family. Similar honor guards have been dispatched to both Mr. Gorham's and Lieutenant Palmer's hometowns where memorial services will be held.

"Now, at this time I'll answer a few of your questions."

A man stood up. "General, it is already a matter of public record that the prototype C-181 Transport has a history of instrument and systems malfunctions and breakdowns. Do you know which one of these might have caused the crash? Or was it pilot error?"

"You're asking the wrong man, sir. Any questions about the aircraft will have to be directed to the Air Force. Or the manufacturer, which I believe is the Fischer-Freelander Aircraft Company of Lawton, Oklahoma."

"General Grady, you mentioned something about photo reconnaissance missions," one of the women said. "How many of these missions were there, and what did they show?"

"There were five such missions launched after the crash, and two the following morning. Those photographs taken immediately after the accident were the ones that showed survivors to be out and moving around. So did a few of those taken the next morning. But because of deteriorating weather conditions during the approach and arrival of that storm, most of our photos didn't show much. On the second morning we got several more pictures, all of which again showed men still alive and active at the crash site. But those were the last pictures we got, the last ones to show any activity. Between the time the final pictures were taken that morning, and the time the climbers arrived, the remaining survivors had died. I'll add here that we have a few photos that will be released to the press. We'll pass them out later."

"Why did you stop the flights after only two that final morning?"

"Because of the high winds at the summit. There was so much new snow blowing around that we couldn't see anything. Further missions were useless."

"Have you gotten others now that the weather has settled?"

"Yes. But you can't see them. They are part of the investigation, and have been classified."

"Would a successful rescue have been possible if there had been no storm?"

Grady sighed. "I don't know. That's very hard to say. Certainly, and as I've already mentioned, the storm held the climbers up. But the survival of those men depended on lots of things. Even without a storm the weather at nineteen thousand feet and higher is brutal. All of the men had to have been injured in the crash; most likely, some of them were seriously or critically injured. They had no medical aid; they had no food, no water, no adequate clothing, and almost no shelter. Survival under any one of those handicaps is questionable, and with all of them . . . well, we don't know how those few we saw in the final photos lasted as long as they did. A successful rescue might have been possible—*might have been*. But a hundred other things could have gone wrong, too. And that is as much as I care to speculate."

"How many men were up and moving on the final morning?"

"All I can say is that there was more than one."

"Why didn't you try a helicopter rescue?"

"Helicopters cannot climb that high. Nor can they maneuver or land in high winds. We were going to fly them up as high as possible, but the winds were too strong. And the only places a helicopter could set down were too far away from the climbing route."

"Are you planning any other ascents up the mountain?"

"None in the immediate future, ma'am. Winter is almost upon us and a winter climb would be impossible. As I understand it, Mount Kota is hazardous under the best of conditions, so it will be a while before we find anybody else qualified to lead another ascent."

"Then how can you expect to conduct an accurate investigation?"

"For the time being, by doing what we're already doing. That may not sound like very much but it's all we can do. Because the crash occurred in such a remote and inhospitable place it will be some time before we can examine the site and its evidence thoroughly. It will be months before we'll be able to cover the most important facts, and we might never find all of them. As I said, however, the media will be informed when new facts come to light and after they are declassified for public release. And on that note, ladies and gentlemen, we will conclude this conference. Thank you all for coming."

"Very good, Tom," said the lanky, balding man who joined Grady in the hallway. "You handled that nicely. I was impressed."

Grady gave his deputy commander a sour look. Brigadier General Martin was always trying to be funny. He could afford to; he wasn't responsible for much of anything. Grady liked Martin, but he was like most deputy commanders—about as useful on the job as a third tit. "Don't you have something to inspect or nitpick about?" he grumbled.

"Two things." Martin smiled, falling into step. "I've already mentioned the first."

"What's the second?"

"You have visitors in your office. They sent me personally to get you. It's hush-hush . . . for your ears only, one of them said. That kind of thing."

They started up the stairway. "Well, who are they, or is that hush-hush, too?"

"One of them is one of your old alumni—General David Kelly of Fort Stanton. Plus a four-star by the name of Mattlock—"

"A *full general*? And we didn't get any word he was coming?" Grady hurried to the stairway.

"I don't know any more than you. All of a sudden, here they were, wanting to see you."

"Good God! Anybody else?"

"A civilian . . . Fairfield, I believe he said. Also from Fort Stanton."

Full generals and civilians, from Fort Stanton of all places. Grady had heard the name Mattlock before, but couldn't place

GENERAL GRADY THOUGHT: Maybe I'm old-fashioned, but a military base should at least *look* like a goddamn military base. And Fort Stanton, Maryland, looked like anything but that. As they cruised along in their drab brown sedan, passing row after row of identical single-level block buildings, Grady had seen only two things to remind anybody that they were on a government installation: a hurricane fence with a strand of barbed wire strung tightly across the top, and a simple gate through which they had entered the reservation. There hadn't even been a sign announcing where they were; no guards, no MPs, no military vehicles. Just an unlocked gate that the civilian, Dr. Virgil Fairfield, had opened for them. He was also their driver.

"Great security you've got here," Grady commented.

General Kelly, the commanding officer of Stanton, smiled and half turned in the front seat. "Oh, it's better than it looks. If you don't believe me, just get out and try to walk in unescorted and unannounced. There'll be at least twenty armed guards on you in two seconds."

Maybe so. Grady had yet to see any guards, armed or otherwise. In fact, he and Kelly and General Mattlock in the rear seat with him were the only people thus far who were even in uniform. Of the dozen or so people they had seen, most of them loading or unloading small, plain-colored trucks, each had been dressed in ordinary work clothes. Grady mentioned this, too, asking if there were any GIs on the post at all.

"We have forty-five hundred working or stationed here right now. About half-and-half. Most of our civilians are like Dr. Fairfield, here. That is, nearly half of them hold PhDs in one thing or another, and most of those who don't are presently working on their doctorates. Ninety-five percent of our GIs are college-educated, and about forty percent of them hold advanced degrees, too."

"The three men you saw back there at that last loading dock collectively have almost fifty years of education," Dr. Fairfield added.

"Aren't they a bit overqualified for what they're doing?"

"We don't like to advertise anything," General Mattlock said quietly. "An ordinary truck driver isn't even cleared to come through the gates. So we do everything ourselves, even sweeping up around the place. It might not look like it, Tom, but Stanton's personnel are the best-educated and most highly qualified people on any military post in the country—including the Pentagon. It's quite a place . . . quite unique."

And the question for that was *why*. But Grady decided not to ask any more questions for the time being. Suddenly, he didn't want to know any more, but he knew he'd be hearing and seeing a lot of what he might not want to learn over the next day or two. They'll tell me, he thought. If twenty-nine-plus years in the Army had done nothing else they had taught him when and where to keep his mouth shut.

"The idea is to keep everything plain . . . simple looking," General Mattlock added. "Most people know what we do here: we handle chemical compounds for the Army. We store and test chemicals, cleaning solvents, petroleum products, explosives and ammunition . . . every chemical mixture the Army might use anyplace in the world, from ink to insect repellent." He gave Grady a wide smile. "And that is exactly what we want everyone to think, so we actually *do* those things. You know, just in case some senator or junior congressman decides to get nosy."

Grady felt a chill. He had been right. But how the hell did *he* figure into all of this?

At yet another row of block buildings they finally turned and drove to the far end. Each building front was identical to the one next to it—a short concrete loading dock with a single roll-up door behind it, and a set of concrete steps leading up to a single door for pedestrians. Every door was painted a neutral tan, the roll-up doors displaying a stenciled number, 1 through 8. Kelly's office was adjacent to number 8. Only two of the sixteen parking spaces were occupied. They pulled into the last one. It didn't even have Kelly's name on it, Grady saw. There were no smartly dressed MPs out front, no American flag snapping in the wind, no mention at all that this was the office

of the commanding general or post headquarters. If it weren't
for the few people they had seen here and there on various
docks and driveways the whole place would have appeared
abandoned.

As Grady climbed from the car he heard a heavy *whump* in
the distance. Mattlock smiled. "Hear that, Tom? We really are
testing explosives today."

"This place comes as close to looking like a military post as
I am to being the king of Norway," he replied.

Kelly laughed. "That's nothing. Wait'll you see my office,"
and he motioned toward the door.

He wasn't kidding. The small warehouse next to Kelly's office was dark and empty except for a few scattered crates and
boxes. His secretary was in an outer office containing nothing
but her desk, one phone, a typewriter, five filing cabinets and
a couple of extra chairs—all surrounded by scratched and battered banker's partitioning that looked as if it had been sal-
vaged from a landfill. The only difference between her office
and Kelly's was that his had real walls and a window, plus three
more chairs and a wobbly conference table. There were no
shelves, cabinets, closets or credenzas; no potted plants, pictures, wall decorations, not even a coat tree. "I've been meaning to requisition one of those," Kelly said, throwing his coat
over the back of a chair, "but we don't usually have much
company here. I'm not here that often, either."

"I've seen field camps that were more lavishly decorated,"
Grady said, and as he spoke, three more men came into the
room. There were greetings but no salutes and no uniforms. All
three looked like the people they'd seen earlier on the loading
dock. Grady was beginning to feel overdressed.

"Gentlemen," Kelly began, "this is Major General Tom
Grady, the CG of Fort Endicott, Montana. Tom, this is
my deputy commander, Brigadier General Bill Turner...
Lieutenant Colonel Dan Gilmore...and Lieutenant Colonel
Chuck Attwood. Colonels Gilmore and Attwood are tempo-
rarily on loan to us from the Blackstone Arsenal in Utah."

"Blackstone? Isn't that the CBR test facility?"

"We're going to be filling General Grady in on everything," Mattlock said to the group, then turned to Grady. "No, Tom, *this* is the Army's chemical, biological, and radiological Test, Research, and Evaluation Facility. Some testing is performed at Blackstone but it's used mostly for stockpiling of CBR weapons."

"And in case you haven't already guessed, Tom," Kelly added, "General Mattlock is the head of all U.S. Army CBR operations." He glanced at his watch. "We've got about an hour before dinner, so we might as well get started. And, Tom, we've got a damned good cafeteria here, too."

"Good . . . fine." Nothing around here was what it appeared to be.

2

WHEN MATTLOCK SAID everything, he meant everything. By the time they broke for dinner, Grady had lost most of his appetite. He had, in one hour, heard far more than he'd ever dreamed of hearing about this place, these men and what they were doing. Nothing about the plane crash, Fort Stanton, this part of the Army or the truth in general was what he'd been given to believe.

They began by going over the details of the crash—specifically, Grady told all that he knew about it. He started with the moment he was called out of bed by the officer in charge at Endicott Center after they learned of the accident, and finished with the press conference he had conducted that morning. He knew very little more than he'd told the public, and he said, "I told them what I understood to be the truth." Because he was certain now that he didn't know the half of it—maybe none at all.

General Kelly passed a paper across the table to him, a copy of an Army hospital patient transfer order. They awaited his reaction.

"Lieutenant Gregory Pommelroy?" he mumbled. "Never heard of him." But he looked at the form again and noticed that Lieutenant Pommelroy had been transferred from General James D. Endicott Army Hospital—Grady's own—to Wheeler

Barracks, Kansas; that the lieutenant had been seriously injured during a climbing exercise. He kept reading. Then: "Wait
a minute . . . I don't know *any* of the names on this thing. And
that isn't *my* signature. What the hell—"

"I had my secretary type that out before I left for Endicott
this morning, Tom," said Kelly. "But I didn't have time to get
the names of your medical personnel, so I borrowed a few
names from our own roster. I had to forge their initials . . . and
your name. But it doesn't matter. The people at Wheeler only
needed a form and they don't care who signs it. The point is,
only three people at Wheeler know who Pommelroy really is.
We don't want any more people than necessary knowing about
him."

"All right, then, who is he?"

"First Lieutenant Gary Palmer."

"Palm...*alive*? But how? Why weren't we told? Good God,
I told the whole world this morning that he got killed on that
mountain! But how did he get down? Who—"

"One thing at a time. You'll have to indulge us for a while so
that you'll fully understand what we're doing, and why. And
what we're about to do."

And that, Grady thought, cinched it, or a big portion of it.
What it all amounted to was covering your ass. Somebody had
screwed up royally. And now the mistake had gotten so big that
they were having to drag him in on it.

"We know what happened at the crash site, sir," Colonel
Gilmore began. "Or we have a pretty good idea, at least, so
we're reasonably sure about what happened to the three
climbers. Had we known about the rescue attempt in time we
would have stopped it. Unfortunately, by the time our facts had
been assembled and checked, your three men were almost at the
summit."

"I was the one who reported to your base camp that everybody at the site was dead," Colonel Attwood added. "I was in
that plane circling above the mountain at the time, talking to
your radio operator.

"At first, we really thought everybody up there was dead, sir.
It wasn't until early the following morning when we were flying
over the mountain again, considering ways to get to the crash,

that we spotted a man wandering down the north face of the mountain—Lieutenant Palmer. We intercepted him before your men, who were taking apart the base camp, saw him. We have no idea how he got down alone, but that isn't important now."

"General," Doctor Fairfield said at last, "you were shocked to learn that Lieutenant Palmer is still alive. We were flabbergasted. Because he should have been killed, and we still can't understand why he wasn't. Or why any of those who lived through the crash survived for as long as they did."

Grady held up a hand. "Hold on, please, gentlemen. What do you mean about stopping the attempt, or that Palmer should have died? What are you trying to tell me?" He wondered if it was what he suspected.

Fairfield paused to light his pipe. "There is a firm in Belleville, New Jersey, with which the Army has done business for a number of years," he continued through a raft of smoke. "The Hammond Chemical Company. They've produced all kinds of cleaning solvents, corrosion preventatives, dry lubricants...those sorts of things. In 1964 they began making insecticides and related products. Right now we're using some of them in Southeast Asia. But a..."

A chemical company. Jesus Christ! I might have known.

"...little over a year ago they stumbled onto something—a complete accident. One of those unplanned rarities that occur to a company perhaps only once during its lifetime. They suddenly found themselves with a herbicide that had been mixed accidentally, and it was by far the most potent herbicide ever concocted. So powerful that it actually frightened them. They didn't know what to do with it. But they continued working with it until the formula was perfected, then..."

And they gave it to the Army. Holy shit!

"...they sent it to us for testing and evaluation."

The basic formula killed all plant life—*all* plant life. It worked instantly, one of its agents halting all nourishment and growth while a second set to work destroying all cellular structure. Plants the size of large bushes and smaller would shrivel and die before your eyes, withering like tissue paper in a fire. Bigger plants, up to the size of large trees, took a little longer—twelve, fifteen, perhaps twenty minutes. After death, however, they could be pushed over by hand. You had to see the stuff work to believe it. It was right out of science fiction—but entirely real.

"But the most amazing and unbelievable thing about it was that it was entirely harmless to animal life. We tested it on five hundred different species of reptiles, mammals and insect life, and in no instance did it harm any of them. The most astounding weed killer ever invented—a fourteen-ounce canister could lay waste an area the size of a football field—yet it would not harm a fly. Amazing," Fairfield said, and sighed.

"So what happened to it?" Grady asked, thinking: *As if you don't know.*

For it to function as they wished, it had to work effectively and efficiently in an atmosphere of high heat, high relative humidity and high oxygen content—a jungle or rain forest environment. And it did, but not nearly well enough. Their first tests were failures because the formula had been designed for temperate climates, and there were occasions when it became completely unpredictable in other atmospheric conditions.

"That's when Colonel Attwood and I were brought in to assist Doctor Fairfield," Gilmore said. "We had to make Swamp Gas—our nickname for it—effective and predictable for use in a jungle. I think we succeeded."

And the rest was now clear to Grady. "So you guys brought in something from Blackstone and added it to your...Swamp Gas," he said. The arsenal contained hundreds of chemical and biological weapons, many of which weren't found in nature. "I didn't know the United States was in the germ warfare business anymore."

"Politically, we're not," General Mattlock replied. "Technically, hell yes. Like it or not, this country has invested heavily in the germ and gas business. So has every other world power, whether or not they admit it. You should see some of the CIA reports we've seen, General Grady. They'd scare the shit out of you. We're only trying to keep up with the Joneses."

"And the orders for development came from...well, higher sources, Tom."

"What *did* you do to it?"

Modifying the gas for maximum effectiveness, Grady was told, meant that additions had to be made to its basic formula.

They added some two dozen different chemicals before they found one that would work—or two, as it turned out.

The first was a fast-acting hemotoxin that suffocated animal life by gobbling up all the oxygen-carrying red corpuscles. Combined with Swamp Gas's natural ability to destroy cellular structure, the hemotoxin produced a side effect: if the victim suffered any break in the skin, even a scratch, he would bleed to death if the gas didn't suffocate him first. Together, both basic formulas acted as a massive anticoagulant along with everything else they did.

The second agent worked even better. They added a super-neurotoxic compound that paralyzed all involuntary muscular action and reacted on most of the nerves like a massive barbiturate. One good whiff of the stuff would collapse a man in seconds, rendering him completely helpless while all his vital organs and functions simply quit on him. "This was the ultimate product on which we agreed," Fairfield said. "A herbicide with all the qualities of an extremely powerful snake venom."

"Jesus!" Grady whispered. "Whatever happened to just shooting and stabbing the enemy?"

"We're interested in any improvement over the old-fashioned bullet-and-gun type of warfare," General Mattlock replied. "Not only that, the projected cost on a per-kill ratio comes down to less than a penny a man . . . which hardly puts this in a class with a nuclear missile or a jet fighter plane."

"General, we could eliminate the population of Red China for less than a tenth of what it costs to build a nuclear-powered aircraft carrier...not counting what it costs to man it and equip it," Colonel Attwood added, smiling.

Grady knew what was coming next. "All right," he said with a sigh, "how did this stuff get on board a troop transport?"

"A screwup," Kelly said. "Pure and simple. We don't have an airfield here, as you may have noticed. Everything coming in or out goes in trucks. We were delivering a forty-gallon canister of Swamp Gas to Blackstone, but we had to drive it down to Andrews Air Force Base where it was going to be put aboard a special transport to Utah. Somehow, it was loaded on the wrong one.''

For shipment, they had placed the pressurized canister back inside the Hammond Chemical Company carton in which it had been delivered to Stanton. It looked exactly like each of the twenty cases of insecticide tagged to go aboard Flight J-440. The plane had stopped at Andrews for that, and other similar cargo, and to change flight crews.

''Christ!'' Grady whispered. ''Then those guys ended up with forty gallons of lethal nerve gas on their plane.''

''While Blackstone ended up with forty-eight cans of bug spray,'' Attwood said, nodding. ''That carton somehow got mixed up with the others while they were loading the plane. After we learned about the mistake it took us a day and a half to track it down. By then, of course, the plane had already gone down and the rescue mission was nearly over. We were in on the tail end of everything.''

''A wild coincidence,'' Gilmore added. ''A million-to-one accident.''

Which wasn't worth a rat's ass now, Grady thought. It had happened. ''So now what?'' he asked, still wondering how he was being fitted into this mess.

Kelly looked at his watch. ''Now, we eat. Before the cafeteria closes.''

3

So now what? meant finding answers to a number of tall questions. The first was Dr. Fairfield's. The crash survivors should have died much sooner than they apparently did. How had they lasted so long? On the other hand, what had killed Doug Gorham and Rudi Gurdler so quickly? If it was Swamp Gas exposure, the features of the gas must have altered radically between the time the soldiers died and the time the climbers reached the summit; if so, what had caused that? How could it have killed so slowly one day and so rapidly the next in the same environment? Or had some—or all—the deaths been caused by something entirely different? If so, what was that? Finally, how and why had Gary Palmer survived at all?

Since all the corpses were for the time being inaccessible and no comparisons were possible, they had to learn all they could from Palmer, the only source of information. But to do that they had to talk with him, examine him and find out what he remembered—which was impossible because he was comatose. All they could do for the moment was what they'd already done—move him to Wheeler Barracks where they could keep an eye on him. Maybe the psychiatrists could pull him out of it. All they could do was wait and see.

At that point they had only theories. The prevalent idea of extended or permanent survival after Swamp Gas exposure was that the atmosphere had altered its action. The addition of the nerve agent had made it ideal for use in a jungle environment; on the mountain it had escaped in an atmosphere of precisely the opposite conditions.

"And we don't know its effects in high-altitude alpine conditions," Colonel Gilmore said. "We've started a few tests under simulated conditions, but we've come up with nothing significant."

"This is where you come in, Tom," Kelly said. "What we'd like to do is kill two birds with one stone, so to speak. In order to answer all these questions with any accuracy, as well as to assist the Air Force people to find out what actually caused the crash in the first place, we're going to go back to that mountain...to the crash site. We have to examine everything there."

"How the hell are you going to do that? We barely got those three men up there as it was. According to my climbers, and every other climber I know of, Kota is one of the toughest mountains in the world."

Nobody, he was told, had said anything about climbing it. "We plan on putting two people up there, maybe more," Mattlock said, pointing to Attwood and Gilmore. "They will be inside a small, permanent station that will probably be located on that spot called the Northeast Plateau."

"We've already done some research about Mount Kota, Tom," Kelly added, opening his own briefcase. He pulled out a thick file and a stack of photographs. Grady recognized some of the material—the information Doug Gorham brought along from Seattle that night, his own notes and pictures. There were also many of Fort Endicott's own recon photos and records, and to all this had been added a stapled set of sketches and drawings. "These are a bit crude because we haven't had time enough to work up a formal design, or even an artist's rendition of our idea. But all of this will come about in the very near future. And we're going to put this thing right on that mountain . . . and put men inside it."

Grady thumbed through the sketches for a minute, mumbling, "How are you going to get it up there? The Northeast Plateau is eighteen thousand feet up."

"17,990 feet to be exact." Gilmore smiled. "We're working on it. In fact, that's the only thing that may hold us up . . . our transportation. Everything else will be constructed or supplied from right here at Stanton. We'll ship it out to Montana, then haul it all up onto the mountain where it'll be assembled."

"I still don't see how."

Still rooting around through the papers and photos, Kelly answered, "With a helicopter . . . but I don't seem to have a picture of it with me. Anyway, it is being developed right now— the same one you've been told about, a high-altitude rescue helicopter. The only question is when the prototype will be delivered. In the meantime, we continue getting everything else designed and ready. And we continue our tests with Swamp Gas."

"And you will be in charge of security around the mountain," General Mattlock told Grady. "Your primary job will be to provide us with any assistance we need, and to maintain full security around Mount Kota. We don't want anybody on the mountain. Before long, you'll be getting a classified memo to this effect which will outline everything for which you're responsible. We're also going to the National Park Service to get the mountain put off limits, and to the Federal Aviation Administration to divert all future civil air traffic away from Kota. But we'll detail all of this later."

"You forgot one thing: What happens to Lieutenant Palmer? He's still alive, and I just told the whole world this morning that he was dead."

Everyone at the table was quiet for a minute.

"This is a matter of national security, General Grady," Mattlock said at last. And the stiff, formal manner in which he used Grady's name and rank made Grady realize that he wouldn't like the answer he was about to hear. "As Dr. Fairfield already mentioned, Palmer is valuable because he represents the only living thing to have ever survived exposure to the modified Swamp Gas. We have to find out how and why. To do this, he must remain under full observation. His official status is 'Killed in the service of his country.' I'm sorry, but that's the way it has to be."

I was right, Grady thought to himself. I don't like it at all. In fact, as the "late" Lieutenant Gary Palmer might say it: *I think that sucks.*

"We've told you all that we can for the time being, Tom." Kelly sighed, getting up from his desk. "And I think we've pretty well got everything covered."

Grady thought, I hope you're right, there, Dave.

GETTING UP FROM HIS DESK, Grady walked to the thermostat on his wall and adjusted it to a slightly higher temperature. His office had always been a little on the drafty side, and during midautumn when the winds from the north became stronger and colder, it sometimes felt as if they came straight through the glass.

It was nearly three weeks since his trip to Fort Stanton. The forthcoming memo that Mattlock had mentioned now existed; his copy lay on his desk. They hadn't been exaggerating about details—nine pages of details—and they weren't kidding about being all business. Serious business.

Examination or possession by any person except the addressees is a criminal offense and punishable by no less than twenty years' confinement in a federal institution and a fine of no less than $20,000.

Among other things Grady had to personally clear every last man from his command who was to be assigned to the project. Not that they would know what was going on—all they would be doing was manning a perimeter around the mountain. They would keep everybody out, and if anyone decided to enter without a special pass, both the intruder and the guard would simply disappear as if they had never existed.

Serious business.

Reports had to be forwarded to the Pentagon at thirty-day intervals, delivered by a special courier. If they didn't hit the right desk at the right time, or if they were delivered by any other means, the deliverer would find himself in command of an ice floe...and within a matter of hours.

There were other details and drawings attached, which illustrated the place they had named Kota Station. It was a building that could house four people comfortably for twelve-week periods and contained a little of everything, from emergency rations to sophisticated—and classified—communications equipment to a fully stocked laboratory and medical facility, plus all the comforts of home. Its structural design could withstand winds of more than two hundred miles an hour; it could be buried under twenty-five tons of snow with no significant damage; and its construction permitted maintenance of 72 degrees inside even if it dropped to 150 below outside. It even had a pressurized, self-sealing door that weighed 550 pounds, cost $28,950 and could ricochet a fifty-caliber bullet. Nothing was mentioned as to exactly what the occupants would be doing inside it, but since its projected cost was going to be in the neighborhood of sixteen million dollars presumably it should be quite a lot. And when the Chemical Corps was finished with it, Kota Station would be given to Fort Endicott for any cold weather or alpine studies they deemed fit to conduct in it.

Grady went back to his desk to finish his coffee, but it had gone cold and greasy looking. He looked at the cup. World's Greatest Dad, it said on it. His younger daughter had given it to him for his birthday back in June; he smiled at her picture, and those of his older daughter and his wife. Somehow, it suddenly felt like a blessing that he and Martha had had only girls. Martha—or Martha, Jr. as they had nicknamed her—had been married more than a year now, and their first grandchild was on the way. She was an architect, and her husband worked for NASA. Judy was in her first semester at Ohio State—probably

already involved in protesting the war in Vietnam. He could not
blame her. Ever since this bullshit about Kota started he'd felt
a few protests rising himself. At least his girls wouldn't end up
in the goddamn Army, doing shit like this.

> First Lieutenant Gary S. Palmer has been pronounced
> mentally unfit for active service by a qualified U.S. Army
> psychiatrist. He will remain confined at the Wheeler Bar-
> racks, Kansas, psychiatric facility... for the remainder of
> his natural life... under medical supervision... and close
> scrutiny... and shall be permitted no contact with any
> person outside the bounds of that institution. His official
> status is "Killed in the service of his country" and shall
> remain as such....

Serious shit, all right.

Dave Kelly had said that he thought they had everything
covered. So. Why didn't *he* think so? Why was it he thought
there was too much left unsaid and uncovered? Why did he
think that this was too hastily planned, not completely thought
out? What had they missed?

World's Greatest Dad.

Here he had been for the past six years—running a quiet little army post in Montana, out of everyone's way, just doing his
job, trying to help and quietly pass the remaining year until his
retirement. How in hell had he been dragged into this mess? He
was nothing more than a front man, a rat, the proverbial sacrificial goat, if anything went wrong. They were trying to cover
too many bases, so all kinds of hidden things could, and probably would, go wrong. And he had been left asshole and elbow out in the wind. World's Greatest Goat might be more like
it.

He stepped into his private rest room, dumped the coffee and
rinsed out the cup. He was about to turn off the light when he
caught a look at himself in the mirror—fifty-five years old, half
of what had been a thick crop of black, curly hair now gone,
and the seamed, lined face reflecting more than ever the two
wars and twenty-nine years of command hassles it had seen. He
was spreading out more, a good deal unlike the ramrod-straight

cadet who came out of West Point so long ago—so idealistic, so certain that he and his comrades could change the world. And they hadn't changed a damned thing. Only they had changed. And it didn't look as if it was for the better.

He shut off the light.

Sorry, Judy, he thought. Your ol' man has gone and got himself mixed up with people who think this is all one big, fascinating game. They play with lives as though they were chess pieces. They lie awake at night thinking of more and more dreadful ways to kill and maim. And they enjoy what they're doing. That's the hellish part—they *enjoy* this shit. General One-Penny-per-Kill Mattlock and his two demented children, Lieutenant Colonels Frick and Frack, like it so much that they're miffed because their superkiller still hasn't been sent to Vietnam so it can gas a few real, live people. But they're real excited about the consolation prize; they're all set to spend millions so they can see up close what it did to some of their own men, and they've got some very powerful people behind them to ensure that they get everything they'll need to play. It's like watching parents helping their children play deadly games. And now they've got me in on it. Fat, dumb, happy me, just sitting here, minding my own business, trying to finish my career as quietly as possible, and they hooked me slicker than a Bible salesman with an old maid. So Judy, baby, if you're protesting any of this, it won't embarrass me. After all, the whole world can see my ass hanging out in the wind.

He walked to a window. He could see Mount Kota in the distance. The peak was hidden by clouds.

I think we've pretty well got everything covered.

He rubbed his eyes. "Well, Dave, do you know what?" he whispered. "I think you're covering your tracks with my ass. Know what else? *I* think *you're* pretty well full of shit. And that this whole business sucks."

PART TWO

★

The KP Project

Any order that can be misunderstood has been misunderstood.

—The Army Axiom

Once you open a can of worms, the only way to recan them is to use a bigger can.

—Zymurgy's First Law of
Evolving Systems Dynamics

CHAPTER EIGHT

HE LOOKED A LOT BETTER than when they brought him there. He was eating properly, resting and exercising. His strength had returned quickly and he seemed to gain more strength every day. All physical parameters had been checked and rechecked, and each pointed to complete normality. Conversations with him—when they could break in on his endless, rapid-fire questions—were lucid, coherent and sensible. He answered questions, too; about his family, home, haunts, hobbies, dreams, desires, even a fantasy or two. And at the end of two weeks his doctors could come up with only two conclusions: one, his mind and body were in proper order; he responded like any 25-year-old healthy male should. And two, no physical or mental traces remained of what had brought him there. He remembered absolutely nothing about any of it.

When was he brought here?

About eight months ago...October.

And he just snapped out of it? Just like that?

Just like that. Scared hell out of one of the nurses.

It had been dinnertime, and the ward was filled with nurses and orderlies scurrying from room to room delivering dinner trays, checking menus against dietary restrictions and sorting out the mix-ups in meals that always occurred in the cafeteria. During the general confusion, the nurse who had just left room 103 heard an odd noise coming from room 104 across the hall— odd because noises never came from that room. All its occupant ever did was sit and stare into space. He might sigh once in a while; he might mumble something that no one could understand; he might point meaninglessly at some inanimate object; or he might sit in the same spot, unmoving, for hours on end. If somebody didn't come in to put him to bed each night they would find him rooted to the same spot, in almost exactly the same position, in the morning. But mostly, he was quiet.

Once a week, perhaps twice, somebody would come into his room, get him out of his chair and lead him gently and slowly to one of the labs for another test or examination. When they were finished, somebody else would lead him back to his room, sit him down in his chair or ease him into bed. He would stay there until another person came in, helped feed him, cleaned him up or took him down the hall for something else. Back and forth. He never seemed aware of any of it. He remained dead silent, letting anybody who came into his room do whatever they wished or take him wherever they wanted to take him.

Many who worked on the ward almost forgot he was there. They had their hands full with many patients who weren't so cooperative or quiet, several of whom seemed to have gone as far as they could go without actually leaving the planet. Yells, screams and gibberish filled the nights. If you worked on the ward you learned which ones to ignore; you learned that a few were beyond whatever most people could do for them. You had only to be sure that they were not given the means to hurt themselves or anybody else. They came from every Army and Air Force base around the world, from every VA hospital in the country, and they collectively represented every major battle-field on which Americans had bled and died since Pearl Harbor. Only God knew what they had seen or done that had landed them in a place like Wheeler Barracks, or what torments they had been through since. So it was best not to listen; to leave their cases and their care to those with three or four diplomas and professional degrees on their office walls. It was best simply to hope for them; to offer a small prayer now and then that they would work their way free of their hellish mazes, and that the guns and cries from their private battlefields would one day be silent. Sometimes it happened—it was rare, but it happened. And one afternoon in the middle of May 1969, it happened again.

A thud came from behind the door of room 104. Slowly, the door opened.

The nurse was about to hand another meal tray to one of the orderlies. The typed card on the tray read: Pommelroy, G.S. 1Lt USA SN 0-55873186 R104. At that moment Pommelroy, G.S., stepped from behind the door, looking around in utter bewilderment. "Hey, what the hell's going on here?" he mumbled. "Where am I?"

The nurse whirled, and the meal tray crashed to the floor.

"The rest of his memory seems fine. There's just no reten-tion of the events in question. Somehow, all of that is a big blank."

"How is he otherwise? Physically and all?"

"Fine . . . as if nothing happened to him. So. What do we do with him?"

"Just as his file says. He's a special case to some very big people."

"But it says here that he's due to be discharged from the service on the twenty-ninth. That's less than a week and a half away."

"Yeah, but it says here *that his discharge doesn't enter into it."*

"Can they do that?"

"You see these signatures? They can do anything they want."

2

"WE HAVE A LOT OF questions, too, Lieutenant," he was told. "And I'm afraid you'll have to answer ours before we can get to yours. All right?"

"Yeah . . ."

It was obvious that he knew, or remembered, everything about himself. He recalled most of his past, most of his personal experiences. So they began with external information. They asked if he had any idea of where he was.

"No. I mean, it's a hospital, but it isn't the one at Fort Endicott."

All right. Next, he was told, try to take a guess at the day and date. "Don't worry if you're not sure. Just take a stab at it, whatever comes into your head."

He had no idea of that, either, and the question itself suggested that he would miss by a light-year or two no matter what he said. He thought for a moment, finally saying, "Umm . . . Tuesday."

"The date?"

"Hell, I don't know...Tuesday...oh, call it the third Tuesday in October. 1968."

"Okay. Now. What was the last thing you were doing before you blacked out? What was going on all around you? And here, we'll give you a clue: you were on a mountain."

"Well, we were climbing the mountain, and—"

"Which mountain? Where is it?"

"Mount Kota. It's in southwestern Montana, in the middle of Mount Kota National Park...about thirty-five miles west of where I was stationed. Fort Endicott."

"Very good. Now, who was on the mountain with you, and what were you doing there?"

"There were three of us. Doug Gorham, Rudi Gurdler and me. We were trying to climb to the summit. There had been a plane crash up there, and all the reconnaissance photos showed that a few people had survived the crash. We were trying to rescue them. To get them down."

"How close were you to the summit when you think you lost consciousness? That is, how much of that area on the mountain can you remember?"

"Wait...hold on a minute. Let me think. I...I think we were very close to the top. I remember seeing a lot of junk...debris from the plane. All over the place. And I remember Karber's Pass; it leads from the Northeast Plateau, where we set up our high-altitude base camp—and we were going through the pass. The three of us. Gorham, Gurdler and me."

"Were you doing anything besides climbing? Were you talking among yourselves? Were you making records of what you were seeing?"

"Uhhh...let's see. I don't know if Gorham and Gurdler were talking or not. But...someone said something to me, I think.... Yeah, they did, I remember. I was talking on the two-way radio. I was talking with the base camp. But there was something else, I think...."

"Try to remember, Gary."

"Yes. I remember that, too. I was taking pictures. I had a camera, and I was taking pictures, that's it."

"Of what, Gary? What were you photographing?"

"All of the wreckage...I guess. I can't think of anything else anybody would take pictures of up there."

"Do you recall taking any pictures at the summit?"

"I...I don't know. I probably did...if we got there. But I can't remember photographing anything there. I can't remember anything at all about the summit."

"Keep trying, Gary. Think. Surely you remember the plane. All of those bodies. The massive debris all over the top."

"N-no...I don't know. I just can't remember the summit. I'm—I'm sorry, but I can't. Nothing comes to me at all about it.... Hey, wait a minute. Hold on! How the hell did I get back down?"

"Okay, Gary, hang on. You may not believe what we're about to tell you."

WELL, THEY SURE HADN'T bullshitted about that. And he hadn't believed any of it, not at first. But it was true. He had been *here*, Wheeler Barracks, the Army and Air Force bughouse, for nearly *eight months*. The mission had been in September; this was May. That long since the deaths of Gorham and Gurdler. Their deaths. They got killed. And he'd been brought from Endicott where he'd been found wandering around near the base of the mountain, blank as a vegetable. Just like Rip van Winkle he had slept right through almost two and a half seasons. And he still didn't know what had caused it. Nobody did.

No, he didn't believe it at first—not until he got a good look out the window at the sea of flatness. Yes, it had to be Kansas. Only Kansas had a landscape that couldn't even be called a landscape. And this had to be Wheeler Barracks smack in the middle of it, because only the Army would establish a post in a place like this. They had a penchant for desolate locations; even if they were offered the Garden of Eden they'd think of a way to bulldoze it, gravel it over, then rain on it. But there he was, in room 104, looking out the window at the only tree for a million miles—room 104, West Wing, Building 3, Wheeler Barracks Psychiatric Facility. He believed it now.

Doug Gorham was dead, his body still on the summit of Mount Kota. Rudi Gurdler was dead, but his shattered body now rested near his home in Switzerland. Somehow, he had fallen from the summit. And just as peculiar—more so in fact—here *he* was after somehow getting back down that mountain alone, and not even remembering how or when or why. There had been no rescue; they had been at the summit but all he had was somebody else's word on it—yet, he had to believe that, too.

They had told him he was all right; except for the lapse of memory about the climb, and some understandable physical weakness, he was perfectly all right. They had poked, probed and prodded anyway, as if convincing themselves, and if they weren't asking questions they were hooking him up to another machine or wiring his head with more electrodes or poking, probing and prodding.

Please do this do that lie down over here over there on that this way that way sit down stand up turn around cough three times roll up your sleeve pull up your top drop your pants relax nothing to this it won't hurt a bit how does that feel? just going to look at this again please answer the question Gary ask the doctors ask the nurses no we don't know because this will sting close it up clear your mind remember what happened next almost done that didn't hurt did it? that's it put your pants on just a few more minutes just turn your head pee into this jar....

They kept telling him how fine he was. And he believed them because he could feel that.

"So, when do I get out of here?" he asked. "If we're approaching the end of May 1969, and we must be because I can see how short the corn is out there in the fields, then I'd like to point something out—and you didn't think I'd remember about things like corn, did you? I'm getting discharged on the 29th. Check my records, and I know you have all my records. The 29th. I mean, *I* remember the 29th even if I can't recall certain other things. I remember my family, my parents. They must be out of their minds by now if they haven't heard from me in eight months.

"What about my parents? Haven't you heard from them? Haven't they been here to see me?"

"We can't answer that, Gary. We don't know about your family."

"Well, can I call them? Look, I have to get in touch—"

"No. We're sorry, but you can't call anybody. At least, not now."

"When?"

"We can't answer that, either."

"When do I get out of here? When do I get to go back home and get my life restarted?"

"We don't know."

"Wait a minute...just a goddamn minute. What's going on here? Are you saying that I can't leave? That I'm stuck here?"

"We don't know."

"Well, what the hell *do* you guys know?"

It was 9:00 A.M., May 22, and he sat in his room staring out at the lone tree just outside the compound. In a short while one of the orderlies would come and get him, and take him to another office where they would ask him another round of questions he couldn't answer.

"What was the object, Gary?"

"A blue and yellow can ... sort of flat. Lighter fluid ..."

"Did you find it?"

"No, Doug did. He picked it up and shook it. There was still fluid in it ... about half-full."

"What about the summit, Gary? The crash site? What did you find there?"

"I can't remember.... I don't remember anything about the summit."

Then he would come back to his room and wait awhile, and somebody would bring his lunch to him. He would sit down on the edge of his bed, put the tray on an adjustable bedside cart and eat, not noticing what the food was. He would be a lot like some of those poor guys he heard down the hall at night; they wouldn't know—or care much—what they were eating, animal or vegetable, alive or dead. Someone would take the tray away; he would sit looking out the window for a while until another orderly came to get him and take him to someone else's office for another session that would lead nowhere. They would ask questions that he couldn't answer; he would ask the same ones he always asked, which they wouldn't answer. He didn't know how much longer this could go on, and if they knew, they weren't saying.

"I want to get out of here. I want to see my family . . . or call them."

"Please answer the question, Gary: What was Rudi Gurdler doing when he fell? Did he slip, or fall over something? Was he trying to climb something? What was it that took him so close to the edge that it caused him to fall? Or did someone push him? What happened to him, Gary?"

"Jesus, I don't know! I can't remember!"

"What about Doug Gorham? What was he doing at the time? Where was he? How did he die? You saw it, Gary. You saw how he died, how both of them died. What happened, Gary? What happened?"

"I don't know! I DON'T KNOW!"

"All right, Gary. Sit down. Sit down, and we'll try it again. From the beginning. Now, where were you when . . ."

When this wasn't going on he usually sat in his room. He wasn't restricted to his room anymore, but there wasn't much more to do than stay there and stare at the tree outside. He had tried the hallways, seeing no more than long rows of floor tiles and locked doors; he'd visited the patients' lounge once or twice with its vending machines that didn't work, the TV that didn't work and the stacks of board games that all had pieces, cards or tokens missing. That left only magazines that were months out of date, all with pages torn out, all looking as if they had been lying on the highway. Pacing the halls brought evil stares from all the orderlies and nurses, and even sitting in the lounge brought the same from some of the patients. None of them—the staff included—appeared in the mood for, or even capable of, concentrating on any game, or watching TV, or doing much of anything requiring complex thinking. As he stared from his room at the tree with the wide and windy Kansas plain beyond, he concluded that these people might actually look forward to one of those famous Kansas twisters. It would be a refreshing change of pace and scenery.

The old jokes were true: if you weren't crazy when you arrived, you would be before long. And there really *were* men in white coats. They were all over the place. And if you gave any of them any shit you would get yourself fitted on the spot for a canvas coat with extralength sleeves.

Gary was polite to these people. He said little more than necessary in fear that if he said too little it might be construed as antisocial behavior; too much could label him a babbling idiot and get him locked up permanently. So it was easier to remain in his room, avoiding contact.

That was another thing about Wheeler—it gave one a whole new slant on paranoia. Paranoia used to be like so many of those lick'em-and-stick'em adjectives like "crazy" and "weird" that were slapped onto the language like bumper stickers. But not now. Not after five conscious days in here. Paranoia now had a new and profound meaning. It was no longer a word to be trifled with.

So he cooperated. Even if they wouldn't answer any of his questions, he still kept trying to answer theirs. If there was any chance of getting out of here he didn't want to screw it up. And he remained in his room, which would afford him the chance of screwing up as little as possible.

Until that afternoon.

3

IT WAS RAINING. He couldn't see a damned thing out the window, barely even the maple tree. He decided to take a walk through the halls.

One of the orderlies at the nurses' station appeared to be a dead ringer for a young Bela Lugosi, complete with the half sneer, dark eyes appraising his newest victim, and the dark, greasy hair hanging in his face. He was everyone's idea of a 1930s back-alley abortionist, and he was helping one of the more sinister-looking nurses unpack a large cardboard box.

Human Parts—Handle with Care, plastic things wrapped in clear plastic bags.

They looked at him as he padded by. He was going to smile and offer a good-afternoon or some other pleasantry, but he kept walking. He kept still. They were watching him. They were noting every move he made, every facial expression; he felt as though he had just escaped from a zoo. As he walked on he almost expected one of them to yell at him to stop while the other called for help. He waited to hear a Klaxon begin a piercing whoop-whoop-whoop in the corridors, as platoons of white-clad orderlies came after him from behind the doors, each of them carrying torches, or baying hounds on leashes. . . .

"There he is, there he is! Shoot! Shoooooot! Kiiilll hiiiimmm!"

But Rosie the Riveter stooped to gather up another armload of plastic bags, and muttered something about having to work this weekend when it wasn't her turn. Bela Lugosi laughed, brushed the hair away from his eyes and paused to take a long drag from a cigarette.

Gary stopped for a drink from a hall fountain. Jesus, he thought; if he didn't get out of here soon he'd be seeing dinosaurs in the shower. He thought about simply making up a story about his forgotten experience on Kota's summit, just trying to tell them whatever they wanted to hear. Anything.

But . . . no. Trying to maintain a complex lie wouldn't be too smart, and with the way those doctors wrote down each tiny detail of everything he told them, they would trip him up in eight or ten whoppers the next time they talked to him. He'd never been much of a liar anyway—which meant, to his way of thinking, that he would never make it as a diplomat. When people asked him a question, he answered with the truth if he knew it; if he didn't, he said so. If they were full of shit, he often said so—which had caused him trouble with superiors from time to time. It also gave him a certain advantage over some people in that he often knew at once when they were lying to him.

And this had occurred to him a short while ago while sitting in his room, staring at the tree and the rain; these people were not withholding information that they didn't know. They knew. They knew that not a damned thing was wrong with him, and that he didn't belong here. They knew that he had undergone some tremendous shock at Kota, and even if they didn't know what it was they knew by now that he could not bring back any memory of it. So, they must not care what it was; they were merely seeing if they could force anything out of him—some of the truth if it could be dredged up, or a bare-faced lie that would prove that they could crack him under stress. And now it hit him that there must be other long, carefully laid plans for him, which didn't include his going home for a long, long time. And since these people didn't care exactly what had happened to him on Kota, somebody else—somebody in a position of power—did. Somebody else was pulling the strings. He was in the middle, caught up in something about that climb or that plane crash that he didn't even know about, but that had affected him in a very big way—so big that he was being kept like a laboratory animal. And that someone might be planning to keep him like that for a long time.

He kept walking through the halls, thinking. The more he thought about it the more he was convinced that he was right. It had to be that way, or something very close to it, and it led him to another thought: if all of this was planned, what had they already planned or put in motion? Suppose, for example, his family didn't even know he was here? What had they been told about the disaster on Kota?

And now, a hundred more questions swarmed in on him— whys, what ifs, might bes, probablys. You couldn't put it past the military to do anything, to say anything, just to get what they wanted. Truth in the military occupied a position identical to what is found in a latrine trench. Was he cooperating with his own imprisonment?

"Dr. Kinkaid, please report to your office . . . Dr. Kinkaid, your office . . ."

Kinkaid was one of the shrinks who had been grilling Gary these past few days. He worked closely with Dr. Byrd, the boss shrink, and a woman, Dr. Rosenbloom, who was shaped like an office safe. Looking around, he noticed that he was outside Dr. Byrd's office, and he was about to grab the knob, stomp right on in and present them with his new theory. Maybe he could demand that they tell him the truth. Maybe if he told them that . . .

"Dr. Tower . . . Dr. Groves . . . please report to reception . . . Dr. Tower . . ."

...he had just figured out what the game was all about, and he was going to blow the whistle, they'd tell him what was going on.

"*...come to reception...*"

And he thought: Who the hell are you kidding? All you're apt to do with a move like that is shit and fall in it. No, the best thing to do was just shut up and listen, and—

The door was opening. He could hear two voices from within.

"*Dr. Kinkaid, please report to your office...Dr. Kinkaid, your office...*"

Kinkaid's office was across the hallway from Byrd's. The door was open, and no one was inside. Gary ducked in, closing the door partway.

"...So that's it?" Dr. Rosenbloom was saying.

"That's it," Gary heard Byrd reply. "We're through with him."

"But I had some more questions I wanted to ask him. And I really think I can get more out of him than he's telling, because I don't think in his case that a total memory lapse is possible. He *has* to remember some of it."

"Maybe. Maybe not. But no more questions. We turn over his files tomorrow morning, along with him. As of 7:00 a.m. tomorrow morning, Lieutenant Gary Palmer is no longer our responsibility."

Smoke from Dr. Byrd's pipe wafted through the open door. It smelled like stale soap. It drifted away after a moment; so did both of the voices.

"*Dr. Kinkaid, please report to your office.... Dr. Kinkaid, your office...*"

The coast was clear, and Gary hurried back down the hallway toward his own end of the wing. He was trembling.

THERE WERE SHAPES...images...things.... They were vague, unformed, hazy outlines appearing, vanishing, returning again as if trying to solidify and be identified, but vaporizing into the mist surrounding him. He couldn't touch them. His body seemed not to be touching anything, not even ground. He was floating, drifting in and out of the fog like the transparencies floating with him...things not quite believable...and yet there all the same.

"By God...now here's the way to climb ain't that right Gary? why look at us we're sailing right over this big son of a bitch—"

"Doug? Is that ... well, of course it is. And over there must be ..."

"Hello again, Lieutenant Palmer."

"Sure. Rudi. Hey, how are you guys? It's been a while."

"Okay, Gary ... can't complain."

"Nor can I, Gary. And you are looking quite fit."

"Uhh ... yeah. Look I hope you don't mind if I say this ... but ... well, you guys are dead, right? That's what they told me, that both of you are dead. I say that because I can't remember a damned thing about either of you dying, and ... well, stop me if I get too personal, okay?"

"Ask away, Gary. Like I said, as long as it's not about my sex life."

"Well, neither of you look too good. Especially you, Rudi. You look awful."

"A five-thousand foot plunge into a pile of rocks does little for one's appearance, Gary. Or one's life expectancy."

"Yeah, Gary, and lying around up here in the snow for the past seven or eight months ain't like a day on the beach, either. Hell, man, I look like a frozen turkey."

"I suppose so. But the one thing I'm not clear about is exactly what *did* kill you guys. Like I said, I don't remember anything, so maybe if you could help me out ... ?"

"You remember the plane, Gary? Where we found a lot of the—"

"Gary? Hey, Gary, shake it up."

"—bodies? You were somewhere else at the moment, but I called Rudi over because I saw something—"

"Yo, Gary! Bean time. Up and at 'em! Let's eat it!"

"—straaange ... about ... theeemm ..."

"Gary!"

With a grunt, Gary jumped up. Someone dressed in white was standing next to the bed. Only when his eyes focused a moment later did he recognize the orderly's uniform.

"Hey, you okay?" he asked, setting the tray down. "Should I call one of the nurses?"

"No . . . no, that's okay. I'm fine." Gary waved, rubbing his eyes. "I just dozed off. I guess I was dreaming." He thought: Dreaming? Some dream, pal. You might have been on the verge of learning exactly what those shrinks have been trying to hammer out of you for a week and a half. They'd never considered that he might want the answers even more than they did. After all, it had been him on that mountain.

"You sure? You still look a little rattled."

"I'm fine, Bobby. Really. I'm just a heavy sleeper. It takes a while for me to wake up, that's all," and he smiled at the only friend he'd made in the whole place. "Now. What are they trying to pass off as supper this time? Cat food?"

Laughing, Bobby removed the covers from the dishes. Gary was grateful for him. He had become acquainted with Bobby only four days before, but in that time he'd come to trust the young orderly. They had talked, and Bobby was the only one on the ward who knew Pommelroy, G.S.'s real identity and probably the only one at Wheeler who didn't give a shit. Bobby was free, loose and generally unconcerned with things not of a more basic or earthy nature. He didn't remember the crash of Flight J-440 or those having anything to do with it afterward; he wouldn't have cared even if he had remembered. Gary envied Bobby because he didn't concern himself with anything more complex than his plans for the upcoming weekend.

"And here we have the pride of hospitals everywhere, the required ration of Jell-O. Ta-da!" Then he sat down for a chat.

"Hey, aren't you supposed to be out there doing something?"

"Yeah, but I'm trying to lie low on this shift. I'm buggin' out early."

"Isn't that illegal?" Gary mumbled between bites.

"As *hell*!" Bobby grinned with a wink. "But it's worth it tonight. I've got a date tonight with a honey I've been trying to line up for six months," he whispered, his eyes bright with excitement. "Finally did it, though, and I've gotta be out of here by nine-thirty. I'm supposed to pick her up at ten." He leaned in close. "A buddy of mine over in the next ward is gonna clock me out at eleven."

Gary laughed. "That must be some girl. I hope she's worth it."

"Let me *tell* you! I'd crawl through a mile of broken glass just to sniff her—" he stopped, his face suddenly flushed.

"If you haven't anything to do, Mr. Carlson," the head nurse said from the doorway, "I'm sure we can find something." She looked at both of them sourly, as if wishing she could put them to sleep.

"Right," Bobby muttered, getting up and following her out the door. He paused for a moment, motioning that he would be back.

Gary waved a fork in a salute.

4

AT SEVEN THE FOLLOWING MORNING, Gary was scheduled to leave Wheeler Barracks with two agents from the Fifth Army Central Intelligence Division. They were to take him to Kansas City, put him on a plane and accompany him to an undisclosed destination where they would turn him over to a pair of high-ranking officers not yet identified to them.

Instead, both CID agents found themselves with fourteen other agents from their headquarters. They were gathered in a conference room inside Wheeler, and the new orders were much simpler, more to the point: Find Gary Palmer. Bring him back to Wheeler as quickly as possible.

"What happened to him?" one of them asked.

It was quite simple—he had escaped. He had clobbered an orderly—one Bobby Carlson—over the head, switched clothing, bound and gagged the orderly and covered him in the bed, then just walked out of the place. The shift change had been at 11:00 p.m., and Palmer apparently strolled out ahead of everyone else. Dressed in hospital whites, he walked by the guard, who paid no attention to him, and drove away in the orderly's car. The local police had found it abandoned in a parking lot about ten miles west of the institution.

"What's the matter with security around here?" another agent asked.

"Nothing that a bigger budget couldn't fix," Dr. Kinkaid said dryly. "This place was never intended as a maximum security institution, and it wasn't designed to prison specifications. It's just a converted World War Two training base. We don't allow our patients to go wandering in or out as they please, but there isn't a whole lot to stop them, either."

"Well, it shouldn't be too hard getting him back," the agent replied, looking over the information they had been given about Palmer. "We're after a runaway Napoleon."

The other agents laughed.

Dr. Kinkaid did not. "That is the first notion you have to get out of your head," he told them. "Palmer is not crazy. He was brought here for special reasons . . . special *classified* reasons. Don't even ask what they are. During the time he's been here, we came to know him, and to know more about him than anybody. He is not unstable or violent or in any way unpredictable. He's as mentally sound as any man. Remember that." And the other thing to remember was secrecy, they were told. No more people than necessary were to know that Palmer even existed. The number of wagging tongues had to be kept to a minimum, and for that reason the agents were advised not to use any local law enforcement agency for assistance. Even the FBI was not to be involved in the hunt unless there was no other choice.

The agents were given as many details about Palmer as could be assembled over a couple of hours—everything except the classified information about the rescue attempt on Kota. It was not a considerable amount, and a lot of it seemed to be mundane information about his past life—everything from his favorite dish to his shoe size to his grandmother's maiden name. There was an eight-by-ten photo of him along with a complete description, which every agent memorized. There was information about his family in Seattle, and as many of his former friends as could be rounded up. "And that list isn't complete," the agent in charge said. "We've got almost everyone on that list covered, though, and we'll know at once if he tries to contact any of them. Anybody else we learn about will just

have to be relayed to you in the field. I know it's like closing the
barn door after the horse is loose, but it's all we've had time for.
We have to get moving.''

Their work was cut out for them. The man they were looking for was smart—smart enough to know that they would soon
be on his ass, and smart enough to move cautiously but quickly.
He would not be that easy to catch unless he made a serious
mistake. Too, there were a number of elements in their favor.
Experience had taught lawmen that most escapees could be
rounded up within forty-eight to seventy-two hours—sometimes less—if they acted quickly enough and followed up on
each lead. The trick was to move faster than their prey, not to
give him enough time to sort things out or to get any plans
working. They had to keep him continually off balance.

In Palmer's case, he might think that a large number of
people would be after him, and they preferred to let him believe that. It could make him overly cautious and slow him
down, maybe even make him afraid to move as they tightened
their net. But as long as he was moving he probably would re-
strict his travel to the hours of darkness; they would have to be
doubly careful about missing him. If he was to stay on the move
he would require assistance at some point, the sooner the better for him. This was a big advantage for them because Palmer
knew no one in these parts. He might have to force assistance,
which would leave a damning clue. He would also need a
change of clothing, food, transportation and money, and he
had none of those. Nor did he have a plan, and this was their
biggest advantage. He had simply clubbed an orderly and set
out for parts unknown. He'd gotten a six-hour head start, but
they were certain that he hadn't had time enough to go very far
or to get any help. He couldn't be too far away, which meant—
if experience served them correctly—that he probably wasn't
more than twenty-five to thirty miles from the room where they
were now seated.

''But we could always be wrong about it, so keep a running
check on all public transportation facilities. Palmer's probably smart enough not to use them, but he might get desperate. Or he might find some money somewhere. He's most likely
still on foot, probably hiding somewhere. He's alone, and in

unfamiliar country. But don't take any of that for granted. Look everywhere."

They would be working in two-man teams, fanning out in every direction, covering each town and road in their sector, and spreading out to a fifty-mile radius. If they had found nothing by then, they would regroup and try again in different sectors. But if one team picked up the trail, the others would be recalled at once and reorganized into a single, concentrated effort until they had found him. It was a simple but effective method.

"Any questions?"

"I have one. I just remembered something. Is this guy the same Lieutenant Gary Palmer who was part of that attempted rescue last September? The one in Montana where that plane crashed on that mountain? I thought he got killed. That's what all the papers said."

No one answered for a moment. Then Dr. Kinkaid spoke. "I'm going to pretend that I didn't hear that question. You are going to make believe that you didn't ask it. And the rest of you never heard a thing."

"Are there any questions?" the man in charge repeated.

There were none, and the men silently filed out of the room.

ONLY A FEW HOURS before the agents separated into their two-man teams and prepared to hit the road after him, Gary was wondering what the hell he was doing. It struck him that he might really be crazy after all, because only a lunatic would try a stunt like this and hope to get away with it. And as he stood alone in the rain, surrounded by the dark Kansas plain, he cursed softly to himself. It seemed hopeless. He was surprised he had gotten this far.

But it was the week for big surprises. What do you do after waking up in an insane asylum five hundred miles from where you're supposed to be, only to learn that you'd been kept there like a houseplant for the past seven and a half months, that you have no recollection of what put you there, and that you will be kept indefinitely in a similar place even though you're perfectly all right? What is the encore? Why, you club an innocent man over the head, steal his clothes, swipe his car, then end up wandering down a deserted Kansas highway in the middle of the night with every cop and Army CID agent west of the Mississippi after you. What else? He was a fugitive. He wasn't sure why he should be one, but a fugitive he was, nonetheless. And, just like a hardened killer running from the law, all he could do was keep going and hope for the best—which at the moment didn't look like much. In fact, it looked like shit.

Lightning flashed in the distant sky, and the thunder rumbled. The rain had lightened up a little over the past half hour, but within minutes it began pouring again.

He stopped and looked up. "Shit!" he mumbled balefully, shaking his head. Maybe he should have stayed where he was at.

Then he thought, No, not really. Anything—even getting drenched out here in the middle of nowhere—was better than what those people had planned for him.

But he had *no* plan to speak of. Beyond getting out, there hadn't been time to formulate any plans, and if Bobby Carlson hadn't stopped by last night to tell about his hot date, he wouldn't have thought of this hasty plan at all. After driving away from the institution he realized that he didn't know where he was going. There were no maps in the car, and he felt uncomfortable about stopping to get one; besides, someone would know Bobby's car and would wonder what the hell he was doing in it. It wasn't too smart to steal a car, then go cruising all over town, and he had no identification, no driver's license, and he was wearing stolen clothing. And let's see you explain that to a cop. He had ditched the car at the far west end of town, and begun walking. He had been walking ever since. All he really knew was that he was traveling west.

He also began feeling guilty about Bobby. Of all the people at Wheeler Barracks who deserved a clout on the head, why did it have to be him on duty in the ward last night? If he got out of this he would have to look Bobby up sometime, apologize, then accept a fist to his nose. Bobby was a nice kid; he hoped to Christ he hadn't gotten him into any real trouble.

But he would have to shove the guilt aside for the time being. Right now he needed a plan, a direction. The first thing to do was find a place to hide while he sorted things out, then get rid of these hospital whites. And that would have to wait until he could find an unattended clothesline somewhere.

Four a.m. found him at the country intersection of state routes 94 and 115/104. A sign pointed the way to Ash Valley twelve miles southwest, and Martin Flats three miles to the west. That settled it. Sunrise would be on him in roughly an hour and a half, so Martin Flats it would have to be. He hoped he would be able to find a dry, safe place to rest. He was cold, tired, hungry and wet, but all he wanted was a place to sleep for a while. And to get in out of the rain.

He began walking west.

Minutes later he saw headlights in the distance, and he jumped off the shoulder and into the ditch. "Shit!" he grunted, landing in cold, muddy water up to his knees. He crouched, and when the car went past it cascaded a sheet of water across his back. "Goddammit!"

Martin Flats. Three miles.

Well, it was a start. Slogging on through the spring downpour, Gary continued west.

5

CID SPECIAL AGENTS William Caldwell and Mel Eaton checked their information one last time before leaving the parking lot at Wheeler Barracks. Their assigned sector would take them due west for fifty miles on a line along Route 94 and areas on either side for twenty-five miles; nine communities had to be checked out along with every farm they came to. They estimated three days for the towns alone. They had no real idea of how long it would take to check all the open country because there was a lot of it; central and western Kansas wasn't known for large settlements.

"They found the car here," Eaton said, looking at the Wheeler city map. "And there's no other way out of town from the west. I'd bet he's somewhere in our sector."

Caldwell backed their plain-looking four-door sedan into the driveway. "No bet," he said, squinting at the sun. "We'll start at the first town outside Wheeler. Which one is it?"

"Let's see . . . a wide spot called Martin Flats."

"Okay. Martin Flats it is."

CHAPTER NINE

LIEUTENANT COLONELS Dan Gilmore and Chuck Attwood were as well prepared for the next phase of the project as they could be. To start with, they had spent nearly six months studying every aspect of Swamp Gas that could be gleaned from the laboratory located in one of the warehouses at Fort Stanton. They, Dr. Fairfield and four assistants had put the remaining supply of the Hammond Chemical Company's herbicide through every conceivable test, both unmixed, and blended with the Blackstone nerve agent. In six months they had used up 150 lab animals and had dissected and examined each animal after exposure to varying quantities, mixtures and strengths of the chemical. They had used it as a gas, it had been tested again and again as a liquid, and they had tried to simulate its use under every type of weather condition found on the planet. Platoons of secretaries had typed reams of reports, test results and anticipated actions and reactions. The investigators had checked and cross-checked each result, and had begun certain tests all over again if their answers were in any way doubtful or contradictory. They had averaged eleven- to twelve-hour workdays six days per week, and their occasional days not in the lab were usually spent in meetings, telephone calls or personally transporting their information from one place to another. Fifteen separate trips to Blackstone had been made and nine to the Pentagon; General Kelly himself traveled at least that often to various locations to ensure that Gilmore, Attwood and Fairfield would have everything they required delivered promptly to them.

During this time, too, General Mattlock turned over the business of running the Chemical Corps to his assistant commander, busying himself with seeing that all facets of the KP Project were completed smoothly, on time and somewhere within hailing distance of the budget. He and Kelly kept a running check on General Grady's end of the project out at Fort Endicott and Mount Kota, and both had visited Grady three times each to deliver or to obtain classified information. At the end of six months, with the most active and critical phase about to begin, they thought they knew more than anybody about Swamp Gas, its potential and its peculiarities. So their last two weeks were spent in familiarizing themselves with their new base of operations and its twin mock-up, which had been erected in a special environmentally controlled lab in another part of Stanton; that completed, they made a fast trip to Colorado for a three-day rock- and ice-climbing course.

"I think we're almost as well prepared for this as an astronaut is for a trip to the moon," Attwood told Kelly when they finished the course.

"And if this stuff is ever unclassified," Gilmore added, "we've got enough background material to write two or three doctoral theses."

Not very likely. Swamp Gas—$DCChX_3D_5Tl_4MO_2O_2MEh_4$ or as it was translated, Dichlorodetrioxymonotrimethanol, mixture no. 4—was hardly the sort of product to use in one's garden. If it never panned out the remaining stock of it would be locked away at Blackstone and simply forgotten as if it had never existed. And that could happen in spite of all their work, because it was still too unpredictable for use against its ultimate target, enemy troops. For that reason, Gilmore and Attwood were going to Montana for their final tests. For that reason, everything surrounding the KP Project was ready by the time they arrived at Fort Endicott.

General Grady met them at Endicott Airfield. Quick salutes were offered, and baggage was taken away to another aircraft except for the heavy leather case handcuffed to Gilmore's left wrist. They stepped inside the small terminal building.

"Any problems, sir?" Gilmore asked.

Grady shook his head. "None worth reporting. We got the station assembled and checked out. All the equipment's been inspected and tested over the past two days. Hell of a lot of it ... I didn't think we'd get done in time."

"I didn't think *we'd* get checked out on all of it in time."
Attwood laughed. "I've never taken so many crash courses on
so much gear in my life."

"If you have any problems we'll send somebody up."

"No," Gilmore said at once. "We'll fix it. Once we're up
there we can't have anybody else with us. And it's not just because this stuff is so highly classified." He pointed to the locked
case at his wrist. "We still don't know exactly what it'll do in
certain situations to a man exposed to it. If anything goes
wrong, we don't want anybody else with us."

"That reminds me, sir, have you heard the latest on that
lieutenant who was exposed?" Attwood asked. "We had daily
reports on him, but we've been out of touch for a couple of
days."

"Lieutenant Palmer. There's been no change that I know of.
That reminds me: the summit was off limits while the station
was under construction. We also thoroughly examined everybody who was working there—no ill effects. So whatever happened was restricted to the summit."

His guests nodded their approval.

"Well, gentlemen, that ramp man is waving to us, so the helicopter is loaded and ready to go anytime you are."

"We're ready, sir. By the way, how did that new helicopter
perform? We heard that its construction and testing had to be
hurried up quite a bit."

Grady pointed toward the end of the ramp. "In a few minutes you may judge that for yourself." He smiled. He had refused to ride in it.

"Ho-ly shit!"

"You mean, that thing actually flies?"

Their amazement with military equipment was renewed. Ever
since the days of the Trojan Horse the military had had an
inexplicable preference for bizarre machinery, and with the
XM-221 helicopter they seemed to have outdone themselves.

"It'll be flying with you in it, Colonel Attwood." Grady
couldn't resist that. "It's just another Army rhinoceros."

"A what?"

"Rhinoceros. A rhinoceros is a thoroughbred racehorse
redesigned to military specifications."

It actually resembled a giant hybrid out of a 1950s nuclear-horror movie—a cross between a cockroach in the front and a scorpion in the rear. A twin-engine, twin-rotor contraption, it had a rear cargo door that could accept loaded forklifts, connected to a rear section that could move up and down something like the bed on a dump truck. It could unload its cargo either on the ground or airborne, simply by lowering the aft end; in either case, it appeared to be in a perpetual state of constipation and trying mightily to take a dump. The overall impression was that it might go skittering away, looking for a place to hide and lay eggs.

Because the XM-221 had a unique job to do, however, it had been designed as one of the most innovative helicopters ever built. Never before had any rotary-wing aircraft been able to work effectively at 18,500 feet while carrying a thousand-pound load, or to do so on virtually any terrain and in any weather condition. It had been given independently pivoting rotors and a special rotor blade design that not only made it more maneuverable than an ordinary helicopter but capable of operation in winds of up to one hundred miles per hour—something unheard-of in light aircraft.

"Any trouble with it?" Attwood asked. If they suddenly had to clear out of Kota Station he would much rather fly than climb.

"A little, but nothing serious," Grady answered offhandedly, as if they wouldn't be interested. "You'll have to ask the pilots what it was. Except for that, its performance has been pretty good . . . as far as I know."

Both of the chopper's engines were already running. The whine drifted across the tarmac, and the drooping rotors began to turn. In the rear the cargo door yawned open, and a crew chief awaited the passengers.

"We'll radio your communications center as soon as we're set up and ready to go," Colonel Gilmore said. "Probably in two . . . three hours."

"We'd appreciate a message at twelve-hour intervals. We have men on duty around the clock in the Center, and we'll have the pilots standing by in case there's any emergency."

Gilmore wanted to say that in all likelihood, if trouble occurred, Endicott would never know about it in time to help, if
at all. In the past six months, they had learned that much about
Swamp Gas and its strange effects on animal life. If it affected
humans in the same way, or in the manner they suspected, there
could be trouble they couldn't imagine.

But nothing more was said except the traditional good-lucks
and goodbyes accompanied by salutes. Five minutes later the
odd-looking helicopter was airborne and disappearing in the
sky toward Mount Kota.

FROM THE MOMENT THEY stepped through the door they knew
at once where everything was. Kota Station was exactly like the
mock-up in which they had trained. The walk-through inspection took only minutes; only briefly did they bother noting all
the hums and purrs from equipment that would keep them
comfortable, assist them with their jobs and help support their
lives over the next eight weeks. The 550-pound door hissed shut
behind them, and an overhead heater came on with a soft
whoosh. Every item had a place—a shelf, a cupboard or a
case—and every container was set in inventoried rows. It was
military, but without the drab monotony; the rooms had even
been painted in different colors.

As you entered the thirty-by-sixty-foot building, the two
rooms on either side of the door were storage to the right,
equipment to the left. They contained heating oil, tanks of
propane gas and the equipment for purifying and distilling their
water. Beyond these rooms was the bathroom, and adjoining
that was a kitchen/dining/recreation area. On the other side of
the central corridor were two bedrooms, and a small laboratory that occupied the northeast corner of the station. The
north wall contained the real business end of the place, holding among other things a 25,000-watt transceiver that produced a signal that could be boosted to 100,000 watts through
a huge linear amplifier bolted to the floor. On a lower shelf was
a receiver connected to a small set of speakers, and a control
board containing some fifty tiny red and green lights. But it was
tuned to listen only to its mated listening devices, small mag-
netic disks each about the size of a half dollar. There were fifty

of them in a box, ready for installation wherever the men wanted them; they could hear any sound within six inches at a range of one mile. And all of this could be wired into an omnidirectional antenna mounted on a concrete base outside. Its ten-foot dish could be aimed anywhere and used for sending or receiving.

"And look at that," Colonel Attwood said, pointing to another shelf. "All the comforts of home." They even had a TV, radio, games and books.

"What do you expect at the price this place cost?"

Attwood began opening cabinets and cupboards. "Food . . . even booze. Somebody thought of everything."

"It's because we can't run down to the local 7-Eleven. Well, I'll signal the helicopter that it's okay to leave."

"Tell 'em that if it's all the same to them, we'll walk down when we're ready to go."

THE HELICOPTER SAT idling, the rotors fanning the air at half speed. The pilots waited for their signal to leave.

"I don't know about you," the copilot muttered as he watched the gauges on his panel, "but I'd just as soon sit here a while longer and let this son of a bitch catch its breath."

"Yeah, but we've gotta get it back down on the ground again if we're going to ground it, you know."

"That might be faster than you think with the way this bucket's running now. It's like trying to fly a goddamn locomotive."

The working ceiling of the XM-221 might be 18,500 or even 19,000 feet, but the more they flew this one the less likely it seemed of reaching it. Every trip only made it worse. This trip, on the other hand, carrying virtually no payload at all, had been scary. Even their passengers noticed it. The effort in getting it to climb to eighteen thousand feet had been torturous. The airframe had vibrated as if being beaten by hammers; every rivet and bolt felt like it was being shaken loose, and the turbine engines shrieked in protest as if ready to fly apart. They made it to the Northeast Plateau, but the landing was hard, more of a wheezing mechanical collapse than a controlled setdown, as if the helicopter had simply run out of breath.

The first few times up to the plateau hauling parts and pieces to the station had been a snap, no sweat. The strain had caught up quickly, and by the seventh or eighth flight they barely made it with the load. So they reduced the loads, first by ten percent, then twenty, then twenty-five. The last few flights carried only fifty percent payloads, and they thought they were doing well to manage that. Every trip up was more of a struggle; each descent became more of a plunge. The pilots consulted with the factory nearly every other day but the designers could offer no more than, "It's an experimental model that was hustled through production in half the time. Sure it's giving you trouble; it's a wonder the damned thing's flying at all. You guys have worn it out."

At last, the station door opened. Gilmore appeared, smiling and offering the wave that everything was all right; they could leave.

"One more time," the copilot mumbled, taking a deep breath. "Just up a few feet, then over. One more time, baby."

"Yeah . . . nothing to it," the pilot said, pushing the throttles forward. The engine whine rose to a shrill scream and the rotors beat furiously, blowing a tornado of snow up around them. "Hail Mary, full of grace . . ."

The ungainly ship struggled to lift itself, the tail coming up first, then settling again. It raised a second time and stayed airborne, and the pilot pulled harder on the stick to raise the forward end. Noise echoed against the side of the mountain like gunfire.

"Come on . . . come *on* . . . get your big ass up. . . ."

At last the chopper lifted and edged its way toward the end of the plateau, clearing by only a couple of feet. When they were in free air, both fliers locked themselves into battle with the controls, trying to prevent the sudden fall over the edge from becoming suicidal.

The aircraft leveled off at sixteen thousand feet, and they eased it downward in slow degrees until they were at only five-thousand feet.

"Hey, fuck this!" the copilot said, breathing again. "I ain't flying this kamikaze plane anymore, not until they fix it. Or get us another one."

"Right. We land this bastard, and walk away from it. Project or no project. I'm calling that general as soon as we land."

STANDING IN THE STATION DOOR, Gilmore had been holding his breath, too. When the helicopter disappeared over the side of the mountain it looked as if it had gone completely out of control. He listened for five minutes, expecting to hear a loud kaboom from the ground, and he was mildly surprised when he saw the ship still airborne in the distance.

"What are you looking at?" Attwood called from the kitchen. "Shut the door, will you?"

"Jesus!" he muttered, shaking his head. One of these days, that damned oddball helicopter was going to kill somebody.

2

"ROGER, ENDICOTT CENTER. It's a little chilly up here but we're fine. Nice and cozy. You people outdid yourselves. Our compliments and thanks. Fine job. We'll get along just fine here. Over."

"Good enough, Kota Station. Get settled in and have a good night's sleep. We'll be standing by here if you need anything. Give us a yell in the morning. Endicott Center out."

"Roger. Kota Station out."

When both radios had gone to standby, Grady was thinking that he might get to go home and spend a rare evening with his wife. That was interrupted of course; a priority message was waiting for him in his office, on his red scrambler phone.

He identified himself.

"Tom? This is Dave Kelly at Stanton. You'll never believe what has happened."

Tom thought, Oh, shit. It's happening already. "What is it, Dave?"

"That Lieutenant. The one they took to Wheeler Barracks . . ."

"Palmer. Lieutenant Palmer. What happened to him?"

"Apparently, he came out of whatever kind of mental condition he was in a few days ago. They'd been working on him, but he escaped last night."

"He *what*? How?"

"I'm not sure, but someone said that he just walked out. Can you believe that? He *walked* out?"

"I suppose no one has any idea of where he went?"

"The CID people have questioned everyone in the place, and they're out combing the state right now. But so far...nothing."

"Well, Dave, what am I supposed to do? You guys were the ones who put him there, and were supposed to be keeping an eye on him."

"I just wanted you to know, Tom. There isn't much anyone can do except try to find him. We don't know where he could go, but he might try to go back to Montana."

"Why? This is probably the last place he'd want to go." But he agreed anyway to keep a lookout for Palmer. When he hung the phone up he couldn't help but grin; then he laughed. It wasn't a laughing matter, but by God, it was funny. Palmer was loose somewhere in Kansas, and the Army couldn't find him.

I think we've pretty well got everything covered....

Then he stopped laughing. The only things covered were their own asses. And the one thing left out in the wind was his own.

3

MARTIN FLATS
Population 50
Elevation 2245

From what Gary could see in the rainy darkness, the town consisted of one gas station, a store of some kind and maybe eight or nine other sagging buildings on either side of the road. There looked to be nine or ten houses scattered at random; three had lights on inside them. The only other lights on came from four dim street lamps. Their reflections against the road were liquidy, and one buzzed and flickered as if ready to go out.

At least the rain had stopped; the thunder rumbled far to the east as the storm moved on. Gary stepped carefully from his hiding place behind a large forsythia bush near the road, then hurried to an oak tree near a building. Just ahead on the right side of the road were a row of bushes, three more trees and a dirty-looking white block building. After he had satisfied himself that the whole town must be asleep he crept to the next tree for a closer look.

There was a rusted pole with a faded and rusty oval sign mounted on top—Esso, he thought it said, or had once said—but the station it advertised had long been given over to whatever landed there. Mounds of trash, garbage bags and a couple of sagging old trailers filled with junk and scrap metal were on one side of the building. Around front were stacks of moldering tires, rusted oil drums and more dark shiny garbage bags, all piled on top of two bashed-in, derelict cars. The building itself appeared to be boarded up, and probably filled with still more debris, but it would be a good place to spend the night. The only place, really—sunup was only fifteen or twenty minutes away, and as he moved toward the old station he noticed that lights had come on in three more of the houses. People were getting up; it was time for him to get out of sight. It would be dangerous hiding in the middle of town, and the abandoned building might be one of the first places anybody would look. But there was no time for any other choice.

Trying not to rattle or upset any of the mounds of junk, Gary worked his way through the mess to the building. All the doors and windows were boarded up and there appeared to be no way inside until he made his way toward the rear corner. One of the larger plastic bags fell off a pile with a soft whump; two or three unseen cans clattered.

"Shit!" he whispered, grabbing hold of the pile so all of it wouldn't fall over. He stuck one hand into a sticky mess of something.

Then he noticed two small windows about seven feet off the ground—the rest rooms. The glass had been broken in the one nearest him, and it looked as if he might be able to wiggle through. Two dogs barked from somewhere across the road. Hell, yes, he thought. I can get through there, and he pulled himself up. It was a tight fit, and once he had squirmed the upper half of his body inside he could find nothing to grab. It was pitch-black in there, too, and he could imagine himself falling to the floor and breaking his fool neck on something. But after a minute one hand found an old oil drum. It felt heavy, partially filled, as though it wouldn't fall over if he put his weight on it. He let the top of his body drop, catching the drum with both hands, then pulled his legs through the window.

Booomp-booomp-booonnng-a-looonnng . . .

"Owww!" he grunted. His head had struck an unseen container sitting on top of the oil drum, knocking it to the floor, and as he tried to right himself and put both feet on the floor he had slipped, knocking something over.

"Clumsy bastard," he hissed, rubbing his head, and hoping that no one had heard all the racket. He might as well go running down the center of town yelling at everybody and shooting a gun. And now, if anybody found him in here they could tack on trespassing and illegal entry to assault, grand theft and desertion. He was building a nice record for himself. Given another twenty-four hours he could work his way up to public enemy number one without even breathing hard.

At least he was inside and out of sight for the time being. And apparently nobody had noticed the noise; no one was rattling the doors, knocking on the windows demanding to know who was in there or threatening to call the cops. Outside, he could hear a vehicle going by, so his entry hadn't been a minute too soon; another car was being started at one of the nearby houses. People all over town were up and moving now.

He began feeling his way around the small rest room, trying to find the door. It was in front of him, and he felt the knob; he pushed. "Dammit, now what?" He sighed. The door was closed tightly, and either stuck or locked. It wouldn't budge. He bumped it with his shoulder, and gradually began moving it an inch or so at a time. Something was wedged against it; it scooted and squawked against the concrete floor, and the noise echoed in the bay of the station. He pushed again, hearing an irritating *booom-errrrk* on the other side, and thinking, You're bound and determined to wake up the whole damned town. The door opened into a single service bay, and after several more shoves with his shoulder he was able to squeeze through.

The sun was coming up. Thin shafts of light were beginning to pierce into the station, and he could see another old, battered automobile parked in front of him, and another large pile of trash heaped on one side of it. This place had to be the town dump. With the doors and windows sealed it should make an acceptable shelter, and he sighed with relief. With a little luck he should be able to stay here until nightfall. Maybe after a few hours' rest he could think of a good plan, think of somewhere else to go. But right now he was too tired to plan anything.

Along the back wall of the shop was a large workbench. It looked as if it was piled high with boxes, cans and assorted junk—like everything else—but there also appeared to be room enough underneath for him to make a nest of sorts. He moved a few things around, and then found an old canvas tarp. "How about that?" he said, smiling. He even had a pillow. Perfect. Not exactly a suite at the Waldorf but you couldn't have everything. He crawled underneath the bench, wriggled around until he was reasonably comfortable, then closed his eyes.

Well, hey! Doug . . . Rudi. Where have you guys been?

Right here where we've always been. Right here where you left us, Gary.

We were talking about something, but I can't remember what it was.

We were talking about what killed us, Lieutenant Palmer. What killed Mr. Gorham, and me. We died unpleasantly, you know.

Oh, yeah . . . yeah, I remember now. But . . . what did kill both of you? That's the part I can't remember at all.

Remember the airplane, Gary? All the dead men inside the plane? Something was very strange about that.

Very strange, Mr. Gorham.

Right. Remember the bodies in the plane, Gary?

No . . . no, I don't. I know I should, but I don't. But please tell me, Doug. Tell me about the bodies.

You were inside looking at them, Gary.

Yes, Gary. You were in the plane. You were in the plane for a long time. Looking at the bodies.

But I didn't stay there. Did I?

No, Gary. You didn't stay there. You came out. And you saw what happened outside. You saw what happened to us. To both of us.

Remember what happened to us outside, Gary? That was strange, too.

Very strange, Mr. Gurdler. And it happened to Gary, too.

What? What was it? What happened to me? Come on, you guys, what . . .

"All right, you just climb right on outa there. Right now."

. . . happened? Tell me . . . can't remember . . . what happened outside. . . .

"I said, get outa there. Now!"

Please . . . tell me . . . tell me. . . .

"Uhh!" Something hard jabbed Gary in the ribs, and as he jolted up his head banged against the underside of the wooden workbench. He rubbed his head and squinted in confusion, and it was a moment before he realized he was face-to-face with a long, narrow object weaving only inches in front of his nose. It moved as he moved, and he thought for a second that he was looking at a large black snake. Then he heard a voice: "Boy, you make a wrong move and you just might lose your head."

"Huh? Who—"

"Crawl on outa there nice and easy. No funny stuff. Now, *move!*"

4

AFTER A FULL DAY'S SEARCHING the only thing they had turned up at all was at Pawnee Rock, inside the bus station. Two nuns bought tickets to Kansas City, Missouri, and a young airman was on his way back to duty at Rantoul, Illinois—those three being the only tickets sold in five days.

No one had reported any sightings of strangers wandering through their sectors, not even a hitchhiker. No vehicles had been reported stolen by any of the local police departments, and there had been no prowlers noticed or break-ins investigated. Eaton and Caldwell had been through the towns of Ash Valley, Vaughn, Pawnee Rock and Martin Flats; tomorrow they would check the communities of Heizer, Albert, Shaffer, Timken and Rush Center. They already believed they would find nothing in any of them either.

One of two things had to have happened: either Palmer had cleared out of Kansas altogether, or he was well hidden and not moving at all—probably the latter. He had no money unless he'd stolen some, and there were no reports of any robberies. But even if someone gave him money, he couldn't buy anything without taking a chance on being spotted. Most likely he wouldn't try to use public transportation, and he wouldn't dare steal a vehicle because it was far too risky. Every cop in the state would be looking for him. No. If he was as smart as he seemed to be he was lying low.

Caldwell climbed into the car. "Well," he said with a sigh, "I guess we don't need to feel like the Lone Ranger. None of the other sectors have reported anything either. It looks like Palmer's vanished."

"Only temporarily," Eaton said. "He's out here somewhere, and I'm betting that he's within ten or fifteen miles of Wheeler. He has to be."

"Yeah, but where? This sector is pretty damned big, and that goes with what I've been saying: we don't have half enough men on this job. I know that Palmer is supposed to be top secret and all that bullshit, but there's still something fundamentally wrong with this whole exercise."

"What do you mean?"

"Sixteen men trying to cover the whole state is what I mean. It's crazy."

"We have others, you know. At the airports, the bus terminals..."

"Yeah, but it still doesn't make sense, not if Palmer's *that* important to the Army. What happens if he gets out of Kansas? If he hasn't already?"

"If he gets out of Kansas there'll be more men looking for him. There's no way we can cover it all, and they know it."

They stared at one of their maps. There was a lot of open country around them. Much of it was still as sparse and desolate as when it was occupied only by Indians. A man unfamiliar with it, especially a man afoot, could easily get lost, and end up walking for days without seeing anything except wide-open spaces. Central and western Kansas was probably the closest thing to a desert in that part of the country without actually being one.

Palmer could head for a city; there were a few around such as Kansas City, Dodge City, Wichita, Hutchinson, Salina and Topeka, to name a few. And if he got out of the state there were places like Omaha, Lincoln and Grand Island in Nebraska, and places all over Oklahoma and Colorado—all of them only a few hours away by automobile. He could last for a long time in a city without calling attention to himself; all he'd need would be a source of money. He could not stay long in any small town without being noticed. Yet he probably hadn't had time enough to get to any city.

All of which brought them back to another certainty: somewhere along the line, at least one other person would have to help him. Unwittingly, unwillingly or voluntarily, somebody would have to assist him. Perhaps somebody was doing so already without knowing or caring who or what he was. Unless they could guess who that might be, finding him might be impossible. Friends and relatives were out of the question; he couldn't contact any of them without being discovered, and he had to be smart enough to know that. That left only strangers. But out here in these small towns, where everybody knew everybody else and trusted no one dragging in off the road, who would that be?

"We're going to have to do some more planning and thinking," Caldwell said as he refolded the map. "Somewhere, we've missed something. We've overlooked something. We're running in circles."

Eaton took out a cigarette from his pocket, and punched the dashboard lighter. He nodded.

"Instead of trying to figure out where he's been or where he might be, we should be thinking of where he can go," Caldwell went on. "We have to get a jump on him. Otherwise, we'll never catch him."

"Nice work if you can get it." Eaton snorted, blowing smoke. "We haven't got the time to keep stopping and rolling the dice. We're supposed to keep moving."

"Well, tonight we're going to stop and think this thing out. If we don't we'll be out here chasing our tails again tomorrow." They had to figure out what Palmer's plan might be or he would vanish; so far he had done rather well at that.

They turned the car around, and drove west out of Pawnee Rock.

"There's one thing that bugs me," Caldwell said. "If he's the same Lieutenant Palmer who got killed up on that mountain last September—or who they said got killed—then I wonder why they had to put him inside Wheeler. For that matter, I wonder why they said that he got killed."

"Top secret." Eaton snorted again. "Remember? We don't want to know why. Our job is to get him back. Besides, you know how the Army operates. Some of their supersecret projects don't make any damn sense at all unless you're in the middle of them. They never tell anybody more than what they have to know. Including us."

"In that case, we'd better get him fast. Christ, I'll bet some of that brass must be shitting in their pants by now. Can you imagine what might happen if Palmer gets hold of a friend or relative and convinces them that it's really *him*, and that the Army was lying? Who knows what secret projects would get their lids blown off?"

"He might not even know that, either. That makes him even more dangerous."

"Yeah . . . but dangerous to whom?"

"We don't want to know."

5

IN THE GLOOM, the gun barrel followed Gary's nose. He moved slowly, easing himself out from under the workbench, keeping both hands up and in plain sight. As he finally got to his feet, reaching both hands higher, he was surprised to see that he stood more than a head taller than the person holding the gun. By then his eyes were beginning to adjust to the dim light, and he was even more surprised to identify the figure behind the gun as a woman. She was short, stocky, wearing a dress, and as he stared at her he could make her out as old, spectacled and white haired.

"Now, who are you, boy? And what are you doing in here?" The gun barrel was perhaps an inch from the end of his nose.

"I—I just needed a place to sleep, ma'am. That's all. Honest. I'm not a burglar or prowler or anything like that. I just needed a place to sleep... in out of the rain. That's all."

The woman had to be in her early seventies, a grandmother at least. In fact, she was built a little like his own grandmother—sounded something like her, too. He couldn't help but think that his grandmother would probably handle this sort of situation in the same manner. And this little old lady, from the way she had handled herself so far, wasn't about to take any guff from some dirty young stranger whom she had caught trespassing on her property. The truth was very much in order here—unadorned, unvarnished and immediate.

"That's the truth, ma'am, really," he went on nervously. "I don't mean any harm. And I won't try anything funny... no tricks. I promise. So please put the gun down."

The gun came up a bit higher. Now it was aimed between his eyes; it was like looking down the barrel of a Howitzer. The old lady studied him for a moment, then asked, "What are you? Some kind of escaped convict or something?"

"No, ma'am, I'm no convict. I'm—"

"Then what are you running from? You've gotta be running from something."

"Yes, ma'am... well, sort of, I guess. But I'm not a criminal. I'm—"

"What are you then? And who are you?"

"My name is Gary Palmer, ma'am. Lieutenant Gary Palmer. United States Army, and I'm—"

"Army? Now who are you trying to fool? That don't look like no Army uniform to me."

"Well, it isn't, not exactly. It's—"

"Then where'd you get it? Steal it?"

"Ma'am, if you'll just give me a chance I'll explain everything."

She thought that over for a moment before nodding. "All right. Start explaining. But you keep those hands up where I can see 'em." The gun remained level with his nose.

Short, sweet and believable, he thought. Please let her believe this, and maybe then I'll start believing it myself. He began with simple statements followed by simple questions: this happened, and did she remember hearing about this or that on TV or the radio? Then, that happened. And so on, trying to be as convincing as possible. The story took about ten minutes to complete. He had no idea whether or not she had bought it. After all, it was a tough one to swallow. And the look on her face told him nothing except the work and worries of her years that stood out. She didn't appear hard or unkindly—only wizened, and very cautious. Light was streaming in through hundreds of holes and cracks in the boards, and Gary could see her clearly now; the white hair pinned up in a bun, the wrinkled face with the wire-rimmed spectacles, the plain flowered dress, baggy stockings, cloppy-looking old-fashioned lace-up oxford shoes...

The Winchester .12-gauge pump.

"...and I ran. I didn't know what else to do. They weren't going to let me go, and I still don't know why except that it's something to do with whatever happened to us on that mountain. And... well, that's what brought me here," he finished. "That's all I can tell you, ma'am. That's all I know."

She looked at him long and hard for a long minute. "Are you going to stand there and expect me to believe that?" she said at last. "No government operates like that except maybe the Russians. But not the good ol' U.S. of A."

"I didn't think you'd believe it." Gary sighed. "I can hardly believe it myself. But I'm telling you the truth, I swear it. The only things I've left out are the things I can't remember."

"Well, then, I guess I'd best get the sheriff out here, young Mr. Palmer."

Nodding, Gary looked at the floor. "You could do that. But I'll tell you this: it won't be the sheriff or any state cop who comes to get me. You'll see a carload of men wearing dark suits who'll throw me in the back. They'll tell you to forget you've ever seen me, and after they've gone you'll never find a soul who will admit that I ever existed. And if you or anybody else asks any questions, some of the same men will take you aside. They'll tell you to shut up and forget everything you ever saw, or you could join me. I'm not kidding, ma'am. That's how these people operate."

"It still sounds pretty fishy to me."

"I know how it must sound. But you caught me here. You do whatever you think is right. You've got the gun."

She gave him that hard look of intense study once again as if stacking up the man's statements against the man, so she could see their depth of substance and conviction. "If you've been through all of that, young feller, why would you give up so easy now? To an old woman?" Now she sounded more curious than hard. Maybe he was convincing her after all, he thought.

"Well, maybe I wouldn't, ma'am. Like I said, I'm worried and scared. I don't really know yet where I should go or what I should do. But I don't deserve to be locked up like an animal. I haven't done anything. And I'm not crazy. I'm not a criminal, either, so my promise of not hurting you, or even bothering you, is good. So, I guess maybe if you tried turning me in…well, I'd have to take off. I might not get very far, and you might shoot me. I don't know. But I won't go back *there*. So I guess you would have to shoot me to stop me from running." And now he held his breath. Those were strong words to be using on an old lady with a gun aimed at his head, and who had caught him trespassing.

She said nothing. The huge gun barrel stayed where it was.

But she was thinking, and she thought about some of the stories she had heard during her life. They had run the gamut, from the ordinary to the fantastic. Many were comically false, stories a child might think up on the spot to avoid punishment for something—like the time when her daughter was five, and let all the chickens out. It wasn't *her*—it was a man in a space-ship who let them out. And her grandson with his BB gun, who shot one of the cats and put its eye out. No, Grandma, the kitty was playing with the gun, and it went off. Honest. He took after his mommy.

Gary waited. His arms were beginning to ache, but he kept them up.

On the other hand, some stories—some of the most improbable and outrageous—often turned out to be completely true. Back when her Henry was trying to buy this station he had gone to Kansas City to arrange the loan. He came back three days later smelling like a French whore drunk on gin; she'd been about to pull this same gun on him and teach him what for. His explanation was that he had been in a department store buying presents—a bottle of perfume for her—when the clerk accidentally spilled the bottle on his suit. Sure enough, before the week was out there was a letter of apology from the store manager along with a check for replacing Henry's suit.

You just couldn't tell sometimes. Maybe this boy was telling the truth. A lot of crazy things were going on these days. The gun dropped a little, and she said, "I don't want to shoot anybody. I would if I had to, but I wouldn't want to."

Gary stood rock still, his hands still held high. "I don't want to get shot, by you or anybody else. I know how you must feel, a dirty looking stranger who's broken into your property and all . . . and then he lays this fantastic story on you. I just wish I had some identification, something to show you that I'm telling the truth."

By then, she didn't doubt Gary as much as she doubted herself. And she had already decided to drop the gun, and let him go. She just couldn't convince herself of what he would do next; despite the gun, he held the real advantage. He might be crazier than a turpentined cat, and he could easily grab the gun and turn it on her, or do anything else he wished. She might be about to sign her own death warrant. On the other hand, if she turned him in to the law she might be responsible for getting an innocent, normal young man put away for the rest of his life just because his memory had gone a little haywire. She wanted badly to do the right thing, and there seemed to be only one hazy indicator of what that was—he still hadn't made a move toward her. She had the feeling that he would not, that his promise of not harming her or attempting anything was good.

And he still stood there, absolutely still. He looked frightened.

So was she; in fact, she was scared to death. She was glad it was dark enough in here so he couldn't see her shaking in her shoes—even her dentures were clattering. Holding a gun on somebody was a statement of intent. You had to be willing to follow through, and she was not. If Gary had tried to run at that moment he would have gotten away easily because she could not shoot anything, especially a man. Besides, the shotgun wasn't even loaded.

The barrel dropped. The old woman held her breath.

Gary exhaled deeply, closing his eyes. He put his hands down. "Thank you, ma'am," he whispered. "Thank you very much."

She exhaled, too, when she saw at once that he meant it.

"You say your name's Gary?"

"Yes, ma'am. Gary Palmer."

"I'm Emma Lockhart. I'll call you Gary if you call me Emma. I'm not used to that ma'am stuff."

Smiling, almost laughing, Gary offered his right hand. "Emma, you don't know how happy I am to meet you."

"You come on with me," she ordered. "This ain't no place to be sleeping. You need a change of clothes…and a good bath, too."

Sniffing his sleeve, Gary nodded—no argument there. She might have found him by smell alone. "I guess I must have made a lot of noise in here. I'd never make it as an Indian."

"Some of the dogs get in here once in a while, and I thought one of 'em was knocking over things until I heard you snoring. I thought my late Henry could outsnore anybody, but you could beat him hands down. Young feller, you're louder than a chain saw. I could hear you next door. I'm surprised the neighbors couldn't hear you.''

FOR THIRTY-FIVE YEARS until Emma's husband died, the Esso station had been a part of a dual business that included a general store. Now there was only the store, or what little remained of it. Old, dark and falling apart at the seams, Emma's store had a little of everything inside, but not enough of anything. What few steady customers there were came around more out of respect and kindness than any real need. She rarely reached the break-even point, and if she hadn't had a pension from her husband and what was left in her savings, she might have starved. Her daughter and son-in-law had tried for years to get her to shut the place down and sell out so she could live with them in Denver, but Emma refused. She wasn't helpless, she said. And she hated being dependent on anybody.

From the moment he stepped inside, Emma treated Gary like a long-lost relative. Her home was in the back of the store and had barely enough room for her; yet Gary was ordered to take over and make himself at home. She began immediately to prepare lunch, and as she clucked about everything coming to mind, he simply listened and looked around.

Her home was spotless. Everything she owned was years old, but cared for, polished and carefully positioned. Houseplants lined the windows and shelves; all the tables were decorated with hand-embroidered doilies set on the woodwork of another age, and again Gary was struck by the similarity of Emma's home to that of his own grandmother. She even had a knickknack shelf that fairly groaned with row after row of delicate porcelain and glass intricacies like the one his grandma had, which he had been warned to stay away from when he was little. One living room wall was given over to a couple of dozen faded portraits and fuzzy tintypes of Emma's stern-looking ancestors. One in particular grabbed his attention, that of a harsh-looking man dressed in a black hat and a stark black suit, and sporting a magnificent handlebar mustache. He bore a striking resemblance to Wyatt Earp, and he too was a marshal; a silver star was pinned to his left breast pocket, and he carried a Colt .45 revolver on his right hip. Now there, by God, was a *lawman*. They didn't make them like that anymore.

"That was my grandpa," Emma said proudly. "Marshal Daniel S. McCuddy, and he really was one of the old Dodge City marshals."

"I wouldn't have wanted him after me."

"You and a lot of other men from what my dad used to tell me. Dad said that he was one of the toughest, meanest men he ever saw. He was too scared to ask if it was all right to marry my mother," and she laughed. "So, my mother ended up asking. But my mother always was pretty spunky. She could be just as tough and ornery as Grandpa sometimes."

Then she came by it honestly, Gary thought with a smile. She had handled herself pretty well with that shotgun.

"Well, Gary, the first thing to do is for you to get yourself cleaned up and into some fresh clothes. The bathroom is right over there, and I'll go get a few things from the store. After that, we'll have us some lunch." She patted his arm as she pushed him gently toward the bathroom.

No doubt about it. She was exactly like his own grandmother, taking charge of whatever she did. Somewhere there had to be a mysterious school for grandmothers that they all attended secretly because this sort of behavior sprouted in every old lady he had ever known. If they were sure you were nice, and nice enough to them, they took over and took care of you as if you were one of their own. And he wasn't about to object. He did as he was told.

Over lunch, however, it was apparent to Gary that she was getting worried; not so much about him now as about the situation in general. He had had a bad break from forces beyond his control, but by her act of kindness she was now in the middle of it. "Do you think I could get in trouble with the government?" she asked. "I've never had that kind of trouble before."

Neither had Gary, and he couldn't be sure of what trouble the government might be prepared to make. He said, "I don't think they'd bother you or anybody else around here, Emma. They're interested in me. Oh, if any agents came through they might look around, or stop and ask a few questions, but that would be about all they'd do. All that stuff about government agents grabbing innocent people off the streets is a bunch of hogwash." But one thing was certain: he was going to leave as soon as possible. He wasn't sure of what might happen at this point, and he didn't want anybody else getting into trouble or getting hurt because of him. "In fact," he added, "I'll leave right now if it will make you feel more comfortable, Emma."

She thought for only a moment before shaking her head, then reaching out to pat his hand. "No. No, you just stay put. You stay right here as long as you want to. Get all your thoughts and plans together. Besides, I'm seventy-two years old, and there isn't much they could do to a tough old bird like me."

That was all well and good, but he still had to make some plans. Fast. He couldn't hide here for long. If those people were as rapid and thorough as he thought, they would soon be here searching door-to-door. He was surprised that no one had shown up yet.

At the same time he had to figure out what it was that had happened to him on Kota; what it was that made him so vital to the Army that they were ready to lock him up forever. But he didn't know where to start. And what would he do with any answers he happened to find? He was starting to feel like a dog chasing a car; if he caught it he wouldn't know what to do with it, and if he wasn't careful it might run over him.

"Is there anybody who could help you?" Emma asked.

He shrugged. "Nobody that they won't know about. They're probably keeping an eye on all my relatives. And most of them live in Washington, anyway, so it—" He snapped his fingers. "Wait a minute, maybe there is somebody. Emma, do you have a phone?"

"Just the pay phone out in front of the store. But somebody might see you."

"Okay. Yeah, you're right. I can't take a chance on that, so I'll wait until it gets dark."

"Who are you going to call?"

Gary patted her hand this time. "Emma, sit right there, and I'll tell you all about her."

CHAPTER TEN

FOR SEVEN AND A HALF MONTHS Janey Burns had done very little but exist. She acted routinely, almost dumbly, with little thought or imagination injected into anything. Every habit became dull, stoic; each movement was mechanical, like the action of an assembly line machine.

She would get up in the morning and pad into the bathroom. She would brush her teeth, and put on some simple makeup. She would get dressed, walk downstairs and join her mother for coffee, perhaps toast or an English muffin with jelly. After a while she would go outside, start up her old car, then come back in for a final check in the mirror, a last gulp of coffee and a muttered goodbye. She would return home from work by four-thirty or five o'clock, and after she changed clothes she would feed and water their two horses, feed the dogs and cats and maybe putter around for a while. When she returned to the house she would help her mother with supper. When that was done, and the dishes were washed and put away, most of her evenings were spent curled up in a chair or on the couch, wrapped in a warm housecoat while she read a paperback book or magazine. Sometimes she would glance up at the TV. By ten-thirty or eleven she would be showered, with her hair done up, and climbing into bed. The next day would be pretty much the same; the only variations came during the harshest days of the Montana winter when they might be temporarily snowed in.

Saturdays sometimes found her working at the bank in the mornings—sometimes not. If not, she would go to town with her mother for their weekly shopping and looking around. Once in a while her mom might call on a friend or two, and Janey would always go along because there was no place else to go or little else to do. By late afternoon or early evening they would be home, and Janey would again take care of the animals, help with supper, get the dishes done, then change into her housecoat for another evening in front of the TV, where she pretended to read a book and listen to Mom while she worked on a piece of knitting or an afghan for somebody. On Saturday nights Janey allowed herself the luxury of staying up for the late movie, whether she wanted to see it or not; she would pay little attention to it, anyway. The next morning she would sleep in, and Mom would drive to church.

They spent Thanksgiving weekend with Uncle Bob and Aunt Phyllis over in Bozeman. When the holidays rolled around, Bill, Jr. and his family spent a couple of days, and her sister Julie came home from college. Four pairs of aunts and uncles came over on Christmas Day for dinner and to watch all the little ones make a shambles of the house. The boys played with the cardboard boxes, and two of the girls fought a day-long running battle over one of the dolls. Later that week, one of the guys from town, a local cop named Randy Hopkins, called and asked Janey if she would like to go with him to the big New Year's Eve dance down at the Moose Lodge. No, she said. But she thanked him for asking, and Mom got on her case again about not going out or enjoying herself, adding for the umpteenth time that she'd end up a sour old maid if she didn't get out of the house once in a while. Janey spent New Year's Eve alone at home anyway, curled up in front of the TV watching a mob scene have a good time in Times Square. Mom went to a church dance escorted by Ira Michaels, a widower from town, and Alfred and Betty Mays. It was her first double date in more than thirty-five years; she was as giggly and excited as a schoolgirl going to her very first spring dance. Janey fell asleep in the easy chair at half past eleven.

Janey did get out of the house, though—twice. One Friday night late in January she took in a movie, her first in six months. She walked out in the middle of it because she was the only unescorted girl in the theater. Too, Randy Hopkins was persistent, so she yielded and went out to dinner with him one Saturday night in March. He talked incessantly about police work, how he would like to work his way up through the sheriff's department and eventually into the Montana Bureau of Investigation, and how there was more crime in this area than people thought. When he asked her about her job at the bank she managed two or three complete sentences before he went into another spiel about how the sheriff's department needed more funds so they could buy more equipment and hire more men, and how could they ferret out crime by working with one hand tied all the time? He was still talking about it when they pulled up in front of her house; Janey was about to say, the hell with it, and just get out, when Randy suddenly remembered what he was supposed to do. He tried that, and a lot more, and it fetched him an elbow in the ribs and a couple of fast observations about his ancestry. Janey's last request was for him to forget her name and phone number as she slammed the door in his face.

Monday, she was back at work in the bank. She worked all day and left at four-fifteen. When she got home she fed the horses, the dogs and the cats, helped her mother fix supper and wash the dishes, watched a little TV, read three or four pages from a so-so paperback novel, then went to bed.

"Janey," Mom said when she came down the next morning, "I want to talk to you. And I want you to listen."

Janey drank her coffee. She said nothing, and she didn't look up. She didn't have to. Mom's talks neither required nor awaited responses.

"Janey, I'm getting worried about you. You've got to snap out of this."

"I'm fine, Mom." She sighed. "Don't worry about me."

"Well, I *am* worried." She took Janey's hand. "Listen, I know how much Gary meant to you. Believe me . . ."

I know what you're going through. . . .

". . . I know what you're going through. But it's not the end of the world. You're only twenty-three years old, Janey, and . . ."

You've got your whole life ahead of you. . . .

". . . you've got your whole life ahead of you. Now, how do you think I felt when your father died?"

It was the end of the world. . . .

"Well, I'll tell you, I thought it was the end of the world. I'd lived with him for more than twenty-five years, had three kids with him, and he . . ."

Was the only man I ever loved....

"... was the only man I ever loved. We had a good life together. So, I was shattered. I thought I'd never get over it."

But you did...

"But I did, Janey. I still miss him, but life goes on. You've got to shake off the hurt ... get tough about it. You have to get out into the middle of things again..."

And get back into circulation, and ... you take it, Mom

"... back into circulation. Get out there and thrash around. Do you understand?"

Right, Mom.

"I was talking to Edna Hopkins yesterday, and she said that when Randy took you out to dinner the other night he could hardly get a word out of you. And when he brought you home that you didn't even say good-night or thank him for the good time. He said that you hopped out of the car and slammed the door in his face. Janey, for crying out loud, I thought I taught you better than that. Is that any way to treat someone who's just taken you out? What do you think the rest of these young men around here will say if that gets around? What will you do for a date then?"

"Mom, listen, I—"

"No, you listen, Janey. Like I already said, I want you to snap out of this awful frame of mind you're in. I want you to promise me that you'll do it. All right?"

"I don't *feel* like it, Mom."

"I want you to try at least. I mean it, Janey."

It was senseless to argue. Mom had formulated the answer—*the answer.* All of her solutions were presented as if they were divine revelations. Trying to change the way Mom saw things would only harden her concrete stubbornness into sheer granite. Of course, a lot of the problem had to do with the fact that Janey was still living at home at age twenty-three, the last place she thought she would be at that age. She was still stuck in Sioux Creek. And as long as they shared the same roof, Mom thought that her advice and opinions still carried the weight they had ten years ago, or that seemed to be her attitude. But Janey had to admit that it was comfortable remaining at home for the time being. She had no burning interests, nothing outstanding going for her just then, and no great desire to venture off into the vast unknown. Right now she wanted nothing more than to remain in neutral, to get herself moving in her own good time and in her own way. If it took another six months, or six years, there still was no hurry—after all, she had her whole life ahead of her, as Mom was fond of reminding her. And if living at home meant that she still had to put up with all the half-baked opinions or an occasional scolding . . . well, that wasn't a large price at all. The Final Frontier could wait.

"Did you hear me?"

"Okay, okay." Janey sighed. "I've got to go. I'll be late."

"Remember what I said."

"All right! I'll see you this afternoon," and she rushed out the door before Mom could think of anything else to add.

Still, Mom was right, and Janey understood she had her older daughter's best interests at heart. Understandably, she was upset at seeing her down this long, and she was right about not allowing it to go on any longer, or Janey's emotional health would be at stake. Janey knew she had been in the trash heap far too long. It was time to pull herself back together, start going out again, doing things and trying to make a life for herself. And of course . . .

Go on . . . say it. Face it.

. . . finding someone else. Well . . . maybe. Later. There was no hurry with that. Maybe someday.

There had been no hurry with Gary, either. There had never been any need for hurrying. They hadn't been marriage oriented, just together oriented. But he had been the one. She had no intention of spending the rest of her life alone; she wanted a family someday, and she had imagined Gary as the father of so many faceless imaginary kids. The image had settled into her, and when it had been ripped out it left a gaping hole that still hadn't healed. And even though Mom didn't know it, Janey *had* told herself time and time again that she should accept the fact, and move on to the world of the living. But she just couldn't quite do it, not yet. And there was a reason.

She tooted the horn as she went by the Mayfield place. Sally Mayfield, a friend from high school, was outside. She offered Janey a big wave and bright smile. Sally didn't have to work.

She already had her talons into the son of the richest man in the county. Sally Mayfield was always bright and happy and smiling and laughing about everything.

Once again, Janey found the thought of moving—just moving right out of the state—crossing her mind. She had friends from all around Montana, and a few from other parts of the country—even one from Ohio. They had always told her over college bull sessions about some of the great things going on back home, or in this place or that place. A lot of it was prejudiced, of course, and yet each one of those friends had returned home. Just as she had never left home. There were the empty promises they had all made, how they would keep in touch, and how they would get together in a few years for a reunion; they had even gone through the motions of exchanging addresses and home phone numbers. But Janey hadn't heard from a single one of them. It was as if they had existed in a dream. Maybe their lives had turned out a little better, and they had each married that certain guy they talked about. Or maybe it had all been bullshit, and they had ended up with someone like these drooling ranch hands or clerks or truck drivers, or maybe even a ham-fisted cop.

No. She wasn't going anywhere.

And this reason had nothing to do with the convenience of remaining home. No matter how she figured things, regardless of how the equation was written or how the elements were transposed, there was one final analysis that always came out the same. And now, driving down Wormann Road, it hit her again.

Gary Palmer was still alive.

She couldn't explain how she could be so sure of anything or where the feeling came from or how it had come over her or, for that matter, exactly what the feeling was. Only that it *was*. It lived almost as surely as if it were growing and breathing. It was real, and it lived inside her, a steadily humming, glowing little generation of light and warmth and power. It was not a hope or a prayer or a warm emotion. It was absolute fact, and the hell with the rest of the sane world. And to hell with the Army reports, the media announcements, the radio broadcasts and the gruesome news photographs. Gary was still alive. She knew it. She just *knew* it.

The feeling hit her again, and she pulled over to wipe the tears and blow her nose. Maybe this was one of those extra-sensory things that they say mothers experience when their boys suddenly buy the farm on some distant battlefield. Perhaps it was feminine intuition, whatever the hell that was. Or maybe it was a sixth sense of some kind . . . or maybe she was a witch. None of it mattered, and she dabbed her eyes with a Kleenex. God, now she looked like a haggard witch, bawling through her makeup like that. She hoped it would never happen at work; but the sudden, overpowering feeling came on her once in a while, and she couldn't stop it. She didn't want to. Because Gary was doing that to her, and he couldn't possibly do that unless he were alive. She knew that, too.

The only way to fix her makeup was just wipe it off and start over. Well, piss on it, she thought. I'll get it in the ladies' room at work, and she pulled back onto the road again.

She felt warm, and she rolled her window partway down.

Gary, baby, you just keep it up. Anytime you want to come to me and massage my soul, you just come from wherever you are. I'll be right here.

2

". . . AND THEY'LL NEED a week's notice at least. But I don't know yet when I'm going. Or where. I hadn't really thought about it."

"Well, good!" her mother said, pleased that Janey had taken some of her advice at last. She'd get through to that girl yet. "A vacation is exactly what you need. In fact, it would do us both good to get away from this place for a while."

She scringed. She was afraid Mom would say that. "Uh . . . I was thinking of going by myself, Mom. I'd sort of like to get away alone for a while. You know, just have a little pri-vacy . . . umm . . ." she ended lamely, thinking, now she'll be hurt, and make me feel rotten, and I'll end up inviting her to go along.

"Oh! Well, I understand. I just thought you'd . . ."

"Mom, it isn't that I don't want you along. I just need some time alone. Besides, I don't even know where I'm going, or if I'm going anywhere. And it won't be for another month or two anyway. This is only the beginning of May. I'll wait for the beginning of summer."

Her mother said nothing, turning back to supper preparations.

Janey tried to busy herself by peeling potatoes. "If I do go anywhere I'll need another car," she said after a long silence. And she added, with a false laugh, "My old Chevy's not up to much of a trip. It barely makes it into town."

Her mother basted the chicken as if she were scraping paint. "That's silly, Janey," she finally answered, making it sound like a life-or-death matter. "You know perfectly well that you're welcome to take my car. It just sits in the barn most of the time anyway. I never go anywhere in it."

With a silent groan, Janey wondered how she got into these things. All she had done was come home and announce that she might—*might*—take a vacation. "Mom, please don't be mad. I probably won't go anywhere...just stay around the house for a week or so. We have a lot of things that need to be done anyway."

"Don't be childish. I already said that you could use my car, so there's no need to feel sorry for yourself because you need another one." She shoved the tray of chicken into the oven and slammed the door. "I've never understood why in the world we need two cars anyway."

Because you'd be without one one of these days when I do decide to leave. Why the hell do you think?

Five minutes passed. Utensils rattled.

"I'll have my car all ready for you. Just try to let me know in time when you're going."

"Yeah, Mom. Okay . . ."

Janey did begin to look forward to a trip. She couldn't decide where to go, or when, only to wait until Julie was home from the University of Iowa so that Mom wouldn't be left alone. Her mother would forget all about a trip with Julie driving her crazy. It was surprising, when she thought about it, that she had seen little of the country. She had never been farther east than Illinois, no farther north than across the border into Canada once, and only as far west as eastern Washington. Denver was the largest city she had ever seen; in fact, Janey knew little about any state except Montana, and maybe a couple of small corners out of Wyoming and Idaho. It soon became a challenge to pick out a place to visit, and she decided at once that she would need two weeks if she was to have time enough to see anything. She thought about flying somewhere. There was money enough, and it would be a much better excuse to give Mom for going alone—she couldn't afford to take them both. Her money would be better spent on a car, and if she drove she would have to buy another one. Or use her mother's, which was out of the question.

She continued thinking about the trip for a couple of weeks, planning little pieces of it. Every couple of days she would buy something. The bank manager reminded her every few days that they would need at least a week's notice so they could cover for her, but she still hadn't decided on a firm date. Her mother gave up asking—formally, that is. She settled on strategically planned silences instead, still hoping that Janey would relent and ask her to go along.

The affair drifted until the latter part of the month.

"Janey!" her mom called from the bottom of the stairs one evening. "Janey! Telephone! Can you come down to get it?"

"Yeah, tell 'em to hold on!" Janey yelled from the bathroom. "I'll be right down!" She appeared seconds later, wrapped in towels, her hair dripping.

"It's a man," her mother whispered as she handed over the receiver. A curious sort of smile matched a strange-looking sparkle in her eyes. No man had called Janey in ages. "I didn't recognize the voice, and he didn't say who he is."

"Well, would you please clear out then?" If it was Randy Hopkins, who for some reason thought he was in the running again lately, she was going to hang up. It was probably her boss about to ask if she could work some overtime.

"Hello?"

3

THEY SHOULD HAVE LEFT the small roadside restaurant and bar before now, but it was much more comfortable than thinking in the car. Too, they both wanted a drink, but all that would have to happen was for the cocktail waitress to come to their table and one of the goddamn field supervisors would show up; they would end up walking back to Kansas City. They settled for thirds on coffee instead. Eaton studied the maps while Caldwell wrote notes.

So far, for all the good they had done they might as well have spent all their time at that table. "Let me see if I've got this straight," Caldwell said. "One: Palmer can't contact anybody without our people hearing about it. Two: that means he can't get anyone to help him unless somebody's already doing so, probably hiding him. Three: there's nowhere he can go without being spotted. And four: even if he had a place to go he has no way of getting there."

"That's partly right," Eaton replied, sipping his coffee and lighting a cigarette. "One: if Palmer has help already he might not have to contact any friend or relative. Two: he's been gone for a day and a half, and if he hasn't left the state, someone has to be hiding him. So he already has help. Three: that same help might be able to take him anywhere he wants to go, and we'd never spot him, which means, four, he would have a way of getting there. So I wouldn't exactly say that he's locked in." He turned back to his maps again and was quiet for a few minutes.

Next door in the barroom, the jukebox started playing "I've Got a Tiger by the Tail." Two couples at a table were laughing about something; one of the men reached down to pinch his lady on the tail. "Ohhh, stop that!" she squealed, delighted that he'd thought to do it.

"I've been thinking about all of this," Eaton said. "And no matter how I add it up, it still keeps coming out the same way. It's just a gut hunch, but I can't believe that Palmer isn't more than fifteen or twenty miles from where we're sitting right now. We've overshot him, overlooked his hiding place. He hasn't had time to make any complicated arrangements. He hasn't had time to get anywhere.'' He made a circle against the paper with his finger. ''He's in this area...right in here someplace. He has to be.''

Within the forty-mile radius Eaton circled were towns they had already checked—Vaughn, Ash Valley, Pawnee Rock and Martin Flats. If anything unusual had happened, or any strangers had turned up in any of those places, a dozen people would have seen and reported it—anything. The most exciting thing they had done in those places was to sit and watch a bridge rust.

''I'm still wondering if he went west at all,'' Caldwell added. ''That's just our theory, you know. Sure, we found the car in the west end of Wheeler, but he could have walked or hitch-hiked from there in another direction just to throw us off the trail. He could be a thousand miles away in some other direction, long gone, while we're out here in the middle of nowhere jerking off.''

Eaton shook his head as he stubbed out the cigarette. ''Nope. No way. That's too complicated for the situation. He was in a big hurry to get the hell out of town and get as far away from there as he could. Going west was the fastest way for him. No, he's out here somewhere.''

''Okay,'' Caldwell said with a sigh. ''Where?''

''I've been adding up a few figures, too. Now, Palmer got away at approximately 11:00 p.m.,'' and he showed his partner an intersection on the map. ''Even a man on foot could get to this spot by 3.00 a.m. at the latest. Now, look at this road.'' He traced his finger along the red line marking Route 94. As they knew, it was the only road out of Wheeler going west. The intersection of routes 94–115/104 was the only place 94 met another road until it reached Route 183. ''See this? If you go south on 115 you don't get to another town for twelve miles. But if you go west on 94 you go straight through Martin Flats, only three miles away. He could have made that easily before dawn.''

''Yeah.'' Caldwell nodded. ''But we already looked there, remember? That place is so small you'd have trouble hiding a rat there, let alone a stranger dressed up in hospital whites.''

But they hadn't stopped there. They hadn't talked to anyone.

They threw the money on the table, wadded their maps under their arms and hurried out of the restaurant.

4

OF ALL OF MA BELL'S PHONE booths he had been in, this one would have to have a working night-light. Gary felt as if he was onstage, under the spotlights; after he dialed the number he pushed the door open. The light went out.

A pair of headlights approached from the east, and Gary turned away, trying to make the movement appear natural. He also pretended to be talking, and when Mrs. Burns answered her voice caught him off guard. He stammered, but finally got the message out. Fortunately, she did not ask who was calling for Janey as she usually did.

And at last he heard her voice. For a second he froze.

"Janey?" he said, shaking. "Is that you?"

"Yes?"

"Janey, hold on. It's me. Gary."

Silence.

"Janey? Are you still there?"

"Listen, I don't know who you are but this isn't funny, and—"

"Hey, Janey, it's Gary. Gary Palmer. It's really me." What was wrong with her? Didn't she recognize his voice?

"Look, you pervert, if you call here again I'll get the cops after you. Now, goodbye!"

"Janey! Dammit, will you shut up and listen for a minute? This is no joke. It's *Gary*, and I can prove it. Please don't hang up."

"Oh, I'm gonna hang up all right, but you—"

"Goddammit! *You* have a mole about half an inch below the nipple of your right breast. You have another one high up on the inside of your left thigh just below the pubic hair line, and I was the one who found it! Now, is *that* good enough for you? Jesus, what the hell's got into you, anyway?"

She flopped down onto the stairs. At the same instant the color drained from her face as if someone had pulled a plug, and she almost dropped the receiver; if she hadn't grabbed it with both hands as she collapsed it would have hit the floor. For a long moment she couldn't speak. She tried, but all that exited was a squeak on her breath. Had anyone else seen her they would have thought she had been struck down by some kind of seizure; in a sense, she had been.

It was Gary. *It really was Gary* on the other end of the line. No other man knew what he had just told her; even her mother didn't know about the mole on her thigh. Tears poured from her eyes, and she began trembling. That was Gary. It was him.

"Janey? Are you still there?"

"Oh...oh...oh, Gar-Gary! *Garrreeeeee!* Oh, it's really you, it's really you! Oh, God, I just knew it, I knew it, I didn't care what they all said, I knew you were still alive and they were lying. I *knew* it! Oh, Gary, *honneee—*"

Ali— The word wouldn't come out. He couldn't have heard that right. Alive? What was she talking about? But if his hearing hadn't played a trick on him, the implications were monstrous.

"Janey. Listen...listen, what do you mean?"

"I knew they were lying, I just knew you were okay, honey, I knew it." She sniffled. "I could feel it—"

"Hold on a minute, Janey. Listen. Who the hell said I was dead?"

"Why...the Army. They said that you got killed."

"My God!" he whispered. Some of this was beginning to make sense now. "What else did they say?"

"Well...two or three days after that rescue mission they announced that you and those other two guys all got killed on Kota. At the summit. They had a big press conference out there at Endicott with all kinds of reporters and brass, and they gave everybody this long-winded report on what happened and that all three of you must have had some kind of accident...uh, they weren't real clear about it, but hey, wait a minute. Where are you anyway?"

On the other hand, a lot of this didn't make any sense at all. What the hell were they up to? They had told him that he somehow made it back down the mountain by himself in a traumatized, almost comatose, state—true enough. He couldn't remember a thing about it. But had they first thought he died up there like Gorham and Gurdler, announcing it to the world, only to have him reappear shortly afterward? No, that didn't seem likely, because they wanted to keep him in captivity. And what better way would there be for that than to announce his death? But why? All of it pointed to the importance of whatever happened to them at the summit—none of which he could remember.

"Gary?"

"Yeah, I'm right here."

"Okay, where's here?"

"Kansas. I'm in Kansas."

"Kansas?"

"Yeah. I was brought here. Right after that mission. But that's all I know...just what they've told me. Something really strange happened to us at the summit, Janey, but it knocked me out. Now, I can't remember anything about it. They locked me up in this place down here, but I regained full consciousness over a week ago, and I'm back to normal now...except for part of my memory. Anyway, I escaped from there, and I'm on the run almost like a criminal. Right now I'm hiding, and . . . well, look, I really need your help, Janey. I haven't got time to explain all of this now."

"What do you want me to do?"

"Could you come down here and get me? I mean, it would have to be right now, just as soon as you hang up. I really need you, babe. I need help."

"Sure. Where are you?"

"A little wide spot in the road called Martin Flats. It's on state Route 94 about fourteen or fifteen miles west of Wheeler, and Wheeler Barracks. Got that?"

"Yes."

"Okay, you take Interstate 70 east to Hays, then route 183 south to a place called Rush Center. Route 94 is about nine miles south of that. When you get to 94, go east straight into Martin Flats, about five miles or so. Got all of that, too?"

She squinted at her hastily scrawled notes and repeated them back to him.

"Good. Now, there's an old general store at the far east end of town. Next to it is an abandoned gas station with a rusty Esso sign in front of it, and a mountain of junk and trash all around the place. They're on the north side of the road. I'm in the back of the store. There's a nice lady here who's helping me out . . . hiding me."

"Gary, what kind of trouble are you in? This sounds serious."

"I really don't know for sure, hon, and that's the hell of it. There's so many things about this fiasco that I don't know—only that the goddamn Army's behind it. And what I do know is just too complicated to explain over the phone. Now, can you tell me roughly how long it'll take for you to get here?"

She had no idea. She would be fumbling through country completely foreign to her. But she said, "Tomorrow night. I'll do my best to be there by tomorrow night. I'll leave right away."

"Great. I'll be looking for you." He happened to look toward the west and saw another set of headlights in the distance. He had to hurry and get back inside—no telling who it might be. "Listen carefully, Janey. Just pull up in front of the store. I'll be inside. And for God's sake, don't ask anybody about me because no one even knows I'm here. Don't trust anybody. If it looks like someone might be following you, go somewhere else, or try to get rid of 'em. They might not know about you—then again, they might."

"They who?"

"I wish I could be sure. I don't know who might be trying to come after me except the Army CID people for sure. And don't tell a soul that I've called or that you know where I'm at, not even your own mother."

"Hey, this sounds scary."

"You're the only chance I've got. Look, I haven't got time to talk anymore."

The headlights were getting closer, now perhaps half a mile away. He had to hurry. It might not be anything except a couple more locals, but he couldn't risk it. Two people had seen him in the phone booth already. And he had imagined seeing people looking for him all day long, people everywhere, hiding behind every tree and bush. He almost had a feeling there might be two or three waiting to grab him as soon as he left the phone booth.

"Gary? I love you."

"Babe, I love you, too. But I've gotta go. Somebody's coming. Oh, yeah, bring money. I'm flat broke."

"How much?"

"All you've got. We might need it. I'll pay you back. I've got about eight months' back pay coming."

"Okay..." She was crying again.

"Be careful coming down here. I'll see you tomorrow night."

"All right. Bye..."

"Night, hon." He dabbed away a couple of tears himself.

In three seconds Janey had bolted up the stairs to her room where she grabbed every piece of clothing handy, hurling them from her dresser to her bed. Whimpering with joy and trying to wipe her eyes, she leaped into a faded pair of jeans and an old pair of run-down riding boots. She put on a blouse so fast that she misbuttoned it. Only when she rushed into the bathroom for a few things did she realize she had forgotten her underwear, but she muttered, the hell with it, and ran back to the bedroom to throw everything into an overnight bag.

"Who was that on the phone?" her mother called pleasantly from the foot of the stairs. "He sounded a little nervous."

All she got for an answer was the muffled commotion from Janey's room. She was about to go up and see what was going on when her daughter suddenly flew around the banister and bounded down the stairs two at a time as if the devil himself was chasing her. She jumped back out of the way just in time.

"Janey? What in the world's wrong with y—"

Janey tossed her bag at the door, then grabbed her purse from the front hall table, and panted, "Mom, how much money have you got?"

"What?"

"How much *money* have you got? Come *on*!" and she dumped the contents of her own purse on the floor, rooting around and muttering something about where the hell was it?

"What's the matter with you? Who was that on the phone?"

"Mom, *now*! Please shut up, and give me all the money you've got. I'll pay you back later. Come on! I've gotta run."

"Run where? What are you doing?"

Janey grabbed her mother's purse, then unceremoniously emptied it on the floor, too, grabbing the wallet, and fishing around in the mess of cards and coupons.

"*Janey!* Give me that!" Her oldest daughter had suddenly gone stark raving mad. "What do you think you're doing?" she screeched.

"*I need your money, dammit!* And I haven't got time to explain!" She fished out several crumpled bills and jammed them into her pockets. "I'll pay you back just as soon as I get back." She scooped up the miscellaneous junk from the rug, throwing it back into her purse.

"Get back? From where? Where are you going? And why the sudden crazy rush? You can't leave dressed like that! You're a mess."

"Can't tell you, Mom, I've just gotta run. I'll be back in a few days. Bye." She ran out the front door to her car.

"Janey! Where are you going?"

The old Chevy roared to life. "Emergency!" Janey yelled over the noise, then threw the car into gear.

"What emergency?" And what had caused this sudden and total loss of sanity? Was this a trick to get away on a vacation without her? She wouldn't put such an elaborate prank past Janey; when she was younger and wanted to get out of doing something, there was little she hadn't tried.

The Chevy jumped backward, gravel clattering in the fender wells. Dust billowed up in clouds, almost obscuring the two pole lights in the yard.

Mrs. Burns ran to the edge of the driveway. *"Jaaa-neeeeee!"* But all she could see by then were the taillights vanishing in the darkness.

5

GARY STEPPED OUT of the phone booth and into the store. Emma had already turned out the lights; there hadn't been any customers all day, anyway.

"Was your young lady friend home?" she said.

"Yes. She's coming here to get me. She'll be here sometime tomorrow evening, if everything goes right."

"Oh, that's nice."

Well, maybe that was nice, but little else was. Everything was wrong. The world had been told he was dead along with Gurdler and Gorham—which could mean that his family had gone out of their minds with grief. The Army had said he was dead so they could lock him away for God-knows-what. He was up to his eyebrows in something so serious that he had to be declared legally dead, and he still couldn't imagine why or what it was—only that it was connected with an airplane crash on top of a mountain, and a failed rescue attempt that he couldn't even remember.

The headlights belonged to an approaching sedan that was now at the west edge of town. It had slowed considerably below the thirty-five-mile-per-hour limit through the village, almost as if its passengers were looking for something.

Gary stepped away from the door and moved toward one of the counters. "Emma?" he whispered across the darkened store interior. "Come here. Hurry."

"What is it?"

"That car out there. Just stand in front of the door and watch it. Pretend I'm not here, but tell me what you can about it." He ducked behind the counter and moved toward a front window.

The car was almost in front of the store.

"Uh...it's a dark-colored car," Emma said quietly. Her voice was trembling a little. "There's one—no, two people in it, two men, I think. They look like they're just looking around...watching everything. They're still driving. No, they've stopped in front of the station."

Oh, shit! "Emma, can you see the license plates?"

"Yes, I think so. I—I don't know what they are, but they're not Kansas license plates— Wait, now they're moving again. Still going east. I think they're leaving."

Slowly, Gary got up for a peek. He was trembling, too.

"Do you think . . . ?" Emma began, and Gary nodded before she could finish.

"I think so. Somehow, they must have tracked me here. I'd better get out. They might come back, and I don't want to make any trouble for you."

She acted as if she wanted to agree, but she shook her head stubbornly. "You'll do no such thing. You'll stay right here until your young lady comes to get you. You wouldn't get ten feet outside this store before they'd see you."

"No. I appreciate it, Emma, but no. I found out something on the phone a while ago. I can't say what it is, but this whole thing's a lot more serious than I thought. Those guys aren't just after me; if they think I'm here, they might take this place apart, and to hell with what the neighbors think. It's that serious, Emma. So I'd better get out while I've got the chance. It's the only way."

Perhaps, but not at the moment. Even as Gary spoke the car had turned around and was coming back toward the store. He saw the headlights reflected against the phone booth. "Dammit! Where's the back door, Emma?"

"No! Now, you listen to me, young man. Just get yourself in the back and stay there. I'll stay here and watch 'em."

"Emma—"

"You do what I say. Now. We ain't got time to argue."

Ten minutes passed before she returned to her quarters in the rear of the store. She was humming to herself as she turned out the lights in a perfectly natural manner, as if she hadn't even noticed the men outside. In the dark she whispered for Gary, who was hiding in the closet.

"What did they do?" he said.

"They stopped in front of the gas station. One of 'em got out for a minute, then got back in. They talked for a little bit, then shut off their car and the lights. They're just sitting there right now."

"Just *sitting* there?"

"Yes. I don't know, but my guess is that they might be thinking you're hiding in the station. They're either waiting for morning to go in, or waiting to see if you come out. So, you'd better stay put."

He was wondering how they had tracked him here. He didn't know, and he was in no mood to try to figure it out because it didn't matter; they were here. So was he. Emma was right; they might think he was in the station. And he'd better stay put.

"Know what else I think?" she asked.

"What?"

"I think you'd better stay awake tonight. And I think I'll stay awake just to make sure *you* do."

"I think you're right, Emma."

"Yep. If they hear you snoring, they'll be in here in a minute."

6

SHE COULDN'T HAVE BEEN SPEEDING—her old car would barely maintain the speed limit as it was. There were no stop signs or lights she had gone through, and she was sure she hadn't been driving recklessly.

Nevertheless, she coasted the Chevy onto the shoulder as the car with the red flashing lights followed, stopping at her rear bumper. Dammit, she sighed, why tonight? Why now? She reached for her purse and started digging for her license. Behind her she could hear the static and radio chatter from the police cruiser, and the thump of the door as the cop got out. He hitched up his pants and strode forward, the leather belt and holster creaking.

"Officer . . ." Oh, shit!

"Well! Good evening. I thought that was you." He put an arm against the roof and leaned toward the window.

"Hello, Randy," she said, sighing wearily. "What did I do?"

"Wrong, you mean? Well, the only thing I can think of is that you're in violation of a Section 555-8417—Failure to Return Telephone Calls. Unless you can think of something else." He smiled, pushing the Smokey the Bear hat back.

Cute. Real cute. That was his phone number. She knew it by heart; her mother had written it on the message pad so many times that she couldn't forget it. And neither her mother nor this jerk seemed willing to let her try.

Locking both hands around the wheel, Janey stared straight ahead. "I didn't know that was against the law," she muttered evenly. "Look, don't you have a couple of cattle rustlers to chase or something? This is a high-crime area, remember? Why are you bothering me?"

"Maybe it's because you bother me."

"Well, if that's illegal, then just give me a ticket and let me be on my way. I'm in kind of a hurry."

He shrugged. "If it was, I'd have you in the County Work Farm. But you can make it up by going out with me again."

Oh, dear God, why me? "Oh, that's real generous of you, Randy. But I'll have to pass. I've got this sick aunt in the Virgin Islands, and if I don't get there by tonight she'll cut me out of her will. So I *really* have to go, okay?" and she put the car in gear. "If I don't get back to you by the turn of the century, you call again and we'll see what we can work out. All right?" She blew him a kiss, then pulled back onto the highway.

Randy stood back and watched her drive away, noting that her rear license plate light was out. He thought for a moment about running her down and handing her a real ticket—the bitch would deserve it—but he didn't. He walked back to his car, got in and listened to the radio chatter for a minute before picking up the mike and calling in.

"No ticket issued," he told the dispatcher. "Verbal warning only."

"Okay, Randy. We have your report on the vehicle now, too. Ready to copy?"

"Go ahead."

"No wants or warrants. License and registration current. State vehicle inspection sticker current...and county tax registration current. Looks like a clean car. Did you suspect anything else?"

"Uhh...suspected possible DWI at first, but nothing to indicate that upon inspection of the vehicle or conversation with the driver. But she—the driver appears to be going somewhere in a very big hurry. She gave me an erroneous story for an explanation. Nothing illegal that I could see, no suspicions I could put my finger on. No apparent reason for further questioning. But . . . well, there was something about it I didn't like."

"Roger, suspected driving while impaired. Do you want me to notify the highway patrol to keep an eye on the car?"

"Uh . . . yeah, roger. Might not be a bad idea."

"Okay. Will do. Dispatch out."

"Unit 15 out. Returning to assigned patrol." He laughed. Okay, honey, if that's how you want it. You be sure to tell that aunt of yours in the Virgin Islands that we're real sorry about holding you up. But, as they say, win a few, lose a few.

NEARLY EIGHT HOURS LATER, nothing looked better to Janey than a couple of hours sleep. She was barely able to stay awake, and her continual yawning kept causing her eyes to water, making everything either fuzzy or blurry. She had already gone through half a box of Kleenex from wiping her eyes every two minutes. She had to have some black coffee and cold water before she wrapped the car around a tree.

The old car, on the other hand, seemed to be the one thing keeping her awake. She needed gas—and oil—and it was the latter that worried her; the old crate was beginning to suck oil like a diesel, and starting to smoke like one as well. Worse, about half an hour ago it had developed a peculiar deep-down sort of knocking in the engine. She didn't know if the Chevy would make it all the way to Kansas or not—probably not, she was beginning to feel. Even if it did, they'd never get all the way back to Montana. But she kept going anyway.

Which was the main reason she was still awake—Gary. Out of the blue, just like one of those stories from "The Twilight Zone," Gary had called. He was in trouble, he needed her, and therefore she would go to him. Not one other thing in the whole damn world mattered.

Ahead, the lights of a Shell station came into view.

The lights from a car behind her turned off at a side road. It was time for some coffee. Besides, the patrolman had been following the Chevy almost since it had entered Wyoming, and for no more reason than somebody had an unconfirmed suspicion of hanky-panky. And the hell with that.

7

THE ATTENDANT MIGHT HAVE BEEN a reasonably attractive young man if he bothered to shave, clean up and get rid of the ridiculous cowboy hat he sported jauntily on the back of his head. As it was he just looked goofy.

Janey caught a look at herself in the mirror. Well, she thought, you're no Playmate yourself.

"Morning," the attendant said brightly, giving her a wide smile, then leaning on one arm against the top of the car, which had to be his best macho pose—maybe he was related to Randy. "And what can I do for you?"

"Just fill it up," Janey said dully, not wanting to look at him. "Check under the hood, too."

"You got it." He winked, pointing a finger at her like a gun.

And that was all she needed. Why was it only nerds came on to her, and whenever she was in the least likely mood to listen? It had to be a family curse or something.

He showed her the dipstick, which indicated that she needed two quarts of oil. He also sounded as if he was beginning a short lecture about engine oil consumption, but she cut him off. "Just throw in two quarts of the cheapest, heaviest stuff you've got," she said, sighing.

He did; she paid; then she started off. She really wanted to take another look at the maps on the seat, but that could wait until she was down the road. If she heard any more devastating lines like those she'd been handed in the past few hours she might run over somebody.

Janey was looking for a spot to pull over before she got to the highway when the Chevy suddenly let go without warning. There was a loud bang followed instantly by a heavy, staccato *rat-tat-tat-tat-tat*. Oily blue smoke boiled from under the hood; the car coughed and lurched a couple of times as she guided it onto the shoulder where it shuddered to a stop. Now, she was wide awake.

Still in mild shock Janey got out and walked to the front of the car, opening the hood. Oil dribbled from the engine; there was a black, shiny trail on the road behind her, oozing from the concrete down into the weeds. Wisps of smoke wafted from the greasy old motor. The Chevy looked like an old dark green animal that had been mortally wounded—which, really, was what had just happened. The car was dead and would have to be dragged to its final resting place. Kansas—and Gary—were still six hundred miles away.

Her eyes watered again. "Oh, no-o-o-o!" she whimpered. Exhaustion, frustration and bitter helplessness all hit her at once. "You stupid old car! You damned old wreck!" She kicked the front tire, and did nothing more than hurt her toe.

The situation went from bad to worse a minute later when she noticed the gas station attendant running to her rescue. He slowed to a walk as he got to the car, smiling, pushing his hat back a bit farther, and looking as if this situation might somehow get him a date. This just wasn't her day at all. With a quiet moan, Janey braced herself; he must be ready to say something like, Hey, baby, got a problem?

Instead, "I saw what happened. Care if I have a look?"

"Help yourself." She shrugged.

"Oh, yeah," he announced. "Yeah, that's what I thought," and he came up from under the hood shaking his head dolefully. "You've had it. Here, take a look." He pointed to the lower left-hand side of the engine. "See that big hole? Where the oil's running out, and with that big hunk of metal sticking through? You threw a rod, right through the side of the block. There's probably a lot more damage you can't see."

"I don't suppose it can be fixed?" Janey asked, knowing perfectly well that it could not.

"Oh, no. No way. You need another engine. This one's ruined."

"Damn!" she groaned. "I need another car. I have to be somewhere by tonight. It's important."

"Well, you'll never make it in this thing. But . . . ah, I think I can help. If you're interested."

Oh, shit, here it comes. . . .

"I can take you into town. There's a couple of rental places where you can get another car. And I'd be willing to buy this one if the price is right."

"Buy it?"

"Yeah. Me and my brother buy old cars and fix 'em up and sell 'em. Or else junk 'em outright and sell the good parts." He began eyeing the old Chevy with that trader's look. "I think we could do something with this one. It's a little beat-up, but it's salvageable." When he looked at her again his smile suggested that she really had no choice. He had her over the proverbial barrel.

The last thing Janey wanted to do—or had ever thought she would be doing—was to horse-trade with some greasy gas jockey at six-thirty in the morning alongside a highway outside Casper, Wyoming. But she was about to do so.

"How much?"

He looked the car over again. "Fifty bucks."

She had more than that invested in it. "A hundred," she said flatly.

"No...no. I'd barely make anything on it. Fifty."

"Bullshit. You'd make at least that on the tires alone. A hundred."

Again, he stared at the car. "I'll meet you halfway. Seventy-five."

"Nope. One hundred."

"Look, I'll have to put another engine in it. That takes time and money. Seventy-five."

Janey reached into the back seat to get her overnight bag. When everything was slung over her shoulders, she said, "I'd like to get where I'm going by tonight. But it's not a matter of life or death. I'll bet I can find another junkyard that'll give me a hundred...maybe more. Do you have a pay phone up at that station?"

The attendant took off his hat and wiped his forehead with a sleeve. It was take-it-or-leave-it time. He sighed, disgusted with himself. "All right...okay. A hundred. Jeez, when my brother hears about this..."

"A hundred, and a lift into town."

"Okay, okay. But you'll have to wait till I get the wrecker and tow this thing back up to the station."

Janey allowed herself a tiny smile. "Of course."

"Come on. You can wait in the office."

"Does this town have a Western Union office anywhere? I'll have to tell my aunt that I'll be a little later than I thought."

"Yeah, downtown. But I ain't got time to be running you all over town."

"I didn't ask you to. I'll get another car and go myself."

Forty-five minutes later Janey was inside the Dairy Creame Donut Shop, waiting for 8:00 a.m. to arrive. She struck up a conversation with a Wyoming highway patrolman who gladly offered her a ride to the Western Union office and the American Car Rental agency. He'd had to rush off to visit sick old aunts himself.

CHAPTER ELEVEN

COLONELS GILMORE AND ATTWOOD had *thought* they were ready for the next phase of the KP Project. That was until they set foot on the summit.

"God Almighty!" Gilmore whispered. "What a mess."

"It didn't look this bad in any of the photos," Attwood added. Eight months and a harsh winter had not made it look any better.

Attwood found it difficult to believe that more than ten men had actually lived through the terrifying crash. And that had been only the beginning. After they had crawled from the wreck, what had they seen? What had they been thinking then? What had they been imagining? And after the sun was up, and they were able to see once and for all how hopeless their situation really was, what had they done then? Attwood wondered how one reacts to the apparent miracle of surviving such an ordeal only to learn that death might have been the better choice. And how do you act when all your friends around you are dying while you can only wait until your own injuries do you in, your turn no more than hours away? Yet that had happened here.

The two worst fears in a war, Attwood knew, are death or being horribly maimed. Most men, if not all, prefer the former. But many combat veterans develop a strange sense of isolation about them, a protective sort of shield through which they are offered an opaque view of death. Death is usually out there, just beyond reach, just outside the shield; a shadow in a dark green uniform, a shape without a face. But the face could be theirs. It might be their own image in the uniform. And since the specter is quite often within view, many men come to an arrangement with it; a sort of agreement, or perhaps a standoff. The next move always belongs to the faceless shape. And it may be through a sense of fatalism or familiarity or perhaps even a genuine disinterest that men sometimes lose their deepest fears of it. Maybe their number will come up next, and the silent specter on the other side of the shield will shatter it like a mirror, reaching through to claim his own. Maybe not. One never knows, and can never be certain. You might worry about death; you might laugh about it; you might ignore it or forget all about it. It might always be there, sometimes visible, sometimes not, but you're not quite so afraid of it.

No, real terror was what had occurred here on Mount Kota—knowing that they were going to die very soon, and being unable to do one single thing about it. Death was a worry, but it usually ran a distant second place to the scores of other demons and monsters lurking through the mossy corridors of the mind.

And one of them got loose inside that lieutenant's head, and something up here let it out.

Attwood pulled the hood on his parka a little tighter. "A lot of work up here," he muttered. "All of a sudden, I'm not sure where to start." It was a little like looking at the ocean—what you saw was only the top.

Gilmore opened a box that looked like a tackle box, and wedged it between a pair of rocks. It was a remote detector and recorder, which would sense atmospheric changes and variations of normal oxygen/nitrogen content in the air. This time tomorrow they would replace it with an identical box, and take this one back to the station for analysis; they were looking for percentage traces of Swamp Gas in the air. So far, they hadn't found quite the level they had assumed they would, and part of what they found had migrated down closer to Kota Station than they had expected. But none of that was cause for alarm, they thought, because the stuff simply stayed in the local atmosphere after contamination. It wouldn't go away; it rose and fell with the local precipitation and humidity.

Staring at the box after he had turned it on, Gilmore said, "This still isn't right. We should be getting higher readings than this. Hell, you don't just get rid of forty gallons of that stuff like you're tossing out the dishwater."

"Maybe the recorder isn't working right," Attwood replied.

"It's fine. I checked it out before we left."

"Turn up your volume." Attwood motioned, tapping his helmet. "I can hardly hear you." Under their parkas they wore full-head helmets similar to those worn by pilots, but with face shields attached and with respirators connected to oxygen reservoirs on their backs. The helmets also contained small radio transmitters and microphones with earphones attached inside. The men would not be breathing summit air at any time.

Gilmore repeated what he'd said about the recorder. "It still isn't right. The ambient concentration is way too low."

"Look, if the recorder's okay, then your reading has to be right. It's another quirk about the stuff. Hell, there's still quite a bit we don't know about it yet, you know." Attwood opened a cardboard box, and removed a handful of small, flat disks.

"There's your damn quirk," Gilmore said, pointing to the objects in his partner's hand. "How many of those things are you going to set out?"

Attwood shrugged, setting the first near the wreck. "Maybe half of them. Anyway, I don't see what you're so nervous about. You act like you don't want them to work."

"I don't. It's no act."

"Come on! You know what that gas is capable of, and if it happens up here, it's a scientific observation, nothing more. It'll confirm what happened in the lab back at Stanton. And we *have* to see if it happens." He set out another disk. Grinning, his eyes crinkling through the faceplate, he added, "Where's your sense of adventure, anyway? Didn't you ever go to horror movies when you were a kid?"

"Go to hell!" Gilmore got up, deciding to leave the recorder alone. "Hurry up, and let's get back to the station. We have a lot more to do than we thought, and we're going to have to plan this out a little more carefully."

He followed Attwood around the site, then down through Karber's Pass as he set out twenty-four of the half-dollar-size motion detectors. All that had to be done afterward was to turn on the receiver inside the station and adjust each frequency; each detector would register its own signal. The last one was set at the lower end of the pass. "That's it," Attwood said. "No need to bug the plateau."

"I hope we don't hear anything but the wind."

"Yeah, but if we do, we've got one of the damnedest weapons you've ever seen."

2

JANEY AWOKE WITH A START, grunting in pain as she cracked a knee against the steering wheel. Squinting, she wondered why it was so hot, and what she had just hit. Where was she? It was one thing to wake up in a strange bed, but quite another to wake up inside a strange car, and with no idea of where the car was parked.

Wherever it was, the place was alive with activity, people all around her, and a constant noise of vehicles coming and going. She wondered dimly if she had parked next to a bus terminal, and as she pulled herself upright, there really was a bus next to her. Then, she remembered; she had stopped in a rest area on Interstate 25 just north of Denver. She had driven from Casper, thinking that she would get to Denver, but couldn't stand it anymore; twice, she had almost fallen asleep at the wheel.

Stretching, sitting up, Janey glanced at her watch, then nearly went into a panic when she saw 7:22. "Oh, no!" she groaned, thinking that she had slept right on through until the next day. But, no...no, she decided. The sun was in the wrong position. Another look at the watch a few moments later told her it was stopped at 7:22. The second hand wasn't moving. She had forgotten to wind the stupid thing.

The rest area was busier than any shopping center the day before Christmas, and no wonder. This was vacationland, packed with tourists carrying cameras and travel brochures, all of them either hurrying kids into the rest rooms or hustling them back out to one of the dozens of campers, motor homes or travel trailers. In fact, her own hometown, Sioux Creek, would be looking like this shortly as throngs of tourists descended on Mount Kota National Park to visit—

No. Don't think about it.

She got out of the car to find herself standing next to a hulking tractor trailer pulling a load of bawling cattle. The truck idled quietly as its driver snoozed in the air-conditioned sleeper cab. One of the cows looked out through the slats at her and mooed sadly.

"I know how you feel," Janey said as she grabbed her case and locked the car. "I don't look any better than you do... or smell any better, either."

It was like Grand Central Station inside the ladies' room, and three times as noisy. A little girl of three or four was having a great time yelling at the top of her lungs and laughing as she heard the echoes; a fat lady dressed in a pair of awninglike striped shorts had brought her son into the rest room. Janey ignored them. She grabbed the first available washbasin, stripped off her rumpled, sweaty blouse and tried to clean up. She wasn't within a country mile of being presentable when she finished, but it would have to do. There was no time for make-up, and this was not the place. Trying to pull a brush through her hair only helped to make it look more bizarre than the wind had, rushing through it all night, so she pulled it into a fuzzy ponytail. Then she rushed back to the car. Twelve miles east of Denver she pulled off the highway for gas, and hamburgers from a grease pit next door. She could eat while she drove. It was already four-thirty, and there were still hours and nearly 400 miles ahead of her.

3

"...WAS ANCHORED IN, and he was coming over the edge. I saw his hand come up and feel around, so I yelled to tell him where to grab. And just like that, he was gone. His rope broke. He ended up bouncing like a yo-yo on the end of his safety line twenty feet below the roof, and *that* line was cut about halfway through. Man, I was sure we'd lost him until I felt the weight on the rope. So, I dug in and started feeding another rope down to him, and..."

So far, Gary had recounted nearly every single fact about his life that he could remember, from each level of grade school right up through college. He told Emma how he got his scholarship to the University of Washington, how he almost joined

Sigma Chi but decided on ROTC instead because the draft was looming steadily larger, and if he had to go in, he wanted in under the best possible circumstances. He talked about his four years in the Army; how he considered himself fortunate because he got the only job he wanted. With an occupational specialty like his, there were no worries about Vietnam. More than three and a half of his four years had been spent right there at Endicott.

Despite being difficult, his job was the most enjoyable thing they could have given him. It was rare being in the military and doing exactly what you wanted to do, and it was because of exactly the opposite that so many good men just put in their time, then told the military to kiss off. What made his job especially good was that each man on each team had to volunteer, then pass a series of tests and requirements to ensure his qualifications. It was one of the few jobs in the military you had to *want*, work your butt off to earn, then requalify for once every year. All of this ensured that they would maintain no fewer than twenty of the finest, most closely synchronized teams they could field. It had always been his pleasure, Gary said, to work with the finest. Most of what the military did was pure bullshit, but there were a handful of desirable positions if you could get them. He had actually considered staying in the service, but finally decided against it—it was too restrictive a life, and there were things he wanted to do that were available only to a civilian. Besides, this episode would sour anybody's outlook on anything to do with the military.

He went on to tell Emma about some of their missions, some of the mountains they had climbed, and a few of the rescues they had performed. He talked about Janey; some of the things he and she had done, and the plans they'd made. He talked about his family—his parents, two older brothers and younger sister; he recalled how his Uncle Jim, Uncle John and his father had introduced him to climbing. He talked about Janey's family; how he had met her older brother, Bill, Jr., and his family only once, her sister Julie twice, and how Janey complained about her mother, and how she had to get out of the house for good one of these days.

Emma took her turn, too, talking mostly about her family, starting with a few details about Marshal Daniel S. McCuddy of Dodge City, and some of the stories told about him. According to legend, he had known Pat Garrett and Bat Masterson; he had once been forced to participate in a real shoot-out on Main Street in Dodge, but it had been against some cowhand who got out of line, beating up a prostitute in a saloon, then taking a shot at one of the deputies. Many of the old western towns, she said, weren't nearly as lawless as TV and movies would have you believe. She talked about her late husband and their daughter, and what a hell-raiser they had thought she was going to be until she married a Methodist minister from Denver and settled right down. Now Emma worried about her grandson, who appeared to be just like his mother.

Emma talked about life here in Martin Flats, which was, as one of the local men once said, a "non-town." She talked about her neighbors, how all of the young people had moved out, and how most of the population were more than fifty years of age. When someone died these days there was no one to move into the empty house, and all you had to do was just look around to see all the empty houses and buildings and abandoned businesses. Once, this village had been an active little place nearly ten times its present size. Hers was the only place of business left, besides that of a man who operated a fleet of dump trucks.

Emma and Gary talked quietly through the night. They were still talking when dawn finally arrived.

And the two men in the dark green Plymouth sedan were still outside.

"In a while, I'll go out and see what they want," Emma said.

"I know what they want."

"Well, they're trespassing. If they give me any trouble I'll sic the sheriff on 'em."

But she never got the opportunity to sic anybody on the two strangers. When she opened the store at seven, they came in.

They seemed friendly enough, smiling and fairly talkative even though they had just spent the night in their car. Emma assumed they had already searched the old station. They opened small wallets and showed her identification cards. She didn't catch their names, but both cards said United States Government across the tops above their photographs. Pretending to busy herself with dusting some of the shelves, Emma asked what they wanted.

They came right to the point. "We're looking for somebody," Caldwell said. "We were wondering if you or anybody else around here have seen any strangers in the past day or two. We have reason to believe that the man we're after is here someplace."

"Nope," she said with a shrug. "I haven't seen anybody who doesn't belong here . . . except you two."

Both of them smiled. Eaton said, "We thought he might be hiding out in one of the empty buildings here, which was why we were waiting outside last night. We thought we might be able to catch him coming out of one of them under cover of darkness."

"We hope you don't mind, but we took a look in that old gas station next door, too. That is your station, isn't it, ma'am?"

"Yes. It's mine. But if there'd been anybody trying to hide in there, I would've heard 'em. And I would have sicced the sheriff on 'em. Now, who is this feller you boys are looking for? An escaped convict or something? Is he dangerous?"

"He isn't exactly a convict, just a runaway that the government is interested in. And he isn't really dangerous. At least not that we know of."

"But we would like very much to find him, ma'am. So any information you could give us would be appreciated. You'll be helping your government."

"Is there a reward out for this guy?"

Now they glanced at each other and smiled. "I don't think anybody mentioned a reward, ma'am," Caldwell replied. "But we'll see what we can do. I imagine the government wouldn't object to some kind of compensation."

"Well," Emma said, sighing, "that sounds okay, but like I said, I haven't seen anybody. Now, I can't vouch for all the folks here in town, but you can bet that if one of my neighbors saw a stranger coming through, then all the rest of us would know about it in short order. You don't keep many secrets in a town this little. But you'd best ask 'em yourselves."

"All right, ma'am. We'll do that. Thank you."

"Oh, and we'll need your name, too, for our report," Eaton said, pulling out a notepad and pen. Emma also saw a shoulder holster and the butt of an automatic pistol tucked under his jacket. But she didn't see Caldwell as he palmed her dust cloth and slipped it inside his jacket.

"Lockhart. Mrs. Emma Lockhart."

Caldwell waved. "Thanks for your help, Mrs. Lockhart." He handed a piece of paper to her. "If you do happen to see or hear of anything, please call this number and just tell them the information. They won't ask your name. And it's a toll-free number so you won't be charged for the call."

"Yes . . . I'll do that."

"Thanks again, Mrs. Lockhart."

"Yes, thanks. You've been a big help."

She stood at the door and watched them as they pulled away, but they didn't visit any of the neighbors. They talked on their two-way car radio for a minute, then drove west straight out of town. When it was at the village limit, the dark green car roared off.

She told Gary what had happened when she saw him standing at the back of the store. "I—I don't know if I helped, or somehow told them you were here, Gary." She trembled. "I didn't like the way they were acting, like . . . like they knew something all along that I didn't."

Gary put his arms around her. "Emma, you did just fine. Just fine. If they thought I was here they wouldn't have left. They'd have called for reinforcements, and started taking the place apart board by board. I think you just got rid of them."

He hoped. At this point he was still guessing about everything. All he might have done was to get this innocent lady involved in more trouble than she had ever seen.

"Son of a bitch!" Eaton muttered. "Well, that's what we get for going so goddamn fast and not stopping to think sooner. Now he's gotten away. He was there, but he's gone now. Goddammit!"

Caldwell stared at the piece of white cotton cloth. It was streaked with patches of dirt and dust and smelled heavily of

Lemon Pledge—an ordinary dust cloth until you turned it over. Which was what that old lady had done when she leaned across the counter to look at their IDs. When Eaton saw it, he had carefully slipped it into his jacket pocket. On its opposite side was an embroidered Army Medical Corps caduceus—the dust cloth had, a couple of days ago, been a left breast pocket of a white smock, part of that Wheeler orderly's uniform. So they had been right all along. Palmer had made it to Martin Flats where that old lady had helped him.

"Maybe we ought to go back and question her some more. She might know—"

"She wouldn't know anything we couldn't guess or that we don't already know. That kid is a lot smarter than we thought. My guess is that while we were sitting there last night waiting for him to make a move, he'd already made it. He's long gone."

"Maybe not. He might still be on foot, you know. So he couldn't be too far away."

"Or somebody drove him out, and I'm betting that's what happened."

"But who? We've got everybody covered."

"We missed somebody, my friend."

"Then maybe that old lady could tell us who. Let's go back and talk to her. Or else we'll be out here running in circles again."

"I doubt it. Look, he had to have contacted a friend or relative, and they came and got him. But that old lady won't know who it was because Palmer's too smart to trust anybody that much. He must have left last night before we got here, and I'm betting he arranged to meet 'em out here in the sticks somewhere so that nobody would see it. Not even that old lady. Now, we've gotta figure out who it was, and where they went." And they would have help for that. In a few hours all sixteen members of the search party would descend on western Kansas. They would meet somewhere, plan their further moves, then fan out again, covering this end of the state, plus Colorado, Nebraska or anywhere else they had to go.

"I don't know..." Caldwell mumbled. "I still think we're assuming a hell of a lot."

4

SIMPLE FATIGUE FINALLY PUT Gary to sleep just after noon. He
didn't think he would be able to sleep, but he dozed off in less
than two minutes, and slept until nearly six. Emma waited on
a few customers, most of whom wondered why she seemed so
edgy; all of them wanted to gossip for a while, and *who* was in
that strange car parked next to the store all night? My good-
ness, Emma, you don't have a couple of boyfriends you haven't
told us about, have you? Well, no, of course not. They were
working for the government, but they didn't say what they were
doing; they just bought a few things and left. But that was just
like the government, not to tell anybody what they were up to,
and as long as it didn't concern her, then she wasn't going to
ask.

And all the time Emma kept watching the road, hoping that
the dark green car, or others like it, wouldn't come swooping
down on her place—or that the young man in the back
wouldn't suddenly begin snoring.

She woke Gary in time for supper. He didn't seem to have
much of an appetite, but that was understandable what with
those men running all over the country looking for him. And
what men those two had been! They were exactly as Gary had
described, just as nice and friendly, and just as sneaky. She
wouldn't have trusted them any farther than she could have
thrown this building. Something else was on her mind, too—his
young lady friend. She smiled about that. She remembered
feeling very much the same way years ago when she was being
courted. Food doesn't count for much when you're excited
about that special someone. Gary managed to get down one
drumstick, a few peas and about half of his mashed potatoes.
He apologized for not being able to finish.

"I understand." She smiled. "Now. It'll be dark before too
long, so you'd better keep an eye out for ... Janey, did you say
her name was?"

"Yes. Janey." The thought hit him like a truck: My God.
She'll actually be here in a few hours. Janey will actually be
here. Now he was nervous. He felt like a kid on Christmas Eve,
sure he wouldn't be able to stand the wait. "Uhh ... Emma, at

least let me help with the dishes or something. It's the very least I can do. I've gotta do something to keep occupied or I'll go right out of my mind."

"No. You get on out of here."

"Really, I'd like to help—"

"No. If there's one thing I've never tolerated it's a man messing around in my kitchen. Men are allowed in here to eat, but that's all. Now, scat."

"But—"

"No. You heard me. Out. Besides, someone might see you at the window. We've gotten you this far, and as my husband would've said, don't screw it up now. So, git."

JANEY CHECKED THE MAP AGAIN. Yes, she thought, this was the right road. This was it. Just another thirty or thirty-five miles to go—just down the road and around the corner. She wanted to ask the attendant about Martin Flats; where it was, exactly, what it looked like, and to assure herself that she was really this close to it. Was this old road map really right? She was so nervous that she was no longer sure if she was in Kansas.

What would Gary look like after all this time? What would he be like? He had sounded like himself on the phone, but that had been a four-minute conversation that occurred a thousand years ago. And how did she look? You are a godawful mess, that's how. You look like Jane of the Jungle. What would he think of her? Would everything still be the same between them once the initial shock was over? Would he still want her, or—

"Huh?" she said, jumping in the seat. "I—I'm sorry, what was that?"

"I said, that's nine dollars, ma'am. Will that be cash, or charge?"

"Umm . . . cash. Just a minute . . . here," and she fished out a twenty from a wad of tens, then realized he had said nine dollars. Shaking, she gave him one of the tens, and told him to keep the change. She told herself to settle down and relax before she went off like a bomb.

"Thank you, ma'am. Come back again."

"Sure, I'll do that," she muttered, exhaling deeply, now more nervous than ever.

As NIGHTFALL CAME, Gary found himself pacing in front of the door. Every two minutes he checked the highway for approaching headlights, seeing a few coming from both directions, and seeing the cars turn off to one house or another. A pair of pickup trucks drove on through town.

What would Janey look like? he wondered. What would she be like? Would their relationship be any different because of what had happened to him?

The past eight months hadn't been months at all. He hadn't given it much thought until now but it was as if he had fallen asleep and awakened a week and a half ago. The mission up Kota had occurred perhaps three or four weeks before.

Eight months.

And now, he and Janey were down to hours, maybe only minutes. He also wondered what they would do when she got here. He didn't have a plan to speak of, no place to go. He had simply broken out and ran, and now he had involved the one person he loved most in the world in this madness. For that matter, he still didn't know the actual depth of all of this yet, only that it somehow tied in with that disastrous mission up Kota to the crash site. All he really knew was what those people back at Wheeler had told him. So, what he needed was a good tactical plan that would not only keep him out of the Army's hands, but would allow him to unravel everything. And he would have to think of something fast because Janey would be here in a little while, and when they were on the move again he wouldn't be able to stop or run in circles. He had to know exactly where to go and what to do.

He started pacing again.

JANEY ALMOST DROVE past Route 94, the turnoff to Martin Flats. She noticed the sign in her headlights only as she went by it, then slammed on the brakes and ended up askew in the middle of the road. Only after her tire-bawling stop did she think to look in the mirror—fortunately, no one was behind her, or they would have rear-ended her for sure. The only other vehicle on the road was coming from the opposite direction. It had to weave off the road to get around her car still sitting cockeyed on the pavement; the driver rolled down his window as if about to say something. But he thought better of it, shook his head at yet another pathetic nut allowed out on the highways and drove on.

Janey waited until he was gone to back up. The sign appeared in the headlights once again.

MARTIN FLATS 5
ROUTE 115-104 8

That was it. And there she was, her stomach tightening, her whole body beginning to tremble. Her teeth were actually starting to chatter. She had never been this nervous about anything in her life.

Relax...you know what'll happen, dummy. You'll bawl and snivel and slobber and make a total ass of yourself.

Her knees were shaking so badly that her foot slipped off the brake pedal. The rented Chevy lurched forward, and she jammed on the brakes again. It was a good thing there were no cops out here to see this, she thought. But she couldn't control the trembling.

"Come on, get your ass moving, honey," she finally whispered in front of a deep sigh. And she turned the car east onto Route 94.

EXCEPT FOR THE FEEBLE STREETLIGHTS and what few lights were on in houses here and there, Martin Flats was completely dark.

Gary leaned against the door frame. He could hear a dog woofing, and the laughter of children playing some kind of game. A little girl screamed excitedly, calling to somebody else; a second dog joined in the fray.

God, how long had it been since he thought about the games he had played as a kid? One of the best he ever knew came one sultry July night when he was ten, and eighteen or twenty kids from all over the neighborhood got together for a super game of Kick the Can. It had gone on for hours, and he ran and hid and booted that Del Monte number 6 peach can five or six times until sweat poured and he was exhausted. And he was

never It. Not once. It was the only time he'd played Kick the
Can without being It.

More laughter came from across the road.

There had been other nights after he and his buddies were a
little older, and they used to creep around looking for girls to
scare—before they discovered how *not* to scare them—or flipping for sodas down at old man Jackson's Gulf station. And
how long had it been since he thought of old man Jackson? Or
his medieval station?

He'd had a soda pop cooler just inside the door, a badly
rusted water-filled container with a broken coin box. You had
to reach inside the icy water for a bottle, and give the old man
your dime. The station, eternally crowded, always smelled like
oil and gasoline and pipe tobacco; things were piled on something else that was atop something else, and they seemed to be
permanent fixtures rather than items for sale. There were fan
belts and parts for long-defunct automobiles, and National
Recovery Act and World War II posters still on the walls. And
there was old man Jackson himself, growling at every kid who
came into the place, or complaining to two or three other men
who were there day and night. But that old man could fix any
bicycle in five minutes, no matter what was wrong with it, and
after Gary got his first car—a beat-up 1949 Chevy with bald
tires and a smoking engine, the first place he took it was to
Jackson's station. The old man taught him a hundred little-
known details and peculiarities of a 1949 Chevrolet, and it was
like pumping up bicycle tires or sticking his hand into that
freezing water all over again.

The old man had died when Gary was a junior in college. His
Gulf station was bulldozed, and a McDonald's sat there
now…and no bottle of Pepsi or Royal Crown or Hires root beer
would ever taste quite the same. No group of kids anywhere
would ever be able to get up a game of Kick the Can like that
one had been. And right now, after all was said and done, Gary
would give anything for the chance of being It just one more
time.

What do you mean? You are *It. You're It in one hell of a way
and in one hell of a game, and if you get caught this time, no-*

*body will ever see your can out and about again. You'd better
stay hidden real good, boy.*

A woman's voice called to the kids in the yard across the road
and through the trees. One of them gave her the proverbial argument: Aww, Mom, do we *have* to? We're not tired. . . .

Gary smiled, then took another look at the road.

MARTIN FLATS
Population 50
Elevation 2245

JANEY'S HEART WAS HAMMERING. She was trying to study each
building she came to, and just barely managing to keep the car
in a straight line. What was it Gary had told her? Something
about the far east end of town and a gas station, but at that
moment she wasn't sure which way was up or down. She was
trying to drive, watch in both directions, look for some kind of
building—a store or gas station, or something—and make sure
she didn't drive off the road or run into someone. It was too
much under the circumstances.

She tried to concentrate. Over there was a store of some
kind . . . an empty building . . . another abandoned building . . . two houses over there . . . two trucks and a car parked
there . . . another old store on the left . . . something that used to
be a station of some kind . . . houses, lights . . . And she found
herself at the far end of town, heading toward the dark plains
and faint lights far to the east. She stopped in the middle of the
road, unable to figure out how she had missed the target. She
turned the car around for another look, trying again to think
of what Gary had said. What was it? An old store. An old store
next to an abandoned station with junk all around it, and just
beyond the bushes were—

Piles of junk . . . next to a . . .

Station. And right there on the other side of it was a gray
clapboard building with a faded sign hanging over the porch—
Lockhart's Dry Goods & General Sundries.

Oh God . . .

And somebody was outside on the porch, next to the phone booth . . . a head peeking cautiously around the corner, looking at her, her rented car. . . .

Oh God, is that . . .

The figure waved, and now she could see his face in the light. A wild, joyous sob of relief burst from her throat as tears flooded both eyes, and she stood on the accelerator, almost hitting the old wooden porch as the car slid to a halt in the gravel. She leaped out, and the figure ran toward her.

5

"ARE YOU SURE YOU CAN'T stay for just a while?" Emma asked for the third time. "You've had a long, hard trip, young lady. You should rest."

Sniffling, Janey smiled and shook her head. She couldn't imagine how in the world Gary ever got here, or how this kindly old lady had befriended him and taken him in. It would be hours before she would be able to ask. Right now, it just didn't matter. She had Gary back. Nothing else mattered.

And they couldn't stay any longer. There was no time for rest until they were well away from this village. The wrong people couldn't be too far away, and if Janey's rented car was seen by too many locals who started asking too many questions, the wrong people would hear about it in short order. So far they had been lucky. They wouldn't be able to push their luck much farther, and there was no time to lose.

"Do you know yet where you're going?" Emma asked Gary. They were such a nice young couple, and she hated to think of them being chased all over the country like a pair of common criminals. And she wished she could do something more than just give them a big smile and wish them well.

"I have a couple of ideas," Gary fibbed with a smile. He reached out to give her another big hug, and he, too, was wishing there was more he could do for her than just leave her behind, possibly to face a wolf pack. If they found out that he had really been here, and she had hidden him, they might make life pretty tough on her. In a very big way it would be almost like leaving a member of his own family behind; and he did not want this to be a permanent goodbye. "Don't worry, Emma. We'll be fine." He was beginning to sniffle again with the women. He hadn't bawled like this since he was a kid.

"Don't tell me not to worry. I'll worry until I hear from you two."

"I'll call just as soon as I can, Emma. I'll have to get some things sorted out, and try to get a few answers. It might take a while. I don't know. But I'll let you know how we're doing just as soon as I can."

Emma patted him, then pushed him away. "I know you will. Now, then, I suppose you're right. You'd better get moving. Like I said, I didn't like those two snakes this morning, so you'd better go before they decide to come back. Run along. And be careful."

And there were no waves or honking horns or calls from open car windows as the red and white Impala drove quietly away into the west—only the disappearance of its lights.

Standing alone on her front porch, Emma Lockhart wiped away another tear. She offered her visitors a small prayer.

IN ROOM 24 OF THE Commanche Motor Lodge in La Crosse, sixteen CID agents were studying the latest information they had about Lieutenant Gary Palmer. Special Agents Eaton and Caldwell were doing most of the talking, adding their own experiences and observations about the past two days. A large map had been taped to the wall.

It had been simple enough, they told everybody. Palmer had had plenty of time to make it to that little town of Martin Flats. An old lady had taken him in, given him a change of clothes, and he had contacted someone who came to get him. Now he was gone; now they had to figure out where he had gone.

"So we're still at square one," one of them said, sighing. "We're still chasing him rather than going to wherever he's headed."

"Not if we can figure out who picked him up," Eaton said. "So, two of us will go back to Martin Flats and check up on the general population to see if anybody's missing. If one of them took him somewhere, we'll know where. On the other hand, if it was a stranger—and I think that's who it was—some of the rest of us will have to figure out who. We thought we had a track on all of Palmer's friends and relatives, but we missed somebody. Caldwell and I will start checking on that."

"You mean, if we know who picked him up, we'll have an idea of where he's going?"

"Right."

"Why not just ask that old lady?"

"You ask her, Johnson. Because I'm putting you in charge of checking that town again—you and Wicks."

"You're the boss."

"I don't think she knows who it was. I think he contacted...whoever, then slipped out of town just ahead of Caldwell and me. He probably met them out in the country, out of sight, because I doubt if he would have trusted anybody that far. Even if he did, and he knew that we were after him, he would know that we'd get the information out of anyone helping him. So, I don't think he told anybody who was coming to get him."

"You sound pretty sure of yourself, Eaton."

Eaton shrugged eloquently and leaned back against the wall. "Berry, if you have any ideas, the rest of us are all ears. Let's hear 'em."

"Well, based on Palmer's past performance, he's keeping things pretty simple. Which to me means that he's thinking on the run, that he hasn't got time to work out anything too elaborate. I think he's out there on foot."

"He might be. And you're gonna find out if that's true. That's your assignment—checking the back roads, checking for hitchhikers, checking all the cross-country truckers who might have picked somebody up. All the truck stops, bars and one-hole dives. Anyplace a drifter might go. You, Blake, and any two other guys you select. Are there any more ideas?"

"If somebody came to get him, they'll have to give him some money, or else have enough for both of them. If you get a handle on that, you'll be closer to knowing who it was...or you'll know exactly who it was."

"Okay, Chambers, that'll be your job. Maybe one of his relatives got away without our knowing about it. Or a close friend. Do a recheck on all the people on that list, plus any-body else you come up with. Anything else?''

Nobody spoke.

''Okay. Let's get moving.''

All of them filed out of the room, muttering to one another. This was the damnedest assignment they had ever seen—one man, and they just couldn't seem to guess what he would do next. If they hadn't known better they would have sworn he was sitting back somewhere laughing his ass off at all of them. They were no closer to getting him than when they'd started.

''Where will you and Caldwell be?'' one of them said, stop-ping in the doorway.

''Right behind you.''

When he was gone, Caldwell asked, ''Where will we be, anyway?''

''We're heading straight to the nearest FBI field office,'' he said, pulling the map down from the wall. ''We're missing something about that boy, and I want to know what it is.''

They collected their things and walked out onto the bal-cony.

''Busy place,'' Caldwell said as they headed downstairs to the car.

''Tourist season.''

''OKAY, THANK YOU, Mrs. Burns,'' said the woman behind the desk. ''How long will you and your husband be staying?''

''Just overnight.''

''All right. Checkout's at 11:00 a.m. After that, we have to charge for another full day.'' She handed Janey the key. ''We have to hustle everyone out so we can get the rooms cleaned in time for the afternoon rush.'' The woman smiled. ''Tourist season, you know. And room 12 is down at the far end of this wing, ground floor.'' Then she sat back down with her copy of *Blazing Romances*, paying no further attention to Mrs. Burns.

Gary was nervous about staying at such a public place, but trying to sleep in the car wouldn't be resting at all. And both of them badly needed a good night's rest.

''Hey, sport,'' she said, smiling as she got back in the car. ''You're not sleeping already, are you?''

"Sleep will be in short supply until this thing's over."

"Well, we can sleep tonight." She pulled away from the door, patting Gary's leg at the same time. "Among other things, of course—" She slammed on the brakes. "Oh, shit!"

Less than three feet from the left front fender, another car screeched to a rocking halt.

"Pay attention, you dumb broad," Janey muttered at herself. She smiled sheepishly at the other driver, who waved at her and went on. "Sleep... definitely. I need sleep."

"Among other things..."

"GODDAMN WOMEN DRIVERS!" Caldwell said as he smiled at the driver of the other car.

Eaton turned around in the seat, noting the Wyoming tags on the red-over-white Chevy Impala. "They must be on their honeymoon," he said. "No wonder she wasn't paying attention."

                              6

AND SO, GENERAL GRADY was informed, Lieutenant Palmer had apparently given the CID the slip. All sixteen agents were combing the country, looking under every rock for him and trying to pick up a trail, but he had vanished. They couldn't imagine where, even though they didn't want to admit it.

"What about that old lady you said helped him? What was she able to tell them?"

"Nothing. She was gone."

"Gone?"

"A couple of the neighbors thought she went to Denver to visit her daughter, but when they checked on the Denver address, no one was home there, either. Neighbors there thought that that minister, his wife and son, and an older lady they understood was his mother-in-law, had gone on vacation. Nobody knew where."

"If they knew where Palmer was, how did he get away from them?" Grady asked.

That was explained.

He laughed. It wasn't supposed to be funny, but it was. One of the bases they forgot to cover had been stolen by a runner who wasn't supposed to be in the lineup.

I think we've pretty well got everything covered.

"What do you want me to do about this?" He stifled another laugh.

Nothing. They just wanted him to know. And they wanted to know how everything was going with the KP Project.

"The project is fine. It's the transportation up and down to it that's just turned to shit."

"EVEN IF IT'S 99.99 PERCENT perfect out of the factory, General," the company representative said, "there could still be something like five hundred things wrong with it. Your flight crew was right to ground it. It can't fly like that."

And Grady couldn't even say why the helicopter's reliability was so critical at that moment—security. The KP Project. Questions were to be kept at a minimum. Those with no need to know would not. All he could do was stand there like a dimwitted idiot and stare helplessly at the exposed mazes of pipes, tubes and miles of wiring that made it go—or didn't.

"What's wrong with it?"

"As far as I can tell right now, the problem seems to be in the intake turbos," the rep said, pointing at some mysterious object deep inside the mechanical innards. "There was a design problem with it to begin with. Some of the engineers thought it might cause trouble after a certain number of hours in the air."

"Well, why didn't they fix it, or design something better?"

"They didn't have time. Somebody high, high up wanted this ship as soon as they could get it. There was no time for changes. They just slapped it together. It's a prototype...or, really, a *proto*-prototype. It's an oddball. They'll never build a production model this way." He explained some of the problems the pilots had noticed, particularly high-altitude control and lack of power. They were going to try to modify it right on the spot, but it would take time and money.

"How much time?"

The rep walked over to the exposed engine. "That's hard to say. You see, what you've got here is an engine that sucks about thirty times as much air as it does fuel. The higher it goes, the less air there is. So, the decrease in air pressure has to be compensated for, and that's the reason for the intake turbos. They provide the engines with adequate air pressure by compressing and injecting additional air and volume through a pair of compensation valves that modulate as the ship goes up and down, and when these valves open up..."

Waving a hand, Grady shook his head. "Hold it, hold it, son," he said. It was just like an engineer to lecture you on how to build a goddamn clock when all you wanted was the time. "Back up. Just tell me how long it'll take to get it airborne again. It's important."

The representative stared off into space for a moment. It was a waste of time trying to explain anything complex to a nontechnical person. If a device had more than two moving parts it was beyond their comprehension. "I don't know," he said, sighing. "It's not like fixing a bicycle. Whatever we do will be a real Rube Goldberg arrangement." He thought about it again. "Four... five days, maybe. If we're lucky."

"All right. Get started. Get whatever and whoever you need. I'll make any arrangements to get parts and people here, but I'll need a list. Work on this thing around the clock until it's flying again," and he turned to leave.

"Around the clock?"

"Yes. It's urgent." He left the hangar before anybody could ask why. He got twenty feet out the door when a runner came to fetch him. There was an urgent message from Kota Station.

7

"RUDI, BE CAREFUL UP THERE... what are you doing? You'll fall... you'll fall, Rudi, get away from there..."

"That was the whole idea, Lieutenant Palmer."

"Doug? Doug, where are you? Rudi's in trouble... Rudi's... in..."

"...trouble. Get back away from... there...."

"Gary?"

"...you'll fall, Rudi, you'll fall off...."

"Gary! Wake up. You're having a dream. Wake up!"

"...you'll fall...."

"Wake *up*!"

"...you'll...huh?" He sat up in the bed.

"You were having a dream. Are you all right?"

Breathing heavily for a minute, he fell back down against the sheets. They were soaked. He felt Janey's hand stroking his hair, and he saw her leaning over him. It was okay now; it had just been another dream. "Yeah, I'm okay," he whispered with a gulp. "I'm fine." He took Janey's hand in his own.

"Are you sure?"

He nodded. "Yeah. I just have this dream once in a while, that's all. The same one...or a continuation of the same one."

"Do you remember any of it?"

"A little," and he swung both feet out onto the floor. "It's me...and Gorham and Gurdler. We're always at the summit of Kota, and they're trying to show me something, I think. Except that they're dead, and I'm alive, but they're still trying to talk to me, and show me...*something*. But I don't know what it is. I've had it three or four times since I came to, back in that loony bin. The doctors didn't say much about it, only that I might have a lot of dreams for a while."

"It sounds like it has something to do with what happened to you up there. As if you remember subconsciously, but that it's twisted, and it can't quite get out."

He got up and padded into the bathroom. "That's what I thought, too. The doctors pumped me for over a week, trying to get me to recall anything about that time at the summit, but they didn't place much faith in what I told them I was dreaming. And now that I think about it, I believe they were badgering me just to make sure I *couldn't* remember anything before turning me over to...whoever."

She sat up in bed, propping her chin against her knees. "That doesn't make much sense."

"Nothing that's happened so far makes much sense," he said over the running water.

"I mean, I did some reading on dreams one time, and how to interpret certain things from your own dreams and nightmares. It said that a recurring dream in which somebody is trying to tell you, or show you, something might mean that you have a guilt complex; that you could be subconsciously blaming yourself about the outcome of an event. You feel guilty because you didn't take action where it was necessary, or you feel that the event was partly your fault. Sometimes, even if the occurrence was out of your control you still might feel guilty because you didn't suffer or pay the same price for its consequences as somebody else."

"Jesus!" He laughed, coming out of the bathroom. "You sound like one of those shrinks. What have you been doing the past eight months?"

"I told you what I've been doing—nothing. Nothing except going to work and coming home again. And listening to Mom complain about how I'm not doing anything." When Gary lay back down next to her, she threw a leg over one of his, moving it up and down gently. "And chasing after oddball lieutenants who call up from Kansas in the middle of the night."

"You didn't even go out?"

She shrugged. "A couple of movies. I had one date...the only one. I told you about him once. The cop. God, what a jerk."

"Did you get horny?"

"A little." She giggled. He hadn't changed at all.

"We've got about seven or eight hours to checkout time."

"Okay, but if you start yelling again, I'm gonna stuff a pillow over your head. Or snoring. Your snoring could bring the plaster down."

"It must be true. You're the third person to tell me that. But I won't yell again." He smiled, bending down to kiss her. "I promise."

"Good."

"Just an occasional yahoo...or maybe a yippee..."

AT SEVEN-THIRTY THEY WERE SHOWERING and getting dressed. Janey listened as Gary detailed the experiences on the mountain up until the final climb to the summit when everything had gone blank, and what he knew of the past few days since he woke up inside Wheeler Barracks. It took nearly an hour to relate everything as he remembered it; the rest was a black void. It wouldn't have been hard for him to believe it hadn't happened at all.

"Those doctors gave me every physical and mental test they had," he said. "A lot of them two or three times. The only thing they could find was wrong was no memory of the time at the crash site. They tried to force it out, like I told you, but I couldn't recall anything."

"How did you find out that they were going to send you away somewhere else?"

"Blind shithouse luck. I happened to overhear it. The day before I was going to be sent who-knows-where, I heard the chief psychiatrist tell one of his toadies that they were shipping me out the next morning. So I started to look for a way out, and I thumped that orderly. God, I hated doing that to him. He was a nice kid. But I had to get out of there, and that was the only chance I got."

Pulling on her jeans, Janey paused and asked, "Now, I've gotta ask the same question Emma Lockhart asked: Where do we go from here? What's next?"

The time had arrived: move it or lose it. He had to come up with an idea right now. "I've been thinking about it. Everything comes back around to the plane crash, and the mountain. I don't know what the puzzle is because too many pieces are missing; I don't know what killed Gorham and Gurdler, or why it didn't kill me; I don't know why I ended up in a place like Wheeler. But all of it is tied to the crash, and whatever we ran into when we walked onto the site." When he looked directly at Janey again, the decision had suddenly been made—not that there was much of a choice.

Janey wasn't moving. She said nothing.

"Kota. That's it. I'm going back to Kota."

She blinked once, and sat down on the bed. "Are you sure you're all right? Kota? Did I hear that right?"

"You heard it right." He said it distantly, as if he couldn't believe it himself. Maybe he really *was* crazy.

"Why don't I just drive you back to Wheeler?"

"Hold on, let me explain—"

"I wish you would!"

"It's the only place where I'll get any answers. Look at the facts . . . what they've done to me. You said they declared me dead. Last night you said that they've got the whole goddamn mountain under guard. I'm right in the middle of something in a big, big way, and I'd like to know what it is. Maybe I'm the key to this, whatever it is, and that could be why I was declared dead, so I could be kept under lock and key while they . . . studied me, or something. Don't you see, Janey? We may not know the name of the game, but the ground rules are fairly clear now. It all started on Kota, and that's where it has to end."

He had a point, and she could see it. She didn't like it, but Gary had nailed it. "But how—"

"I just thought of something else: Kota is the last place where they'd expect me to go. And it's the one spot in the world where they'd never be able to reach me."

"You're going too fast. Gary, whatever happened up there killed Gorham and Gurdler. It put you in the funny farm for eight months. What if it kills you this time? What will that prove? And, like I said, they've got the whole mountain guarded, something like twenty or thirty guard stations all around the base. How would you get past them? And even if you did, could you climb that thing again? You've only been up once, and you can't even remember how you got back down. What about all of that?"

He was quiet for a minute. "All right. Where would *you* go? What would *you* do?"

"Good question." She sighed after a long moment, and shook her head. "I don't know."

"Well, that's it, then. I don't know what else to do. I don't even know if I can do it, and I'll have to make things up as I go along. But I can't see any other choice." He got up from the bed and walked to the window. "I can't think of one other logical thing for me to do."

"Us."

"Us?"

"Us," and she looked at him with those dark eyes boring into him like two lasers. "We. The two of us. If you go up Kota again, so do I."

"Hey, whoa, wait a minute. Who the hell said anything about both of us going up Kota?"

"I did. Just now. You go, I go."

"Hold it, hold it," he said, arms waving. His towel fell off. "Look, I don't know if *I* can get up there, and it'd be stupid to risk your life, too. No, I can't do that."

"You listen to me, soldier boy, I've gone to a lot of trouble to get you back. You ain't gonna get rid of me that easily, no way. You said that I'm probably already in trouble just by coming to get you, just by knowing your whereabouts. So, forget it. If you climb Kota, I'm going with you. And I'm not such a bad climber myself, you know. So don't send me home while you go off on this crazy windmill, buddy. Or I'll just take my rented car and leave you stranded here." In a softer voice she said, "Please don't send me home."

"You're even crazier than I am." But he was smiling as he said it.

"Then we're stuck with each other."

"I wouldn't call it a laughing matter."

"I'm laughing because you look silly trying to make a point in your birthday suit."

He hadn't noticed that his towel fell off. "Well, I still mean it."

"So do I. You're stuck with me, nature boy."

8

THE FBI FIELD OFFICE IN HAYS was cooperative; the place was theirs, Eaton and Caldwell were told. Was there anything the personnel there could do for them? They had heard about a CID manhunt in progress.

"How did you guys hear about it?"

"We're the FBI."

"We'll need a secure phone, and your telex machine."

"The phone's in there. The telex will be waiting. Help yourself."

"I'm going to call the commanding general's office at Fort Endicott. While I'm doing that, you get hold of the phone company and put a trace on that phone booth outside Mrs. Emma Lockhart's store. Check on any long distance calls made from there over the past forty-eight hours."

Five minutes later, Eaton met Caldwell outside the secured, soundproof room; both of them were grinning. They didn't know why they hadn't thought of this before. "Let's grab a quick lunch while we're waiting," Eaton said.

And when they came back to the office, the agent in charge handed them two pieces of paper—a yellow sheet torn off the telex roll and a phone company message. "Is this what you guys were looking for?" he asked.

"This is it." Eaton smiled.

"Man, is this it!" Caldwell said, and he scribbled down the name and address on the telex sheet. He hurried to another phone to call the Montana Department of Motor Vehicle Registration.

NAME:	Burns, Jane Charlotte
DESCRIP:	White female 5ft-4in 110 lbs hazel eyes brunette
FAM/PERS HISTORY:	Born 13 Aug 44, 2nd of 3 children—William Dwight Burns (died 4 Oct 63) & Charlotte Bidwell Burns; Brother Burns, Wm. D. Jr., 30 (18 Mar 38) Rancher—Billings, MT Mar. (3) children; Sister Burns, Julie Rachel, 20 (22 Sep 47) Student—Iowa State Univ, NM, No children
EDUCATION:	HS Sioux Creek Community HS, class of 1962; COL Sioux Creek Community College; AB Business mgt/admin 4 Jun 64
EMPLOYED:	Cattleman's State Bank & Trust Co, 334 West Main St Sioux Creek MT—Teller, Asst Commercial Loan Officer

MAR STATUS:	Single NM No children
POLICE RECORD:	Speeding ticket (Montana Highway Patrol) 19 Jul 65 (Fined & Dismissed)
PERS ACTV:	No political/community memberships or activities; Hobbies/interests unknown
CURRENT ADDRESS:	Box 15, North Wormann Road, Sioux Creek MT 77701 (Phone 555-3009); (Lives w/widowed mother)

Gentlemen: Miss Burns presently gone. Departed hastily approx 2 days ago according to mother. Whereabouts unknown.

> T. Grady, CG, Ft Endicott

"That's it," Eaton said again, and he turned to his partner. "Let's get everybody rounded up just as soon as we get a make on her car. We'll all meet them when they get to Montana." He thought for a moment, then added, "One more thing. We'll call the Montana Highway Patrol. Ask them to keep a lookout for that car, in case they see it before we do."

Now, Caldwell thought, that was the first thing that made sense. This would probably be their last chance to grab Palmer. With a police force helping them, they couldn't miss—because if they missed this time, all sixteen of them would end up buried and forgotten in the deepest files section of the CID until they retired.

EVEN THOUGH JANEY had been driving most of the day, it was Gary who looked beat, nearly exhausted. "Worrying takes a hell of a lot out of you," he said.

And he had worried about everything. He had distrusted each person they met, and he couldn't help it. Each person was watching them, reporting their movements, whispering among themselves. Everybody was suspect. They lurked behind trees, they peeked through windows and around corners. They were watching at gas stations and rest stops and rest rooms. Any car staying behind them more than a mile was tracking them.

It was all *their* fault. Oh, those guys were fiendishly clever. They'd probably stopped at all the motels and restaurants and gas stations, showing his picture around, telling everybody what to do. Turn this boy away. Give him nothing, no help, not even the time of day. He's ours, and we're gonna keep him out there on that cold, hard road and run him right into the ground before we take him back. By the time we're through, he'll be begging us to take him back just like a whimpering, tuck-tailed puppy.

"Relax," Janey told him. "We're doing fine."

"Easy for you to say..."

"Why don't you get to work on a list of supplies and equipment we'll need for Kota. That ought to keep your mind off things. I thought we'd stop in Boulder. There are all kinds of alpine shops there."

Kota. Now, *that* was crazy. What made him think he would be able to get within a mile of that mountain, much less actually climb it? "I should have left you out of this, Janey. Hell, I'm not even sure of what I've gotten either of us into."

She gave him a dirty look. "Yeah? Well, I don't think you'd have gotten out of Kansas without me."

"I didn't mean it that way. This is my problem, and I shouldn't be involving innocent people."

"Well, somebody has to help you, and that has to be someone you can trust. And you haven't exactly been up to your neck in trustworthy friends these past few months." She signaled and steered the car onto an exit ramp.

"Why are we turning off here?"

"Make yourself useful. Get a phone book, and find a good alpine shop."

He found one. It was located just north of Boulder in a small, out-of-the-way shopping area. And the man who owned it was one with whom Gary had become familiar eight months ago.

CHAPTER TWELVE

THERE WERE REASONS why Swamp Gas had been called Swamp Gas. The first and most obvious was its appearance—in its natural gaseous state it was a slightly greenish color. Too, there was its chemical name, which few mortals could pronounce and fewer still could spell, and which cried out for a reasonable nickname. But it was the half-forgotten allusion to the Air Force's explanation of UFOs during the 1950s that finally produced the name. *"Your eyes was playin' tricks on you, boy, and that wasn't no spaceship from Neptune. That was swamp gas."* Swamp Gas and optical illusions. And only if you'd seen it work as it had during test number 33A at Fort Stanton would you understand illusion. You might easily believe that your eyes had been playing tricks on you.

All of this lent itself to the name KP Project, an abbreviation for Kota Phenomenon. Unmixed and working by itself under intended conditions, Swamp Gas was something of a phenomenon anyway. But then the Army mixed in one of its most bizarre nerve gases. And then came test 33A. The Kota Phenomenon.

The A designation on any of Stanton's tests meant that it had been originally unplanned; usually, an unexpected side effect had occurred that had to be investigated. Because Swamp Gas was unique, Dr. Fairfield ordered that any test leading to an alphabetic designation would be filmed for their permanent record. Four videotaped copies were made of 33A, the most unusual of all their tests. And even though 33A was the only time the phenomenon was actually witnessed it became the focal point for the whole project. It produced results that convinced them of what had occurred at the summit of Mt. Kota.

Gilmore and Attwood had a copy with them at Kota Station.

The film jumped and flickered before a red-on-white warning appeared, announcing that it was classified Top Secret, and listing the penalties for illegal possession or viewing by unauthorized persons. It was an official United States Army Chemical Corps motion picture.

After the title had faded, a technician, dressed in a bulky insulated suit and helmet, came into view of a camera set inside one of Stanton's laboratories. He carried a steel-mesh cage containing an adult male rhesus monkey, which was hanging on with both hands and feet. The small furry head looked here and there, both of the black eyes flitting in fright. Twice, he tried to reach out and grab the man; when that failed he began gnawing at the wire mesh.

In a corner of the lab was an eight-foot square glass cubicle to which a maze of hoses, ducts and wires was connected. The technician entered the chamber and set the cage on a small steel table. He flipped on a few switches and adjusted several controls, and the monkey scampered about in the cage, looking for an escape. But the rhesus could find no way out, and after the technician closed and sealed the heavy glass door behind him, the monkey settled down as if resigned to his fate.

The screen then split into a dual-image projection. The second camera was pointed toward a cluster of instruments and gauges mounted on the rear wall of the enclosure—a thermometer, humidity indicator, barometer, relative pressure in atmospheres, nitrogen/oxygen content indicator and double-faced clock that measured both real and elapsed times. Hanging by itself was a vertical tube in which a column read zero to one hundred percent, its indicator changing colors as it rose to the top. It measured percentage amounts of Swamp Gas mixed into the cubicle atmosphere.

A moment passed, and all the needles and indicators began creeping slowly in one direction or another. On the opposite half of the screen was the monkey in his cage. He looked around the cubicle in confusion, then took hold of himself, shivering, then hugging himself ever tighter. His fur was rustling, then blowing. The thermometer's reading dropped steadily, continuing to fall until it leveled off at a negative thirty degrees. A velocimeter, measuring wind velocity, was giving a variable reading of twenty-five to thirty miles per hour with gusts going up to forty and forty-five.

Trembling, the rhesus monkey tried rolling himself into a tighter ball.

Three minutes passed.

The relative humidity had dropped to sixteen percent; the oxygen level was at less than sixty percent of that at sea level. The interior of the enclosure began to fog slightly as injected water vapor was introduced, turning immediately to a kind of artificial snow flurry in the wind. When ten minutes had elapsed on the dual clock, the chamber environment approximated weather conditions found at nineteen thousand feet in the mountains during a storm. The monkey shivered uncontrollably, burrowing his head under an arm, and wrapping his tail around himself.

Another minute went by, and the instrument camera focused slowly toward the Swamp Gas indicator. The percentage level began creeping upward, the colors brightening as the meter climbed; white up to twenty percent; yellow to forty-five percent; orange until the saturation reached seventy percent. Everything above that was indicated in red. The level inched up for three or four minutes until it steadied itself at sixty-five percent, the estimation of saturation at the crash site on Mount Kota. They couldn't know for certain, of course, but it was about what they could expect from forty gallons spread over the summit. Calculated at that relative percentage, its overall strength was estimated at eighty-six percent of total potency. If it behaved as they thought, it would still kill, but take a little longer doing it.

The monkey looked up once. He was terrified and unable to understand why he was being tortured.

Another five minutes passed. By then, three-quarters of a liter of modified Swamp Gas had been injected into the chamber atmosphere, or roughly enough to kill a herd of fully grown elephants. Looking up a second time, the rhesus appeared confused, dazed, if such expressions were possible for him. He seemed to become steadily more disoriented as the minutes passed, until he appeared not to notice the extreme cold anymore. His tail flopped to the bottom of the cage like a discarded rope and he unwrapped his arms. They fell loosely to his sides. He acted as if he was about to come to his feet but had forgotten how to manage it. Instead, his eyes closed, he fell back to a slumped sitting position for a moment, then toppled over.

The film flickered and faded for a few seconds. When it came back on, someone held a sign in front of the camera that read Phase 2. The screen split into a dual image again with the second camera aimed at the clocks. Three and a half hours had elapsed. The rhesus monkey still lay exactly as he had fallen, his fur blowing with the artificially created wind. Snow had collected around the body. The first camera then zeroed in toward the mesh cage until it filled the screen. The monkey lay motionless, both eyes closed, mouth slightly open, exposing one of the long incisors.

Nothing happened for a moment; then the tail twitched. It lay still for several seconds, then twitched again, flopping against the cage. The small black fingers and thumb on the left hand flexed slightly, and the left leg gave a sudden kick. By then, the tail was flicking almost rhythmically, and the right-hand fingers and thumb were flexing. The left arm then jerked upward, fell back across the torso, and the body rolled over. The tongue slipped out as the head lolled slowly back and forth. And there the monkey lay, still for several seconds before his body started flinching again.

The laboratory was now filled with excited activity as people dressed in sealed, insulated suits and helmets hurried back and forth in front of the camera. One technician waved for another to bring something to him; a second pushed a cartful of instruments to the chamber door, and a third rushed out of the room. Someone ran into the camera, knocking it toward an observation booth installed on the far side of the room. Dr. Fairfield and two other men inside were frantically directing their technicians here and there, and when the camera was reaimed toward the chamber, two white-suited men stepped aside. The picture was refocused onto the monkey inside the cage.

By this time, nearly ten minutes had elapsed, and the rhesus was jerking spastically, rolling from side to side, both legs kicking. Both arms were under the body and it rolled face-down where the legs bent at the knees, pushing its bottom up. With its tail still twitching, the monkey pushed himself up to his hands and knees.

Thirteen minutes, nine seconds. There was a quick shot of the clocks, then back to the monkey. He had taken hold of the wire mesh with both hands and although he rocked back and forth as if ready to collapse he remained on his knees still gripping the cage. He hung there for nearly two minutes, then pulled himself to his feet. He remained standing for just over four minutes before falling down. On the cage floor the rhesus continued kicking, hitching and rolling about, acting as if he was trying to get to his feet again.

The second camera came on once again, now aimed toward the chamber instruments. At once, all the indicators began dropping or rising, and in five minutes the chamber interior was returned to the same levels as the outer lab environment. The Swamp Gas was evacuated, and two of the technicians entered the chamber with a tray filled with medical instruments.

Lieutenant Colonel Gilmore shifted uneasily in his chair. The end of the film always made him nervous—more so now that he and Attwood were actually there on the mountain.

THE DAY BEFORE TEST 33A WAS FILMED, three technicians had been finishing the modifications of the glass chamber. An artificial alpine environment was necessary for the next portion of their tests, and they had spent two days rerouting and re-connecting all the required gas and liquid lines through the glass walls. They were testing all the connections, and the chamber itself, for leaks. One of the men had entered the chamber, sealed the door behind him and was adjusting his suit when somehow the Swamp Gas had accidentally been turned on. No one knew how it had happened, or how long the man had received full exposure. All they knew was that after several minutes in the chamber the man became woozy and disoriented before he simply collapsed to the floor. They weren't sure how long he had lived after hitting the floor. Before they could evacuate and purge the interior, the man was dead.

A full autopsy had been planned, and the body had been moved to a makeshift morgue in another building. It had rested all night in a locker set at thirty degrees.

"It was a perfect opportunity," Fairfield said later. "Grotesque to be certain, but we all felt that there was no other choice."

THE FILM WENT MOMENTARILY blank, came on again and two technicians rolled a gurney up to the chamber door. Two other men removed the steel table from the chamber, and the body, dressed in white coveralls, was moved inside and placed on the floor. After the door was sealed and the chamber pressurized, the second camera came on, aimed at the chamber instruments.

Once again the internal temperature plummeted, the relative humidity fell, the oxygen dropped and a fan came on; the chamber environment stabilized at minus twenty-eight degrees, sixteen percent relative humidity, and with a gusting wind of thirty to thirty-five miles per hour. More water vapor was introduced and when those in the control booth were satisfied with the conditions, Swamp Gas was injected.

And everybody waited.

One minute. Then two. Three.

A hand flinched, twisting at the wrist. The fingers flexed slightly, and the opposite hand bumped against the floor.

The camera moved in a little closer.

The first hand moved again, and now one of the legs was beginning to flex. A foot jerked slightly at the ankle, and the leg came up a bit higher before sliding to the floor. The head rolled toward the right, back again, then to the right a second time. And now an arm jerked upward, suspended itself with the hand in the air—fingers still flexing—and fell across the face. It lay there a moment before falling to the floor, and after it had moved away from the face, the jaw began working.

Four minutes had passed.

The jaw moved as if there was a walnut in the corpse's mouth—opening, closing partway and grinding from side to side. The tongue fell out, and teeth clamped down on it, nearly severing the tip, and as the head began rolling from side to side a little faster, the loose end slapped both cheeks.

Now both arms were working like loose tentacles, hands banging and flopping; the legs bent, straightened and kicked. A foot rapped against a heavy glass panel. The entire body seemed to be in motion, arching at the back, then dropping. It almost looked as if the man was having a terrible nightmare about fighting off attacking insects.

Nine minutes.

The body stretched, then acted as if it would roll over. But it fell back. The head came up off the floor, fell back, came up again. It turned toward the camera, jaw still working, the end of the tongue still hanging by a raw string.

Gilmore looked away. This was the part he couldn't stand.

The eyelids snapped open. They appeared to look directly at the lens.

Still kicking, one of the legs caught hold of the floor and the toes dug into a corner, giving the corpse enough leverage to turn over. As with the rhesus monkey earlier, the hitching and kicking pushed the posterior up. Instead of gripping something and pulling itself up the rest of the way, the body only straightened out with another kick with both legs. It rammed its head into the glass door where it continued kicking and jerking before rolling over on its back again.

Twelve minutes, thirty seconds.

The corpse never came to its feet. But it did sit up. Head drooping and shaking, legs splayed out, arms still flopping about brokenly, the body arose. The right leg bent under as if to try to get up, but kicked out instead, and the body fell to one side against the glass. Sliding down to the floor, the right arm swung straight around, hitting the glass panel hard enough to move it, and a moment later the head came up, then down, crashing against the same panel. The impact broke the skull, and a noticeable flat spot appeared against the glass. Far more serious was the hairline crack that suddenly split across the bottom corner of the glass.

Test 33A was halted at once. The chamber was evacuated and purged, and three technicians hurried to open the door.

The corpse was still kicking violently.

A fourth man appeared on-screen, carrying a tray of medical instruments like those brought in for the rhesus. All four men grabbed the corpse, and as three of them held it pinned to the chamber floor the fourth technician hurriedly set to work with the instruments.

They were connected a minute later, and the camera focused in on a set of small screens now registering dots and blips. Or *not* registering them. Blood pressure: 00/00. Pulse: 0. EKG activity: None. EEG activity: None. It was, after all, a corpse they were holding down to the floor.

2

ATTWOOD STOOD BEHIND GILMORE as he shut off the TV and removed the videotape. "That damned thing gives me the heebie-jeebies every time I see it," he said with a shiver. It was also the reason he had placed motion detectors all around the crash site and down through Karber's Pass.

"What's for supper?" Gilmore asked. He didn't want to talk about the film. And now that they had been to the summit, he didn't want to think about it.

"A couple of steaks, potatoes and corn. Baked potato or hash browns?"

"Baked."

"How do you like your steak?"

"Medium-well."

Attwood shook his head in mock sadness. "Burned steaks. What a waste. I might as well cook up one of your boots and serve it to you Charlie Chaplin style."

"I'd rather have it that way than rare."

Opening a can of creamed corn, Attwood replied, "Stunned. Just trot it past the fire and throw on a little salt."

Gilmore got out fresh vegetables and began to make a salad. "Well, don't take it personally if I refuse to watch you eat the damned thing. I never could stomach watching a cannibal at work."

Besides watching their diet, which had been planned by a Fort Stanton dietician, they were under orders to ensure that no activity was overdone. They could work outside no more than four hours at a time, and after any exterior stint they were to eat, drink and rest for at least two hours before going back out. Every activity had been as carefully prearranged as those followed by the astronauts. If they didn't do as they had been ordered, anything could go wrong; and any one thing going wrong might be disastrous. The very least that could happen was that the whole project would fail because of one or two stupid mistakes. At the worst they would end up the late, great so-and-so. They were getting only one crack at this, and they had to make it count.

Gilmore didn't want to talk about the film or test 33A, but as they sat down for their meal they were talking about them anyway. They talked about the other tests, some of which they had conducted or assisted with, and they discussed tests that were still going on. None had been conclusive; nobody could quite figure it out. No one was certain of whether 33A had been an isolated fluke that would never occur again, or whether it had been their only actual success. All they knew was that it had happened only once; but then, so had many of the other results. The only tangible result was that both of them were now eating their meal inside a research station high up on a mountain.

"Is that steak black enough for you?" Attwood grinned.

"It's okay. How's yours?"

"Just needs a little salt." With a wider grin, Attwood stabbed a bloodred hunk, chewed it with his mouth open and let the juice run down his chin. He winked and licked his lips.

"Fucking carnivore!" Gilmore looked at his food. Plants and animals, he thought. His thoughts had been turning more and more to living things lately—a new appreciation for life perhaps. And maybe it was because there was so much death so short a distance away. Even if there had been no plane crash and no Swamp Gas, a place like this wasn't meant for life. It didn't lend itself even to the appreciation of life. Mountains, like so many things in nature, were intended to be a part of the scenery, a pleasant backdrop with which to complete a picture. Nature was a paradox; it had created life but seemed to have little respect for it. And man, with all his built-in weaknesses, should never attempt interference or try to get into the game. Because when nature cut it to the bone and got down to its most basic and primitive, man wasn't equipped to handle it one-to-one.

No respect for life.

What they were fooling around with was no respecter of life, that was certain.

"Think about that," Attwood had said the first time they saw the crash site. And you couldn't help but think about anything else, not when you were standing in the middle of it with your nose right down in the bloody mess. You could only imagine what those men had been through, what they must have felt and imagined when they crawled from the burning wreckage. Add to that all their injuries, watching their buddies die off one by one, and the overwhelming trauma of being in so helpless and hopeless a situation, and it would be enough to drop the strongest and most willful man.

And then they had been poisoned.

"Just *think* about that!" Attwood continued. "You'd be half out of your mind anyway—hurt, freezing to death, no hope of rescue—and all of a sudden you see all your dead friends start kicking and jumping around like spastic puppets...goddamn!"

But Attwood's reaction of horror was exactly what Fort Stanton and certain others wanted. Not only did the modified Swamp Gas have the potential of becoming a superb tactical weapon, but a psychological weapon of extraordinary power. For an enemy soldier to survive a gas attack after seeing every other living thing around him wiped out would be demoralizing enough—presuming a few survivors still existed—but the rest of what he would witness could cause wholesale battlefield desertions. If an uneducated, superstitious soldier suddenly saw his dead comrades come lurching to their feet, the psychological implications were truly amazing. Entire battles could be won without firing a shot, without risking a single one of your own men. Swamp Gas might introduce a new dimension in warfare.

No. It did not respect life at all. What they were fooling with didn't even respect death. And it hadn't occurred to Gilmore until that moment that perhaps the same things could be said of him and Attwood.

But that was beside the point now. They were here. They were supposed to try to figure out what had happened, and all they really had at the time was a hunch. Because if they weren't sure of how the gas worked, then they were doubly uncertain when Lieutenant Palmer came into the picture.

When they learned which plane the misplaced forty gallons had been on the authorities thought they had simply lost it, but were prepared to advise any recovery team of the potential danger. Almost immediately they heard there were survivors, and that three climbers were going after them. By the time anyone was in the area, the attempt was near its conclusion, and they thought: Oh, shit, they've had it, and we're too late to stop it. And then Palmer appeared—injured, catatonic—and nobody had a clue about what had happened to him. For a long time all they had to go on was Palmer's final radio transmission, and they had listened to it dozens of times. Linguistics experts had tried piecing it together, studying carefully the emotions behind every word, the inflection in each syllable. Other experts had tried to analyze some of the background noises picked up by Palmer's radio after it had been dropped: the heavy breathing, grunting, panting and humming everyone had heard before contact was finally broken for good.

Dead. Everybody in the plane. Dead. You . . . you . . . you're dead. And the final word which had everybody stumped: *Deeeathhh.*

They had concluded that either of two things had taken place: either someone was alive up there with Palmer, or he had been alone. The double-talk reply was explained to mean that if Palmer had been under the influence of a chemical agent he might have made all the guttural noises himself. If not, somebody else could have—probably one of the two other climbers. Probably Doug Gorham. But they really didn't know, and there was no way to find out.

Three months later, test 33 came up in their standard battery of physical gas tests—then 33A. Now they thought they had something. It appeared that Palmer, while under some unknown influence of the gas, had witnessed a primary exam-

ple of the Kota Phenomenon. He might have been at least partially hallucinating when he had seen one or more of the corpses
up and stumbling about. And coupled with whatever was taking place in his mind at that point, he had deserted the house,
leaving only the porch lights on. And, ironically, the last recon
photos that launched the final rescue attempt, must have captured some of the same corpses as they were lurching around.

Gilmore thought about some of those woolly statements:
must have been...appears to be...probably...looks as if. Cut
to the nub they all meant, we don't know. Anything could have
happened. And Palmer, their only living link to all of it,
couldn't help them. Right now he couldn't even help himself.

Attwood put down his fork. "Hey, is everything all right?"
he said.

"Everything's fine. Why?"

"Because you haven't said more than five words since we sat
down. You are a million miles away."

No, only 1100 feet. "I'm okay. I was just thinking, that's
all."

Attwood got up to pour the coffee. "About what?"

"Oh, about all the work we have up here, I guess."

"Since when is that anything new? I haven't seen a project
yet where everything went the way it was planned. All we can
do is try. It all pays the same, whether it works or not," and
Attwood sat back down at the table. "But I'll tell you what I
think about whenever a project is going badly. I think about
where I'd be if I hadn't gone back and gotten my advanced degree in chemistry. Without that I'd be leading a line company
through some goddamn swamp chasing after a pack of slants
in black pajamas and cone hats. Probably with a bunch of
potheads and dopers just waiting to frag my ass. You've got
your good duty and your shit duty. And *this* ain't bad."

No. It wasn't bad duty at all. This multimillion dollar marvel had been put here just for them, Gilmore thought, just for
their comfort and safety so they'd be able to do a better job.
And look at the job: he and Attwood were the only people in
the world doing this, doing anything like it. They were part of
a handful of experts working on one of the most exclusive
projects on the planet. Perhaps fifty people knew of the proj-

ect's existence, and less than half of them knew what it was all about or where it might lead. Most worked only on small, disconnected pieces of it. What he and Attwood were doing here could one day revolutionize modern warfare—all from the accidental discovery of a weed killer whose presence on a troop transport had been a stupid mistake. And if they could figure out how it worked the end product might make obsolete the most destructive and complex weapons in the world, and its ultimate cost would be less than a penny per kill.

If they could figure out how it worked.

3

WHEN THE PROJECT ENDED and all the bodies had been recovered, the remains were to be shipped to eighty-one separate cities and towns all over the country. The order for 128 caskets—two extra for Gorham and the "late" Gary Palmer—had already been sent. They would be delivered to Fort Endicott and stored until the bodies were brought down.

In the meantime, Gilmore and Attwood had to collect dog tags, after which those men killed by the Swamp Gas would be segregated and autopsied. They had a passenger manifest and a crew list, and they would check off names one at a time as they came to the bodies.

The work began at eight-thirty the following morning. They trekked to the lower end of the plateau and up into Karber's Pass, and before an hour had gone by they were reminded again of how no project ever goes quite as planned. They had thought this portion of the job would be the easiest; they had also thought that their look around the site yesterday had prepared them for their work now. Respectively, it wasn't and it hadn't.

From the upper end of the pass to the lower end of the summit they identified bodies and collected ID tags. They checked each name off their list. They worked for four hours, digging frozen, mangled corpses from the ice, snow and rocks, and there was nothing easy about it.

Many of the bodies had to be turned over; most were frozen fast to the ground and rocks. Clothing ripped away in their hands, some of it partially rotted or burned. Most of the victims couldn't be moved by hand. Ice had buried many of them, and even those who were found faceup had to have ice chipped away with hammers and chisels and picks so they could get to the dog tags. But most had to be pried away from where they had fallen. For this they were forced to use pieces of structural ribbing and spars from the airplane, and to pry the bodies loose as one would move a rock with a wrecking bar. Dull, wet cracks and pops filled the pass as they went methodically from corpse to corpse, broke it loose from the ice and turned it over. They hammered and chipped away jagged chunks of ice from chests, necks and heads and grabbed one of the two pressed aluminum identification tags each man wore. Bones snapped as bodies were wrested from their death positions. Flesh and muscle tissue ripped like paper where they were frozen to the ice. Many of the dead men seemed more mutilated than before; they just hoped that the later recovery parties wouldn't ask too many questions.

They tried not to think about what they were doing. They tried to look past it. And they found themselves pausing often—for a breather, they told themselves, but just to look the other way for a moment, to stare at something else—the rocks, pieces of the plane, the sky...anything at all.

The diversions were rapidly becoming fewer as they approached the summit. Near the end of the pass there was little else to look at except still more bodies and pieces of bodies—arms, legs, feet, hands—everything poking up from drifts of snow and patches of ice at twisted angles, as if this were a graveyard of mannequins.

Attwood spotted a body roughly ten feet above the pass in the rocks. He climbed up to it, telling himself that things could be worse. He knew that was exactly right, that things could always be worse no matter what you were doing. But after nearly four hours of this he was at something of a loss to imagine just how much worse things could be.

Gilmore had gotten a picture stuck in the front of his mind a couple of hours earlier. He couldn't shut it off. It was a film he'd seen once, taken by British troops who had liberated one of the Nazi concentration camps—a film of thousands, tens of

thousands, of bodies. They were being tossed into massive open
pits, huge graves; bodies being rolled or tossed in by captured
SS guards; bodies being pushed in like so many tons of gravel
by bulldozers; bodies being carried in, dragged in, by gloved
and masked Allied soldiers. Thousands of bodies. Each pit
contained at least five thousand; several held twice that many.
An endless procession of grim, fatigued men dragging corpses
along the ground as if pulling heavy chains. The film ran over
and over in his mind, rewinding itself, and always, for some
reason that baffled him, started with the same body being rolled
into a pit by one of the guards—the body of a young woman.
A nude body. She'd had a nice shape, and she hadn't been
starved down to skin and bones like most of the others; she'd
been shot point-blank in the side of the head. You could see the
dark, gaping hole, the powder and bloodstains, and as she was
dropped over the side she landed on the bodies of several young
men. Her breasts jiggled, and one hand struck a man's face—

*Christ Almighty, stop it! Stop it! Why the hell am I thinking
about that? About a poor, helpless victim of torture and per-
version? What's the matter with me?* Gilmore took a deep
breath and looked up at the sky, trying mightily to think of
something else.

Above him, Attwood struggled to get a piece of wing spar
wedged under the body lying in the rocks. It was frozen solid
between a pair of large boulders, twisted into a position that
made moving it almost impossible. He'd had to hammer out a
place under the body and jam the spar in, and now he was
trying to pry it out of the ice. He heard clothing rip as he
pressed down, and he felt the sharp end of the spar suddenly
sink into the dead man's rib cage with a dull crack.

"Oh, shit!"

He moved the lever, working it under the shoulders, then
down by the man's legs. The body broke loose at last, ice
snapping and cracking from around it, and he pushed it up and
to one side, reaching for the dog tags.

And it fell, rolling down the rocks away from him, bouncing and thudding, more bones snapping like pencils. He opened
his mouth to yell at Gilmore below him, but before he could,

the stiffened left arm hit a rock and broke off completely like an icicle. It landed on the trail, the hand striking Gilmore's leg.

Gilmore leaped and grunted in fright like a startled cat. "Goddamn! Will you be careful of what you're doing? For Christ's sake, man!"

"I'm sorry. It rolled away from me before I could grab it."

"Well, Jesus, man, take it easy! If you can't move one, say so, and I'll help you. Look at this guy. We're supposed to identify them, goddammit, not mutilate them any more than they already are!"

"All right! It was an accident. Hell, we're going to see a lot worse than this. Settle down."

Gilmore was quiet for a moment, presumably trying to settle himself down. "What time is it?" he finally asked quietly.

"Eleven fifty-six. What happened to *your* watch?"

"Nothing. I was just asking. All right?"

"Okay, okay..."

"I count forty-three identified so far. How many do you count?"

"Forty-three... forty-four with this one." He bent down to retrieve the ID tag stuck to the man's chest. His hand brushed against the fresh hole made by the wing spar. There would be some answering to do about this guy.

"Okay. To hell with it, let's go on back down. We're going to be running low on oxygen before long, and I think we've had about all we can handle for one morning."

Especially you, Attwood thought. But he said, "Yeah, you're right. Let's get the hell out of here."

As they started down the pass, Attwood recounted the names, nodding to himself. Forty-four. Forty-four out of 126— not a bad start for four hours' work, and so far they hadn't run across any remains that couldn't be identified. Most of the bodies were in remarkably good shape, all things considered. Some of them were missing limbs and violently mutilated, but most were reasonably whole. The freezing cold had preserved them well. Even the remains of the airplane had been left intact, so that you could easily tell that it had been a plane. Most crashes left only smoking heaps of rubble; many of the passengers were destroyed completely, with nothing left to recover. This crash didn't look all that bad by comparison, and you could see how there might have been survivors; Attwood said so to Gilmore.

"Well, I wouldn't call it a thing of beauty," Gilmore grunted. But he knew what Attwood meant. That everything was in as good shape as it was could be attributed to the fact that all the plane's fuel had been carried in the wings, both of which broke off on impact. One landed far below near the South Face before smashing to pieces and burning, and the other landed a fair distance away from the fuselage in the rocks above Karber's Pass where it exploded harmlessly. Nearly all the loss of life had occurred from the sheer weight and energy of the plane slamming into the mountain and flying apart; most of the victims had been hurled into all the lethal flying pieces.

"I didn't mean that it would make a nice postcard. What the hell's wrong with you anyway?"

"Oh, nothing at all! I've just been digging through more dead bodies than I've ever seen before, and this afternoon I'll get to go back and do more of the same. That's all. Wrong? Why should anything be wrong?"

"Well, do you think I'm enjoying this shit? It came with the territory, you know."

Gilmore stopped. "Look. I'm sorry. It just got to me, and...well, I didn't know it would affect me like that. Let's just talk about something else for a while."

And within three minutes they had something else to talk about.

"Who was the last one out?" Gilmore asked as they paused, then walked to the door of the station.

"You were."

"Yeah." He had been. But he'd closed the door behind him. He was certain of it. When you had to swing a 550-pound door closed and you heard the hardened-steel double-action lock snap shut as you did it, you remembered doing it; and when it was the only door to the only building on the entire mountain, you remembered doing it.

They stared at the open door for a moment, swung it back and forth a couple of times, and twisted the knob. The knob worked; the latch worked. When they went inside, closing the door behind them, the latch clicked solidly against the striker and the door sealed.

Attwood pulled his helmet off and disconnected his oxygen mask. It was cold inside—of course—and he could see the white vapor from his breath hanging in the air. He tested the door twice, opening and closing it. "You must not have closed it," he said, looking at the door.

"Of course I did."

"Well, the wind sure couldn't have blown it open."

"I *closed* the goddamn *door*!" he yelled above the roar of the ceiling heaters. "I closed it, and it latched." He looked around for a moment, then hurried to the radio. "I closed it," he said again. "Somebody else has been up here."

Gilmore was in no mood to be argued with, so Attwood pretended to study the door and latch once again. Maybe Gilmore was right; maybe somebody else had left it open. Maybe someone had flown up this morning, come in, found them gone, then left. Maybe. Except no one would come up here unannounced and without a damned good reason. Kota Station hadn't been put here for social calls, and that peculiar helicopter hadn't been developed for joyriding.

"Endicott Center, Endicott Center, this is Kota Station. Do you copy? Over."

Checking the latch and knob again, Attwood dropped onto one knee and watched its action as he turned the knob back and forth. It locked with a tempered steel dead bolt that snapped out above the latch like a thick railroad spike. Locked, the knob wouldn't turn; to open it required a full ninety-degree twist. The assembly was not the sort you could buy at the local hardware store. Nor was it apt to fail.

"Endicott, are you certain about that? Over."

"Affirmative, Kota. Will repeat: there were no flights authorized to Kota Station this morning. To repeat SOP, no one goes up there at this time unless you guys request it. In fact, the helicopter was grounded yesterday. Repeat: the XM-221 helicopter has been officially grounded until further notice. I guess someone forgot to tell you that. Over."

"Oh, that's fucking great!" Attwood muttered, closing the door.

Gilmore glanced up at the ceiling, adding, "No shit, Endicott. Someone forgot to tell us all right. What do we do in the meantime? What if we have an emergency and one or both of us have to be evacuated? Over."

"Uhh . . . no word on that, Kota. Over."

"Well, when will it be airborne again? Any word on *that*? Over."

"No exact word, Kota, but they're working on it day and night to get it in the air again. They estimate at least two, possibly three, days at the longest. We'll just have to let you know. And I'm advised to tell you to check the integrity of your door hardware for possible failure. Over."

"We checked that, Endicott! The door is fine. The hardware is fine. And we do not leave the door open when we leave the station. Somebody else was up here. Somebody else had to be here. Do you understand? Over."

"We have no idea who it could be, Kota. Nobody could get past the security around the mountain," another voice from Fort Endicott answered. For a moment they didn't know who it was. "Be advised also that yelling at my operator won't get you any answers. We suggest you check the door again, and make certain it latches when you leave the station. And we'll radio you the minute the helicopter is airborne again. Now. Is there anything else you wish to report? Over."

"Nothing, General Grady. We'll advise you when we have something. Kota Station out."

"We're standing by. Endicott Center out."

Both men were quiet for a while. The only noise in the station came from the four overhead heaters, and they began shutting down one by one as the interior warmed up. Gilmore sat at the radio, staring at it as if he wanted to smash it. Attwood looked here and there for any damage from the cold, but could find nothing. Everything was humming efficiently—the generator, the water purifier, the refrigerators in the dining area and lab, and the storage unit in which they could place three corpses. One of the water heaters in the equipment room came on with a quiet *fwooom*.

"Well, I guess we could change latches." Gilmore sighed, still staring at the radio.

Remembering how jittery and jumpy he'd been earlier, Attwood said, "Why don't you do that after lunch? I'll go on back up, and you can come up later after you're done."

"Okay."

"What do you want for lunch?"

"Anything but raw meat."

GENERAL GRADY CALLED the airfield and asked about the grounded helicopter. Before picking up the phone he knew what they would tell him—"two days minimum, just like we said the last time you called"—but he called anyway. It was his job; it was what you did when you were in charge and had little else to do, and when in fact very little was actually under your direct control: you badgered your underlings. You belabored the obvious. Thou shalt make phone calls. He didn't care if that silly-looking thing ever flew again, or if the whole stupid project it supported fell flat on its stupid face and rotted where it lay. But he called the airfield anyway because it was expected of him. It would have to go into his reports, and thou shalt make thy reports whether they say anything or not because that was how you played the game if you were stuck in the middle. You passed the ball (or buck) with your left hand while keeping your right hand safely and securely over your buns. That was security, Army style. Basic survival.

Now, he thought, what was he supposed to make of the latest report from Kota Station? This, of course, would have to be detailed in full in his report to Kelly and Mattlock—that the $28,000 door had failed to latch. That meant they had had an equipment failure, which meant going back to the manufacturer for testing, retesting, verifications and possible design changes—which meant phone calls, paperwork, a lot of finger-pointing and meetings and opinions and guesses, and all of it would lead to the final verdict: take that latch off, and put on another one.

Maybe it hadn't been installed correctly in the first place; maybe the door was out of kilter, causing the latching mechanism to loosen; maybe the cold temperatures at 18,000 feet had affected the metal parts in a way not anticipated; perhaps the door frame was out of alignment, causing an improper latch; or maybe the whole damned wall was slightly out of plumb.

Oh, we tested that and that, and we thought of that, too, and we checked all that out beforehand, and it's our opinion that it wasn't installed right because you guys didn't follow the instructions, so it's your fault and we claim no responsibility, but we'll sell you new latches, all of them you want....

And you were right back to Go again. Paperwork, phone calls, verifications, new equipment specifications, meetings, time, money and manpower. Take the defective latch off. Put on another one. Close the door. Cover your ass. All because someone up there was jerking off instead of making sure he'd shut the door behind him when he left the building.

Grady talked with the chief technician in charge of the crew repairing the helicopter. "This is Grady. I just wanted to see how you're doing."

"You're kidding," the man answered with a doleful sigh.

"Afraid not. I just got a call myself. I was ordered to check again." He sat down on the edge of someone's desk, trying to picture the haggard technician—unshaven, red-eyed, grouchy, arms in grease up past the elbows—trying his best to get the aircraft repaired in the face of constant hassling from Grady. "Look, I don't like bothering you guys, believe me. But that helicopter is supporting a very important project right now. The lives of two men may depend on its being able to fly when we need it, and . . . well, I'm getting a lot of pressure from above me. If it was up to me I'd leave you alone and let you fix it in peace. But they won't leave me alone." It sounded almost like a plea.

The technician said nothing for a minute. "Two days, General. Maybe less if a couple of parts we've ordered get here early."

"Understood."

"That's what you said the last time."

"Well, that was before this . . . call I just got. Is there anything I could do to help get the parts delivered a little earlier?"

"I doubt it. They have to be hand-tooled in one of our shops, and they're working day and night now to get them finished.

But it's like everything else—it takes a certain amount of time. Besides, we're . . . well, we're doing the best we can."

"I know you are, and I appreciate it, even if it doesn't sound like it. And I'll try not to bother you again."

"I would appreciate that, General Grady. And if it's any consolation, I think I understand your position, being in the middle and all. I'm glad it's not me. We'll get this thing in the air again, and you'll be the first to know when we're finished."

Grady looked around the communications center, at his men working quietly and efficiently at their monitors and boards and panels. He thought again about the men inside the hangar who were working feverishly day and night to get that oddball helicopter in the air; the two men on the mountain picking through the remains of a terrible airplane crash, their multimillion dollar shelter perched 18,000 feet up on a flat piece of cold rock; and he thought of an innocent lieutenant who had been locked away in an asylum like a diseased animal, who had been declared dead by men he didn't even know just so they could keep him for study.

I think we've pretty well got everything covered. . . .

Uh-huh. The wonder weapon isn't acting like you thought it would, or you wouldn't need Kota Station or those two men up there in the first place; your young guinea pig, Lieutenant Palmer, isn't behaving like you assumed he would, and has, as they say, fled the coop; your CID agents can't seem to find him; and as a matter of fact, your two mountain men can't even remember to close a door.

All because a couple of your educated, highly trained, superbly qualified geniuses went and delivered a box to the wrong loading gate.

Well, Tom, you play this game a lot better than I do. And I can think of only one thing you've covered successfully.

CHAPTER THIRTEEN

CRUNNNCH ... CRUNNNCH ... RUNNNCH ... runnnch ...

Gilmore stopped his inspection of the door and latch and looked over his shoulder toward the far end of the building. Attwood had left the microwave receiver on and the speaker turned up. Lights were flashing on the control panel as each of Attwood's movements were picked up by the motion detectors scattered through Karber's Pass and across the summit.

... crunnnch ... crunnnch ... crunnnch ...

Attwood had probably left everything turned on just for his benefit. He thought he was real damned funny sometimes. Gilmore turned back to the door, trying to ignore the noise.

For the fifth time he opened and closed the door, his nose almost on the knob as he tried to figure out how the door had come open. He couldn't figure it out at all. You had to give the knob a full ninety-degree twist in either direction to release the latch. The latching mechanism itself consisted of a heavy steel bar that slid in and out of a slot inside the door frame. You couldn't push or pull the door open if it was closed; you had to turn the knob. Shut, the door sealed against an insulated lining set inside the frame, the entire assembly working something like a pressurized cargo door on a plane. And it couldn't have blown open by itself, he thought as he worked the latch again. No way.

... crunnnch ... runnnch ... runnnch ...

The noise was beginning to get on his nerves, and he started to get up to go turn the receiver off. But he thought better of it. If Attwood got into any trouble up there, he might not be able to contact the station; the motion detectors might be the only way he'd know of any trouble.

The door, he thought. Get the door fixed so you can get back up there to help him. He laid out a set of screwdrivers, a pair of pliers, a crescent wrench and a hammer on the floor. Then he opened the box with the new latch and knob assembly—or parts, he was dismayed to see. The whole damned thing was unassembled.

"Goddammit," he moaned, opening the directions and drawings. Attwood should be doing this. Gilmore was Mr. Thumbs when it came to anything mechanical, and even though there were drawings and exploded views of exactly how the thing went together, he could barely read them. He tried: this piece went into there, but only if that thing was properly fitted into that funny looking doodad attached to the thingamajig here, and if that spring was not set properly into the slotted hole, then this bunch of pieces connected to that mess of parts wouldn't fit when the anklebone was connected to the legbone....

He cursed again, throwing down the drawings. The words ran together and the lines twisted into ancient hieroglyphics.

...*crunnnch*...*crunnnch*...*runnnch*...

Christ, wasn't Attwood at the top yet? What was keeping him? He was supposed to be working, not wandering around like some tourist.

Gilmore tried the door another time, wincing at the cold, stiff breeze that blew in. Well, the hell with this. As far as he could see, not one damned thing was wrong with it. All the pieces seemed to be moving properly, and the door held fast when it was closed. He got to his feet, collected the tools and the box of parts, and stuffed the mysterious instructions back inside. There was no need to fart around with a perfectly good mechanism. As his dad used to say, If it ain't broke, don't fix it. Good advice. Hell, even the Army had an axiom of their own about fixing things—something about not replacing anything unless it was necessary. Besides, as klutzy as he was with tools and loose parts he'd probably only screw it up so badly that it wouldn't work at all. They had far more important things going on up here than screwing around with a stupid lock.

He went into his bedroom and retrieved his parka, coveralls, boots and helmet, then got another oxygen reservoir from the storage room. It was time to get back to work . . .

Counting the bodies.

And he set the reservoir on the floor. He didn't move for a long time.

2

"FORTY-FIVE . . . FORTY-SIX . . . forty-seven . . . forty-eight," Attwood muttered to himself, marking the adjoining names on his wadded list and checking them against the four sets of dog tags he held. Private First Class Carl M. Sherman; Sergeant Peter S. Krugg; Private Eugene V. Lawson, Jr.; Private First Class Wayne B. Householder. Those four were the last of those found in or around Karber's Pass.

He looked off in the direction of the airplane. Dozens of bodies lay all over the place, none of them officially identified—kind of a dumb attitude, he thought, an identification process that didn't recognize a person's existence, or former existence as it were, unless the officer in charge checked them off his list. They weren't there until he got to them. "Stupid . . ." he mumbled. But at least his charges would wait patiently.

It occurred to him while looking at them that if he and Gilmore were ever going to get around to their primary purpose for being here, they would have to end this quickly, or somehow simplify it. Besides, it was starting to get to him. You just couldn't look past all the broken, bloodied bodies and think of them as only things; you couldn't look upon the shock and horror permanently etched into all the frozen faces without thinking about what had caused it. You couldn't get used to it. You couldn't ignore it. This was not simply a distasteful job because these bodies had been living, breathing, laughing people once. They had been husbands, fathers, sons, brothers, uncles and friends.

He recalled that these men seemed to represent a whole cross section of purest Americana, someone from nearly every re-

gion of the country. Like that guy right there—PFC Householder, late of Richmond, Indiana. He couldn't have been more
than nineteen years old—slightly built, dark hair, almost delicate looking. He didn't belong in a set of jungle fatigues, or
carrying an M-16, and it was hard to imagine so young a face
greased up in green and black camouflage paint, on a man
sneaking through a jungle looking for someone to kill. That
face hadn't even grown a beard yet. And Sergeant Krugg—a big
man built like a football player. Crew-cut blond hair, a thick,
round face, massive hands and a lot of upper body muscle.
Legs like tree trunks. What the hell was he doing here? Why
hadn't he been on some college campus, with a hawk-nosed,
gaunt coach dressed in shorts and a windbreaker yelling at him?

And that guy down there, who had been nearly cut in half by
a section of wing skin—Private First Class Sherman. His body
was a sickening mess, but everything from the chest up was
completely unmarked. He appeared to be in utter peace, as if
not at all surprised to have died this way. In fact, he still had his
glasses on, and how had that happened through so fearsome an
accident? He had been from Boston. College graduate? Har-
vard? MIT? Boston College? Probably not. If you can afford
to put your kid into one of the big Ivy League schools, you can
afford to keep him out of the service. Maybe Sherman had been
a raving maniac or a bloodthirsty killer, but he looked as if he'd
spent his life behind a stack of textbooks.

Finally, Attwood walked away from the spot and toward the
wreck. He couldn't stand there all day imagining things about
the victims. They had to speed up the identification process so
they could get to work on the gas victims, and they still had to
find who the gas victims were. He began a quick count of all the
corpses he could see around him; seventy-eight should remain
to be examined.

He pointed with his pencil. "Twenty...twenty-one...twenty-
two..." and he wrote down 22, then looked off into the opposite direction. "Twenty-three...twenty-four...twenty-
five..." All but eleven were accounted for. According to the
manifest, there had been a flight crew of four, and an officer/
senior NCO list of twelve. And there they were, trapped inside
the forward section; and there they would be for some time, he

saw as he walked slowly around the smashed wad of metal. Only one body was visible, plus part of a leg lying in the ice next to the hulk. An arm hung out from the body, streaked with frozen red; the face was frosted over like meat hanging in a freezer, and the left eye was open. It seemed to stare at him as if questioning his presence here.

Will you help me?

Quite suddenly, Attwood found himself wanting to do just that, to climb up to the body of the lieutenant. He stared at it. The opened eye felt as if it were moving, following him, and then he wanted to climb up and close it, turn the head away.

Don't look at me like that.

Please help me....

It wasn't a stare. The eye cut right through him. It was the eye of a lost, hungry child begging silently for help.

Please help....

He half expected to see the mouth move, to actually hear the words exit with a slow and painful whisper. He thought he might see the arm extend out toward him so that he could take hold and help the poor man out of the plane. And he wanted to; he wanted to lay the lieutenant down on the ground where he should be. He had been trapped there for eight months waiting for someone to pull him away from the jagged spears of metal that had pierced his body.

Please...

Don't. Don't...say that. I can't help you. I'm sorry.

It was awful seeing the man like that. It was obscene having to leave a man like that, skewered like a hunk of raw beef.

The wind blew, and the stiffened arm moved, bumping against the side of the fuselage.

All right...if you can't help...

And now Attwood found himself wishing he could somehow explain things more appropriately, because these men deserved that much. They should know how and why this had happened to them. They deserved far better than they had been given, and the least one could do was to tell them why so suddenly and with no warning their lives had been taken from them.

Attwood walked to a place between the two halves of the wreck.

They were all dead. PFC Householder of Richmond, Indiana, was dead. So was PFC Sherman from Boston, who should have been inside some library or study hall. And which university was missing the physical prowess of Sergeant Krugg, who should have been helping to open holes in somebody else's offensive line?

He stooped to retrieve something sticking out of a jacket pocket—an Instamatic shot of a '57 Chevy with its front bumper and grille removed, a pair of huge racing tires on the back, and an A-shaped tow bar bolted to the frame. It carried Ohio tags; it was parked under an oak tree, and next to it was a pretty girl dressed in a skimpy bikini. She had one leg bent, and one hand pushing up her blond hair from behind as if making fun of the classic model's pose. She appeared to be on the verge of the giggles.

The jacket had been lying unattended in the snow. To which of these men—men? Most were barely out of boyhood—did the photo belong? Which one had been her boyfriend, or husband?

Remorse, huge and painful, rose in his chest. "God, I'm sorry, you guys," he whispered, and he felt as if tears might bubble over any second. "I wish I could explain this. . . ." And the tears came then. He sniffled. And he pushed up the faceplate on his helmet so he could blow his nose and wipe away the sudden and overwhelming sadness on his face.

3

GILMORE LISTENED TO THE faint noises coming from the receiver. Attwood must be back to work, moving around up there.

Among the bodies.

He looked at his equipment lying on the floor, then back to the receiver. He should get his gear on. He should get out of here and back to the summit so he could help Attwood. Except . . . except that it didn't seem to matter that much. Really, now that he considered it, there would be little difference whether he was out the door in the next two minutes, or not at all. Besides, if the truth were known—*and truth is why Attwood and I are here, isn't that right?*—he didn't want to put his gear on. He didn't want to go through the door or back outside or up to the crash site again. He did not wish to leave the relative security of this building, thank you very much, and he didn't want to go poking around all those . . .

Corpses.

He walked to the table and sat down, thinking. What was wrong with that? he wondered. What was wrong with Attwood doing all the outdoorsy work? Nothing that he could see now that he thought about it. Not one thing seemed wrong about that. Attwood didn't mind it up there, so let him fetch those bodies down here. He, on the other hand, would remain right here. He would do all the lab workups on the bodies. That was a much better arrangement; he was far better suited for the delicate lab work anyway. Attwood was like a gorilla inside a laboratory. Why, for that matter, he would do all the work here in the station. Everything, even the cooking. Attwood would not have another chore in here, not even picking up after himself. Surely he would agree to so simple and logical a shift in responsibilities.

Now he got up from the table and paced the room. It was a good idea, Attwood doing the work at the site, him staying here, and as he thought about it he could find only one hole— that he would be checking and examining and prepping all those bodies. He would be here in the station with them. *Alone.*

Gilmore couldn't quite decide what he should do. There was no way he could avoid contact with the bodies. Whether he helped Attwood to identify, classify and pack them down, or whether he stayed here to poke, probe, cut and examine, he couldn't get away from them. And what if something caused that gas to take effect again? That could happen. They didn't know quite what caused it, but the effect could sure as hell happen again at any time. But there he would be, alone in the lab, Attwood nearly a quarter mile away, while one of those bodies began hitching and kicking and vibrating in there on the table, flopping around, arms flailing, sitting up . . .

With its eyes open.

He shivered. He could almost see it happening, and he thought of the videotape over there on the bookshelf. Oh, mother, if that happened while he was working on a corpse, he'd shit and go blind at the same time. Nothing about Swamp Gas or what little they had learned about it so far suggested that any of its effects were one time only. Among the many unanswered questions was how long it remained active inside a dead body; it could be active for almost as long as it took for a corpse to decompose.

And decomposition hadn't happened up here on this mountain. Everything was still nicely preserved. The mechanism could be as potent as ever. For that matter, there was nothing in the rules that said these dead men couldn't get right up and lurch their way from the summit and down through Karber's Pass . . . right down here.

Now he could see that happening, too. He could just imagine opening the door only to find the station surrounded by those . . . *things*. Dozens of them, perhaps, stumbling down through the pass, crossing the plateau, trying to beat their way into the building . . .

. . . *crunnnch . . . crunnnch . . . runnnch . . . crunnnch . . .*

He jumped at the sudden noise, whirling about to see green lights flashing up and down the board. Five of them were modulating; the noises were coming from the upper end of the pass. It was amazing how much local movement could be picked up through one of those little disks. If you shouted through one of them the noise would blare through the station louder than a freight train. He watched the lights, and listened to the noises. The lights were flashing down the board; Attwood was coming down. He was coming back hours earlier than planned, so he must have run into some trouble. Or, more likely, he was pissed because he'd been left up there alone.

. . . *crunnnch . . . crunnnch . . . runnnch . . .*

Gilmore stared at the control panel, watching the lights, thinking about Attwood. He'd get over it. And he'd just have to understand that he would be working by himself on the summit from now on. There was no other way.

The wind whistled softly, and snow and ice cracked underfoot. Rocks clacked and clattered. Gilmore stared at the lights. Attwood was coming down, and suddenly this was the most forlorn place in the world—so lonely and desolate. Why would anyone come up here if he didn't have to? Why had those mountain climbers spent so many years trying to climb up here? Why would anybody in his right mind do something like that? You could go right out of your mind up—

. . . crunnnch . . . crunnnch . . . runnnch . . . crunnnch . . .

Pulling up one of the chairs, Gilmore sat at the control panel. Three of the green lights were flashing near the lower end of the board—the approximate center of the pass. And so were four others from near the upper end of the pass.

4

FOR SEVERAL MOMENTS after he had pulled back the canvas tarp hung across the end of the fuselage, Attwood stood motionless. It was nearly all he could manage; he could barely hang on to his flashlight. And he hoped that what he was seeing was his imagination.

Then he stepped up into the wreck. With a deep breath he played the light around the interior.

"Jesus . . ." Oh, there had been survivors—ten, maybe fifteen, of them. But this hadn't been in the script. Survivors try to survive. They might kill in order to survive. But not like this.

Trembling, he stepped over the bodies next to the opening. The light shook as he moved it, and he had to force himself to look at the remains, to try and determine what might have happened in here. That's your job, he told himself, and he muttered it aloud twice. He was supposed to report. Measure. Cross-check the facts.

Some facts . . .

His light passed across the body of a man whose head had been split open—that is, split right down the middle, whack, like you'd halve a fire log, and now it lay open like a split apple.

Propped against a bulkhead next to him was the body of a tall, black sergeant first class, one of the few who seemed unmarked except for what looked like crash injuries. But next to that, lying across the body of a black private lay a buck sergeant, his head thick with frozen blood and matted hair; a closer look revealed that the opposite side of his head was nearly gone, smashed to jelly.

The facts would be there, they had been told, because J-440 had been a fairly tidy crash as plane crashes go. Finding the facts would be easier because: 1) the crash occurred high on a mountain, and all the evidence should be preserved; 2) They would not have to comb through the debris with sifting screens and tweezers because most of the evidence would be of manageable size. It didn't blow up or burn down. Finally, 3) Nobody had messed with the evidence. Everything they were looking for was undisturbed. All they had to do was find it. None of these factors was true when one of these huge airplanes did a swan dive onto an unyielding strip of tarmac. All that was apt to be left after a crash like that was about what you'd find in an ashtray.

Now Attwood's light found a man dressed in two extra pairs of pants and two extra field jackets. Something had hit him in the head, too, hard enough to flatten one side of it, and to rip part of his neck in the process. The same violence was evident on the body next to that, and the one propped up against that.

Okay, I've found it. Now what?

Maybe the eggheads at Stanton had left something out. Maybe this was yet another of the many bizarre things unknown about Swamp Gas. Oh, it is strange all right; it just flat kills everything, mowing down all life in its path like some freakish biblical plague. And if by some miracle or accident you happen to survive an attack, it goes to work on the neuromuscular system of the corpses of those it just killed, and here they come boogying at you like so many zombies from a horror flick. A nice little touch. If it doesn't kill you outright it gives you a coronary seizure. Nice . . . real nice.

The light traveled to the opposite bulkhead. It found two more bodies with ruined heads before it paused, illuminating a pair of PFCs and two corporals lying in a green and frozen-red heap. One of them had had both hands bandaged with rags; a second man had wrapped rags around his head like an old woman wearing a dirty scarf; three of them had suffered almost identical violent damage to their heads—terrific blows that had flattened their skulls on one side or the other. But something else was wrong with one of the corporals, and it took a moment to find it.

Then he saw it. "Shit!" Part of the corporal's left leg was missing, and he saw the end of a broken bone sticking out. And all around the wound were deep, heavy—

Attwood lost control, and whirled around toward the opening.

—teeth marks. A dozen of them. There was no mistaking the half-moon rows of bites.

Lunging back outside, Attwood barely got his helmet off before his last meal arose like a volcanic eruption and splattered all over the snow. Five minutes passed before his head came back up. He coughed, spitting out the bile; his throat burned, and it was hard to breathe. Great, he thought, just fucking great. They hadn't known anything about that gas at all, and wouldn't they be pleased at all this nicely preserved evidence here now? Guess what, boys? Just guess what else this shit does to you? Just wait until you see what happens to someone who lives through an attack. If they don't die outright, they go stark raving mad. One hell of a product there, gentlemen. It causes you to kill, mutilate, dismember and then feed on your friends before it finally kills you, and animates your corpse. One hell of a product.

He spit, and wiped his mouth. A little of the shock had been diluted, and he was thinking again, trying to tell himself to do what he had come up here to do. He had to go back for another look. Accurate and impartial observation was required here. He had to make certain of what he saw. Measure. Crosscheck. Analyze. Report.

Okay. Okay, here goes: I saw the remains of men who had had their heads smashed and ground round like raw hamburger. I observed that gallons of frozen blood, brains and remains had been spilled and splattered all over the inside of that airplane as if someone had started a grotesque pie fight. And

*it was my observation and expert opinion that each of the crash
survivors had been murdered after the fact. Yes, that's what I
said:* murdered. *Each victim displayed extreme violence on his
person. One had been dismembered, after which his severed
limb apparently became an entrée on some lunatic's menu. I
cross-checked these facts, gentlemen, and the above is my
analysis. You may measure for yourselves what it all could
mean because I have no such intention. And I offer only one
personal opinion:* Fuck this. *Find yourselves a new under-
taker. You started this shit, and you'll have to finish it. I quit.*

And to hell with the rest of the impartiality and accuracy. He
was going to go back down to the station right now, get on the
radio and tell Endicott to send that helicopter back up here
pronto. The Stanton experts would have to figure this one out,
which was what should have happened in the first place. Let
them stay up here.

Behind him inside the plane, Attwood thought he heard
something bump against the metal. It startled him, and he
turned around, the light on again, looking into the interior. The
wind snapped the canvas tarp, and a few loose hunks of metal
skin creaked; one of them bumped against another. He thought
that was what had caused the noise until the light found two
bodies lying on the floor. One had no face left; the second lay
next to him, facedown, his arm thrown across the first man's
chest.

The piece of metal banged again.

He was about to turn the light off when he noticed that the
arm of the man on the floor appeared to have moved from the
other's chest. He watched the arm for a moment. It didn't seem
to be moving now, but there was no question that it *had* moved.
He was sure of it. And now he thought about Test 33A—about
corpses kicking and jerking and moving.

Slowly, he passed the light beam from one side to the other.
He looked at all the bodies: some exposed, two or three under
tarps and rags, or with other corpses lying on top of them.
When the light again found the two men on the floor in front
of him, the arm that had been across the chest now lay on the
floor. The body had shifted slightly to one side.

"Gentlemen, what we witnessed today inside that chamber was totally unexpected, an effect for which we have no explanation. But since it occurred twice, and there may be evidence that it has occurred before at the site of the plane crash, we believe it will be part of the basis of this research. For this reason we shall name this project as the KP Project in reference to what we have come to call..."

The dead man's leg moved, bending slightly at the knee. Attwood had the light right on it; he saw that.

He backed away from the plane.

"...the Kota Phenomenon."

5

THERE WAS NO MISTAKING IT; there were two sets of lights flashing, two sets of noises being transmitted from the motion detectors in the pass. Gilmore watched them, listened to them. He had no idea of why there would be two, hundreds of yards apart, or who—or what—was making the noises. But he should go up there and see what was going on. He should get off his ass right now, get his gear on and go see if Attwood had run into trouble. He should.

But he couldn't get out of that chair. He couldn't take his eyes off the control panel. There was movement coming from two different locations up there, and it had just dawned on him why. No way could he go out there now.

But at least Attwood was on his way back down, and thank God for small favors. The silence and isolation were starting to get to him. All kinds of crazy things had been flitting through his mind like so many bugs buzzing around a yard light. Kota Station seemed to have changed while he sat there alone, almost as if it were shrinking, as if the walls were closing in on him. That couldn't be, of course. Kota Station had not been equipped with movable walls; the U.S. Army did not feature a sense of humor about any of its facilities. Some of the vehicles, perhaps, but not its buildings.

No. He was just worried, that was all. And the walls weren't moving.

At least not when he turned to look at them.

And he turned to look at all the walls, all the rooms, all the equipment surrounding him. Not a single thing had moved, either in front of him or behind his back. He was almost certain of it.

He got up from the chair. Looking. Listening.

Ordinarily, Gilmore's imagination was limited only to those things related to his job, and then only in controlled quantities. He was proud of that; it kept his observations neutral and unbiased. Too much imagination caused one's mind to wander, a bad situation when one was looking for the heart of a problem. If you worked in a place like Blackstone or Fort Stanton, you could not allow your mind to wander while looking for solutions to problems.

He thought about what his imagination had already done. He and Attwood had come down from the summit a while ago and found the door open; he had radioed Endicott, accusing them of leaving it open. Stupid. No wonder Grady became angry with him, because there was only one explanation—he was the last one out this morning, so he had left it open. And there was nothing wrong with the door or its latching assembly. He had simply forgotten to close and latch it. He had screwed up twice, actually—leaving the door open, then blaming somebody else for it. No, three times; Attwood was still working alone, and *he* was still in here acting like a scared little kid at a Saturday afternoon spook show, thinking about moving walls. . . .

No. . . moving corpses.

And Attwood. His partner was still out there somewhere in the pass.

He glanced at the microwave receiver once again, but now there were no noises, no sounds of movement coming from outside, no noises registering on the control panel or coming through the speaker. None of the green lights was flashing or modulating. He watched the board for a minute, then hurried across the room to where his gear lay on the floor. Throwing on his parka, he pulled open the heavy door and stepped outside.

Nobody was out there.

"Chuck?" he called, looking toward the pass. "Attwood? Where are you?" and he took a few steps toward the lower end of the plateau. "Attwood? Are you out there?" He could see nothing; he could hear nothing except the wind. But damned if he couldn't *feel* something . . . almost as if someone was hiding behind one of the rocks watching him.

He stopped, then stepped backward toward the building. "Chuck?" he said again, his voice now dropping to a whisper. "What the hell are you doing? Where are you?"

6

"*. . . AND WHILE NO ACCURATE METHOD yet exists to determine any latent or long-range effects of the agent, it is assumed for the time being that if the host organism is in some way preserved it can continue to provide a vehicle in which the agent may interact for an indefinite period. Such a potential mechanism is not only possible, but may very well be occurring at the site of the . . .*"

Well, guess what, guys? Attwood thought as he hurried down the summit toward the pass. Ain't no maybe, no assumption, no head scratching about it. This shit works, and you can go take a look for yourselves. You'll excuse me if I don't. I've seen enough, thank you, you're welcome, over roger and fucking out.

He scrambled around the section of aileron blocking the pathway, jumping over two of the bodies. He had turned both of them over this morning to get their dog tags. He almost slipped on another piece of junk, but just caught himself and stepped gingerly over a third corpse lying faceup in the snow.

Got a problem there, buddy?

"What?" he choked, then looked down. The corpse's eyes were open, a quizzical sort of expression frozen on the features. And now it rolled its head up, facing him. Heart hammering, he looked at it, thinking, No . . . oh, shit no, they can move they can kick and jerk and roll around but no way no fucking way can they—

Ice cracked from around the bloodied mouth. The corpse grinned at him. *We all got problems, don't we?*

Shaking, Attwood backpedaled away from the body, unable to take his eyes off it. He was ten feet away, still moving, still trembling badly, when he slipped on the ice and went down, his arm striking another body he had had to move earlier that day.

The man rolled over toward him. His eyes were frozen shut, his mouth set in a half-open sort of O shape. But that changed as it transformed into a broken grin. The eyelids opened slowly.

Problems, problems, problems...

"No—"

Legs pumping, Attwood scrambled to his feet. And ran.

7

As HE STOOD THERE, Gilmore remembered something he had once heard from a huge black master sergeant instructing him and his men about night infantry patrolling: "You is the hunt-*er*. They is the hunt-*ee*. You gotta remember that so that when you finally meet up with 'em that'll make *you* the kill-*er*, and *them* the kill-*ee*."

Good advice: always take the offensive. And why had he recalled that now? Why did he have this feeling that taking the offensive might just save his ass?

He looked around the plateau again. "Attwood? Are you there?" and he still could see nothing moving. A disquieting thought occurred to him then. Suppose Attwood ran into some kind of trouble with the gas up there. It was possible, possible for both of them, and Attwood could have been exposed to it. Their protective equipment was supposed to prevent that, but there was still so much they didn't know about the stuff that even the most trivial mistake could be a disaster. There were always accidents, and Attwood could have had one as easily as anyone else. Even a mild exposure could affect you badly, which was what they assumed had happened to that young lieutenant last September. And the gas was certainly around. It had to be, even if the concentrations were less than they had expected. Tests had already proved that a concentration of forty gallons spread over an area the size of the summit would remain for something like 275 or 300 years before it dispersed to harmless amounts. And between now and then, you just couldn't get rid of it, and given the right atmospheric conditions, the stuff could migrate for short distances. Gravity and precipitation would bring a little of it down to some of the lower elevations. In fact, they had been warned to expect trace amounts at the plateau level. The only reason it would be of little concern was because the station was pressurized and filtered, so none of it could migrate inside—

Unless, of course, one of them pulled a real boner—such as leaving the door open.

As it had been earlier. And as it was right now.

He turned to look at it, confirming that he had fucked up again. "Oh, shit!" he moaned, sagging. And there he stood— no coveralls, no helmet, no mask, no respirator. One hell of a time to be remembering all the important little details, he thought, cursing again. So maybe the gas had gotten to him, as it had to that lieutenant eight months ago.

Well, now, he had to think. They had to react. There was no telling how it had affected him, and if Attwood had suffered exposure up top where the concentrations were the highest, he could be in real trouble. They had to get the hell out of here right now. He had to look for Chuck, help him, carry him down this mountain if necessary, and there was no time to lose.

"Chuck? Chuck! Where the hell are you? Ch—" and he saw something around the corner of the building, or thought he did. He walked toward it, thinking that Chuck might be half out of his mind by now or that something worse could be wrong. "Chuck? Is that you?"

8

CHUCK ATTWOOD HAD RUN down the pass. He was more than halfway down before he stopped, out of breath and still in something of a panic. He tried to think, and he remembered only then that he was missing a helmet and the rest of the equipment that went with it.

"Oh, God, no!" he groaned, collapsing against a rock. "You dumb shit!" He remembered what he had done. Now he might be a walking dead man.

Like those men up there.

He took a furtive look behind him up the pass. Nothing was there. But there had been; he'd seen them, heard them. Sure he had. There had been bodies moving, coming to life—one inside the wreck, three or four others outside. Dead bodies, things that should be forever immobile, forever silent...moving. Talking.

But no one was there now.

His head began to clear, and it occurred to him that nothing had happened to him so far. He had run away from the summit, from the bodies, and he now stood halfway down the pass. He was still alive, still breathing, still thinking. He felt fine—winded, still half in a panic—but all right. And now that he was thinking, how could a corpse rise or follow him? It could not. Impossible. If the dead bodies were really moving they were being animated by the gas in the atmosphere. That was it, all it could be. And maybe it had caused him to see things, to imagine he had seen bodies moving.

He sighed, relaxing a bit. Some of the questions didn't seem quite so mysterious now, and he was thinking that he'd just learned something important about Swamp Gas, something they hadn't considered before. But he would have to sort it out with Gilmore, and together they would have to talk it over with Stanton.

He was still considering some of the new details when he turned to see who—or what—had followed him down the pass.

9

GRADY WAS LOOKING FORWARD to a quiet evening at home: a leisurely meal, some light conversation, then perhaps a good book in his easy chair. Or maybe a game of chess with Martha, and he smiled when he thought about that. People were surprised that she not only played chess and played the game well, but that she had taught it to her husband and daughters. And none of them could beat her. Grady had often joked that she should be the general because she could maneuver and connive much more skillfully than he.

Walking from his office, a feeling came over him. He should go straight down the hall, he thought, down the stairs and out the door to the parking lot. Get in the car, drive home and take the phone off the hook, he told himself.

Instead, he walked across the hall and into the communications center.

The officer in charge spotted him before the door was closed. "Glad you stopped in, sir. I was about to see if you'd gone home for the day."

"What's up?" Grady said, taking a deep breath.

"We may have a problem, sir."

Shit, what else is new? "What is it?"

"Kota Station. We can't seem to raise them." He led Grady toward their main radio console. "We were checking about their earlier problem with the door, and whether they'd gotten it corrected. That, and it's past their check-in time."

The radio operator sat at the control panel, trying quietly to get someone at Kota Station to respond. He repeated his message over and over.

Grady looked at his watch—7:03 p.m. They were supposed to have heard from Gilmore or Attwood no later than six. "I wonder if their radio's out?"

"No, sir." He pointed to a set of lights on the control panel. "Our indicators say that it's on and they're receiving. No one's answering."

"Well, maybe their radio is turned down."

The OIC nodded. "Could be, sir. But they're not supposed to do that."

An hour overdue, and no word since noon. Plus Gilmore and his strange accusation: *"Somebody else was up here. Somebody else had to be here."*

"They could still be away from the station," the communications officer went on. "Maybe they found something that required more attention."

Or maybe something found them, Grady wondered. But he nodded, pretending that it was nothing to worry about. "Keep trying to raise them. Call me at home if you still haven't made contact in a couple of hours."

"Yes, sir."

IF HE MOVED THE RED BISHOP into position to take out the rook, her knight could take his pawn, and place his king into check. His one remaining rook would be taken by her queen if he moved it to try and guard his king. No other piece was in position to do any good, so there was only one move; back his king up diagonally away from her knight, which meant it would probably cost him his rook anyway.

He sipped his coffee. "Damn! How do I get into these messes?"

Martha's chin rested in her hands. She smiled sweetly at him, but her eyes betrayed her; she was ready for the kill. "I keep telling you," she said with a shrug. "You have to plan your opponent's moves, too. And you always seem more interested in seeing how many of my pieces you can take out instead of concentrating on the opposing king."

He sighed, and moved his king back. "Hell, go on, rip my throat open." He waved. "You're the most bloodthirsty woman I've ever seen."

She did. Two moves later it was checkmate.

And then the phone rang. It was the OIC at the communications center. There was still no response from Kota Station.

PART THREE

★

The Kota Phenomenon

Once a job is fouled up, anything done to improve it only makes it worse.

—Finagle's Fourth Law

Things always get worse under pressure.

—Murphy's Law of Thermodynamics

A sudden idea will always work better than anything carefully planned.

—Anonymous

CHAPTER FOURTEEN

"YOU PEOPLE HAVE JUST two things you've gotta remember," they were told. "One: nobody gets by your post and into the perimeter without this pass, and I mean nobody. Two: if anybody tries to get in without that pass, you stop 'em. You already know how. It'll be your ass if you don't."

Short and sweet; anyone not in possession of the special Class AAA-1-101 Kota Post entry permit was to be warned only one time if they tried to enter, and that warning would carry with it the sincere promise to shoot if they did not halt. If that failed, ka-pow. The guard issuing the warning would shoot to kill—no further warnings, orders, arguments or questions. Whoever the interloper might later prove to be—bum, general or the President—was secondary to keeping him out of the area. And if any guard failed in this duty it was not merely possible but damned likely that he would vanish faster than yesterday's shit.

But at least any potential intruder would have had ample warning. The perimeter—an unbroken barbed wire barrier that twisted its way around the entire base of the mountain—was constructed high up near the edge of the timberline. There were also warning signs—five hundred of them all around the mountain—that had been erected all through the timber just above all the hiking areas and campgrounds. Each was as subtle and tactful as a load of buckshot in the ass. Even if all of this failed to warn someone away, the sight of the barbed wire and heavily armed guards probably would. Most civilians were respectful of such things if not out-and-out scared shitless.

With their two primary orders, the guards were told to ignore everything except aggressive movements against their posts. They would speak to no one except their commanding officers, or among themselves; they would answer no questions, offer no information, and make no gestures that could be construed as friendly. For all purposes, the world on the opposite side of the perimeter did not exist while they were on duty, and when they were off duty they would make no mention of it. Any breach of security would not even be discussed—only punished, swiftly and thoroughly.

"Sounds pretty serious," one of them commented during the briefing.

"You don't even want to know how serious it is."

"Is there anything else we should know?" a second man asked.

"Yeah. Don't fuck up."

Since the park was closed from September 30 to May 1, nearly all of the guards' tours of duty had occurred during long periods of inactivity. Most of their time had been spent simply manning the guard shacks all around the perimeter and walking their posts, and almost all of their conversation centered on the harsh mountain winter. One of the officers in charge would come by in a jeep approximately every four hours; once in a while they might see one of the park rangers on regular patrol, but they, too, had been warned of what was going on around the mountain, so they stayed away. The guards' meals were taken up to them, and they were relieved at eight-hour intervals. They worked seven-day shifts, then had two days off.

The only change of pace came when the park opened and they began seeing all the tourists in the areas below their stations. That was where they had been told to look for potential trouble; some of the hikers and campers would wander up toward the perimeter by accident; others would get close out of curiosity or gleeful disregard of all the warnings. But in two weeks, the only incident reported had been two hikers who came up to about two hundred yards from the barbed wire near Post 14. They stared at one of the signs, pointed toward the wire, then shrugged as they walked away.

With nearly six thousand acres under guard, twenty two miles of continuous barbed wire to watch and walk, and twenty-two guard posts to man—all of it set dead center in a large national park—it was a remarkable lack of activity. By no means had the security become complacent, but with nearly eight months passing in utter solitude and quiet, the men had become used to having nothing to report. Even near the end of May when the park had filled up with tourists, some of whom ventured closer and closer to the perimeter, nothing had happened. The intimidating signs, the vicious-looking barbed wire and all the green-uniformed men carrying automatic rifles and submachine guns seemed to be causing the desired effect. The guards reported hourly to their commanding officers on the field telephones; they watched the civilians on the trails and in the campgrounds below their outposts. They heard the noise of laughing children, and once in a while the smells of barbecuing hot dogs, hamburgers and steaks wafted up to them on the breeze. Everything was quiet, under control.

And no one offered the slightest attention to the faded, dented old GMC pickup truck that drove quietly to the back of the campground just below Post 19.

And stayed there.

2

DOUG GORHAM ONCE SAID, "There are only three routes up Kota. Two of them are no damned good at all unless the weather's perfect. The third one ain't much better." Later, he'd shortened the declaration. "There ain't any such thing as a good route up Kota."

John Karber had never been heard to say anything about their climbs, or the routes they had discovered and used. Steve Woodhull, on the other hand, had an opinion: "That's bullshit." Shorter, straight to the heart. That was Woodhull.

"Look," he told Gary, "I know you're not supposed to speak ill of the dead, or whatever the suitable phrase is, but it's high time for a little truth about that friggin' mountain, and everything else that went on. Especially if someone's gonna climb the son of a bitch again."

Woodhull didn't look quite as Gorham had described him, and almost nothing like the solidly built, muscular man Gary had seen in the old photos. But, Gary thought when he first saw Steve behind the counter of his store, time passes and things change. Woodhull was much heavier, his face thicker, and the copper-colored hair had a tinge of gray at the edges. But the shock came as Woodhull climbed down off the counter stool to greet his customers. He was barely able to walk, hobbling painfully with the aid of a heavy cane.

"Morning!" He smiled, flashing the wide expression toward Janey. It caught her off guard, the first time Gary had ever seen her blush. It was Steve Woodhull—no mistaking him, or the smile Gorham said used to paralyze women in their tracks. "Can I help you folks?" And before Gary had a chance to reply, Steve waved his cane at the woman across the store, who was stacking boxes on a shelf. "Judas Priest, Debbie, the hammers go down there!" And as if nothing had happened he turned back to Gary and Janey, smiling again. "What can I do for you?"

"We need to be outfitted for a climb," Gary said.

"That we can do. Rock? Alpine? Both?"

Gary handed him a list of equipment, and Woodhull studied it for a minute. Most of it ran to alpine gear, and a lot of that seemed more high-altitude gear than anything else. He guessed that whatever mountain they were planning was a lot taller than any local peak. "It would help to know which mountain you're climbing," he said.

"Mount Kota," Gary said quietly.

The reply seemed to jolt Woodhull, but only for a moment. He looked at Gary with a quick half smile. "Kota? Why that one?"

"I've been on it before, about eight months ago. With a late friend of yours. Doug Gorham. My name is—"

The smile vanished. "What the hell are you talking about?"

"Gary Palmer. Lieutenant Gary Palmer, U.S. Army. I was stationed at Fort Endicott, Montana. And eight months ago I was with Doug Gorham and Rudi Gurdler, and we climbed Mount Kota on an attempted rescue mission going after survivors of a plane crash that occurred on the summit. We—"

A hand came up; for an instant Gary thought the cane might come up with it. "I'm in no mood for jokes, Mr.—*Lieutenant* Palmer. I remember the plane crash. And I remember that all three of those guys got killed up there." He shoved the list into Gary's pocket. "There's the door. Use it."

Gary didn't move. "Mr. Woodhull, I'm really Gary Palmer, and I can prove it. I've been on Kota. I've been to the summit. And I can prove that. Just give me a few minutes."

Janey grabbed his arm. "Gary, let's go. You don't need any trouble."

He stood fast. "No. We need to talk to him."

Woodhull stared at both of them long and hard, as if sizing them up for a fight. Finally, he backed away a couple of steps. "All right. I'm listening," he said quietly. The tone of his voice suggested that Gary had perhaps a minute, and that he might get bashed with the cane if Woodhull didn't like what he heard.

Well, he had told it all to an old lady who had pulled a gun on him; a recital to a man about to club him with a cane seemed par for the course. So he repeated the story he'd told to Emma Lockhart, but added specific details about the mountain. Woodhull kept nodding as he talked, and when Gary finished he said, "You believe me, then?"

Steve nodded. "You were there, all right."

There must be something about the way I tell it. Gary sighed.

"Keep going," Woodhull added with a wince, hobbling back to the stool behind the counter. "I can't stand too long on this leg."

"Well, if you believe me—"

"Go on anyway. I want to hear all about Gorham." He sounded angry.

Gary continued the story for another five minutes, right to the point where the three of them had started up Karber's Pass, when Woodhull stopped him again. "How come they said that all three of you got killed? And if you're in the Army, what are you doing here?"

"I was getting to that. This is where..."

Two customers walked in.

"Do you have a place where we can talk in private?" Gary asked.

"What's wrong with right here?"

"It's a long story, and it's not one everybody on the street should be hearing."

Steve got up, motioning for Gary to follow him. "In the back. What do you mean, not for everybody?"

"I mean, as in classified. Military secret. I mean, this thing is about to get weird."

"It's already weird." He gestured toward a tiny office where they sat down. Steve fished two beers from a small refrigerator.

"What did you mean, you wanted to hear all about Gorham?"

Popping the top, Woodhull took a long drink. "You want weird? And you think you told *me* a weird story? Well, I'm about to see your capacity to believe stretched asshole tight over an oil drum. *I'm* gonna tell *you* about Doug Gorham, because I believe your story. Hell, I have to from your description of Kota…that, and because I don't think you're the type to come in here with shit like that made up just for my benefit. But before we go on, what do you want from me?"

Gary's story finished with everything he knew about the mountain's summit and crash site, and what had become of him afterward. "So you see what I'm up against? Since the only way to stay out of their reach and to find out what happened to me is to climb up there again, I'd like to know how the hell I got down. It couldn't have been the same way we went up. I was catatonic. I can't remember any of it. So, anything you can tell me about the mountain would help."

Woodhull stared off into space for a moment, but this time his thick, creased face contorted alternately with expressions of anger and what seemed to be pain. When he looked at his guest again, Gary suddenly knew that he was about to hear far more than he'd expected.

He waited.

Steve drained his beer as he collected and rearranged his thoughts.

"I think I know how you got down. But there's a hell of a lot more to it than . . . well, shit! I guess the only way to explain it is to tell you the whole friggin' story. But it all stays here."

Gary nodded.

"Remember that little cave where you guys spent the night? What did Gorham tell you about it, anyway?"

"Not much. He said you found it on your seventh ascent. We didn't see anything unusual about it until the next morning when Gurdler and I noticed that all those rocks had been stacked where they were. We felt cold air blowing through the cracks. We asked Gorham about it, and he said you put them there to keep the wind out; that the opening went back into the mountain about sixty or seventy feet. But that you'd never explored it. He got mad when we kept asking questions about it."

Woodhull shook his head. "That son of a bitch!" he muttered. "Oh, I'll bet he got mad. You're lucky he didn't get worse than that."

"What do you mean?"

Settling himself down, Steve went on. "Okay, now for some truth. Hang on. Karber found that thing on our *tenth* climb. Shit, man, we'd passed it by two or three other times because we didn't know what it was. All the rocks had rolled out from the inside, and it didn't look like a cave. Then, Karber happened to take a look at it, and his goddamn light wouldn't even reach the end. So we moved the rocks away, and went inside for a look. And that was the beginning of the end. I almost wish we'd never seen the friggin' thing. But that was Karber. He was forever spotting all the little details everyone else missed. I don't know why he didn't become a detective or something because he would've put that friggin' Sherlock Holmes to shame.

"But once we were in it, we saw that it went back a hell of a lot farther than any sixty or seventy feet. We were more than a hundred feet back, and it was still going, and at a hundred and fifty feet or so it went up, following the contour of the mountain. So Karber and I said, 'Well shit man, let's see how far this thing really goes,' because we couldn't see the end of it anywhere. It just kept going on up and up and friggin' *up*. We must have been inside a good four hundred feet or better when we finally turned back."

"Why did you turn around?"

"Gorham! Oh, man, he was having a shit fit, madder than hell at us. He was yelling at us, 'What the hell are you doing, climbing a mountain, or exploring caves?' I mean, he was screaming like some nutty old woman. And he just flat refused to go any farther. So we had to turn back just to shut him up. We were afraid he might get violent, or that all his screaming would start an avalanche or something."

"Are you saying that you and Karber thought it might go all the way to the summit?"

"Damn right. And after hearing your story, I'm pretty sure it does, or damned close to the top. If you were in the kind of condition you described, I can't think of any other way you'd have gotten down alone.

"But, like I said, we turned around because of Gorham. Hell, we needed him. You know, it's like taking one of the wheels off your car. You can't go on if one member of the team just friggin' lays down on you. But what I was getting to is that I think John found the upper end of that thing on our last climb. I think . . . I'll never know for sure."

"Where was it?"

Woodhull quieted for a moment. "Well, here's where it gets bad. And weird, like I told you.

"See, Gorham was always a little funny about that mountain. He was the one who did all the research about it, and who brought us there to climb it. Hell, he could've told you every detail about every expedition that ever went up the thing. That was a problem we never saw until years later: Kota was an obsession with Gorham right from the beginning; a full-blown psychological obsession, and it seemed to get worse with him every year. You could see it. Each year you could see him get a little madder, a little more frustrated, and more and more desperate. He *had* to be the first man to the top, and there were times when he'd friggin' *talk* to himself out of frustration, almost like he was in a trance. After nine or ten years of that shit, Karber and I were starting to worry about him. We should have stopped the whole thing then and there. I suppose we were a little obsessed by then ourselves. All of us wanted to get to the top. But it was eating Gorham up.

"But the thing Karber and I didn't see until the ninth or tenth climb was that he acted like it was his mountain, like he literally owned the friggin' thing. It was like we were no longer partners, or part of the team. He was trying to run every detail of every climb, almost like some friggin' drill sergeant. See, we never had an expedition leader because we never felt like we needed one. When we first started out we worked pretty well together without any one of us taking over. But the last few climbs, Doug wouldn't have it that way. You know; we were climbing *his* goddamn mountain, so we were gonna do it his way. He wouldn't stand for anything else, and he acted like he'd get violent if we didn't climb that thing like it was supposed to be climbed.''

Woodhull reached into the refrigerator for two more beers.

"It was the last climb that tore it all to shit. There was something we didn't tell Gorham. Before we ever started, John and I decided that if we didn't make the summit that time, the hell with it. That would be the end of Kota for us. We were getting burned-out on it, but we were really tired of all of Doug's shit. We just weren't gonna put up with it anymore.

"What happened was that it started out perfect. Oh, Gorham started right off wanting to go up that friggin' Lunatic Wall again, but Karber and I said, 'Fuck that, we're going up the North Col and buttress. Let's make it easy on ourselves for a change.' He didn't like it, but we thought, screw 'im, and that's the way we went. And that was when we made the god-damnedest discovery we ever made up there: taken in perfect weather, the Northern Route becomes a walk. You will not run into one single obstacle that'll hold you up. To prove it, we started at seven in the morning, and we got to the cave about five that afternoon. We couldn't friggin' believe it. The climb was no tougher than hiking down a country road.

"Man, did that gall him! By the time we got to the cave, he was about ready to explode. That wasn't mountain climbing at all to him, and sure as hell not the way we were supposed to be climbing his mountain. He was so mad, I thought he might start breaking rocks with his fists. And that was when Karber made *the* discovery, and he picked absolutely the wrong time and place to say the wrong thing. He said, 'Well, would you look at that shit. If you take the Northern Route to here, then go the rest of the way up in this cave, it's a climb anybody could make.' And by God, it was true. We'd never seen it before, but there it was. When you stood there looking down, then up toward the cave, the route was easy to see. Of course, we still didn't know if the cave went all the way up, but even if it didn't you could still avoid a lot of the obstacles above us. So, we stood there looking up and down at a route that anyone with hiking shoes could take.

"Son of a bitch! Here we'd been busting our balls for eleven years trying everything we knew to climb to the top of that thing, and the easy route had been there all the time. Right in front of us. Like I said, Karber noticed the details. Well, we felt like total chumps, dumber than a bag of bricks. Then Karber started laughing; then I started laughing. All of a sudden it was the funniest friggin' thing we'd ever seen, and we were howling like a couple of stoned hyenas, rolling around in the snow. All those *years*, man! All those times we damn near killed ourselves trying to get to the top of a rock that was easy. Hell, a good rider could've taken a motorcycle to the summit.

"But that did it to Gorham . . . caved him right in. I guess it all hit 'im at once; all the years of planning, working, danger, trying to do everything a certain way. We had to use all the techniques, all the right tools, lay out the routes, do everything exactly right, and in one fell swoop—just one quick look up and down—it all added up to nothing for him. He snapped right there on the spot. He went into another rage, only a lot worse than the year before. He was screaming, throwing things . . . completely hysterical. We were laughing at *him*, laughing at *his* mountain. And when we tried to calm him, he broke down. No shit. He collapsed into the snow, crying, blubbering, wailing like hell. Well, Karber and I knew then that we had us a fucking problem. What the hell do you do when one of your climbers has a breakdown at sixteen thousand feet?

"Well, John and I started picking up to go back down. Shit, man, that was it, no more. But Doug's little fit ended then. He was calmed down, he got up, collected his stuff, then damned if he didn't apologize to us. He was talking calmly, explaining what happened, how it just got to him for a minute, and that he just didn't see anything funny about the situation. He insisted that it was over, and he was fine. He felt good, no problem. And then he said that maybe we'd better forget any future climbs up Kota, and that if we didn't make the summit this time, we should forget the whole thing. Did that sound okay to us?

"Holy shit. It was the most reasonable thing he'd said in five years. He sounded like the old Doug Gorham again. Karber and I were stunned for a minute. We didn't know what to make of it. Then Gorham added that as long as we were this far along we might as well try and finish it because everything else was going so good. And John and I just found ourselves agreeing.

"Well ... now I know. I know we should have hog-tied him and carried 'im back down there on the spot. That was the worst mistake we ever made—agreeing with Doug Gorham right after he'd had a breakdown, so we weren't all that bright either. And I'll have to admit that we wanted to get to the top almost as badly as he did. We were within three thousand feet of it, everything was going good, and there didn't seem to be any reason we couldn't make it that time.

"So, we kept on going. We forgot the cave just to keep him calm. We got to the Northeast Plateau in good shape, set up camp, had a nice rest, and all the while Gorham seemed perfectly normal. We just didn't know that he'd cracked. The next morning while we were looking around for a route to the summit, he seemed to be in a kind of euphoria, more talkative and happy and friendly than he'd been in years. Dumb, dumb, *dumb*! Jesus, were we stupid! Then, maybe an hour or so later, Karber located the entrance to the pass. That's what finally caved him in for good. You remember Karber's Pass, don't you?"

Gary nodded. He remembered most of it.

"Think about that for a minute. People had been trying to climb Kota for more than fifty years, and no one had done it. It's got the worst reputation of any mountain in North America. People were terrified of it, even some of the best climbers in the country. So, to Doug Gorham, it was his mountain, the one that made his reputation. Everybody would know who he was—leader of the first expedition to climb Kota. And a lot of people were watching our last climb.

"Then look what happened. Look what it turned out to be. First, the Northern Route, then the cave, and finally the pass. They were easy. If you took the right route, it was nothing but a walk. Hell, your grandma could handle it. Kota was the biggest, tallest mountain in the country, and it was a pussy. Nothing but a great big empty dream.

"Gorham was shattered, man. Hell, I think he was bawling again halfway into the pass. But don't get me wrong because Karber and I were a little disappointed, too. Hell, you don't spend eleven years trying to achieve something and then have it fall apart like that without feeling something. It was like none of us wanted the final victory handed to us. But Doug couldn't handle it at all, and it shoved him over the edge. Anyway, you can see now what he did to you guys."

Gary had been thinking about that. You had to feel sorry for someone like Gorham, but the anger Gary felt growing could barely be contained. Woodhull was right; Gorham was a son of a bitch. "He risked our lives going up the Northeast Route," he muttered. "And if we'd taken the Northern Route, we might have gotten to the top hours, maybe a day, earlier."

Steve nodded. "You might have had a successful rescue. But Gorham was still protecting his mountain."

"I'll be damned. Now I know what it feels like to be had."

"Oh, it gets better—or worse—than that. There was all that bullshit about how Karber supposedly fell. But that was Gorham's version. I didn't see it happen. All I've got to go on was the frame of mind he was in."

"What do you mean?"

"Going up the pass, Karber was in front, Gorham was behind him, and I was maybe a hundred feet back. There was a place where the pass bends to the right and levels out a little, and they'd gone around the bend where I couldn't see them. All of a sudden I heard this shouting ahead of me, Gorham yelling at Karber. I ran up to see what was going on but I couldn't find them for a few seconds. I heard more yelling, this time above me in the rocks, only it was Karber yelling at Gorham. I still couldn't see 'em, so I started up to where they were. Then here comes Gorham back down. I yelled, 'What happened' and all he said was: 'Karber fell. We've gotta go back down.'

"Well, that's when *I* almost flipped. I told you Gorham was in bad shape, but when he came down from those rocks he had the strangest look on his face I'd ever seen on anybody. I can't describe it except that it was friggin' scary...all red-faced, wild-eyed, like some goddamn loony or something. And when he said that Karber fell and we had to go back down it sounded like he was asking for the time, or he had to go take a shit or something. There was no emotion at all except for that weird friggin' look on his face. So when he got down, I threw him against the rocks and yelled at him. 'What do you mean, Karber fell? What the hell happened up there, anyway?' Oh, man, I was ready to beat his friggin' brains out.

"Then he grabbed me, and the punches flew. He decked me once, and he just turned around and started back down. I yelled at him again: 'What the goddamn hell happened, you son of a bitch?' and he whirled around and came up with his ice ax. No shit. If I'd made another move I'm sure he would have attacked me with it. And he yelled, 'Karber fell! That's all! Are you coming back down to get him or not?'"

"Wait a minute," Gary said, eyes wide. "Are you suggesting that Gorham might have *killed* Karber? That he was looking for the upper end of that cave, and Gorham pushed him?"

"I don't know. I'll never know for sure, and neither will anyone else. All I can say is maybe, and that'd never hold friggin' water in any court. All I had to go on was the way he was acting, the condition he was in, and I sure as hell ain't no psychiatrist. The only support I could give it is everything you've told me: there he is, five years later, leading a rescue party that's supposed to get to the top as fast as possible, and he takes you the long way around. Hell, even if you couldn't have outrun that storm you could've used the cave...assuming you'd have known where it went."

Quite a few things might have been possible, Gary thought. And now some of them appeared likely, including his own mysterious descent. But something else occurred to him, and he looked Woodhull straight in the eyes. "If you knew all of this, where the hell were you while it was going on? Why didn't you say something? You could have saved us a lot of trouble."

"I was in the hospital." He pointed to his leg. "That's why I'm walking around on sticks right now."

"What happened? Climbing accident?"

"Oh, don't I fuckin' wish! But it was nothing that glamorous. A car hit me. I was going into a liquor store a couple of miles down the road. I was walking in front of an empty parking stall when this friggin' drunk came wheeling in, and boom! He rammed right into me—almost put me through a plate-glass window. If the curb hadn't been there, I'd be a Buick hood ornament today. Broke my leg in three places, jerked the thighbone clear out of the pelvic socket, and totally fucked up my knee. I'm lucky to be walking at all. And the asshole who hit me still has his driver's license. And I run my shop, and yell at Debbie all the time. Like they say, life's a bitch, ain't it?

"But now that I've heard all of this, the real bitch is that my accident happened the day before that plane crashed up there. The evening before. I spent that night all doped up in the hospital, and half of the next day in surgery, then another day or so doped up. By the time I was watching any TV or reading the papers, all that shit on Kota had already happened. Then they said that all three of you guys got killed up there, so I said, Well fuck it. I'd just let it all die with Gorham. Everybody still thinks Kota is the number-one badass mountain, and I saw no reason to tell 'em any different. Especially not after all the shit that's happened up there now. I still think so. I still think it'd be best for everyone just to stay away from the friggin' thing and enjoy the view ... from a long distance."

Gary smiled. He wished he could take the advice. "If you'd had no accident, and I'd called you that night, would you have taken us up?"

Steve shrugged. "Six years ago I said I'd never go near that thing again. I wouldn't have wanted to, that's no shit, so I probably would have just told you how to get up to the top. Really, I don't know. But not climbing it again had nothing to do with Karber, like everyone thought. It was Gorham I was worried about. If I'd have even thought about going near Kota again without him, I think he'd have come after me with a gun. He was in that frame of mind. And I'd bet that the five years between our last climb and the plane crash must have given him the drizzlin' shits, too. He was always afraid someone else would beat him to the top. I still don't know why he didn't go on up, as close as we were, even after Karber got killed."

"That's right!" Gary said, surprised that he hadn't noticed it. "You guys turned around... You didn't make it to the summit *that* time, either."

Woodhull smiled sadly. "Nope. Close, but no cigar. We missed it by a couple of hundred yards or so. Then, not long after the accident I started hearing these stories about Karber's dreadful fall, how ironic it was that he was so close, and all this shit about how we tearfully bestowed his name on the pass he discovered. What a friggin' crock. But everyone thought we made it, and Gorham just agreed with 'em. Then he started telling everybody how tough it was, and how other climbers should stay away from it. He was still protecting his mountain. I can just imagine what he was thinking when you told him that someone went and crashed a plane on it and scattered people all over the friggin' thing."

"He tried to talk us out of climbing it."

"Sure he did. Now you know why."

Gary drained his beer, refusing a third one. "Why didn't you tell anybody the truth about the mountain? Or about Gorham?"

"Nobody ever asked me," and he pushed himself back to his feet. He had to go back and mind the store. "But... Gorham was a friend once. Maybe he died a happy man, and I can't help but hope that much for him. At least he died in the one place where he always wanted to go. All of which makes you the only man who's been to the summit and lived to tell about it."

"Yeah, and I can't even remember it."

3

BOTH VEHICLES WERE IGNORING the twenty-five-mile-per-hour speed limit through the park. As General Grady looked out the window through the billowing clouds of dust, his mood became even more sour. It was already one of those days, and it had just started. Everything—his breakfast, his morning coffee, even the air—tasted bad. Everything felt bad; even his uniform felt as if it belonged to somebody else. And the day, he knew, was about to get worse.

Because it was happening at last. The dam was cracking, splitting. Water was starting to trickle through and about to burst.

I think we've pretty well got everything under control....

And when was that, Dave? he thought disgustedly. Exactly when did you have it all under control? And what was it that was under control? You based this project on control of an unpredictable product; you put your test facility in an uncontrollable and unpredictable environment; and now your main test subject has gone out of anyone's control and pulled, as they say, a Houdini. No, Dave, if you ask me—and I wish you would—control of this damned project was never really yours or anybody else's; except your guinea pig, late of Wheeler Barracks, Kansas.

He glanced over at Caldwell in the seat next to him, and nudged him, pointing to a pair of the many No Smoking and Watch Your Campfire signs posted along the road.

Caldwell muttered something, then put out his cigarette.

Goddamn yo-yos! They hadn't even known that Palmer had a girlfriend. They hadn't even considered it because they hadn't found one back in his hometown. Caldwell's partner, Eaton, in the ranger's truck up ahead, had let that little screwup slip out. Eaton had also been the one who said, "Well, don't worry about it, General, because we've got him now, by God. We know where he's going, and we'll be there to greet him." Within a few hours, every CID agent available had been rushed to Sioux Creek. The county had been salted with bogus utility linemen, mailmen, meter readers and even a make-believe land survey crew that kept a special watch over Wormann Road, and that girl's mother's house. They covered everything except Mount Kota National Park.

And now, here they were, heading toward the north side of the mountain—specifically, to Post 19 of the security perimeter.

GRADY STARED AT THE OFFICER in charge of the perimeter. "Captain," he said, sighing, "I presume you briefed your people on the security and urgency of all this." He looked toward a ring of guards surrounding an old GMC pickup truck parked under a spruce tree.

"Yes, sir, I certainly did. We don't know how this happened. We're trying to find out so it won't happen again."

"Well, since it's already happened I believe your men would be more beneficial to security back at their posts. That truck poses no risk." For that matter, his own presence here was less than necessary. He was here only because Caldwell and Eaton, who were now in charge of the CID operation in Sioux County, insisted that he come out. For reasons they had yet to explain, they wanted through the security barrier, and they wanted him to personally let them in. They had had some crazy idea about going up the mountain after Palmer, until they got a good look at the mountain. Now, they pretended to be miffed at not having been informed of the security barrier, and they were flexing their authority by commandeering Palmer's old truck. Grady was amazed by the way they operated; no wonder Palmer had slipped past them so easily. You guys ought to apply for jobs with the Chemical Corps and Fort Stanton, he thought. You'd be right at home.

"You're sure about the truck?" he said to Eaton.

Eaton nodded. "Palmer bought it from a Mr. Stephen Woodhull of Boulder, Colorado. He owns an alpine shop, where Palmer and an unidentified woman bought more than six hundred dollars' worth of climbing equipment. Yesterday."

By then Caldwell had joined them. "He really pulled one on us," he said, staring at the flanks of the mountain. Helicopters flew back and forth, searching for the two climbers. "We were trying to track his girlfriend's car, but she ditched it for a rental car before she ever picked him up. Then they ditched that one in Boulder, and bought this truck." He couldn't bring himself to admit the rest of it aloud—that Palmer had enlisted the aid of two women the CID hadn't known about until it was too late, and switched vehicles twice, or that he and Eaton had overshot their mark on at least two occasions. And to ice the cake, Palmer not only returned to a spot right under everybody's nose but was entirely out of their reach. He almost had to admire the guy; all that had taken balls.

It wasn't until then that Grady made the association with the name Woodhull. He had to force down a grin. Steve Woodhull—the last surviving member of the team that had beaten Kota. Palmer had known exactly where to find him. And even if he hadn't planned a single detail of his flight from Wheeler Barracks, he was still pretty damned good at thinking on his feet. He had been ahead of the CID all the way; they hadn't even been close.

"Well, General," Eaton said with a sigh, "he's out of our reach. Can you send any of your people up after him?"

"No. Out of the question."

"Why not? You have a whole base full of climbers."

"No. None of them have ever been on Kota, and it's too rough a mountain for them to train on now. They'd never get him in time anyway."

After a glance at each other, Caldwell and Eaton started to ask the same question at once. Caldwell got it first. "Get to him in time for what?"

"Yeah, what the hell's going on here?" They had to get Palmer back somehow. The CID had been made to look foolish and inept, something that set as well with their superiors as dog shit on their desks: *"Goddammit, you two are gonna stay there until you get 'im! If you can't go after 'im you'd better hope he falls off or you'll be there until he dies of old age!"*

"As I said earlier, gentlemen, you don't want to know what is going on around here," Grady replied. And he hated telling these two what he had just thought of, but it was his duty. "There are a couple of alternatives, however. You'd have to be patient while they develop."

"What are they?"

"Number one, you simply wait. Wait him out until he comes down. He has to come down sometime. Or, number two, we might be able to fly you up to...a certain place."

"*Fly* us?"

"I didn't know any helicopter could go that high."

"We have one—a prototype. And it's grounded right now, so you'll have to wait another day or two. But now that I think about it, it would be best for one of our men who's connected with this...well, project, to go get him. Things are going on up there that you aren't supposed to see. How does all of that sound?''

"Like we have no choice.''

With a smile, Grady nodded. "Afraid not.''

"Uh, pardon me, sir. What about the two guards?''

Grady turned to the guard captain. "What two guards?''

"The two who were on duty at this post last night. I'm holding them for disciplinary action, and I wanted to know—''

"Let 'em go, Captain.''

"I beg your pardon, sir?''

"Captain, if anybody gets their ass burned for the security break it'll be me. There's no reason to drag two men down with me just because of a low spot in a ravine no one happened to see.'' And if they failed to stop Palmer, he thought, the damage was as good as done anyway. "The guards will be of a lot more use to us if they're on duty. Later on you can stick them with an Article 15 and maybe a fine or restriction, but let them go back to work for the time being.''

"Whatever you say, sir,'' he muttered, shaking his head. What the top brass said and what they did always seemed to be 180 degrees apart.

"Well,'' Eaton said to his partner, "I guess we hang around Endicott for a day or two and see what happens.''

Welcome to the club, gentlemen. But the statement gave Grady an idea, and he walked back to his car to call Endicott Center.

"Negative, sir,'' the operator told him a few minutes later. "We've still had no contact with Kota Station. The situation hasn't changed. Their radio is on and receiving, but we still can't raise anyone. It's been nearly twenty hours since the last contact, sir. Should we declare an emergency?''

And do what with it? he wanted to ask. He said, "No, not yet. I'll let you know what to do when I get back. I'll be on my way in a few minutes.''

"Yes, sir. Endicott Center out.''

As he switched off the radio and hung the mike back into its holder he happened to look at the summit of the mountain high in the clouds. It appeared windy up there; snow could be seen blowing against the deep blue sky. From down here the sight looked so peaceful, so serene; a quiet, white solitude. You'd never guess what was going on up there; and right now, they couldn't.

And down here around him in the rugged evergreen forest, twenty-two cheap-looking metal huts had been installed like so many portable shithouses. More than twenty-two miles of evil-looking concertina wire had been strung around the mountain, making the place look like a fire base in a combat zone. There were hundreds of intimidating signs pounded into the ground to remind everyone that they were unwelcome here, and that they might get shot or killed just for venturing too close. The only things they hadn't done were to set out land mines and position artillery pieces and mortar pits—probably because no one happened to think of it.

"It looks like hell," he whispered.

And despite all of it—the carefully laid plans, the coordination, the fantastic sums of money spent and all the elaborate security arrangements made—the shit was going to hit the fan anyway. By all accounts, Palmer was a fine climber, and he was already well on his way to climbing this mountain another time. And there wasn't a damned thing any of them could do to stop him. He was their one vital key, the living link, to their project's success. And yet he was its potential executioner.

. . . *got everything under control . . .*

Right. And now he had to notify Kelly and Mattlock. They would want to know all about these latest developments in their long series of carefully controlled events. And wouldn't they be pleased?

He waved for his driver. "Let's get the hell out of here."

4

WITH THE SNOW AND ICE beginning to melt at the lower elevations, and in a half-solid, half-slush condition farther up, the Northern Route wasn't quite the walk in the park Steve Woodhull had suggested. But it wasn't the Lunatic Wall or the Northeast Route either, so Gary and Janey were making rea-

sonably good time. They found the slopes steep in places, rough
and slow-going in other spots. Where the snow was gray slush
the ice underneath would sometimes break, and they sank past
their ankles. They were forced to drag the backpacks along to
lessen their own weight; it was worse than picking their way
through sticky mud. Only as they neared the lower end of the
buttress where the ice was solid and the snow became more
powdery and dry was their progress faster.

Not that it became easy. Gary was out of shape after lying
around since last September, and even though Janey had always managed packing her share of the load on their climbs,
this was Kota. Whenever she looked up it appeared that they
would be climbing halfway to the moon. At daybreak, after
they had stopped for their third rest, and food and water, it felt
as if they had been climbing nonstop for the past five or six
days. She looked up once again toward the summit. It appeared miles away. They had barely gotten a good start.

"I know what you mean," Gary said after he heard her
groan. "But we'll make it. We'll get there. I can tell you right
now that we're at least a thousand feet higher than we were this
time on the last climb. It's a good route. We're just taking it at
the wrong time of year." He looked up toward their next obstacle, the Meataxe Ridge. He had not been on it before—consciously at least—and if it was like most ridges at this elevation,
the snow drifted and piled on its edges was in exactly the right
condition for an avalanche. Kota's slopes had a history of them,
most on the western face, but a few on the northern slopes. A
few years ago, park rangers had deliberately set one off; it had
become airborne, and was clocked at over 195 miles per hour.

Too, they weren't yet out of aircraft range, and if anyone had
tracked them to this park they would know at once where he
and Janey had gone. Gary could picture whole parties coming
up after them, the skies filled with helicopters and bullhorns.
They wouldn't be out of reach until they were at least halfway
up the North Buttress, and until that time they would be fair
game, dodging and hiding for most of the distance.

"How are you feeling?" he asked, breaking a chocolate bar
in two and handing it to her.

Janey nodded. "Okay." She smiled. "A little winded, but all right. I'm just . . . well . . . sort of worried. I feel like we've broken into a secret government installation or something."

"We have."

She bit off part of the chocolate bar. "I guess so," she muttered, chewing. "What are you going to do with all the classified information you assume you're going to find up there?"

"I'll think of something."

"When?"

"When I see whatever it is, I guess." But there had to be something up there, and something big from the looks of it. He hoped he could think of something big to do with it.

They had entered the park yesterday before dusk, signing into one of the camping areas as Mr. and Mrs. Gary Burns. Immediately, they began scouting for a good place to start the climb, which was when they came upon the security perimeter. And in only one glimpse, Gary's decision to climb the mountain again was reinforced. The whole damned mountain was under armed guard, as Janey had said. And up there somewhere were his answers.

They found Post 19 right at sundown. It seemed to be one of the most obscure and heavily wooded, and the closest to the spot Woodhull had suggested they begin climbing. Gary looked around, pretending to search for a place to set up camp, and within half an hour he had located a small ravine some hundred yards west of the guard shack; it looked as if they might be able to make it under the wire there. The guards didn't appear concerned with watching it, and observation of the place told him that it was visited by the officer in charge only at 4-hour intervals. "That's it," he'd whispered to Janey. "We'll just wait until they're over there by the shack, then sneak through under the wire. Once we're into those trees up there we're as good as gone. They'll never know we were there."

"That's what I'm afraid of."

"You know what I mean."

"Yeah, but are you sure, Gary? It doesn't look that easy to me. Look at those guns. And those two goons look like they're just itching to use them on someone."

"Don't worry about it. Hell, I even know one of 'em, the big one with no hair. Carrying the submachine gun."

"Well, so what? He doesn't appear conversational. He looks like he might take his job a little too seriously."

"Yeah, but he's not exactly a mental giant. I don't know how he was picked for something like this."

"Maybe because he's a good shot. And he won't hesitate to shoot."

Maybe. But there had been no shooting. They spent the remainder of the evening getting their equipment sorted and ready for the climb, and after a few fitful hours of sleep, or trying to sleep, they saddled up and crept to the ravine. Four a.m. found them at the timberline where they worked their way diagonally to the north face of the mountain.

And now, with the sun shining, they were on the most exposed side of Kota. Gary found himself checking the sky often. The winds seemed filled with the sounds of thumping helicopter blades, and voices shouting at them to halt where they stood. And a little while ago, the helicopters had appeared, flying from east to west and back again in steady, crisscross patterns. The Man was closing in.

It could be worse, he kept telling himself, and he tried to imagine where they would be if he hadn't stopped to talk with Steve Woodhull. And if Woodhull was right, they would meet few obstacles, none of them along the Northeast Route.

They began climbing again.

"I've been meaning to ask you if you remember any of this?" Janey said behind him. "You know, maybe coming back down this way."

He had been looking around just for that, hoping that he would find something that might jog his memory. He had to have descended somewhere along this route, but nothing he had seen so far was familiar. "No," he called over his shoulder, "I don't recognize a damned thing. For all I know, someone might have carried me down."

"I just wanted you to know that I think we're still doing a pretty good job."

"Don't thank me yet."

"No, really. And you might even be doing this subconsciously, knowing the route without being aware of it."

"Maybe." All he consciously recalled about it was that Gorham had said something about coming back down this way. But, then, there were quite a few details he had conveniently forgotten to mention.

Janey paused to adjust her backpack. It was fairly light as backpacks go—about thirty-five pounds—because Woodhull had insisted they wouldn't need all the equipment they normally carried. But it was getting heavy and awkward all the same. By the time they neared the summit even her toothbrush would feel as if it weighed ten pounds. "I'll keep throwing little reminders at you all the way," she said when she was under way again. "Maybe one of them will jolt your memory."

Smiling, Gary stopped and pulled her up to him. He gave her a light kiss. "Hey, lady, you jolt me anyway."

"No time for that, soldier boy. We've gotta climb."

5

THE LOCAL CID OPERATION was officially disbanded in General Grady's outer office by Caldwell and Eaton. The people at Fort Endicott would be assisting in the apprehension of Gary Palmer from now on in, the agents were told. Also, each of them was to forget all about what they might have heard about some supersecret operation going on around this military base, and at Mount Kota National Park. Whatever they saw, they didn't see it.

Grady then called General Kelly at Fort Stanton, Maryland. He moved the receiver away from his ear after he had delivered the message.

"Wh-what?" General Kelly stammered over the red scrambler phone. "Tom, you've got to be kidding. He's *on the mountain? Right now?*"

"I wish I was kidding, but it's true. Hell, those CID guys never even came close to catching him."

"Oh, Jesus! If he gets all the way to Kota Station he could screw up everything. Tom, you're going to have to stop him somehow."

Grady wanted to ask how the hell Palmer could screw things up worse than they already were, but he said, "Dave, I'm afraid I've got a triple whammy for you. It's a lot worse than all that. He's climbing, but we can't go after him, at least not yet. That helicopter is still grounded, and the last word was that it will be until sometime tomorrow. There's no way we can get him without it. Even if I sent climbers up, they don't know Kota. They'd never catch him. He's got at least a six- or seven-hour head start on us."

"Dammit! What else can go wrong?"

"That's what I was about to tell you. For some reason, Kota Station isn't answering their radio. They've been out of contact for almost twenty-three hours now, and we have no idea why. We know their radio is receiving, but they're not responding. So I wanted to ask you if you thought that gas might have done something to them."

Kelly thought about it for a minute. "I . . . I don't know. It's possible, I suppose. There are things we don't know about it. But we've taken every possible safety measure we could think of. I really don't know. Have you declared an emergency?"

"I will if you want me to. But there isn't a hell of a lot I can do about it. I launched another photo recon mission a while ago, but even if we see that something terrible has happened, we can't do a thing about it."

Kelly was quiet again. Then, "Well, Tom, you'll have to send some climbers up after him. It's the only way."

Just like that. For some reason everyone seemed to regard Mount Kota as little more than a big hill in the middle of a meadow. "No, I can't do that, Dave. Absolutely not. No one around here except Palmer has ever been near that thing. I will not risk any men on some crazy windmill."

"Goddammit, Tom, are they climbers or not? I know it's a big mountain, but you've gotta get something moving now! Palmer is jeopardizing this entire project! You have to stop him. That's your responsibility!"

And with that, Grady had heard enough. This wasn't his project. He'd been sucked into it against his will and against all the common sense he had ever developed. For the past eight months they had played with his men, his equipment and a hell of a lot of his time and patience just for this stupid game of theirs. He was only a half-assed overseer with no authority over any of it, and now that leaks had popped, *he* suddenly was being held responsible. Well, enough of that shit. "Don't you lay any of this on me now, Dave," he growled. "We're doing everything we can! Until that helicopter is flying again, we'll all just have to sit tight. And from here on in, if you want me to act with any authority, then *give* me the goddamned authority. I'm on your side, remember?"

"All right, I'm sorry, Tom. What do you want to do?"

"Well, your project is in an emergency situation right now. For that matter, there could be two or three emergencies. But they're all out of our control, at least for the time being. Now, with a little luck I might be able to round up Palmer. That'll be touch and go, and I can't promise anything. I'll try. But if your two men, or Kota Station itself, are in trouble, I don't think I'd know what to do. You guys are the experts there. So, can you come out here and give me a hand with all of this? Otherwise, I'm still working half in the dark, and with one hand tied."

There was a long silence from Fort Stanton. That didn't surprise Grady. Finally: "Well . . . I suppose I could. If you really need the help . . ."

"Well, shit, Dave! Don't get so enthused about it."

"I was only thinking how soon I could get there."

Right. "Okay, then. I'll see you in a few hours. Right?"

"Sure, Tom. Okay. A few hours."

Grady laughed when he hung up the red phone. He only wished there were some humor in all of this.

But the mood changed when he walked into his outer office. Eaton and Caldwell were lounging there: smoking, drinking his coffee, trying to charm his secretary. When he saw them, he smiled, wide and tight. The humor was genuine.

Time to go to work, boys. "Would you gentlemen follow me, please?"

His secretary recognized the smile and gallant manners in a second; she had seen them before, and combined, they meant that someone was about to get his ass roasted. She turned back to her typewriter, and the keys suddenly began snapping like a string of firecrackers.

"I've given this some thought, and had a conversation with others involved in our project," he said to them in the hallway. "We've decided there will be no risk in getting you gentlemen involved, after all, because you are good security risks."

They smiled; he smiled.

"We also decided to give you the opportunity to get Palmer first. Understand, you'd still have to turn him over to us immediately afterward, but you would be the ones to catch him. It would help heal the shiner he gave the CID."

"Sure, General," Eaton answered eagerly. "That was always the idea."

"Yeah, we're all for that."

Now the smile stretched even wider, almost exposing teeth. And dressed as he was in dark green fatigues, the combination of the two caused his expression to take on an amazing similarity to that of a hungry reptile. Only then did Eaton or Caldwell suspect something might go wrong. "Good!" Grady said. "Now. Have either of you ever done any climbing?"

EXACTLY ONE HOUR LATER, all the information from all the sources lay on Grady's desk in front of him. First of all, Kota security had been alerted to allow two men identified as Eaton and Caldwell access onto the mountain. Secondly, the ring of guards surrounding Kota had been doubled, with each man out there placed on twenty-four-hour alert. Half of them had been ordered to watch for unauthorized movements from outside as always; but the other half would be watching for anything coming *down* the mountain. There were now four people up there somewhere, any one of whom could show up anytime, and soon there would be six; if any of them did, they were to be held at the nearest guard shack until further notice. The third task Grady handled was to place all the operators in the communications center on full alert. In unceasing eight-hour shifts they would still be trying to raise Kota Station. And finally, he made two calls to the airfield—the first to order the recon flight over the mountain once again, the second to make a final check on the progress of the helicopter's reconstruction. The photo plane, he was told, had just taken off, and with luck, the XM-221 should be airborne sometime tomorrow morning.

Grady sat back in his chair. He could think of nothing he had left undone. All he could do now—or again—was wait. And by the time Kelly got here—assuming he didn't weasel out on some lame pretext—there would be nothing for him to complain about. Everything—

Hands across those buns, gentlemen.

—had been covered. Besides, Palmer was the one holding the hole cards, whether he knew it or not. How he might choose to play them was anybody's guess, but one thing was certain—he was not bluffing.

CHAPTER FIFTEEN

THE CLIMB BECAME BOTH easier and more difficult at the same time. It was easier after Gary and Janey had traversed the North Buttress where the ice solidified and the snow was drier and more powdery; their progress became much faster, and they soon passed the ten-thousand foot mark with relative ease. There, the Northern Route began a long bend toward the Northeast Route to the left. They would merge just below the sixteen-thousand-foot elevation, or some five hundred feet below the lower end of the cave Woodhull spoke of. Too, Gary could just make out certain landmarks he remembered from his first climb. They were still far away, but at least if he could see them they were on the right trail.

The difficult part had been simply getting there, and the route had nothing to do with it. Someone had found their truck in the campground and put two and two together, and by 11:00 a.m. three helicopters had appeared. They flew over the lower end of the north side of the mountain, going slowly back and forth from east to west, then back again in a search pattern. All three were stair-stepped one above the other, and as they turned around the helicopter below would follow the route just taken by the one above; each pass moved them a few hundred feet higher up the mountain, and they continued the ascent until the lead, or upper, helicopter could climb no higher. After that, they would start the pattern over again in a methodical attempt to cover every foot of the mountain between the northeast and northwest edges. The attempt almost halted Gary and Janey; from 11:00 a.m. to 3:00 p.m., as they dodged from rock to rock and zigzagged their way up, they gained only six hundred feet. And the only reason they were not seen from the air was because they wore white canvas pullovers on top of their bright red parkas.

They thought the search had ended at three when the helicopters flew back to the base of the mountain and landed. Instead, one of them returned about half an hour later, landing near the lower end of the buttress. Two men got out. They were wearing climbing gear and carrying backpacks. They talked briefly with a couple of men who remained on board the helicopter, then began walking as the chopper took off and flew back to the base. Minutes later Gary saw all three helicopters take off toward the east, presumably going back to Fort Endicott. The two men began climbing.

"Oh, wow," Janey mumbled. "I was wondering when they'd get around to that."

Gary watched them through a small pair of binoculars. They were too far away to be recognized, more than a mile below them. But he was worried; Endicott wouldn't dare send anybody up Kota unless this whole situation was one hell of a lot more serious than he'd thought. And now that they had, he wondered who they were. They would have to be damned good climbers—or so the illusion of Kota still suggested.

"Can you see who they are?" Janey asked.

"No. I can think of a couple of instructors who might be good enough, but they're still too far away to tell." He put the binoculars back in their case. "Let's go. I'm not going to wait around until we can see the whites of their eyes." And if they were any good at all they would soon notice what Woodhull had said about the Northern Route; they would be able to see how easy it really was, and they might call for reinforcements. He just hoped they wouldn't notice the lower entrance to the cave—assuming they got that high.

Gary looked up. The cave was roughly four thousand feet—give or take a few hundred feet—above them. And above that . . . well, he wouldn't think about that yet.

SOME 5400 FEET BELOW THEM, both men stopped. They looked down the mountain toward the timberline far below, then up to the intense glare of the snowy summit. It appeared to be miles away. The aluminum-framed packs felt like boulders strapped to their backs. The equipment belts clinked and clanked with strange-looking tools they'd never seen before and barely remembered how to use, and their gaudy-looking clothing felt hot and awkward; they felt totally awkward and completely helpless.

"We're fucking crazy, you know that? How did we get into this shit?"

"Yeah, well, I wish you'd quit saying that. What the hell were we supposed to do? Sit around in Grady's office for the next week? I don't know about you, but it's been a long time since I was out job hunting, and I don't feel like going out looking for another one now."

"That's for sure. Look at this son of a bitch. Do you see how high it is? We'll never make it!"

"Look, all we have to do is make a show of it, just give it some kind of effort. They can't fault us for that, not if we try. Come on. Let's go."

"Fucking crazy..."

AT TEN MINUTES PAST FIVE, Gary and Janey arrived at the upper end of the North Buttress. The cave was just ahead. They had made good time, excellent under the circumstances, and there was at least two and a half hours' climbing time remaining before nightfall. With a little more luck, and a bit more muscle, they could hole up somewhere inside the cave and be at the summit early tomorrow morning.

For a few minutes after he'd dropped his pack to the ground, Gary stared at the cave entrance. He remembered it, of course; he remembered every detail of its interior, or what little he'd seen of it. And over there, to their left, he recalled the outer route over which Gorham had taken them eight months ago. It seemed like last week, and he supposed that by the strictest interpretation, it was. Everything about it was clear; it couldn't have occurred that long ago.

The next traverse from here was along the edge of those rocks, and the exit was up past an area they couldn't see from here, a snow-covered ledge that opened up near the bottom of a ninety-foot ice wall. Once that was climbed the path wound across four more ledges—and you had to know which ones or you'd have to back down and start over—until you were out near the far northeast edge of the mountain. From that point

the route went up, but it was a complete 180-degree doubling
back that went west for nearly a quarter mile before stopping
at the bottom of another wall shooting straight up just over one
hundred feet. At the top, the trail began another back-and-forth
passage through a confusing maze of ice- and snow-covered
rocks and trenches filled with snow that was ten to fifteen feet
deep in places. Only when that was cleared did you finally exit
at yet another short ledge, which ended abruptly next to a 5500-
foot straight drop off the mountain. It looked like the end of
the trail, but that was where you pulled yourself over a short
wall. And then you found yourself standing at the far end of the
Northeast Plateau, 17,997 feet above sea level, 1166 feet below the summit. Gary remembered it all, nearly every step of
the route. He recalled the plateau, Karber's Pass, and all the
destruction scattered through it. He remembered everything
except what had put him in a Kansas military asylum—the
thing that had somehow gotten him down off this mountain
alone. And so far he had seen nothing that had shaken loose a
single detail lodged inside that dark blank spot in his memory.

Janey stepped cautiously inside the opening. She called to
him a moment later, and when he walked inside, she pointed to
the rocks. Many of them had been pushed from the neat stack
Gorham had made, and were lying all over the cave floor.
"Hey, I guess Steve Woodhull was right," she said.

Apparently. They had been lying there for some time from
the looks of it, and it was easy to see they had been knocked
down from the inside out.

Eight months ago.

"Looks like it," Gary whispered. Beyond, the cave was a
black hole into the mountain. There was a cold breeze gusting
from an unseen source, and water dripped into a puddle somewhere back in the void. Gary found a small flashlight, and
when he had snapped it on he saw that Woodhull's memory of
the place had been on the money; the cave went farther back
than the light could reach. Back and back and back. The eerie
darkness and moaning wind made it look exactly like a frozen
catacomb.

"Sure is dark in there," Janey muttered, as if saying it to
herself.

Gary took her hand. He knew what she was thinking because he was thinking the same thing: I know how you feel, babe. I don't want to go in there, either. "Yeah," he finally answered, a chill running through him. "Well, we'd better get the packs. And check on our friends below."

He'd had an idea earlier about redisguising the cave entrance with some of the rocks, making it appear as it had when John Karber found it. Three expert climbers had completely missed seeing it on two or three climbs, and that might work again. It could keep their pursuers well in back of them by forcing them to find the outer route to the Northeast Plateau. But when he brought the binoculars out to see where they were he said, "Well, I'll be damned!" and he laughed. "Here. Take a look at this. You won't believe it."

Janey looked. They were so far away she could barely see them. "What are they doing? If I didn't know better I'd swear they're dancing."

"They might as well be. Hell, those two have barely gotten above where they started. They're just standing up, then falling down."

"That doesn't make sense. Why would they send up two people who can't even climb? Who could they be?"

Gary put the binoculars away and grabbed his pack. "Who knows? And who cares? They won't be catching us. But let's get the hell out of here just in case somebody gets lucky."

Lucky, he thought. There was that word again. They had been damned lucky so far. They probably weren't even aware of all the pitfalls they had barely avoided over the past three days. If he really had a guardian angel she must be nearly ready for an ambulance by now, and all he could think was, Ma'am, just hang in there a little longer. Get us through this and I promise I'll become an accountant or a clerk.

"Got your flashlight? And an extra battery and bulb?"

"Right here."

"Okay, just put 'em in an upper pocket, and zip it shut. We won't use them unless we have to." He checked to see that he had a battery and bulb ready in his own pocket. "Leave your pack loose, too. Steve was saying there were a couple of places kind of tight, so we'll have to take them off."

"Do you think we can get all the way through in just a couple of hours?"

"I don't suppose it makes much difference. It's a lot darker
in here than it'll be outside. Well, you all set?"

"All set," she said with a deep breath.

"So am I. Let's do it."

2

AT 150 FEET INTO THE TUNNEL, it went up. Gary and Janey
wriggled between a couple of rocks, pulled their packs through
behind them and started the climb. The tunnel ascended at
varied angles, twisting this way and that, sometimes veering in
either direction at nearly right angles. Over the next 250 feet or
so Gary counted eighteen places where they changed direction, twelve spots where the path leveled off slightly before
going up sharply again to the left or right. It was a slow, twisted
and difficult ascent with no place where the roof was more than
six and a half feet in height, occasionally down near five feet,
and less than that in one spot. Added to that was a rough floor
strewn with thousands of dislodged rocks from the size of
gravel to twice as large as a man's fist. With nearly every step,
dozens clattered and rolled into the darkness behind them,
many clacking and bumping into their larger cousins that
formed the walls. And with each clatter and thud, Gary
cringed; he hoped feverishly that they wouldn't accidentally
cause an avalanche that could easily bury them in here. Off-
hand, he couldn't think of a worse way to die.

As they continued he began thinking that Gorham had been
perfectly right to insist that Kota be climbed in a more conven-
tional fashion. This was crazy, stupid. There were sharp out-
croppings of rock jutting up, or out from the walls, and they
continually stubbed toes, cracked shins, knees and elbows and
bumped heads against one obstacle after another. They tripped
and slipped clumsily on loose rocks and the icy dampness covering the floor; Janey almost fell flat when her feet slid out
from under her, and Gary did fall as he reached for a protruding spire that snapped off like a rotted branch. Worse, it was

dark. With the light off—and Gary accidentally snapped it off twice—the cave became a black, howling shaft. As such, it afforded no good way of measuring their progress. Gary was too busy trying to move from one handhold to another, and Janey was doing the same behind him, too busy and too worried to look at the time. No outstanding landmarks existed anywhere; most of the interior looked the same behind and ahead of them. They simply kept moving, watching whatever came into the light while all at their rear was swallowed in blackness.

But they were on track; Gary pointed to several places where the rocks were already dislodged. He had come this way before.

That was their only reference point to reality—to keep going and concentrate on what lay ahead; to stay busy, remain calm and keep their minds constructively occupied. Without that, all the grips and stops and anchors to the real world would disintegrate. In fact, it occurred to Gary that perhaps that was the ultimate reality—when someone was forced to come to terms with the most brutal kind of realism—the kind you'd face in a war, or anyplace where you never thought you'd be. He thought of himself as a sort of cottage expert on the subject; he had, only a couple of days ago, been walking the halls of a place that dealt with that kind of ferocious awareness. It almost happened to him. And maybe that was where some of those poor bastards were at right now—lost inside the corridors of some black subconscious cave. It was probably all too easy to do in the middle of a battle. You ran from the shitstorm into the nearest available shelter, and if you went too far you could get lost among the unremembered twists and turns. Your own mind became a Byzantine maze.

He stopped and looked at the passageway ahead. Some leader he was; escape from the maze in his mind and dive right into this one. And what if John Karber had been wrong, and this cave didn't open up at the top after all?

"Why are you stopping?"

"I'm a little winded...not quite in shape for this. But I think we're getting pretty high. Notice how thin the air seems to be getting?"

"Yeah, I noticed that."

And they began climbing again. It was too late in the day, too late in the trek, too late in the whole scheme of things to be stopping or backtracking. They were committed; stuck with whatever was about to happen.

Ahead, the tunnel narrowed again. The rocks closed in like the aperture in a camera. They would have to get down on all fours to get through it.

He checked the flashlight. It was still bright and strong, almost glaring in the deep gloom. After all, he told himself, it contained a new battery and light bulb, and both were working just fine with many hours of light available—more than enough to see them through here.

Nine lives, you know . . .

Besides, they had spare batteries, spare bulbs and an extra light. They were well prepared, just like a couple of Boy Scouts. But he checked the light again anyway because this darkness was so thick and heavy you could feel it. It almost seemed to try and eat the light up, and he found himself shielding it, protecting it.

Minutes later, they had wriggled through the narrow opening. The area on the upper side was suddenly much larger, a good eight or nine feet across and nearly that high. For the first time they could stand up side by side, and as Gary shone the light around they were amazed. By comparison the cave was now a cathedral. The path ahead was still uphill, of course, steep and strewn with loose rocks, but it appeared to be much easier going—at least as far as the light could reach. The cold wind in their faces seemed a little stronger and sharper as well, and its mournful howl had gone.

"Weird mountain you've got here, Palmer."

"No shit."

"Can you remember any of it yet?"

Gary shook his head as he played the light around more slowly. "Not a damned thing."

It was impossible to tell exactly how far they had come, but they couldn't be too far from the end because of the wind and the increasing cold, and because breathing was getting more difficult. The oxygen was noticeably less than it had been where they started at sixteen thousand feet. Gary checked his watch

again; it was 6:42, which meant they had been climbing more
than an hour and a half. He didn't know, but he said, "I think
we may be at about plateau level . . . around eighteen thousand
feet. It can't be much farther to the end."

They wriggled the packs onto their backs—plenty of room
for them now—and set out again.

3

AT 6:55 P.M. THE commanding officer of the Photographic
Reconnaissance Section delivered pictures to General Grady.
He selected four or five, explaining, "These were the only good
ones we got, sir. And they aren't that good, either."

Thirty of them had been shot during three passes across the
mountain. Most were different angles and views of the summit, but five caught both the plateau and Kota Station, and
different areas of Karber's Pass. Only two showed anyone to be
up and moving; a pair of sequential shots taken within a couple of seconds of each other. They showed somebody stooped
over a body, and he was either engrossed in whatever he was
doing or simply ignoring the airplane because he was looking
down. And because of the angle of the shots and many of the
long shadows created by the setting sun it was impossible to tell
which of the station occupants it might be. The final photo—
or, rather, part of it—showed that the same man had started to
move away from the body. There, they could see that the corpse
was facedown in the rocks with only the lower half of its body
included in the picture.

The captain apologized for the poor quality of the photos,
saying they should have loaded the cameras with a different
speed film, and have set everything to eliminate all the shadows. "But we'll do that right now, and send up another plane
if you like, sir," he quickly added. "We still have daylight left.
Or we could set up for a night mission."

Grady studied the pictures. They looked like five hundred
others they already had on file. He was starting to get tired of
looking at Mount Kota, and the wreck of Flight J-440. They'd
be better off all around just to put the mountain off limits for

good, and leave things as they were up there. All the studying and checking and examining and looking and talking in the world wouldn't bring a single one of those men back to life. He sighed, thanking the captain for the offer. "No . . . no more missions for the time being. We'll use what we've got."

"Yes, sir. But there is one thing, though."

"What's that?"

"Well, for us to offer an accurate analysis of this, it might help if we knew what that man is supposed to be doing."

Grady smiled, and shook his head. "Afraid not. It's classified. Even *I* don't know everything he's doing." He passed a magnifying glass across the eight-by-ten glossy black and white. The man was stooped over a body, and he appeared to be the only man moving around in any of the pictures. It looked as if he was examining the body, doing his job—not a pleasant job, but it came with the territory. He studied the picture silently for five minutes, and when he'd put the magnifying glass down he was satisfied that he knew what the man—the one still alive—was doing. "I can't tell you exactly what he's doing, Captain, but I can say that he appears to be doing his job."

"Very good, sir. If it's satisfactory to you, it's satisfactory to us. And I won't take up any more of your time." He stood and saluted.

So, Grady wondered after the captain had left, just what the hell was he doing? And which one of them was it? A photo analyst he was not, but damned if Gilmore—or Attwood—didn't look exactly as if he was picking the dead man's pockets. And in the second photograph where he had started to move away from the body, the body itself—or what little of it could be seen—didn't . . . well, somehow just didn't *look* right. He couldn't pin it down, and for several minutes he had his nose almost on the magnifying glass as he tried to think. *What's wrong with this picture?* If he had done nothing else over the past months since the crash he had looked at pictures: pictures of the mountain, pictures of the crash and pictures of all the bodies lying in the snow. He was probably more familiar with pictures of corpses, and where each of them lay up there, than anybody. And yet something about this one seemed out—

Out of place.

"Holy shit!" He jumped up from his desk and ran out of the office. He caught the captain in the parking lot. "Get on the phone and get your best analyst over here on the double."

SERGEANT KENSOR, they learned, was on a two-week leave home, and home was Tampa, Florida. "Damn!" Captain Sailes muttered as he put the phone down. "He's our best analyst . . . he and Lieutenant Goodwin. They're the ones who've studied all the Kota photographs."

"All right, get Goodwin."

He tried. Lieutenant Goodwin lived off post in an apartment he shared with another single officer, who told them Goodwin was gone for the evening. "He had a hot date with a girl in town," Sailes reported. "But we could send a couple of MPs to try and find him."

Grady thought about Palmer, and his girlfriend from town. Hell, didn't these guys date WACs or Army nurses anymore? He said, "How good are you at photo analysis, Captain?"

"Not as good as they are, but I can do it, sir."

"Good enough. Let's do it," and he shoved the pictures across the desk. Pointing to the last one, he asked, "Do you see anything unusual about the dead man? Compare it with the other pictures. Compare that body with all the others."

Sailes studied the photo for a minute, then saw it. He looked at Grady, then back to the picture. "He looks dead, but he sure doesn't look like he's been lying there for the past eight months."

"He doesn't look that way to me, either. And I'll tell you something else: I've looked at enough pictures by now that I'm probably as familiar with the top side of that mountain as anyone. We have photos of almost every square foot of it, and in no other photo was there ever a body in that part of Karber's Pass before now. You can look through all of these—" and he thumped the thick stack "—but you can take my word for it."

"Then who is he, sir? One of the men who are supposed to be working inside that building?"

"It would appear that way. It looks to me like one of them got himself killed somehow, and the other is examining his body. But if that's true, why the hell hasn't he reported it?"

"I wouldn't know, sir."

Then it was time he did know. "How much do you know about all of this?"

Sailes shook his head. "Not much, sir. Only Kensor and Goodwin were cleared for this thing."

Grady told the captain certain details about the KP Project—mostly information about Gilmore and Attwood, and what some of their responsibilities were. He didn't mention anything about the gas, and he stayed clear of the project's main intent; but he did say that there were peculiar circumstances surrounding the deaths of the crash survivors, and the rescue climbers. "That, and the fact that we've been out of touch with Kota Station for nearly twenty-eight hours now. And it looks like one of them is dead, we have no idea of what the other one is doing, and we don't know what the hell's going on."

"Then based on what you've just said, sir, that would be my guess, too," Captain Sailes replied. "I'd say that one of them died somehow, and the other is looking at the body. It could be a serious injury, of course, but you'd have to assume the worst until you know differently."

"Of course." There didn't seem to be much else left to go wrong with the project, short of the building blowing up or the mountain falling down. It was a good thing he was nearing retirement; when word of this failure got out the army would be reluctant to put him in charge of a latrine.

Sailes dug through the stack of photos. "There was something else I noticed a while ago, sir. It's probably nothing, but I'll mention it for whatever it's worth."

"What's that?"

"Yes, here it is." He handed the general one of the pictures of the plateau and Kota Station. "Right here," he said, pointing. "Maybe whatever happened up there happened suddenly. See that? Somebody left the station door open."

4

GARY WAS RIGHT. It wasn't much farther to the end of the cave.

The cave had enlarged, and wasn't nearly so steep a climb, or its pathway so littered with fallen rocks. It was still quite dark, though, and cold. The breeze felt as if it was getting stronger, not quite so gusty. They had to be near the exit—and near the top of the mountain. The climb was almost finished. They would soon find whatever there was to find up here, and perhaps that was what made them go more slowly.

Janey stayed next to Gary, hanging on to his parka once in a while. She could feel the tension and nervousness building in him, and in herself, too, almost as thick as the gloom around them. Not so long ago this climb was talk, nothing more. She had thought Gary really was out of his mind when he'd decided to sneak back to Montana and climb this thing again. It was a crazy idea, almost like an armed robbery of a police station. Only as the miles passed, and the reasoning behind the idea began to take hold did it begin to make sense. After their stop in Boulder and Gary's talk with Steve Woodhull, climbing Mount Kota not only seemed possible and probably the only route left to Gary as he had insisted, but it became exciting. Yes. The whole idea was intriguing, almost like a heady sexual anticipation. Why the hell *not* do it? Everything they had seen so far pointed to exactly what he had been saying all along. They had lied, saying he'd been killed; they had secretly locked him up in a Kansas asylum; and now they were chasing him all over the country. Gary stood dead center in something very big and very devious, something that he had no control over. He had very little knowledge of what it was, but someone had casually decided for him that he should give his life for it. There had been no choice. He'd been given no choices about anything since that airplane crashed up there. So he was perfectly within his rights to demand something from them, an explanation at the very least. If they wouldn't give it to him he had every right to make the choice for himself. He had to defend his personal freedom, his free will, and he sure as hell had the right to struggle for his own survival. She was proud of him, and glad to be with him.

In here. She looked around, listening to the wind. They were
groping their way along through a black, freezing cave like two
kids inside a haunted house on a dare. She happened to think
about one of those old Nancy Drew mysteries she used to read
as a kid—Nancy Drew holding a flashlight. Nancy was *always*
in some dark passageway, holding a flashlight on every cover
while exploring a place like this one. *Janey Burns and the
Mystery of the Haunted Cave...*

She took hold of Gary's parka. All sorts of imaginings were
beginning to pop up now. What *would* they find up here? What
had happened that was so serious that the Army felt it necessary to lock up Gary, then ring the whole mountain with armed
guards? What had she and Gary been so eager to step into?
And what would become of them if all of this failed and they
got caught? Visions of her mother, her family and friends, her
father, her past suddenly came into view. . . .

Anita McAllister...the *Kaleidoscope*: Jane Charlotte Burns
(Goobers); JV Cheerleader 1,2; FHA 3,4; Chorus 2,3,4; Stu-
dent Council 4.

"Hey, did I ever tell you that back in high school my nickname was Goobers? Dumb name . . ."

"What?"

And she just started talking. Her voice echoed in a high,
nervous pitch inside the darkness as if she had taken leave of
herself and she was watching in amazement at her own babbling. Goobers had been bestowed by Anita McAllister, one
Saturday night at the movies, when she and Janey and three
other girls nearly got thrown out of the theater while trying to
get four football players to pay attention to them. She couldn't
remember the name of the movie; only that it was a western
that starred Audie Murphy, and man, was he *cute*. The nickname stuck all through the rest of high school, long after it
stopped being funny or cute; even her date for the senior prom
called her Goobers. Really, she didn't care all that much for
Janey because it sounded too cutesy, something you'd call a
little girl—which was her size when her dad gave the name to
her. So she supposed she would always be called that; she'd be
Janey until she was bent-over, cucumber-tits old, and it did
sound a hell of a lot better than Goobers. Besides, that name

always reminded her of something you might find squished up in a baby's diaper....

Gary squeezed her hand. Janey stopped talking as suddenly as she'd started, as if the words had been wrung from a washcloth. He opened his mouth to say something, but halted in his tracks and put up a hand.

Ahead, the path split into two branches. Gary aimed the light toward the one on the left, then the right, and then he turned the light off.

"Gar—"

"Shhhh..."

She could hear nothing except the wind. It seemed to be getting much colder. "I can't hear anything," she finally whispered.

For a minute, neither did Gary. He relaxed a bit and took a deep breath. "My imagination, I guess. But I could've sworn that I—"

He heard it again, a distant sort of scraping noise, as if someone was dragging something across the cave floor. It stopped as he was trying to decide which tunnel it was coming from.

"Did you hear that?" he whispered.

"I think so."

He turned the flashlight back on, and after another moment's hesitation he motioned toward the left-hand tunnel. It appeared straight, almost flat. The lowest obstructions were just above their heads.

They began walking slowly, listening, and trying to make as little noise as possible. Janey clung to Gary's parka. All Gary wanted to do was get the hell out of there before dark. Karber's Pass was supposed to be an easy traverse, if you could call it that, but it wasn't a good idea to negotiate any obstacle at night—especially not on this mountain. The best thing to do on Kota was find shelter. And stay there.

And this cave wasn't shelter.

They kept walking; it seemed as if the cave was never going to end. "Do you think we took the wrong turn back there?" Janey said.

"Christ, I hope not."

And they hadn't. Sixty feet ahead was a shaft of light coming through the roof. Gary stopped and turned off the flashlight to make certain it was really sunlight they were seeing. "Well, look at that," he said with relief, taking Janey's hand. "And you were worried."

"Let's just get the hell out of here. This place gives me the creeps."

They hurried toward the light, watching it carefully as if it might suddenly move or go out like a candle. When they were beneath it at last they saw that it was a simple hole in the wall; a rounded opening that poked through the rocks at an angle. It was a natural exit.

But the rocks below it, piled into a crude set of steps, were not.

Gary examined them. Apparently, the architect they heard moving around a while ago in the darkness had been busy. There were things strewn all over the floor. Gary moved the light around to see what they were. He found pieces of clothing tossed into a careless pile, part of a wooden crate, bits and pieces of bent metal from the airplane, a wooden lid from another crate, a few torn, soggy cardboard boxes, a combat boot and several lengths of canvas strapping.

"Dear God!" Gary whispered. "Someone survived the wreck after all." His light found still more junk scattered all over the floor. "Jesus! I wonder how long he lasted up here."

And Janey caught it out of the corner of her eye. "Is that—" *Him?* she started to say, but choked. As the light reached the shape she'd seen, she had to stifle a horrified scream. A shock jolted through her.

It was a body, propped against the wall in a half-sitting position—frozen, head down, arms locked down on either side. Both legs were amputated at midthigh. Broken ends of bones jutted out from flesh that looked as if animals had been chewing on it.

"Shit! Don't look, Ja—" and Gary nearly choked. Now he could see bones scattered around what looked to have been a small camp fire. Human bones. Dozens of them. They lay everywhere.

With a choked cry, Janey scrambled up through the hole in the rocks.

Gary was right behind her. The flashlight slipped from his hand and rolled into a corner, the light still on—pointed at another small pile of bones. But he didn't see that.

If it hadn't been for all the wreckage littering the rugged landscape the view would have been breathtaking. Here, you were on top of the country.

But no one there at that moment was taking the view. The two sat on the rocks, in the glaring sunshine. Janey was whimpering for air, and nearly ten minutes passed before Gary remembered their oxygen bottles. As hard as he was trying to help her, he couldn't seem to calm himself. He trembled so badly that he dropped a bottle, then couldn't seem to get the tubes plugged in, the valve opened or the mask slipped around Janey's face. For a moment, she didn't notice it, and when she did, she held on to the mask with both hands and buried her face against Gary's shoulder. He finally got his own bottle operating and the mask on; then, he hugged her. And they sat there. Holding on to each other.

He tried to think. Woodhull was right. He had to have exited this mountain through that cave even if he couldn't remember a moment of it. It was easy, too, to see from up here how Karber could have been pushed over the side. It wouldn't take much, maybe only a sudden gust of wind. Just a few feet behind where they sat was a straight, heart-stopping plunge into oblivion, and to the north, less than twenty-five feet away, was another violent plummet down to the northern slopes and walls far below. Only in front of them was there a safe way down into the pass. One way only. A path. And somebody had used it many times; somebody knew his way around up here. He had made himself a home in this place.

Janey removed her mask. She took a long look around, and it occurred to her that this was it—end of trip, nowhere else to go. The great adventure was a trap. She whispered to Gary, "Now what?"

He thought, Good question.

5

THE TECHNICIAN AND ONE OF the two engineers clipped the leads to the master instrument circuit panel and turned the breaker on; in the pilot's seat the second engineer waited for the okay, and when he got it he snapped a black-handled toggle switch to the On position. The panel in front of him lit up and all the instrument needles and indicators suddenly jumped to life. He looked at each of them, writing down their readings, then checked their operation by pushing an On/Off/Reset button installed under each one. When he was finished, every instrument was noted on his list as being in acceptable working order.

"Primary power okay," he called to the other two men.

"Primary okay on test module," came the response. "Switching now to auxiliary power."

"Starting auxiliary instrument test," and he began the instrument check again from a backup power source.

So far, half an hour had been used for both tests. The engineer wrote down the second set of readings, making a note to modify the wiring so that the test could be accomplished in two steps instead of four—four because the whole thing would be repeated in a few minutes with the second set of instruments on the right side of the cockpit. All this double-testing was getting to be a royal pain in the ass.

He sighed, hoisted himself out of the left seat and moved to the right. When this was finished they would move on to the radio gear; next would come the radar, then all the avionics equipment. The only system this model didn't have was a fire control system, something that would take more than two hours by itself. At any rate, if their control panels and consoles were acceptable and in airworthy condition they would be able to stop for some food and badly needed coffee before beginning the tests of both engines, all the engine electrical control circuits, the electrical and hydraulic flight controls and all the mechanical and manual/auxiliary override controls.

Assuming they could get it all finished by sunup tomorrow—assuming that they found nothing wrong—they would have to go for a two-hour ride while the pilots checked everything out once again under actual strategic operating conditions. Only then could the ship be turned back over to these people.

The engineer settled into the right-hand seat, yawned and rubbed his eyes. He was hot, tired and as dirty as a barnyard goat. None of them had seen a shower, bed, razor or change of clothes for nearly four days. Shortly after arriving at work three and a half days ago he and the other engineer had been hustled onto a company jet and dropped off here in Outer Mongolia without so much as a how-do-you-do or even permission to call home. They had been told simply to assist the technician in getting Fort Endicott's XM-221 operational again, and that anything needed to do so would be at their disposal. That had been easy for *them* to say; what they found was a sagging, beat-up hulk of a prototype that had been flown to death. No one at Endicott was willing to say what had been demanded of the ship but it was obvious that it had been battered far beyond its design capabilities. These guys didn't need a complex, sophisticated aircraft; what they should have had was a diesel tractor with wings.

The engineer wiped a sleeve across his forehead. His wife would have to burn this shirt. His suit trousers were probably ruined as well what with all the grease, oil and hydraulic fluid spilled on them. He had long since lost his necktie and chip-diamond tie tack, and ruined a good pair of dress shoes along with it.

Just get it into shape, they'd said. Sure. Just like that. It was like asking for a demolition derby wreck to be restored to showroom condition. And even if by some wild quirk the damned thing actually hoisted its own ass into the air tomorrow morning, he sure as hell didn't want to be riding in it.

"Hey, are you ready in there?" the technician called.

Yeah, yeah, yeah, he thought, offering a weak wave out the window. He answered, "Primary power on. Starting right-hand instrument check."

6

WITH NIGHTFALL COMING, and both the summit and cave out
of the question for campsites, the Northeast Plateau was their
only choice. The plan, such as Gary was able to create from
minute to minute now, was to set up camp, get some rest, and
climb to the top tomorrow morning. Then...well, he hoped he
would be able to think of something else. So far, so good, but
this seat-of-the-pants bullshit had to stop. He needed answers.

They climbed down from the rocks and started the descent
through Karber's Pass. Long shadows were beginning to fall
over much of it even though there were at least forty-five minutes of daylight left. Dark or not, it still felt one hell of a lot
safer and better out in the open, and Gary had already decided
that their descent would be down the northeast route. Anything was better than going through that cave again.

He told Janey. She appeared to be settled, outwardly, at
least, and he hoped she was in a receptive mood, even if she still
wasn't talking much. She tended to babble if worried or a little
frightened; she clammed up entirely when she got scared.

"If we last that long," she muttered. It was her longest
statement in more than half an hour.

"We'll be all right."

"Oh? You think so?" That response came out two octaves
higher than normal; she was still scared, but getting angry.
Now, she would talk.

"Yes, I think so," he said stubbornly. "We've done all right
so far."

"Then, what about that...that mess back there in the cave?"
she demanded, stopping and pointing. "Who did that? And
he's still around, you know. We did hear someone moving
around in there."

"Yeah, I heard it, but we don't know that it was some*one*.
There's a lot of wreckage; it might have been the wind blowing
junk around or something. Besides, how could anybody survive up here for eight months?"

"Well, it looked to me like somebody did a pretty good job
of it!"

"Look, if there's any real danger, we'll clear out first thing in the morning, Janey."

"Don't you think there is? If there's someone running around up here, I'd call that dangerous. And what if he comes after us? We'd be the first hot meal he's had in a long time."

"Then we'll have to watch out for 'im! What else can I tell you? We'll just have to be careful."

"Oh, that's brilliant! He chews up a bunch of big, strong troopers, but *we've* got nothing to worry about. Gary, let's get out of here while we still can."

Gary was silent for a moment. "How? Where?" He shrugged. "It's getting dark. We can't climb down in the dark unless we go through that cave, and I don't want to go through it again. At any rate, Janey, it's a little late for all of that. We're here. And we're stuck with whatever we find."

"I know we're here! Like I said a while ago, now what?"

"I don't *know* what, dammit! I don't have the answers! That's why I came up here, remember? An airplane crashed up there, and a lot of people got killed, and a lot of other bad shit has come down since that happened, and it involves me somehow. But I don't know what it is. You've seen everything I've seen, and you know everything I've learned, so now we're still trying to put the pieces together. I never said this would be pleasant, or easy. For all I know we might find witches and vampires up here. I just don't know. All I can do is look."

They were silent for a long time, each looking in different directions. When he turned to her again he put his hands on her shoulders and looked directly into her eyes. She was still frightened. "I don't know what else to tell you, babe," he said softly. "You think I'm not scared? I'm scared shitless. Now, I don't know what the dangers are, and I don't know where they are. And I've got you here with me...and that worries me more than anything."

Janey nodded, trying to smile. "But your ass would still be in Kansas if it wasn't for me," she whispered.

He grinned. "No shit!"

"No shit."

They started down again. They walked perhaps two hundred feet.

"Gary . . . oh, God!" She turned and grabbed him.

"Take it easy." He pushed her gently aside for a closer look at the body lying in their path. He thought for a moment that it was another crash victim; but no. There had been no bodies this low in the pass, and another look told him that this one was a lot different from all the soldiers up top. This man was dressed in climbing boots and white insulated coveralls. In the rocks next to him was an oxygen bottle, the hose and face mask lying next to his head; the plastic mask was smeared with frozen blood. He also wore a helmet, now pulled halfway off his head, and the snow beneath it was stained in red. Gary knelt and pulled the body faceup.

"Oh, shit!" There was little of the man's face left, and what remained had been smashed almost flat. The nose was flattened, the jaw driven backward, and the shattered forehead was pierced with skull fragments. The helmet had a full face shield, but that too was smashed and filled with blood. He looked as if he had been hit straight on by a speeding bus.

A climber? Gary thought, but noticed the dark green name tag sewn above the left breast pocket—Attwood, it said. And on one side of the collar was sewn a silver cloth oak leaf; the opposite side displayed the Chemical Corps insignia. Who the hell was this guy? There were no climbers at Endicott who were lieutenant colonels, and certainly none who had been assigned to the Chemical Corps. He'd never heard of a man called Attwood.

He rolled the body back facedown. "It's all right, Janey. Just step over it." He extended a hand to her.

"Who is it?" she gulped.

"I don't know. But he wasn't on the plane. He must have been sent up here to investigate the crash." He wondered, too, how he got here. Had someone else discovered that cave?

"What happened to him?"

"I'm not sure, but it looks like he fell," Gary lied, thinking, My ass, he fell. Someone tried to take that bastard's head off. So we really do have company up here. And he was from the Chemical Corps? Why would they have a man here? "Come on. Let's get out of here."

She was shaking, but she tried to ignore the body. It wasn't easy.

"I'm not sure what he was doing, but it looks like he was trying to climb up into those rocks," Gary said, trying again to calm Janey—and himself. "Maybe part of the plane is up there. But I don't think he was a real climber because a climber wouldn't try to climb up there. Those rocks are pretty loose and unstable. But if we could find out what he had in mind, we—"

And they stopped. They were at the bottom of the pass, just above the plateau. Janey pointed at it. "What's that?"

7

THEY WERE STANDING on the plateau before Gary could answer. "A building," he muttered, stopping again to stare at it. If it had been a flying saucer he wouldn't have been any more amazed. But it was a building. And now, the mystery surrounding all he had been through had just gone from the peculiar to the outrageous. A building? he thought. When had they put that up here? How? And why?

The lights were on inside, spilling yellowish canted rectangles onto the drifted snow. Footprints tracked from the door across the plateau to where they stood; others went around the front and rear. The door stood open, almost like an invitation, but there were no signs of activity inside—no people, no noises, no movement of any kind. Light fantailed out from the doorway; snow had blown inside and was drifted against one of the walls.

"Well," he said at last, "let's have a look."

"Gary, I don't know..."

"Janey, it's nearly dark. There's no place else to go now. Come on."

Gary started inside, paused, stepped in a second time, then stopped again. They stood at the edge of a tiled hallway that was dusted with snow. The door had been open for some time.

"Hello?" he called. "Anybody here?"

No answer.

"Anyone in here?" and when there was still no reply, they walked inside. The place was divided into several rooms, each of them filled with equipment. Someone obviously had planned on staying for a while, and the building could not be anything but permanent.

"Anyone here?" Gary called again. "It's empty. Let's look around."

"Wait. I don't like the looks of this, Gary."

"Relax. We've got the place to ourselves." And among all of this, he thought, were the answers he was looking for. They had to be here.

"I know where one of them went," Janey whispered with a shiver.

Rooms were on either side of the hall, each filled with different equipment; some of it was to keep the building operating, but most was intended to support whatever the occupants were supposed to do here, from the looks of it. But the farther they tiptoed inside, the more strongly Gary sensed that something was all wrong. Janey noticed it, too, and it was more than each room being in a slight disarray. Boxes and cartons were out of place, some opened and others stacked improperly; cabinet doors hung slightly open here and there; some items were out of kilter, or seemed to have been moved as if someone was searching for something; other boxes had had their contents removed and simply tossed to the floor. Nothing appeared broken or deliberately damaged, and they could see no destruction. In all, the interior couldn't have been called ransacked or vandalized. It was as if somebody had made a quick, haphazard search for an item he couldn't find, then hurried out before getting caught. And to Janey, the sight was worrisome and uncomfortable, as though they had just missed seeing it happen.

Gary dropped his pack to the floor.

"What are you doing?"

"I'm gonna get a shovel or something to get this snow out of here, and get the door closed. Come on, give me a hand."

"Wait a minute. Something's happened in here...it's...it's all wrong. I think we should leave."

All he could find to shovel with was a large cardboard flap. He went to work throwing snow from the hallway.

"Didn't you hear what I said?"

He kept working. "I heard." And when he finished, he pulled the heavy steel door shut. "There. Now it'll warm up in here."

And now the building wasn't so quiet. The ceiling heaters whooshed, and other appliances hummed and clicked, regulating themselves automatically. The building seemed to have its own preordained metabolism and life.

"Gary, let's *go*. Please!"

"Where, Janey? We've already been through this. It's dark outside, and there's no way we can go anywhere in the dark." He tossed the cardboard into a room. "We're safe in here. A hell of a lot safer than out there." When she didn't answer that, he went on. "I've been thinking about this. Take a look around, Janey; just look at this place. Somebody went to a hell of a lot of trouble putting it up here. The only way I can figure that they did it was by airlifting it somehow, and then they'd have to use a whole crew of men to put everything together and make it work. And just look at this stuff, Janey. Every item in here is the very latest in technology, the very best. Hell, some of it is so new that I can't even identify it. My God! This place had to cost millions, maybe tens of millions. And for what reason? The investigation of *one* plane crash? Bullshit. This was put here for other reasons; it's probably connected with that crash, and it's definitely connected with *me*. So, now that I'm here I'm gonna find out what it is."

"That's the point! There were people here. We found one of them. For all we know, the others could have ended up the same way. Let's go while we still have the chance."

"No! Janey...don't you see? The answers are *here*. I'll bet anything that everything I need to know is right here. Hell, we're lucky. At least we don't have to clomp all over the crash site looking for anything." He went to her and held her. "There's nowhere else to go. This is it, the end of the line. If we leave now, and we get picked up, you can bet your cute little buns that we'll never see each other again. We've got this far; we can't quit now.''

Janey said nothing. After a moment she dropped her backpack on the floor next to his. Because he was right, even if she couldn't quite bring herself to admit it. Of course they couldn't leave while it was dark, and it would be stupid to even consider it at this stage of the game. The smartest thing to do was make the most constructive use of their time and, as he'd just said, consider themselves lucky that they weren't huddled up out there in the snow somewhere. He was right about the building; something happened up here last September besides a plane crash, or all of this stuff wouldn't be here, and he wouldn't be in this predicament. It was now a major top-secret operation. The thing to do was quit bellyaching and help him look for whatever answers there might be in this place while they had the chance; after all, this was a very big start, the very thing they'd been looking for. Wherever it all led, they had to see it through. Together. They had come this far, much farther than they had expected. So, get to work. Do something, she told herself.

Which, of course, wouldn't make it any easier spending the night in here. It didn't explain how and why that man up in the pass had died so violently. Or where the other people had gone, and there had to have been more than one man up here. And why they had fled the building so fast that they didn't even close the door.

CHAPTER SIXTEEN

ENGINES WHINING, THE SMALL business jet with the U.S. Army markings rolled to a stop next to the main hangar. In the cockpit, the pilot and copilot talked, shutting off switches and removing their headsets. Minutes later the door opened, and General Kelly was the first one out.

There were salutes and greetings as Grady stepped forward to greet his guest, who ignored everyone except the host.

"Good Christ, what a mess!" Kelly muttered.

"It's real nice seeing you again, too," Grady said with a snort, falling into step next to him.

"Well, I just didn't expect this. I've seen things go wrong before but not everything at once. What the hell's happened, anyway?"

They climbed into Grady's staff car, where he instructed the driver to take them straight to his office. "We'll talk there," he said. The ride was in complete silence.

"I repeat," Kelly said before Grady's office door had closed, "What the hell has happened up there? I went over all your earlier information with Dr. Fairfield and everyone else connected with this thing, and no one can imagine what could have become of Gilmore or Attwood. Have there been any changes in the past few hours?"

"One at a time, Dave: one, we're still not sure what's become of Gilmore or Attwood, but there is a new piece of information you won't like. Which brings me to two: almost nothing has changed. And we were hoping you could tell us a few things."

"What do you mean, a piece of information I won't like?"

Grady told him about the man lying facedown at the lower end of Karber's Pass. He showed him both of the photographs and apologized as Captain Sailes had for the poor quality of the shots. But there could be no mistaking the dead man, or the lower half of the body visible in the picture. No way could he be one of the crash victims. "But we can't tell from this which one of those guys he is. Are you able to identify him, Dave?"

"God!" Kelly groaned. Grady handed him the magnifying glass, and he looked at the pictures. He came up, shaking his head. "No, I can't tell which one it is, either," he said, dropping the photo. "Both of them are about the same size and build. The only way I could tell them apart from behind would be to look at their heads. Gilmore's hair is lighter, and he doesn't have as much of it." He glanced at the pictures again for a moment, then shook his head again. "Son of a bitch! What could have happened?"

"We don't know. And we can't understand why the other one hasn't reported the death . . . or won't even answer the radio." Grady grabbed a third photograph. "Take a look at this one, too. See that? The station door is hanging open. Why is that? I thought that one of them got into trouble, and maybe the other came running so fast that he just forgot to close the door. But that doesn't make much sense when you consider that he apparently hasn't come back to the station yet." He put down the photo and stood. "It looks like it adds up this way: the one still alive—*if* he's still alive at this moment—must have been affected by that gas. Somehow, despite all the precautions, one of them, or maybe both, were contaminated. And for all we know, the plateau level, and maybe even the station, were contaminated."

Kelly thought about that for a minute. He finally nodded. "We didn't think that was likely at first, but you could be right. We thought the only way they could get in trouble was if they were somehow contaminated at the summit—which still might have happened—but you could be right. Dammit, there's so much we just don't know about that stuff."

Grady shrugged.

Kelly asked about Palmer and his girlfriend.

Another shrug. Grady explained that Palmer was an excellent climber, and he had been to the top of Kota before. They knew very little about the woman with him; she might be holding him up, but they had to assume the worst—that she must be a good climber as well or Palmer wouldn't have taken her along. And because they had been climbing since early this morning, and climbing conditions were good and the weather excellent, they might be at, or very close to Kota Station. Nobody had been able to spot them anywhere on the mountain, and nothing he was aware of had stood in the way of their progress.

Grady deliberately did not mention the two CID men, who would not have presented a problem to Palmer, anyway.

"Well, that doesn't make sense, Tom. If everything was that perfect, why didn't you send a team up after them?"

Here we go again. "I already told you why. And I'm not going to explain it again."

"Then we'll have to hope that somebody answers the radio, and we can tell him to intercept Palmer."

Grady got up and started pacing. "Come *on*! The other man could be dead, too. They've been out of touch nearly thirty-four hours now."

"All right, all right. But I was thinking—even if Palmer gets to the station and learns all about the project, what's he going to do with the information? As you said, he still has to come back down, and then we've got him."

"And what about the woman with him, Dave? What do you do with her? You can't make her disappear like you tried to do with Palmer. She's a local, and she'd be missed, you know." He stopped pacing and stood at the window. "Part of your problem is that you're assuming too much. You have to stop assuming that Palmer has painted himself into a corner, because he seems to have gotten out of two or three of them quite easily so far."

Both men were quiet for several minutes.

"What about the helicopter?" Kelly sighed.

"Tomorrow morning. We'll have to sit it out till then."

"I'm going to assume—if you'll pardon one more assumption, Tom—that Palmer can't climb in the dark. It looks to me like we're all sitting things out till then."

Grady nodded. But, then, what was another night? He had been sitting things out since this damned project had gotten under way. "There is one more possibility, though," he said quietly, still looking out the window.

"Which is . . . ?"

It was difficult bringing it out, and Grady had to think before he spoke. "Palmer doesn't know about the gas or contamination. If he does happen to make it to the summit, he'll be unprotected. It could kill him. You would no longer have your subject for study, but there would be no further outside threat to security, either." He could see Kelly's face light up in the reflection in the glass.

"Yeah...yes, that's a possibility," Kelly muttered. "And we could consider it. We could give him enough rope to hang himself with. Yeah, Tom, you might have something there." And now he was smiling.

Yeah, I've got something. It's called a big fucking mouth.

2

JANEY REMAINED IN THE CHAIR while Gary conducted his own search through the building. She refused to move because she was still worried and scared, and now that they were in a place where they clearly didn't belong she felt like a burglar and a vandal on top of it. Somebody seemed certain to appear outside the door at any time. But that in itself was cause for even more worry because why would someone be out after dark? Where would he be? If there was no place up here to run *to*, it made you wonder what there might be up here to run *from*. And if everybody who was supposed to be here was dead— murdered, girl, let's get it straight—then the killer or killers couldn't be far away. Damned if you do, damned if you don't; there was more trouble in her and Gary just being here than her mind could sort out in one sitting. She didn't know about any- one else, but she had trouble thinking straight when she was scared shitless.

There was a consolation, though—at least the door was locked. From Gary's description of the door, nobody was apt to be beating it down or kicking it open in case of a raid. Locked and sealed, this building was secure.

Gary's search through most of the rooms turned up little that they couldn't already see. Only when he looked inside the room in the northeast corner did they begin to suspect the full grav- ity of whatever was going on here. The room was a combina- tion medical center and laboratory, fully stocked and equipped for both. A little poking around inside made it suddenly clear that someone was supposed to be examining bodies, among other things. The room held a stainless steel autopsy table, bottles of preservatives and instruments like those used by undertakers, and a three-drawer refrigeration unit set into a wall, and *that* sure wasn't intended to store your beer in. A corpse would fit quite nicely into each drawer. All of this led to another big question: why go to all this trouble for crash victims? Their deaths had been fairly straightforward. Also, it was the only room that appeared to be unused, so what else had they been doing up here?

Gary also found papers—stacks of them along with typed reports, books and a pile of manuals nearly four feet tall. There seemed to be something technical written about every single item the building contained. He brought everything he could find over to the table. "Now, we study," he said.

"We?"

His reply was to flop one of the thick bound stacks onto the table in front of her. "*We*. You read through that one, and I'll start with this one. We'll go through them one at a time until we find something." His material was about a project of some kind; it was classified Top Secret. Hers had been stamped Confidential.

"Hey, won't we get into a lot of trouble for reading this stuff?"

"No more than we're already in. But, no, not really, not if you don't tell them. If someone should ever ask, you didn't see anything, and you didn't read anything. Neither did I."

Well, he nailed that one. It was hard to see how anyone could get themselves into any more trouble than this. But at least it was something to do besides sit rooted in this chair trembling and flinching at every little thing moving. And maybe someday she might even look back on this and, as they say, have herself a good laugh. *Oh yes, kids, Mommy and Daddy went up a mountain to see a wrecked airplane and oodles and oodles of gory-looking dead bodies all over the place, and later we sat down and read a whole bunch of closely guarded military secrets. That was just before they put us in jail.*

She opened the cardboard cover.

KOTA STATION
High Altitude Research Facility
Parameters
Primary, Secondary, Tertiary Functions

"Kota Station," she mumbled. "That's where we are."

"Kota Station? Good name for it." He got up from the table. "Are you hungry? I'm starved. It looks like they've got enough to feed the Third Army in here." He began digging through the cupboards and refrigerator.

"I don't want anything." Fear and worry didn't do much for her appetite, either.

"Well, I'll fix you something anyway. We haven't had anything since noon."

Yes, Mother. She turned her attention back to the book.

As far as Janey could tell, Kota Station was—or might be— an interesting place to visit, but it made for yawning, eye-watering reading. Approximately two-thirds of the report was little more than specifications, justifications, and cross-references to more of the same. Separate reports and technical manuals covered everything in the place, and each was mentioned with appropriate secondary information including acceptable contractors and subcontractors. After a couple of hours Janey began to pity those who had had to assemble such a boring mess and wondered how they had done it without going crazy. Only as she came to the end of the 487-page report did she see anything that Gary might use. "Why didn't I read the end first?" she mumbled to herself.

"What did you say?"

Kota Station, she said with a yawn, had been put here to investigate the crash of Flight J-440. It could house four people, but only two had been assigned to this project. And because of the nature of their work, much of the equipment and facilities had been specially modified. The laboratory, for example: ordinarily, it would be a medical facility equipped for limited treatment. For this mission it had been converted to a small but full-blown research laboratory. "But it doesn't say what they're researching," she finished. "It isn't specific about anything else."

"Well, it fits with this report," he said. The specialized work had been named the KP Project. There was no reference to what KP meant; only that Flight J-440 was directly involved because of an error that was supposed to be explained in the second half of the report. "They keep mentioning some sort of mistake or accident that wasn't discovered until the plane went down. And look at this." He turned the report around for Janey to read. There were two pages, complete with photographs and parts of their service records, concerning the two men who were supposed to be there: a Lieutenant Colonel Gilmore, and his partner, Lieutenant Colonel Attwood—the man lying up in Karber's Pass.

Gary mentioned the Chemical Corps insignia he saw. "I wondered what somebody from the Chemical Corps was doing here, and now I think I know. See this? Both of them are from the Blackstone Arsenal, and they've been involved with this project, which originated at Fort Stanton, Maryland."

"What about it?"

"The Blackstone Arsenal is the Army's Chemical Warfare Center, Janey. They handle all kinds of weird biological and chemical weapons. But I didn't know Fort Stanton had anything to do with that. I thought they were just a storage depot where ammunition and explosives were tested." He looked at Janey. "But I guess not—" And then it hit him.

And Janey, too. The eyes of both widened in fear. The implications suddenly were hammered home. "My God! Gary, do you suppose . . . ?"

"It sure looks that way," he whispered. Now it was beginning to make some sense—the deaths at the summit, whatever happened to him, his confinement, and all of this. "Maybe that's what this accident was. Maybe someone accidentally loaded some sort of chemical or biological thing aboard that plane. And this project is to find out what happened to it. Or better yet, to study what its effects might have been. Hell, that's probably it. The Army doesn't give a shit if they kill anybody, but they'd want to know what their weapon did to the victims." And, he wondered, just what *did* it do to the victims? It could have killed the crash survivors, Gorham and Gurdler, and it did something to him. He thought of that Colonel Attwood lying up in the pass with his head bashed open like a watermelon; and he thought about the missing Colonel Gilmore. Maybe something had happened to him, too. Hell, anything was possible.

"Gary, we have to get out of here *now*! Please!"

"No. Not yet." He flipped to the back of his report.

"What! Are you crazy?"

"Janey, we need more information. We need—"

"You've *got* information! What more do you need? Do you have to get us killed to prove a point?"

"We haven't got anything yet. We have to learn all the specifics, all the details. We have to have absolute proof... something they can't deny. Janey, if I tried to tell anybody what little we know now they'd just lock me up again. We have to learn all about this weird project."

"No-o-o! We're in danger! Let's leave now!" She jumped up from the table.

Gary jumped up to grab her. "Janey, will you listen? We're safe in here. Nothing can get us unless we let it in. And I'm only gonna say this one more time: we can't climb down this mountain at night. We're stuck here until morning, like it or not. So let's use it to our advantage. If we don't then my escape and this whole damned thing would be a waste. We'd climb back down, and if they didn't just shoot both of us on sight, we'd both get locked up. We wouldn't accomplish anything." He let go of her arm.

Janey turned away from him.

"Hon, do you think I'm not scared? Well, I am. I'm scared shitless. All of this happened to *me*. I'd like to know what it was. Please don't quit on me."

She said nothing. She turned and walked to the nearest window. Snow ticked against the Plexiglas, and Janey shivered. Not with cold, but trembling with dread now creeping over her like a blanket of frost. Tears came. She couldn't stop them; they had been threatening for hours, and she was unable to contain them any longer.

Gary remained at the table, now deep into the second half of the material about the KP Project.

THIRTY-FIVE MILES EAST of the mountain, inside Endicott Airfield's main hangar, a shrill whine filled the building. Rotors turned, slowly at first, then with steadily increasing speed until the thudding echo hammering against the walls shook everything. Steel roof trusses rang and doors and windows vibrated. Heat waves poured from the engine exhaust and the whine became a banshee scream as the engineers poured on full power for ten uninterrupted minutes.

Fifteen minutes later, after both rotors ground slowly to a stop, one of the engineers asked how the instruments looked on the control panel.

All right, he was told, and he asked what the test modules and dynamometer readings looked like.

Good, was the answer; full horsepower, torque and RPM. Of course this was only a ground test, he was quick to add. The results could be quite different in the air. But they wouldn't know for sure until morning.

THIRTY-FIVE FEET SOUTH of Kota Station the footsteps dragging across the Northeast Plateau came to a stop.

3

GARY KEPT READING. What was it? he wondered, brushing over page after page of the report. It had to be mentioned in here somewhere. The men aboard Flight J-440 had been ordinary infantry, regular GIs. Grunts. Groundpounders. The most complex weaponry in their company inventory would have been automatic rifles and machine guns; the only thing even remotely qualifying as a chemical weapon would have been white phosphorous hand grenades; no regular infantry company would have been issued anything else. And none of those things—hand grenades, ammunition, and certainly no such thing resembling a chemical or biological agent—would ever have been put on the same plane with them. And so far, all the second half of the report mentioned was this or that reference to the mysterious accident with only one paragraph hinting vaguely about what might have happened—an unspecified cargo stop at Andrews Air Force Base, Maryland. Fort Stanton wasn't too far from Andrews, so maybe the accident occurred there before any cargo was ever loaded. Or maybe there

had been no accident at all. There were truths, and there were
military truths.

He turned another page.

And stopped. "Holy shit!"

Preliminary Analysis

Dichlorodetrioxymonotrimethanol

$DCChX_3D_5Tl_4MO_2O_2MEh_4$ Mixture #4

He read the page twice to make certain he wasn't seeing
things, then read it a third time before going on. There were six
pages to the preliminary analysis about some kind of thing
known as Swamp Gas, and when he had finished them he was
trembling.

"Janey?" he mumbled, his face still down in the report.

She sniffled and said nothing.

"Janey? I've found it."

She turned away from the window. "Found what?"

"What we were looking for. We were right. There *was*
something on the plane. God, you should read this."

"You mean, a chemical?" She walked to the table.

"Chemical isn't the word for it. Listen: Fort Stanton had
been fooling around with some sort of superpowerful weed
killer, something that could destroy any kind of plant life. Then
somebody got the bright idea to mix in one of the nerve agents
they have at the Blackstone Arsenal, and they came up with the
damnedest thing you've ever seen." He looked up at her. "It
just kills everything it touches . . . just wipes it out."

"And that's what was on the plane?"

Gary nodded. "Yeah. They were sending forty gallons of it
from Fort Stanton to Blackstone, and somehow it was misplaced and put on the wrong plane. And that's it. That's why
this building is here, and why those two colonels were here.
They're supposed to be studying the effects that this stuff might
have had on the few people who survived the crash."

"And they didn't even tell you guys about it?"

Gary took her hand. "They didn't know it at the time. They
didn't know it was on this plane until later."

"Now you know! Gary, we've got to get out of here. On top
of everything else, there's a poison gas in the air up here!"

"Janey, listen—"

She pulled away from him. "No! Are you crazy? There's a poison gas that probably killed everyone on the plane! It probably killed those two men you were climbing with! Maybe it even killed the two men who are supposed to be here in this building! What more do you want?"

"*Proof!* I want proof, Janey. Stop and think: if the gas killed the crash survivors, why did the recon photos show people out and moving around a full day after the crash? Why did they show people moving around on the morning before we got here? And if it killed Gorham and Gurdler, why didn't it kill me, too?" He picked up the report. "According to this, the gas works in seconds, Janey. It kills as soon as it's released into the air. Don't you see? The stuff apparently didn't work like they thought it would, and that has to be part of the reason for all this investigation. No doubt that was why they had me locked up; they probably didn't know what it did to me, or why it worked on me differently than it did on the others." He put the report down, then got up from the table. "Since we can't leave here yet, the best thing to do is learn all we can about this. You know: ammunition. I don't want either of us getting locked up when we leave here."

"You really are crazy."

"Probably." He smiled, then gestured toward the table. "Do you feel up to some more reading? There's still a lot of stuff here to go through."

Her face blank and drawn, she sat back down at the table. Wordlessly, she picked up another bound stack from the pile of papers.

Gary went into the recreation area. He found the AM/FM radio.

"Radio Sixty-three...!

"And here we are at 9:15 in the p.m., with Steve Schell comin' atcha till midnight. This is the Box Tops and 'The Letter...'!"

Much of the information on the table seemed to be technical data relating to the equipment in Kota Station. There were operational instructions, maintenance instructions and repair instructions about everything contained in the station. Everything—right down to the personal items and each stick of furniture, all of it in alphabetic order, piece by piece. If you had time enough to plow through all of it, Gary said, you'd learn how everything worked, half a dozen other uses for each item and how to build another one if necessary. It was far more than two people could cover in only one night. "If you could remember half of this," he said in amazement, "you could qualify for two more college degrees."

Well, that was fine for him, Janey thought. But she understood almost nothing about the technical information. She had trouble playing a radio. When her old Chevy blew apart a couple of days ago, she might have sat there until now trying to get it started if it hadn't been for that gas station attendant. So she gave up on the technical manuals, concentrating instead on the laboratory. It, too, was difficult to understand, especially all the references to certain medical tests and procedures that could be performed there; many were supposed to be conducted by a qualified M.D. under normal circumstances. But she soon learned that the KP Project was nowhere near the realm of the ordinary, and two highly trained researchers from the Chemical Corps were all that anyone wanted to risk for the time being. And, as one set of instructions pointed out, no one knew for certain what they might find here, or exactly where they should look for anything. It seemed that all they intended to do was look for whatever they could find, then subject their findings to certain tests so that a few unmentioned theories could be proved or rejected. "It looks like part of their work was to identify the crash survivors, then bring them down here to the lab and run certain tests on them," she said. "But the lab is untouched. I don't think they were here for more than a couple of days."

"Then there probably wasn't time enough for them to learn whatever they came up here to learn," Gary said. "And something killed them suddenly and violently just as they were getting started."

"They?"

He nodded. "I'd lay money on it. I'd bet both of them are dead."

Then he showed her a couple of photos stapled inside one of the manuals—pictures of the XM-221 helicopter. "This is how they got everything up here."

"I wonder where it is now?" she said. "I mean, with two people dead, you'd think that this place would be crawling with Army officials right now."

"You'd think that, wouldn't you?" Gary muttered. "Makes you wonder, doesn't it?" Unless, he thought, the second man—Gilmore—had been evacuated; that what they had found was so bad, they simply ran away from it, leaving Attwood's body where it had fallen.

And that brought up another possibility. Perhaps Gilmore had experienced much the same thing Gary had eight months ago; maybe the gas hadn't killed Gilmore, but had done something to his mind. Maybe he had gone crazy, and killed his own partner. Which meant—

Maybe you went crazy and killed your two partners, ol' buddy. And ain't that a hell of a thought?

"Hey, is something wrong?" Janey said after a few minutes.

"No, everything's fine. Why?"

"Because you've been reading the same page for almost ten minutes. Is that a manual, or a girlie magazine?"

He smiled. "Don't I wish. But it's a manual, for that radio over there," and he walked over to it.

4

"THEIR RADIO IS ON and receiving," General Grady was explaining to General Kelly, "or this set of lights wouldn't be on. If they were talking, these two lights would be flashing, or modulating."

"And there are no possible malfunctions that wouldn't show up?"

Grady shook his head. "None. We've been through the system twice, and everything's working."

"Then what's happened up there?" Kelly whispered. "If one of them got killed, why hasn't the other at least reported it?"

Grady said nothing. He was holding to his opinion that the remaining man—if there was a man remaining—had suffered effects from the gas, and might now be running about like a madman. He might even have killed his partner. On the other hand, he might be dead now, too.

"None of this is making any sense," Kelly went on. "We knew what some of the effects would be, but nothing like—"

"Sir!" the radio operator interrupted.

"What is it?"

The operator was pointing to the control panel. "Look. The lights just went out. Somebody just shut Kota's radio down."

"Oh, shit!"

Grady grabbed the nearest telephone. "Get me the airfield...*fast*. And then get me the photo recon section."

5

GARY KNEW LITTLE ABOUT RADIOS except for those the climbing teams carried with them on missions. It wasn't until he'd switched it off that he knew what he'd done.

"What happened to the lights?" Janey said behind him.

He shrugged, turning back to the manual. He quickly saw that he didn't have to be an expert to appreciate this radio; in fact, radio didn't seem to be an apt description for it. He began comparing items with the manual, twice getting out of the chair for a look behind, and underneath, the console. This was one hell of a radio. With its linear amplifier turned on, the signal could be boosted to 100,000 watts, making it by far the most powerful transmitter at this end of the country. All you had to do was adjust the power output setting, aim the antenna dish to any direction, then key it up and start talking. It could be set to any AM or FM signal, and if cranked up to full capacity it would make coleslaw of an ordinary transmitter or receiver.

He was still fiddling with all the switches when Janey sat down at the adjacent control panel. Lights were flashing on a board. "What does this thing do?"

"I don't know. I haven't got to that yet." He handed one of the manuals to her. "Here. You check it out."

"I don't understand any of this stuff."

"Just read through it until you know what it does."

"You read through it," she said, handing the manual back to him. "I've had enough for one day."

She looked it; she appeared ready to drop. "Okay." Gary smiled. "Go get some rest."

"Where?"

"There's two bedrooms over there. Make yourself comfortable."

Comfortable? She would feel more comfortable in a graveyard. "You are kidding? I feel like Goldilocks about to be discovered by the bears."

This corpse is too warm, and this corpse is too cold...

Only here, the bears devoured you and spit your bones out like watermelon seeds.

... but this corpse is just right....

"Well, try to rest anyway," Gary said. He was already involved with the manual and the light-filled board. He was reading the manual alternately with some kind of handwritten list he'd found lying on the desk. After a few minutes he opened a drawer and pulled out a cardboard box filled with loose objects.

"What about you? When are you going to rest?"

He studied one of the objects from the box. It was a round, flat disk about the size of a half dollar. One side looked perforated, like a tiny speaker, and the other held a smaller circular device that looked like the head of a screw. He studied it for a moment, then turned the page in the manual.

"Gary?"

He looked at the panel in front of him, glanced quickly back at the book, then reached toward a switch.

"Gary, are you listening?"

"Mmm..." Opening the desk drawer, he fumbled around until he found a screwdriver. He picked up the disk, twisted the screwdriver against it and flipped the switch on and off.

"Gary? Did you hear me?"

"Yeah...you said something..."

"Yeah, I did. Mom and I are starting a whorehouse there at home. We wondered if you'd like to be the piano player?"

He put down the disk, reached to the control panel again and made two or three more adjustments she couldn't see. "What did you say?" he mumbled.

"Nothing...forget it. What's that?"

He tossed the disk to her. "Well, if I've fixed that thing right, what you've got is a low-frequency listening device. A transmitter. Just like the ones they use in the spy movies."

"You mean, a bug?"

"That's it. Say something into it."

She stared at it. "What should I say?" and as she said that, the twenty-fifth green light on the board flashed brightly. The adjacent VU meter jumped to the far end of its scale.

"Hot dingies, it works! That's the transmitter, and this is the receiver. These lights and meters show the strength of the signal; how close something is to the disk. I thought this list was a secret code, but it's a list with all twenty-four bugs on it."

"What?"

"They planted twenty-four of these things between the summit and the bottom end of Karber's Pass. The list tells which one is which," and he pointed to the board. "They're in sequence; number one at the bottom, number twenty-four at the top."

Janey shrugged, handing the disk back to him. "I still don't understand why they would bug anything. What is there to listen for?"

Gary shook his head. "I have no idea. Every time I think I've found an answer, two more questions pop up behind it. The more I look, the more confusing this thing gets. And now they've put bugs..." and he stopped. He looked toward the ceiling. "Do you hear that?"

She heard it. "It sounds like a plane."

Oh shit! Gary thought as he ran to the door. As he opened it he expected to see that weird-looking helicopter settling down on the plateau, and perhaps a dozen or so heavily armed Special Forces troopers leaping out to rush the building. Someone had to know by now that they were up here.

But it was only an airplane. Gary looked at the dark sky in time to see it roll gracefully to the left, east of the mountain, then head eastward. In a minute it had disappeared into the night.

"Gary?" Janey called from the doorway.

"It's all right," he said, and waved. "It was only a plane. It's gone now."

Yes. The plane was gone. But as he looked out at the blackness of the great mountain and the sky above the sensation hit him that something else was there instead. He couldn't identify the strange and uncomfortable feeling for several moments, and he found himself looking toward both corners of the building as if getting set to run across a street against traffic. Then he knew. It was an eerie sensation of being watched. That was it. Something out there in the dark was watching him. It was staring at him as if he were its prey. He was sure of it. He could feel it.

He stepped away from the building. *Where are you?*

He could see nothing except the black walls of rock—cold monoliths against the sky. He could hear nothing except the wind. Yet as the minutes passed and as he looked and listened carefully, the sensation grew until it became frightening. He shivered, trying to imagine who or what was out there... watching him. They had to be close, perhaps just out of reach of the lights. Over there, maybe, or up there, or maybe over there. Two eyes.

He took two more steps away from the building.

Eyes. Unblinking. Flat, lidless. Observing every move he made. And it was not some wild quirk of his imagination, no daydream, no idle thought, no way. Somebody was out there, probably the same somebody they had heard moving inside the cave, and it had followed them down here to the plateau. The feeling was real, almost alive, almost like raw power thrumming through his nerves. Something was watching him, the building....

"Gary?"

The sensation became stronger as he moved away from the station. He was getting closer to it, and with it came the feeling that if he got too far away he—

"Gary? What are you doing?"

—might not get back.

He stopped. The sensation grew. The eyes were getting closer, moving through the darkness toward him, and suddenly he froze, looking around, trying to get his eyes to adjust to the blackness, his ears attuned to the wind....

"Gary! What are you doing?"

And the sensation left him as if the unseen eyes had blinked themselves away into the mountain night. He looked all around him, toward the walls, the sky, the building. But nothing was there now. He stood alone in the cold, staring at empty darkness.

"Hey, what are you doing?"

"Nothing, just looking around."

"At what?"

"Oh . . . I thought I heard another plane."

"Radio Sixty-three . . . !

"And this is another reminder, boys and girls, for you to get those postcards in by June 15, and maybe you'll be the big winner of the Beatles collection. Enter as many times as you like, but as they say in Chicago, vote early, and vote often!

"Steve Schell, KSCM, and here's The Who, riding their 'Magic Bus.'"

The eyes watched the building.

6

FORTY-FIVE MINUTES AFTER Grady sent for the photo analyst, he, Kelly and Childs examined the latest set of photographs. Six of them clearly illustrated Kota Station—the lights were on, and somebody was home. A seventh picture showed the dead man facedown in the rocks at the lower end of Karber's Pass. They still couldn't identify him. And they weren't sure who was inside the station, or who it was outside looking through one of the windows.

7

SHE MIGHT NOT HAVE BEEN ABLE to make herself comfortable, but at least Janey had managed to get to sleep. Less than ten minutes after Gary came back into the station she had stripped down to her thermal underwear and collapsed on one of the beds.

Gary then walked through the building, turning lights out and making certain the place was buttoned up and locked; he had called to her that he would be right in, but got no answer. When he looked into the room, Janey was already asleep.

He smiled. That, he told himself as he watched her for a moment, is one hell of a woman you've got there, son. And somehow you've got to get her safely out of here and down this mountain. She comes first.

He left the room to turn off the rest of the lights, leaving only one on at the far end of the building in the recreation area. He was still too keyed up to sleep now with a thousand new questions storming around in his head, and he had to stop and wonder again if he had done the right thing. Oh, he was doing what he had set out to do, or thought was the best idea on the spur of the moment, but now that they were here . . . well, as Janey had said, Now what? How do you turn all of this to your advantage? How do you get out of here with all of this in your head, even if you do find answers to every question, and take it to the right people? Who down there among all the guards and Army officials waiting for him, or about to come up after him, was likely to listen? There seemed to be only two possible results of the climb: one, he had either made things much worse and would be locked away for the rest of his life when they caught him; or two, if he could play this out to the end and somehow think of a way to do it right, they wouldn't dare touch him or Janey. They would have a shitload of explaining to do. And who were the right people? Who could help him?

He sat down at the table and stared at the green modulating lights on the detector control panel, and he tried to think.

INSIDE THE FIRST BEDROOM Janey stirred, tossing a little and moaning softly.

Janey had never quite come to terms with death; consciously, she doubted that she ever would, or that she was likely to try very hard. Death might be one of the two most natural things in the world; it might be the great phenomenon and the route to the better world lauded in song and story by the men on the pulpits of the planet. But none of that, no flowery philosophy, would ever set it straight in her mind or make it acceptable. Death was far more than mysterious or worrisome. It was panicky, frightening, sometimes terrifying. Facing it was unimaginable.

She first met it head-on when she was seven. Her grandfather died. She seemed puzzled at first, perhaps even slightly curious, until she found out exactly what had occurred. The pretty pictures of heaven and winged angels playing harps in the clouds and the Big Guy with the white beard suddenly vanished because she *knew* then what had happened to Grandpa. After the doctors got done with him they handed Grandpa over to a man who set about doing awful things to him, fixing it so that he could never get up again. During the funeral she realized that they were going to lock him inside that box, plant him in the ground like a potato and leave him there. She began crying at the funeral, and it hadn't been the service, the sad music or the grief of others causing her to cry; she was genuinely shocked because Mom and Dad and all the aunts and uncles were allowing such a terrible thing to happen. No amount of rationalization or reasonable explanation would ever convince her that Grandpa wasn't really Grandpa anymore. Of course it was Grandpa. She had been bounced on those knees, held in that lap, fallen asleep on those shoulders. The big callused hands had held her own tiny ones when she was trying to learn to walk, had taken her for hundreds of walks later and had even picked flowers for her. That kindly, careworn face with the wrinkled smile, twinkling blue eyes and bushy, scratchy white mustache had shown her a thousand expressions as it told stories, offered advice and gave occasional warnings. Grandpa was the man who had been indirectly responsible for her being there in the first place. It was still Grandpa in there. *That was him.*

It happened again years later—and after she had thought she was grown up. Her father died, and once again all the tormenting demons cackled as they wriggled out of the grave and came after her. But she was a woman by then, or very nearly so, and she was able to see how badly her reaction was affecting Mom, who needed comfort and understanding almost as much as she. So Janey simply put her father out of her mind, the only way she could cope with his passing. She managed to ease herself out of the event, and looked back on it only after years had placed it at a safe distance.

Whenever a loved one of a friend or more distant relative died, all Janey could do was cringe, withdraw to a suitable distance and offer what sympathy was available at an arm's length. She seemed cold, distant and perhaps even a little cruel to those who didn't know her well. It was this misunderstanding that had resulted in no contact between her and Gary's family eight months ago, and none since then. Not that they knew one another; Janey had talked with Gary's mother only once over the phone, months before the plane crash, and had written only a couple of letters to her during the two and a half years she'd known Gary. But there wasn't even a note of sympathy passed, either from Sioux Creek, Montana, or Yakima, Washington. Janey isolated herself, seemingly crawling into her own mind as if that were the only shelter from the world. For three days after all the official announcements had been issued she moved about in more or less a dreamlike state. Weeks passed before she edged back to reality, and then only to be struck with the hazy and intuitive sensation that the whole show had been a sham, a fraud—that somehow Gary was still alive. For a long time she couldn't decide whether or not to trust the feeling, and she had finally decided to do so partly because it felt better and more comfortable to believe it—but partly because the other side of the same intuition caused her to believe it was true, that Gary really was alive somewhere.

When it happened, death had been driven away, cheated. Her feelings had been on the mark, and she had beaten death back for the first time in her life. And for the first time it had seemed as though she might be able to face its harsh realities the next time it reared up. And that might have been possible only a few days ago.

But now she was surrounded by death. She was smack in the center of scores of horrible deaths, inside a place constructed for the sole purpose of studying death, built by men whose careers and fortunes had been made by the discovery of new and more bizarre ways to cause death.

Janey Burns was in mortal terror, sleeping now only because her conscious mind was something like that of a punch-drunk fighter; after you get hit so many times you hardly feel the pain. And because her body was simply bone-weary. Her slumber was not peaceful by any means.

ONE OF THE CEILING HEATERS came on with a soft whoosh, bringing Gary back to reality. He looked at his watch; he had been sitting at the table for a full ninety minutes, and he was no closer to solving his final problem than he'd been when he sat down. Even if he knew every fact there was to know up here, he still did not know what to do with those facts, where to take them.

Again, he stared at the motion detector control panel. Green lights winked and VU needles quivered. He got up; walking to the panel, he turned a black knob marked Master Volume, and noise came from two small speakers mounted on the back wall. It was soft wind noise, marked with the occasional needles of snow and ice striking all twenty-four disks in the pass and on the summit. He listened for a minute, then turned the volume down to one notch above its lowest setting.

An electric motor came on in the back equipment room; inside the bathroom, the water heater pilot turned itself on with a quiet *fwooomp*. He could hear the main generator humming above it, a soft but steady whizzing. Kota Station needed no human supervision, it seemed. Left completely alone it would still hum and click its way along with quiet efficiency. If it were a vehicle it would need no driver.

Gary sat back down at the table, picked up another equipment manual, browsed through it, then tossed it aside. He had read through most of them, and of the ones left there was very little that would do him any good. What he needed was more information about Swamp Gas and about this thing they called the KP Project. But he had read everything available on both, and right now he couldn't begin to go through it all again. He was getting tired, dull, and even if there was something he'd missed earlier he was sure to miss it again. So what he really needed was more time to digest this and to look around; he needed to remember what had happened to him at the summit eight months ago; and he needed an out. He needed a person or place where all of this could be taken.

And he needed sleep.

The green lights were getting blurry, the VU meters fuzzy, out of focus. He should go to bed, he thought dully. Go in there, crawl in next to Janey and pull those covers up over his head and drift away. That would be so nice. . . .

"...on KSCM, Sioux Creek..."

So peaceful...

"...reminding you that the camping season is upon us again. The National Park Service and all the county fire departments are saying that if you plan on doing anything weird out there in the woods, do it without starting any forest fires. You have to make sure those camp fires are out, boys and girls, and don't build any unless it's absolutely necessary. If you do, be sure to douse 'em good, even if you have to dump all your beer. And as the bear in the drill instructor hat likes to say, 'Only you can prevent forest fires.' If you torch their homes, all the critters will do their thing in your living rooms.

"Steve Schell, KSCM, Radio Sixty-three, getting back to the Grass Roots, and listening to their 'Midnight Confession.'"

Head down, arms crossed, feet up on the table, Gary dozed off.

Down the hallway behind him, the doorknob twisted.

8

JUNK...PIECES...WRECKAGE...

We are...about halfway through Karber's Pass....

...debris...cargo...crates...engine blades fuel lines tubes... Survivors?

Negative. Nothing. No. Bodies...bodies, yes. No survivors...only bodies up ahead. Rocks. Bodies.

Black box...colored wires...ribs...wing skin struts junk trash bodies Do Not Adjust... No Step... Piles. Nothing whole. Sheet metal fatigues boots bags arms legs blood.

Concentrate. Report. Understand.

Yes, sir.

Faces, limbs, bones, bodies...Ronson lighter fluid...class ring Chevy hot rods girlfriends mom dad...*Playboy*...

Survivors?

No...a foldout. Big tits, big smile...

Don't have to be that descriptive and that's an order Palmer do you understand that's an order report observe take pictures...

We've arrived. Ahead. The wreck. J-440, God what a mess!

Center... fuselage. Check it out. Center fuselage. Check it out Cen—

On my way, hold on, Doug... he's waving, he's found...

Lieutenant?

What the hell caused this? Who knows? Happened after the fact. Keep out the wind. Windy. Bad, bad storm, you know. Keep out the wind with a friend.

But who? What? How? Why?

Lieutenant? Do you copy?

I don't know... haven't seen him. Anybody know where he went?

Palmer! Report! What is happening? Report! Report!

Weird... really weird...

What's weird? What? Report, Palmer, report report report report report...!

Well, this is, what do you think? They're dead. They're all dead, don't you know, General... Grady... Tom, ol' buddy ol' sport. Everybody in the airplane. Dead.

Palmer! Report! Report! Report!

Jesus, Tom, is that the only word you know? What do you mean, get rid of the oxygen? That an order? To quit breathing? What kind of climb is this?

Palmer!

He fell... Gurdler... he fell...

Palmer! Report your situation! Answer! Respond!

Oh-ho... whoa, there, hold on. Back up. Uh-uh, buddy, can't be. *You're dead. You're dead...* Sit...chew...aaa...shunnn? Bad. Oh, wow, bad. All dead, and I don't feel so hot myself, and goodbye....

"...N-no...dead. You're dead, you're—ummm-mmm!" Gary bolted up in his chair. A long minute passed as he looked around at the interior of the station and finally remembered where he was. Yes. He remembered now—the lights. The green flashing lights on the control panel, that was it. He'd been dreaming.

He thought about it. It was like chasing down stray papers blowing across a field, but he remembered what the dream was about....

The climb. The summit. Eight months ago.

He jumped up. The details were muddled, and some of them blew away before he could examine them. But a few were still there: Gorham... Gurdler... and himself.

And something else... But what? He didn't know. But that wasn't important for the time being. The events lost so many months ago on the summit were starting to edge back into the light.

He started to sit down again. He badly needed to think, to concentrate, and to try to prod whatever else was in there to the surface. But something else caught his attention.

It was the control panel. Several of the lights were flashing a brighter green than the others; a couple of them gave off a steady green glow that bent the VU meters to the far end of their scales. He watched them for a moment. Numbers 16, 17 and 18 were registering the strongest signals.

Then he reached for the volume control.

...unnnnch...crunnnch...crunnnch...

17...18...19...

He felt a slight shock. Something was moving out there. It was walking up Karber's Pass.

...runnnch...crunnnch...crunnnch...

"Jesus!"

HE CHECKED ONE LAST TIME to make certain that he had everything he needed—and he had no idea of what he really needed at all. But a full pack wasn't necessary, so he dropped it to the floor; neither food nor medical supplies would do him any good on this little jaunt. Besides, the summit was only 1100 feet away—a walk. No, what he supposed he needed was a gun, or a big club or... or that. An ice ax. He wasn't certain of exactly why he felt that he needed protection except...well, there was no telling who might be moving around out there. There was supposed to be the second half of the research team who had occupied this place, out there somewhere. He might now be just as dead as his partner, but if not, then unnecessary protection was better than protection left behind... or whatever the suitable phrase might be. Anything was possible. Anything could be moving in that pass.

"Ax, lantern, rope," he muttered, zipping up the insulated white coveralls, and grabbing a parka. "That, too," and he took one of the helmets and oxygen/respirator units. Each was good for four hours of air. You should be back long before then, he thought.

You hope.

But he did want to be back before Janey woke up. She'd fly right off the high side if she woke up and found him gone. But just to be on the safe side—assuming there was a safe side— he'd left her a note.

As he stepped from the storage room, he listened. She was still asleep in the first bedroom. At the far end of the building he could see all the green lights on the panel. They all seemed to be modulating, as if fifteen or twenty people might be running up and down Karber's Pass.

He set the helmet on his head, plugged in the reservoir and tested the respirator. He zipped up the parka, pulled on his gloves, then picked up the ice ax.

Now. Did he still want to do this?

Hell no! he thought. This was insane. He might be taking a foolish chance with his own life—to say nothing of Janey's—by leaving her down here all alone. All he really had for the moment was an idea—and a piss poor one at that—but the only one he could come up with. It was a lame hunch. If it worked, he might find out what had happened to him. If it didn't...well, he couldn't live forever. But there were no more choices. He had to grab an opportunity as soon as one was presented, however left-handed it might be. And he had come too far to stop now.

One final check—the radios were off, and everything else was turned down. There was nothing in the building to wake Janey.

He drew in a deep breath.

Okay, hero, here you go...your big chance.

He unlocked the heavy steel door, pulled it open, then slipped quietly into the cold, blustery night.

CHAPTER SEVENTEEN

ONCE AGAIN HE HAD TO STOP and rest, and he fell back against the rocks, gasping for air. The trips up and down were difficult and getting harder each time. They caused everything to hurt. But everything hurt anyway; everything hurt or ached or stung or burned. It didn't seem possible that so much pain could be contained in places so small, or that so many kinds of pain could issue from only one or two places.

His lungs rattled and wheezed with congestion, his throat burned, and when the coughing started, as it did more and more often now, it was uncontrolled, sometimes going on and on for what seemed like hours. The coughing caused the other pains to intensify, and tears were forced from sore, burning eyes. His stomach hurt so badly that dry heaves occurred almost every day, and even if something had been forced down earlier, brownish crimson came back up. His hands and fingers were black with grime, and mottled with a score of open wounds, and for some time now there had been little or no feeling in six of his fingers; the nails had blackened on four of them. He had much greater difficulty walking now, and when on the rocks it was hard just to stay upright. His feet, still encased in the same battered, ripped boots never intended for sub-zero snow and ice, issued an unbearable stench from the dead, frostbitten tissue. It hurt to stand; it hurt to walk; it even hurt just to remain still. Open sores stung his face, irritated by the shaggy, unkempt growth of beard; intense pain came from both ears, too long unprotected from the icy winds; and the brilliant glare from sun against snow had long since damaged both of his eyes. And the whole pain-racked frame on which this misery was carried had deteriorated to less than half its original and proper weight—an animated skeleton covered in limp, filthy rags.

Yet, incredibly enough, there was a strength and determination that forced movement and life. Whatever the body had lost seemed to have been at least partially regained by a single-mindedness that only eight months of torturous solitude could have given. And inside the mind that remained existed a purpose; so far as it could remember, there had never been any other. And it was the only thing left in the world pushing him.

He hauled himself to an upright position. He had to go on, he remembered. Picking up his weapon, he restarted his shuffle upward through the snow and rocks.

He wasn't far from death—or, to put it a more accurate way, death was not far from him. He had managed to keep it away, to keep it off balance for a long time now, and it had gone somewhere else where its collections had been easier. But it hadn't forgotten him, no. It was back. And he knew it.

I'm coming for you, boy. Won't be long now.

True... but it still had never fooled him. He had been able to see through its many disguises. It might be wearing one, or several, of its countless faces. It always came back in one form or another, and it had tried often to trick him. It hadn't succeeded because he was getting to be an old hand at spotting it. Yes. He wasn't that easy to fool, not him.

But sooner or later, it would get what it came for. Yes. He knew that, too. You couldn't cheat it forever. It always knew where you were, and if in the right mood it would allow you to play its game for a while. It might allow this, or let you do that, and you think you're outrunning it or hiding from it or cheating it. But you aren't. No. You couldn't, at least not for long, because it was an old, old hand at playing its game, and it had been playing far longer than you. It knew all the tricks of the deal, and the ins and outs, the little quirks. You were allowed to play the game only if good enough, a worthy opponent. Otherwise it would grow weary, bored with you... and it had you.

You gave it a good shot, boy. But the time's almost up. Gotta get on with business.

Well, you don't play this long without learning something. And there were times when you could dictate your own rules, your own little changes. You might be able to say, Hey hold on there, I'm not finished yet. Let's go another round. You didn't have to give in just because it said so. That was another in its bottomless bag of tricks—making you think the game was over, and that you'd lost. If a small lie didn't work, one of its many powerful suggestions or intimidations might do the trick if you weren't careful. You had to be on your guard. It could come at you from any direction. The trick—*your* trick—was to be watching so you'd recognize it when it appeared. If so, you'd be there for another hand.

Just as he was doing right now.

And he laughed.

Because it was right down there. He had seen it, coming from—how many was it this time?—four...yes, four different faces. Two earlier, two new ones now. Oh, it was clever. So many false faces, and only one real one in the bunch, and you just never knew which one it was....

And that had been the first thing he'd learned about it. Never trust any of the faces. Death could be hiding behind any one of them.

THE STORM WAS DYING DOWN, the wind ceasing. He could tell. He had been listening. And there was no better place to listen to the wind moan than from there...where he was.

Where he'd been hiding for hours.

Lonely...oh, so lonely in that fearsome shelter where the wind howled like a hundred loosened banshees. On and on and on and on...

And he could stand it no longer. Death was in here, screaming through the tunnels, screaming in his ear, and he could stand it no longer. Whimpering, his chest heaving uncontrollably, he climbed from the gaping hole in the mountain. He stumbled down the rocks, falling, landing painfully against sharp edges, stones, jagged protruding pieces of metal now cropped out of the rocks like hellish weeds. He got up, and he fell; the wind knocked him down. Up again, and he tripped over...

Bodies.

Even in the blowing snow and wind he could see them. Everywhere. Dozens of bodies. The storm covered them; uncovered them; covered them again.

Here. Look. Your friends, George. Your friends. Here. Over here. Look here, and here, and here, there are more and more and more...

No! No! No, please! Pleeeeeaaassse...

He ran to the plane. He would be safe in there. Safe from the howling, the voices, all the death faces, the screams, the cries... safe from death. In the plane. He wouldn't have to see or listen or think....

And he found the metal hulk in the storm at last. He could hear the canvas as it popped and snapped, and he jumped inside, scrambling over the rows of bodies stacked to keep out the screaming wind.

Oh, yes. He remembered the bodies there. Good idea, wise move. It keeps death out. If it saw them its appetite might be sated for a while, and it would leave him alone after it had seen how much it had already taken. And there was movement in there. He could hear them moving.

He landed on the floor. He could see their shapes. Yes, they were moving. Moving all around him. He could hear them, see the shadows. Four... five...

What...?

Anderson? What's going on?

Richardson? McDaniel? Is that you? What are you guys... doing?

Damon?

Why are...are you moving like that? What's the matter with you?

Oh, God!

Answer me. Hey, answer me, okay? What is this? What's wrong? What's going on in here?

Oh, God... God...

Answer me somebody. Please.

Please! Answer meeeee! Say something! Saaay soommm-thiiinnng!

HE LAUGHED AGAIN. Oh, yeah. Death had broken him in real good, had shown him real fast what kind of game it played, the type of opponent it was. And he'd taken care of it then; shown it what kind of adversary *he* was, and by damn, it hadn't taken to that kind of nasty trick since then.

But it was still there. It was always there somewhere.

Near the toe of his boot was another of the small metal objects it had left in the rocks just out of the pathway. Clever. Oh, you had to be on your toes all the time with death stalking you. It wasn't infallible; it couldn't be everywhere at once, so it used sneaky little tricks like this to keep tabs on you. It tried to fool you into thinking you were safe while it kept a running check.

Gonna get you, boy. Better make your peace, and get yourself ready.

Maybe. He nodded with a chuckle. Maybe. But at least it was in a sporting mood.

And he was primed for another go. With a silent giggle he nudged the small, round piece of metal with his boot. Yeah, death. It's me again. I'm still here. Just thought you'd want to know.

Then he shuffled away back on up the pass.

"*Shalll weeee . . . gaaath-errr . . . at the . . . riiivvv-errr . . .*"

2

GARY COULD HEAR NO NOISES except for the ones he was making. It was so quiet in the pass, unnaturally quiet, as if everything had stopped to watch him as he made his way up. And the higher he went the more he felt like the prey in a grim game of hide-and-seek.

No . . . trick or treat. Or maybe just trick.

He was roughly one-third of the way through the pass. A hundred feet behind him lay Colonel Attwood's body. He had forgotten about it still lying across the path, and had nearly stumbled over it, and that little jolt of adrenaline almost made him glow in the dark. But it was the darkness that bothered him most of all, because it was almost pitch-black in the pass. The moon afforded some light, but only when the thick black clouds weren't in front of it, and they passed in front of it every few minutes. He didn't know which was more unnerving—the cold reflection from the moon, or no light at all. The former caused the pass and its surrounding spires and walls to look like some eerie, alien landscape from a distant planet; the latter, which forced him to use the lantern, made it look as if the walls were closing in. Anyone of a claustrophobic bent would have been reduced to a case of the pants-pissing shakes by then.

The moon reappeared in the sky, and he clicked the light off. He didn't want to use it. The beam was like a neon beacon, and he didn't want to advertise the fact that he was up here. He wanted to get a look at things without making his presence known—even though it had to be known by then—because he had a vague idea or two about what might have happened to him. And, hard as it was bumbling his way along in the dead of night, this seemed the only safe way to get a look, or to jolt his memory.

He stopped as the moonlight was blotted out again. But, he thought, maybe that was the best way to move, using only the moonlight. That, and to try and be quiet. The problem was, he could hardly hear anything with the helmet on. Somebody could come clanking up behind him in a suit of armor and he wouldn't be able to hear them.

Three minutes passed before the moonlight illuminated the pass once again, and now he could see junk up ahead: small pieces once from the plane, scattered personal belongings. He could make out bits and pieces from the cargo, parts from vehicles. There were a few dull reflections here and there in the rocks, and in his path was a waterlogged wad of writing paper; next to it was part of a neck chain holding a single dog tag. A Gillette safety razor lay on top of a torn hunk of sheet metal stamped with the words Access Panel.

Get your ass moving, he thought. You didn't come up here to take inventory. So far nothing appeared familiar, but he saw that a lot of it had been moved around. Parts and pieces had been taken from the rocks where they landed and stacked. And when he finally came to the first soldier's body, it, too, had been disturbed; the fatigue shirt was torn open. Those colonels had probably been collecting dog tags. He didn't know how far into the pass he had gone, but it had to be more than halfway. There was a lot more wreckage ahead, and much of it included bigger, heavier pieces. He could also see at least three or four more bodies.

So he walked until the light faded again, then paused next to a jeep's axle poking up from the rocks. It was an uncomfortable four-minute wait before the moon reappeared, and the next twenty minutes consisted of short hikes among and around bigger and bigger piles of debris. It was the pauses between that began to get to him; they were worse than seeing all the destruction. The loudest noise on the whole mountain seemed to be him and the thudding of his own heart. A sensation of dread was growing, and he began to feel that he was being watched again. He thought about going back. Maybe this could wait for daylight. He couldn't shake the mounting sense of an impending disaster, which seemed to be only waiting for his arrival.

Stupid. Stupid, stupid, stupid . . . the dumbest fucking thing you've ever done. You oughta get the hell out of here while you can still walk.

When the moon was in full view again he looked back down the pass, then up. Neither direction was inviting. No, he thought, neither of them looked worth a damn. But he was getting close to the top. So far he'd stepped over ten or twelve bodies, and the junk was sizable. Only twenty feet ahead was a large portion torn from a wing, too large to be moved out of the path. Just beyond the trail turned toward the right, and he thought he recalled that as being just below the summit. With a deep breath, he turned toward the section of wing and walked to it.

Dumb, dumb, dumb . . .

There was no graceful way of stepping around the wing section. Gary pushed himself into the rocks behind it and leaned on it to balance himself; he was about to step back down into the path when the wing suddenly moved. He slipped, falling against it and dislodging a pile of rocks, and everything began tumbling at once. Rocks banged and clattered against the metal, and the wing section moved with a groan. Gary fell forward in front of it; if the wing fell on him he would be lucky to get away with only three or four broken bones.

"Shit!" He rolled and kicked to get out of the way. As the wing boomed to the ground, he landed in the rocks in front of him—and on top of one of the corpses lying in the path. Illuminated in the moonlight, the ice-covered features—the broken nose, half-opened mouth, and both eyes frozen open in a dead stare—were inches from his face. The right side of the head was broken like a melon above the ear. For a moment, he was struck with a wild impression that he had somehow awakened the man. The gaze looked positively alive as it stared back at him, almost as if about to ask for Gary to please get the hell off his chest.

He nearly choked. But he tried to scramble to his feet, at the same time trying not to touch the body. When he was up and moving in a drunken sort of stumble, he couldn't help but look behind him. He had to run. At that moment he wouldn't have been too surprised to see the dead man sit up and say something.

And he fell over another corpse.

Clouds passed in front of the moon once again, leaving the pathway in darkness. Gary could see nothing for a minute as he tried to get up, fell, got up again, then fell across the same body a second time. He could hear nothing except his own panting and strangled grunting. But he could feel. And he felt stiffened, frozen limbs, torsos, pencil-like fingers, hands ... they were everywhere, all over the ground around him. Every square foot he found seemed occupied by a dead man, sometimes two or more. He couldn't get away from them, and the harder he tried, the clumsier and more desperate he became. He lost track of the path; he was lost among rocks and ice and snow with more dead bodies than he could count.

"Dammit ... shit!" he whimpered, falling over another one.

It seemed as if an hour passed before the moon shone again, and now Gary had to stifle an outcry of utter terror—there *were* bodies all around him. They were everywhere, scores of them. They lay in the path; they were leaning against the rocks, propped up against each other; they were sitting, lying flat, kneeling, and one was even propped up standing. He was surrounded by dozens of battered and mangled corpses frozen solidly in their positions of death; where they still existed, limbs were twisted and broken like piles of sticks; heads were cocked at peculiar angles; bodies were crooked and stooped as if frozen in the middle of some insane, horrifying dance. And the faces—dozens of bizarre, frightening faces stared at him in expressions of pain and fright and outright terror, even those with features that didn't even look human anymore.

But Gary fought the panic rising inside him. They're dead, he thought. They appear horrifying because they went through a plane crash, and they've been dead for months. But the panic was doubling back on him because none of these men, he suddenly realized, died *here*. Each of them had been moved to this spot—*because someone up here knew he was getting company,* he thought. *This is his calling card—our greeting.* He wanted to know what had happened up here. Now, he was beginning to find out, and he thought perhaps that some of this was beginning to turn the rusted gears of his memory.

With a deep breath, he walked on.

The letters U.S. AIR FOR were on another hunk of metal, but partly obliterated by black streaks fanned across its surface. Nearby lay part of an engine exhaust. He concentrated on each piece of debris he saw, and a dim sense of recognition seemed to come over him. He wasn't sure if it was genuine memory or images being forced to the surface just to fill in the blank spots; but he thought it was recollection. It might have been a stupid idea to come up here chasing noises, but it seemed to be working. As he thought about that, the rock walls of the pass dropped away on both sides. The moonlight became much brighter, reflecting against larger areas of snow and ice, and just ahead he saw larger sections of the plane; and over there was the top of a spire—the western boundary of the summit, he remembered. Yes. He was remembering objects, landmarks, and just around that spot was the—

There it was.

"I'll be damned," he whispered. Bathed in full, silvery illumination and surrounded by the stark blacks and whites of rocks and snow lay the wreck of Flight J-440. The summit.

He stopped, taking it all in again slowly. Maybe he had seen all of this before, but now there came traces of understanding of how such a sight could be forgotten—even in the darkness it was too much to handle in only one look around. And maybe that's what happened—or partly. Maybe his mind had overloaded or short-circuited, refusing to register or classify such a disaster. The eyes had photographed and printed the sight, but some self-protective device never allowed the pictures into the active files. The only ones he could see now were those accidentally dropped in the hallway while being hustled to the vault.

He could see nothing moving. The place was as silent as a graveyard. Hell, he trembled, that's exactly what it was. It was just that nobody had dug any holes.

Well, there was only one way to finish this and that was to go the rest of the way up for a good look. Check it all out once and for all. He might even scare up whatever had been walking around up here earlier, and they sure as hell had to be here somewhere. And that—whoever or whatever—might give him the answers he sought—whatever they might prove to be. Or else lower the curtain and turn out the houselights for good.

Too late for debate or worry, pal. You're here. Right where you wanted to be. So get this damn thing finished.

He started toward the wreck.

Some two hundred yards below, one of the two dozen or so corpses that had been positioned around the pass eased himself down from the rocks. He was grinning. He chuckled as he picked up his weapon, swung it once, then started toward the summit. Yes. He really had death on the run this time. This was the best contest he'd had with it yet. And he was enjoying it.

"...ga-a-ather...with the sa-a-aints...at the...ri-i-ver...that flo-o-ows by the throne...of...Go-o-od..."

3

JANEY SAT UP IN BED, staring at the darkness and listening to the quiet. She looked around sleepily, aware that she had to use the bathroom, but momentarily confused by the strange surroundings. She got out of bed, noticing then that Gary wasn't with her. There was no snoring from the opposite side of the bed. She had quickly gotten used to it again; even after only two nights with him it seemed as if he'd never really been gone. Her bed at home, in which she'd slept since she was three, would have been foreign with him there. But all the others—bunks, even sleeping bags—were strange unless he shared them.

Maybe he was still sitting at the table, reading, she thought, leaving the room. Or he might be in the bathroom himself—and probably reading in there, too, as most men like to do for some oddball reason. She remembered her own father sitting for hours in the bathroom, keeping a rotating supply of magazines and paperback books in a rack.

But Gary wasn't sitting at the table. Nor was he sitting in the bathroom. She didn't see him anywhere.

"Gary? Where are you?" she called, suddenly aware that he wasn't in the station, but hoping against the growing panic that she was wrong.

And she was not; moments later, she found the note he'd left on the table.

Janey—
Went to the summit. No time for explanation, but urgent. Won't be gone long. *Stay here* and don't follow. Too dangerous. And don't worry. Back soon.

Love,
Gary

"Oh, no!" she moaned. The summit? At night? Now? What did he think he was doing? What could be so urgent that it couldn't be put off until morning? And if anything happened to him up there—assuming that it hadn't happened already— then she might as well jump off this mountain because she could never get back down alone any other way.

She wadded the note up and threw it, hoping it might break something. "Damn you!" she whimpered, trying to keep herself under control. *Don't worry.... Back soon...* He was making it sound like a jog down to the corner market for a loaf of bread. *Won't be gone long....* Well, he really was out of his damn mind, and that gas, or whatever it was, must have gotten to him again if he'd walked out of here in the middle of the night, leaving her here all alone.

With dead bodies lying all over the place.

But she thought then, Since when have I listened to everything you've said, soldier boy?

Since he called you the other night.

Well, the hell with that. And the hell with not following him because it might be too dangerous. She had gotten this far with him, and she wasn't such a bad climber herself. She could do it, especially if the route through that pass was as easy as he'd said. What she'd seen of it didn't look bad, so all she would need were some tools and a light and . . .

Every ounce of guts you've got, lady.

The only thing not required was her sanity. Check it at the door. To leave here in the middle of the night and go after him would be a complete disregard of all the common sense she'd ever collected. And so what? she thought. Swamp Gas or swamp fever or whatever, she wasn't staying down here by herself.

She hurried into the bedroom to collect her clothes, and was pulling them on as she went from there into the storage room. You ungrateful son of a bitch, she was thinking as she laced up her climbing boots. I go to all the trouble of smuggling your skinny ass from Kansas to Montana, finance this little excursion, and you do *this* to me? Leave me down here all alone with only a note for an explanation? You just wait, Palmer, just wait till I get my claws on you. . . .

She had no idea where anything was kept, so she began ripping open boxes and cartons, or throwing things off the shelves, until she found what she needed. It took several minutes for her to get everything rounded up; she was busy, making a lot of noise. She didn't hear the ticking against the window. And she didn't notice what was looking in at her.

Not until she had pulled her parka on, put on her heavy gloves, set a fur cap into place and found a flashlight—and opened the door.

4

THE SHORT WALK up to the wreck took about fifteen minutes, a meandering sort of route that took Gary through the heart of the disaster. He wandered about in a kind of daze, pausing now and then to stare at something, to study for a minute whatever he happened across, to think. The first minutes were passed in horrified fascination at the disaster, amazement at the sheer volume of wreckage strewn over so small an area, and of all the death it had caused. It didn't seem possible for so much of the airplane to have come through it intact, and that made survivors of such an accident easier to accept. And yet it was incredible that anyone could have lived through it. But here an extraordinary number of victims had been left reasonably whole. He guessed that it was because the plane hadn't exploded on impact, as planes tended to do when they crashed. It had bellied in onto the summit; the wings and engines had broken off, and the main portions of the fuselage had stayed at least partly intact. And now that he thought about it, the scene looked just a little like a multiple bus accident, and he began remembering. He remembered that the three of them were surprised when they found everything in this condition. Even though it had been picked through recently, with a lot of the junk and bodies having been moved around for examination, the site still appeared almost as it had last September. The forward flight deck was still smashed against the rock spires, and all the bodies were still trapped inside; the center section where all the survivors had taken shelter looked pretty much as it had when they first saw it eight months ago—somewhat the worse for wear, but about the same. And right up there to his left, in those rocks, were the remains of the broken tail section, and—

Dear God!

Gary stopped in his tracks, every muscle suddenly freezing. It was happening. Straight out of the blue, without a thought being given to it at that moment, it was happening. The events of that afternoon so long ago were beginning to roll. Not all of it—but more than he expected. The film was old and scratchy; the frames clicked and flicked disjointedly, out of sync, and there were places where it had been crudely spliced and patched. But it was running at last. He was remembering.

"We are . . . halfway through Karber's Pass . . ."

Doug and Rudi were ahead. They stooped to pick up small items lying here and there . . . shreds of canvas . . . papers . . . a can of Ronson lighter fluid . . . a green sock draped over a rock as if left there to dry . . . a metal box with five or six wires attached, and stenciled lettering—Do Not Adjust Unti—

"A lot more junk up ahead now . . . parts . . . part of a wing . . . a bed and tailgate from a truck . . ."

Burned, melted aluminum . . . fuel lines . . . No Step . . .

"Lieutenant, has there been any sign of survivors?"

No. Negative. None yet. Bodies . . . ahead. But no survivors.

"Pass levels off . . . turns right . . . stop and move junk out of the way. Large wing pieces . . . flaps . . . ailerons . . . heavy . . ."

Help move it . . . hold on. Up there, in the rocks . . . where Karber went.

"Is something wrong? Over."

Oh, yeah. You should see what's wrong up here, Tom ol' pal, ol' buddy. Move out. Yes. Don't stay here. And there they are... bodies... buried in the snow... both sides of the pass. Fifteen... maybe twenty... maybe more, maybe less and we're going past some of them right now and I don't want to look don't want to see... take pictures.

"Upper end of the pass now... more victims. Arms... legs—"

"Settle down... slow and easy. Concentrate on your job... report what you see... understand?"

Easy for you to say. Doug just uncovered an SP5's arm, and that's all folks, just the arm with a gold high school class ring on the third finger. Steno pad... runny ink... "Dear Mom and Dad... you'll never guess what happened to your little boy"... *Playboy*... nice smile... bright blue eyes... huge big tits... Doug's leaned over for a look too....

"Just tell us about the site—"

Oh, yeah. Well, guess what I see now, Tom?

"We've arrived. Just ahead is the wreck."

Screw the pictures. Right. Go and check out the center section of the fuselage. Look for survivors... gotta be survivors up here someplace, right? Why else would we be here?

"On my way, sir... I think... Doug... he's found something. Hold on..."

What'd you find? Take a look. Okay... step up there... turn on the light....

"Holy Jesus! Did you see this?"

Didn't go in... wanted you to do that.

Oh, thanks a hell of a lot. My dear God... smashed faces... blood... skulls shattered... broken features...

"Lieutenant, are you copying?"

... ruined bodies... teeth smiling through the blood... smashed, twisted, shattered broken... Damned if I know it wasn't the wreck this shit happened after the fact and that means... murdered. God... somebody killed them....

"Lieutenant?"

"Where's Gurdler?"

Gurdler? Don't know... can't imagine... couldn't say... haven't the slightest...

"Weird... really weird..."

"What's weird? Report! Report! Report! Repor—"

Yes...report...dead...all dead...everybody in the plane. Everybody on the ground...in the rocks...in the snow...dead. All dead. And maybe we don't feel so good ourselves...and maybe that's what's weird. And now you're saying...get rid of the oxygen? *That's* weird....

And so is that.

"Gurdler!"

Careful there, Rudi, you'll...

"Palmer!"

...fall. And he did. Son of a bitch if he didn't. Gurdler fell. A perfect swan dive I'd say.

"Report your—"

Sit...sit...chew...aaa...shunnn. Oh. Oh, yeah. Bad. Bad situation. You ought to see it. Everybody's dead. Rudi...and maybe Doug wants to be dead, too, because there's a dead guy bashing his brains out right now. Ohh! Ugly! Situation? Not worth a shit, and getting worse because now that dead guy's coming after...

Me. Oh, wait a minute, here. You're dead. Dead. No, hey, you're...

"Deeeathhh!"

GARY WAS IN A SLIGHT DAZE as he wandered around to the far side of the plane. Two bodies lay there, both having been moved recently. He looked away from them; one of them was Gorham, and that was all he wanted to see for this night. No way could he look inside the plane. Instead, he moved to the edge of the summit, and stared at the scenery—the nearby mountains, the dark forests and the distant lights far below. He tried not to think about all that lay behind him in the rocks.

The rest of his dream, or what could be dredged up, was truly abstract, fuel for the shrinks. For some unknown and unimagined reason, a river was the central object, and it was as if he had been placed into a boat, then kicked away from the dock where he drifted down the dark, quiet stream—a subterranean river maybe. He didn't recognize it. All he was sure of was that it was...well, pretty. A beautiful river. And so peaceful. Not at all frightening as one might expect a dream or nightmare object to be. Unseen voices called from the shore, and once in a while he could hear his name from one of them. At other times he could hear singing coming from flutelike voices, an ethereal chorus. They sounded as if they were singing about the river...how beautiful the river was, and how they should all go to the river. He wondered if he should answer them; perhaps he had but couldn't remember it. But it wasn't important. Nothing seemed as important as lying there and floating silently along the glasslike river; nothing was more important than this undisturbed peace.

He didn't know how long he remained like that, how long he was on the river. Only that the time was too brief before the river narrowed and became rougher, faster. The voices along the shore were still there but they weren't singing anymore; they sounded harsh and unpleasant, and yet they still called to him. Now, he didn't want to answer them, didn't want them to know where he was. All that seemed likely was that the river would end sometime, and he thought he could see bright lights in the distance. Noises were getting closer—clinks, clatters and rattles—and other voices. The farther he went the closer they came; some urgent, others calm, still others issuing commands that sounded strangely familiar—

...And *this*. There were walls...a door...a small table...and a bed. He was lying on a bed.

"Hey, what the hell's going on here? Where am I?"

Slowly, the night came back into focus. The stars became stars again, and all the lights in the distance were seen once more, and recognized. There was no river—only the cold solitude of the mountain and the remnants of a disaster all around him. The summit and its desolate wreckage had taken on the look of an ancient ruined castle in the center of a medieval battlefield. For an instant Gary could almost see barbaric figures shouting, scrambling up ladders and wielding axes and flails as they stormed the stone walls amid spears and arrows zipping past them.

But it was only the wind. This was a smashed airplane, the birth and death of which had been the results of fathomless twentieth-century technology.

"...the bu-teee-full...the bu-teee-fullll...riiivvv-errrrrr..."

And those..."warriors" had been scarcely more than boys. Most of them had faced nothing more brutal than boot camp, and their battlefields had been sandlots, baseball diamonds and basketball courts.

"...*gatherrr with the saaa-ainnnts...at the...riiivvv-errrrrr...*"

But he remembered now, or a good portion of it anyway. Answers had begun to make themselves known, even the shards from his eight months in the Land of Nod. It was making sense.

Except for that dream about the river.

"...*that floooowwws...by the thronnne...*"

A river. What river? Was it real or imagined? It seemed real, not an off-the-wall detail that came out of most dreams. And he could almost hear those voices again, telling him how they should gather at the river, and—

Voices?

He whirled.

"...*uhhhf...God!*"

5

"*FUCK!*" HE CHOKED, backing away and staring in shocked wonder at—who? what?—the tall figure advancing on him, not ten feet away. A club of some kind was held high, readied for business. The form holding it inched ahead from the shadows and into the moonlight. Giggling. Singing softly to himself. Gary's heart stuttered. A fearsome insanity grinned at him from behind a shaggy filth-encrusted beard and a pair of wild-looking eyes.

He moved backward, his mind racing at light-speed for a solution—no, an escape. The madman was now fully visible; there would be no reasoning, no talking. The eyes glared at him, looking like two golf balls. Blackened teeth grinned like those set in a skull.

"...*with the saaa-aaaints...at the...rivvv-errr...*" he whispered brokenly. The club came up a little higher.

Now it occurred to Gary: the river. The darkened underground river. The cave...and that haunting voice always in the distance. He remembered. He'd simply run from the summit into those rocks above the pass; he found the opening to the cave, dived in and kept going. And this fruitcake had—

"*. . . by the thronnne*"

Gary put up a hand. He tried to yell.

"*...uhhhf...God...*" With a short whoop the club arched toward him with surprising speed and power. Gary leaped to one side; the move saved him at least two broken bones, but the club boomed against the airplane and bounced off, slamming into his upper right arm and knocking him off balance. He grunted in pain, and as he tried to shield himself he stumbled and fell into the snow.

The club swooped down at him again.

"Aaahhh Deaaaaaathhh!" the crazy man bellowed.

As Gary kicked frantically and tried to roll out of the way, the last thing he heard was the loud crack of his own helmet splitting open.

Clever. Oh, how clever it was. This trick, that trick, a misdirection here, sleight of hand there...it never gave up. One face after another, one attempt after another. This was no mere game; it was an art, a science.

But you missed again never came close never touched me...

He laughed. Still humming to himself, he shouldered the heavy club and started down the summit toward the pass.

6

JANEY NEVER GOT THE DOOR closed. The thought never occurred to her. The momentary hesitation in which she screamed and nearly fainted at the sight was all it took to let him inside.

He was horrifying. Walking death stood not more than a few feet away, then came at her. In that moment, Janey froze in utter shock. She was able to move again only as the grin on the face suddenly broke into a wild and violent howl, and the heavy steel bar he carried crashed against the door. She couldn't even find another scream. Falling against the wall, Janey stumbled backward along the hallway wall as the madman entered, club held high.

Easy. Easy, easy, easy. Nothing to it this time. You must be getting tired of the game. What is it? Am I getting too good for you? Have you met your match?

He came down the hallway after her, laughing and giggling. Mumbling to himself. The wild-eyed grin wider than ever. All Janey could do was try to stay clear of him as she backed up clumsily, fumbling against the furniture behind her, never taking her eyes off him. She tried to control her whimpering and to get hold of herself, to think of something, anything—

Oh God dear God who is he what is he where's Gary what happened—

"Gaaarreeeeee!"

But Gary wasn't there. She knew that. She knew she was on her own.

A weapon...something. This place was supposed to contain a little of everything, so there had to be something she could use as a weapon. Anything. A club or a gun or a knife or—

She bolted for the kitchen, knocking over two chairs in her path. He was right behind her, puffing, trying to bellow like an animal, and she heard the huge metal club crash into something. In a second she was yanking drawers from their runners, and utensils crashed and clattered to the floor.

God, where are they....

The club slammed into one of the chairs. She jumped at the loud whacking and splintering of wood. The table buckled under another loud boom, and when Janey whirled about the man was stepping over the mess. Two more chairs were hurled out of his way; one of them smashed into a bookshelf, and the contents sailed all over the floor in a white flurry.

But she found a knife, and she brought it up, both hands gripping the handle. She could barely see him through her tears, but he had stopped.

Oh, ho! Another trick. Hide in the form of a defenseless woman so you can lure me into a trap. Is that what you're doing?

Laughing softly, he backed away. The club stayed up like an ax, but he backed off for some reason, and he didn't stop until he was fifteen feet away. He was only partly visible in the half light coming from the storage room, and Janey heard him laugh again, louder. And he waited. She had no idea of why he suddenly backed off. What was he doing? Surely he wasn't afraid of her. If he came forward now he'd have no trouble at all in finishing her off. No way could she stop him. The knife was only a desperate bluff.

But she realized then that he didn't have to come forward. She was in the corner, trapped. All he had to do was wait her out, and he obviously had nothing but time. The next move was hers.

The standoff lasted for a minute. Two minutes. Except for the whistling of the wind through the door, Kota Station was utterly silent. Three minutes passed, and Janey thought she would come apart. She couldn't control the trembling of her body, the hiccuping, or the flow of tears. She felt almost like giving up, just dropping the knife and inviting him to do his thing. It seemed hopeless. Gary must be dead out there somewhere. This lunatic must have killed him, just as he probably killed the other two men. And if she blinked at the wrong moment, she'd get the same.

The lights on the control panel glinted dull green reflections against the knife blade. The man still hadn't moved. His club remained high, readied for business. She could see about half of his face in the light—the black teeth set into a grin, and one eye opened wide and white, almost protruding with excitement. He was breathing heavily and it sounded as if he was humming to himself. He was enjoying this.

And, almost like an accident, Janey moved. She was hardly aware of it because it wasn't even a full step—only an involuntary move forward. She knew only that she couldn't stand there helplessly much longer. So she moved, hoping that her knees wouldn't collapse. They already felt like cold syrup.

The humming stopped.

She ventured another step. Then two. She wanted to wipe her eyes, but was afraid to take them off him. Three steps. Four.

The crazed grin faded slightly, and—incredibly—he backed away.

This is crazy you're gonna get your fool head split open....

The club stayed up. She could no longer see his face, but she could feel his eyes upon her. There was only a shape wheezing in the darkness.

Another trick...another clever trick. But you can't fool me, no no no...

Very slowly and uncertainly, she made her way around the smashed table. Now she was barely out of his reach. Her only idea was to watch him and hope that he didn't suddenly attack. Beyond that, there was no plan except to run like a bat out of hell and hope she could get away. But she was thinking now, and if she could get him to retreat a few more feet she might be able to make it to the door.

If. Might. Sure, right. *If* she pushed her luck, he *might* make a lunge and smash her skull. She was dealing with a complete unknown, a wild guess.

She moved again. But he did not. She could hear him giggling.

Gonna beat you...yes, I am. Gonna beat you again but you can't touch me.

He laughed quietly, brokenly. A dry wheeze.

Janey sniffled. She couldn't stop shaking. She wanted to wipe her eyes but didn't dare take either hand off the knife. Cold air gusted lightly down the hallway, ruffling her hair. If she could just get outside she might have a chance. So she took another step, sideways this time, to her right. Very carefully, very slowly. Toward the open door at the far end of the hall. It looked as if it was half a mile away.

The man watched her. His club moved slightly.

Another step.

Please let him stay there please let me get outside please...

Janey was watching him. She didn't see the overturned chair. She tripped and fell toward him.

This is it!

"Aaaaahhhhh!" He brought the club around with a sudden whoop, grinning ear to ear.

And missed. Janey fell against him, screaming, and the force of his swing threw him off balance. Both of them fell to the floor, and the club left his grip, sailing across the room, booming against a wall and clattering to the floor.

The searing plunge into his right shoulder was a complete accident.

Ohhh! A trick! A dirty, dirty, sneaky trick! You tricked meeeeee....

Janey scrambled madly to get away, unaware that she had stabbed him. She rolled away, grunting in mortal terror;

jumped up; fell flat. Then she kicked and launched herself toward the doorway, the madman's screams ringing through the station.

She fell again. Something locked around her ankle; eyes blurred with tears, she kicked furiously at the arm and hand holding her. She could see his face again, pained, confused, but filled with murderous anger. Only then did she see the butcher knife protruding at an angle from blue parka, buried halfway to the hilt. The quilted material was soaked black.

"Tr-trick..." Janey heard the man gasp brokenly. *"Dirrr... dirrr-tee triiiiick!"*

"Let me goooo!" she wailed, still kicking.

To her shock, he did. Panting, muttering, he released her ankle. His head dropped to the floor.

With a cry, Janey pulled away, then jumped up and ran for the door.

It was just getting light outside.

7

DAWN FOUND GARY MOVING, too—such as it was.

He could barely move at first, but as he finally did the first thing coming to him was what had happened. No memory loss this time—he remembered everything, even the whys and wherefores. He had been caught daydreaming, forgetting all about the ghastly remains they'd found inside the cave and one of the two colonels—and there was no mystery about what had become of the other, even if they hadn't found the body. He remembered—this time, and eight months ago. Everything.

And you're damned lucky to be able to remember, he thought, gingerly touching the back of the helmet. It had been the only thing that had saved him, and only then because he'd caught the shot in the back of the head where the outer material and inner padding was the thickest. Had the blow come across the faceplate... Even then his faceplate was cracked and loose. It was stifling in there, too, and a look at the pressure gauge said that his oxygen had given out hours ago. The only air he was getting was through the cracks, so he tore off the faceplate.

The cold air tasted good, despite his head feeling like it had been mashed flat. He started to remove the helmet, but a huge bloody lump back there was wedged into the padding. He sat still for a minute, breathing, and trying to get his eyes to focus.

Then he remembered where he was. And what else was up here besides a wild man with a club.

"Shit!" he mumbled, pushing himself up to his feet, head pounding, the whole summit beginning to spin. When he was erect, a woozy sensation hit him, threatening to bowl him over again, and he bumped against the side of the plane. He had to remain on his feet. He had to get the hell out of here. This place was alive with that strange gas. He had to get down now, to get back to the plateau, to the station, especially before Janey discovered—

Janey! "Oh, God!" he moaned, his gut suddenly churning. He had almost forgotten about her and that she was down there all alone. And, God, that maniac with the club had to know that she was by herself because he'd known that he was coming up here; he'd been waiting for him, laying a trap. And now . . . there was no telling what might have happened if he'd gone down there to find her alone.

Gary tried to hurry. He fell twice before he had gone sixty feet. Both times it was more difficult getting back up and harder still to keep standing. His vision was blurred a bit more, his head hammered furiously, making him feel sick and dizzy. If he'd gotten only a concussion out of this, he was lucky. As it was the back of his neck was soaked and clammy from the bloody lump; he could feel the blood trickling down his back. And each time he moved his head the pain made him want to scream.

But he was moving again—slowly, uncertainly, a lot like a drunk trying to dance, he thought, but moving. And as he started again for Karber's Pass he just hoped that he wouldn't run into that crazy bastard with the club because he'd be as good as dead. In fact, he wasn't sure he could make it to the plateau at all without passing out.

But he did get into the pass. He was making his way around some of the junk when he heard somebody coming.

CHAPTER EIGHTEEN

SEVEN-TWELVE A.M. ENDICOTT AIRFIELD.

Kelly and Grady held on to the bills of their service caps and stepped back as the XM-221 helicopter came to life. Both rotors whooshed in slow circles and the turbine whine rose in intensity, and within minutes the rotors were hammering the cool morning air. Those watching squinted and turned away from the tornado of small debris churned up from the pad.

In the cockpit, both pilots talked to each other and to the trio of factory engineers aboard. They had filed through the loading hatch weighted down with portable instruments, blueprints and boxes filled with strange-looking test devices. It had taken them an hour to hook it all up and preflight the helicopter, then another forty minutes of checking and rechecking their work. Grady began to wonder if they'd ever take off, but they were ready to go at last.

Grady hoped it would be worth all the trouble. So far, the cost for parts and for having the three engineers here to put them in and fix everything else was closing in on three-quarters of a million dollars. And all of that, as far as he was concerned, was for something that didn't work as it was supposed to. Well, it was a lesson if nothing else. He had been looking for something to do after retirement, and now he'd found it—the defense industry. Being a supplier to the world's richest and dumbest customer had to be the world's most lucrative business.

Finally, the rotor beat became heavier, strained, and the helicopter flexed and twitched like a runner on the starting blocks. Slowly, it eased itself off the ground, climbing to treetop level where it hovered for a minute. So far, so good. And then it angled itself up and off into the sky.

Kelly and Grady stood on the tarmac and watched until the ship became a dot on the northern horizon. Once again, all they could do was stand by and await the results. Things were not in their control, and Kelly began to see what Grady had been talking about. Even when they could give the order to fly back up to Kota Station they would have to stand and wait again. That had been the story of this whole damned project, and Grady's participation in it. He had never been given so little control over so much. He could determine or decide almost nothing; and he could not ask, answer or tell anybody a damned thing. All he could do was stand around and play with himself while waiting.

They turned back toward the main hangar. "How long will they be gone?" Kelly asked.

"At least an hour, according to the pilot," Grady said. "Maybe longer. They filed a local flight plan, so they'll be within a fifty mile—"

The airfield duty officer came running up to them. "Sir?" he said with a quick salute. "Don't leave the field yet. We have a plane coming in from Andrews Air Force Base with a Dr. Fairfield aboard. He says it's urgent, and he's requested to see both of you at once."

"Fairfield?" Kelly said as though he'd never heard the name before.

"Now what the hell are you doing here?"

Fairfield looked as if he hadn't seen a bed, shave or change of clothing in three days—which was very close to the truth. And all he replied was, "Where can we talk?"

"In my office," Grady answered. "Or in my car if it can't wait."

It couldn't wait. In the back seat, Fairfield unlocked his briefcase and removed a stack of wadded and disordered papers that had been stuffed into a manila folder. Most appeared to be hastily scribbled notes with a few charts and graphs, and some marked-up computer printouts. He fumbled nervously through them, dropping several papers on the floor before locating the ones he needed. He handed them to Kelly, who glanced through them and handed them back. "You're the scientist. What is this stuff?"

"This 'stuff' is the latest data on Swamp Gas. Our latest tests. You took off yesterday before I had a chance to show them to you. To shorten a long story, what it all means is that we no longer have a project.''

Grady and Kelly looked at each other. ''What tests?'' Kelly said. ''What went wrong?''

''Tests.'' Fairfield sighed wearily. ''Molecular structure and density...stability...variants, variables, compositions, alterations...tests. Nothing went wrong because no chemical compound behaves in a manner that's right or wrong. It either works or it doesn't. And it doesn't necessarily adhere to any physical law.''

Grady motioned for the papers from the front seat. ''Then I take it that this one didn't, either.''

''No, not exactly.''

On top of the test results was a copy of a report addressed, with yesterday's date, to General Mattlock at the Pentagon. Grady quickly read through it, whispering to himself. ''...must have dispersed with the storm, but probably killed those in the plane due to estimated higher concentrations...lower concentrations remaining outside...levels estimated less than deadly...summit concentrations considered safe for up to three or four exposures...enough to cause *hallucinations*—'' He stopped, looking at Fairfield in amazement.

''Read on, General Grady,'' the scientist said, looking at the floor.

Grady rattled the paper and continued. ''For the agent to be of full usefulness at one hundred percent effectiveness under battlefield conditions, concentrations of approximately double what was originally thought, plus an overall strength of about two and one-half times that originally intended, would have to be released into the local atmosphere. Even then, the agent's maximum killing capabilities and postdeath animation are entirely subject to only slight alterations in local weather conditions, as well as individual metabolism...'' He paused again.

''Keep going.''

''The opinion of those of us who have been working with the agent throughout the life of the KP Project are unanimous that: A) In 89.9 percent of the test cases the product has proved itself wholly unreliable. And B) In every case, the results have been inconclusive and unpredictable. A great deal more testing is necessary before such a product can be considered for use, or even stockpiling, for any U.S. military agency." Grady put the report down. "What the hell does all this mean?"

"It means," Fairfield said, sighing and running a hand through his hair, "that we think it killed those men who survived the plane crash eight months ago, but only because they were subjected to a heavy concentration, which the storm probably blew away. It means that when Lieutenant Palmer and his partners arrived at the summit, there may have been enough left to kill two of them, but to cause him only hallucinations, probably due to differences in their metabolism. It means mostly that we no longer have a project. Mattlock ordered it abandoned late yesterday, which is why I'm here—to terminate the whole thing, and to collect Gilmore and Attwood."

Grady wanted to hit something. But he should have expected something like this. Nothing else about the KP Project had gone right, so why should the prime ingredient be any different? "After all we've gone through," he muttered, "and now you're saying that this shit doesn't even work. And that Lieutenant Palmer hallucinated for eight months!"

"We still have to look at him to be certain, General. But we doubt if anything is wrong with him. There would be if he were exposed several times, or over an extended period—probably some form of permanent brain damage—but not after only one exposure. As a matter of fact, we'll probably look him over, then turn him loose."

"Holy Christ!" Kelly groaned. "*Now* we find it all out!"

"What do you mean?"

"Well, it's a little late for all of this, Dr. Fairfield," Grady said. "Palmer escaped from Wheeler Barracks three days ago. And we don't know what's become of Gilmore or Attwood." He told Fairfield all that had transpired over the past three days. He was surprised that the doctor hadn't heard about any of it. He finished with a question: "Any ideas about Gilmore or Attwood?"

Fairfield was shocked. "No...no. I—I can't imagine what's happened to either of them. Are you sure about all of this?"

"We know that one of them is lying dead up in Karber's Pass right now," Kelly said. "We don't know which one, but he *is* dead. And we're almost certain that Palmer and his girlfriend are up there somewhere, too."

Which puts us two up on you guys, Grady thought. So far as he could tell, there wasn't one swingin' dick at Stanton that knew much of anything.

"I...I just don't know what could be wrong." Fairfield shrugged.

"Tell me about it!"

"Well, when could we fly up there for a look?"

They could hear the helicopter approaching in the distance. "We'll find that out in a few minutes."

2

THE XM-221 HAD BEEN INTENDED for some of the most adverse operating conditions. It could remain airborne with any three of its electronic systems completely out; it was capable of full maneuverability at maximum altitude under the worst weather conditions and would still work almost as easily as it did at ground level; and it could even deliver full firepower in support of any ground troops under any of these conditions. It could perform like no other helicopter ever built.

But it couldn't do everything. And it was never intended for the beating it had sustained during the construction of Kota Station.

As the test flight progressed it was soon apparent to everyone aboard that they were lucky to remain in the sky at all, and it wasn't so much a matter of anything in particular being wrong as it was the sensation of something about to go wrong. All the instruments on the control panels said that all the parts and systems were functioning. The engines were running within specs. All the lights were green. The pilots flipped switches, pushed buttons and manipulated the controls; the ship responded. Everything appeared to be in order and working properly. But little of it *felt* that way, and they all could feel and sense the same thing—the elusive seat-of-the-pants sensation that the whole machine was on the verge of flying to pieces. Its tolerance levels had been passed. Little was left of it.

"Jesus!" one of the pilots said after they had landed. "Am I glad that's over with. Did you feel that shit?"

"Who didn't?" The other one shrugged, removing his helmet. "Like all of a sudden this thing would come apart, and we'd be sailing along up there holding onto nothing but our peckers."

ONE OF THE ENGINEERS STARED at Kelly and Fairfield in open-mouthed amazement. "Didn't you hear what we just said? That thing has had it."

"You guys said you could fix it! What the hell's wrong now?"

"General, it's no longer a question of an overhaul," the second engineer put in. "It's been completely worn out. There's nothing left to fix."

"Our modifications would have been beneficial to a new aircraft," the third man added. "But not on that thing." He waved at it in disgust. "I don't know how, but in two weeks you've reduced it to a wreck."

"Well, what the hell good is it if it can't stand up to a little abuse? Or if it ever has to go into combat? What kind of junk is the Army buying?"

"Well, you guys sure know how to abuse it all right! You people would probably screw up an anvil."

Kelly ignored the last comment, turning to Grady instead. "I don't know what the hell to do. We have to get up to Kota Station somehow."

Grady said nothing. Welcome to the club, Dave.

"The helicopter is our only chance, General Grady," Fairfield said. "If there's any emergency, we must find out immediately what it is, and if that thing will fly at all, we have to use it."

"Dammit, I can't order anyone to fly that helicopter if it's no longer airworthy. What if it crashes? I'd only have two or three more dead men on my hands."

"General!" Fairfield said, reaching for his arm.

Grady motioned for the pilots. "Do you guys think it could handle one more trip to Kota Station?"

"No, sir."

"Okay, that's it then," he said to his guests.

Kelly started to protest again, but was interrupted by the airfield duty officer who came running from the tower. "Excuse me, gentlemen, but there's an emergency," he said to Grady. "They want you at the communications center right away."

"What's wrong?"

"They didn't say exactly, sir. Just something about a broadcast coming from Kota Station."

3

I KNOW I HEARD SOMETHING, Gary thought. It came from down there ... in the pass. He had hidden behind a piece of wreckage until he could see what it was. It could be anything.

He remained motionless as he waited and listened. But he could hear nothing except the wind, and an occasional groan or creak from one of the larger pieces of junk. He waited, and when nothing approached, he ventured a peek around the hulk of bent metal.

He was greeted by faces, at least twenty of them, maybe more. Bodies. Some were in the path, others in the rocks on either side. Their limbs were as rigid as wood; their bodies twisted, bent and broken into bizarre shapes. Heads were cocked at curious and improbable angles, and faces stared at him in frozen expressions of grief, pain, confusion and fright. Two or three faces held no expression; others had little or no face left. Yet they all seemed to look at him from where they were—sitting, standing, lying, leaning, propped up. One was only three feet away from his own face, seemingly staring at something past him. The eyes were open; the mouth was open; the tongue protruded. The man was in a position that suggested that he was about to get up but had stopped halfway.

Think I'll stay right here.

"Wh-what?" Gary whispered, looking at the man in astonishment.

I believe I'll stay right here.

Now he looked very closely at the man—the torn clothing, the face covered with thick ice, and the frozen patch of redness underneath, matting the blond hair. No. No way. Uh-uh, buddy, no sir, no way no how . . .

Very slowly, the man's head turned toward him. An arm dropped, and all four fingers flexed.

Gary's breath caught in a sudden choke.

The man's head continued turning until his face looked straight into Gary's. And now the opposite arm was beginning to move.

Why can't I stay here?

"Nnnn-n-n-no . . . !"

Why not?

Yeah, why not?

Why can't he stay right there?

"N-n-n-nnnn . . . !"

A man with no face turned toward Gary. Ice cracking away, his mouth split into a horrifying grin. Next to him, leaning against a rock, another man flexed an arm as he laboriously pushed himself up into a standing position. His opposite arm, nearly severed at the shoulder, fell to the ground with a rotten rip of material. He paid no attention to it. He stared at Gary.

"Nnnnnn . . . !"

One by one they moved. Rocks rolled and thudded; ice snapped and cracked and fell to the ground from the frozen arms and legs and torsos and dead faces as the men of Charlie Company sat up, stood up, turned their heads and opened their eyes . . . and spoke to Gary.

We want to stay.

We all want to stay.

There were a dozen voices, three dozen, a hundred. Gary turned around, and all over the summit the men were moving, coming from out of the airplane, from the rocks, coming erect from out of the snow. Sheet metal groaned from the strain of being pushed away by bloody hands and stumps, and more ruined faces appeared.

"Nnnnn . . ."

Eyes opened. Mouths moved.

We want to stay here.

Voices long silent cracked in mournful timbre and moaned with the wind.

We're all gathered here.

Shaaalll weee gaaathhh-errr at the riii-vverrr . . .

"Nnnnnnoooo—" and Gary ran from his hiding place. He didn't stop running until he was halfway down the pass, when he ran into Janey.

IT WAS A LONG TIME before either of them could manage a coherent word, and longer still before they could let go of each other. But at last Janey helped Gary remove the helmet. She winced at the bloody lump on the back of his head, and he managed to explain how he got it—that, and everything else.

"Is that why you went up there? At night?"

"I'm sorry. I shouldn't have left you alone. But I had to find out what was up there, and I thought I'd remember everything. And I did. But we have to get out of here before he comes back."

"He's dead."

"He's what? Dead? How?"

"I killed him," and both eyes clouded as she said it. She was trembling as she tried to explain what had happened. "He came into the station . . . swinging that club. He was trying to kill me . . . and I got a knife, and he made a lunge at me, and I fell against him. It was an accident, but I killed him . . . Oh, God, who was he?"

He was truly amazed; Janey actually killed him. He should have taken her with him. He hadn't even heard the guy coming. "A crash survivor," Gary finally said, holding her again. "He killed Gorham, and I think he killed most of the others who survived the accident before we ever got there. I remember him now. But there's no time for that. We have to get out of here, and off this mountain."

"It's about time."

They helped each other up. "I think I've got all the information I need now, so all I have to do is tell the whole . . . world . . . about . . ." and he stopped, staring into space for a moment.

"Gary? Are you all right?"

When he looked at her again it was straight in the eye, and a look of excitement suddenly hit him. "I'm gonna tell the world about it," he said again. "And I just thought of a way to do it. Come on."

They hurried down to the station. The door was open, and they stopped short of the entrance, shocked at what they saw—a thick trail of fresh blood smeared across the tiled floor of the entryway—and no dead man. The snow and rocks near the doorway were stained red for nine or ten feet.

"God!" Janey choked, backing away. "I—I killed him."

Gary stepped inside. "Apparently not," he said, pulling her in behind him. Carefully, he checked the building, but found it empty. And with the door closed and locked behind them, he said, "Okay, start collecting equipment. I'll be with you in a few minutes. But first I've gotta put something on this bump... and then talk to some people."

"Talk with who?"

He grinned. "Whoever's out there."

GARY WASN'T SURE if he could even turn the complicated radio on—he had only read through the manual briefly—but he began playing with it, and as soon as the numbers on the panel looked right, he picked up the mike, and muttered, "Well, here goes."

Janey stopped what she was doing to watch him.

"Pardon the interruption, ladies and gentlemen, but I urgently request your attention for a few minutes. My name is First Lieutenant Gary S. Palmer, and I have an extremely important message for everyone listening.

"Eight months ago I was a rescue team leader assigned to the Second Search and Rescue Battalion at Fort Endicott. I am the same Lieutenant Palmer who was with the rescue party last September, which climbed Mount Kota in an attempt to rescue the survivors of Air Force Flight J-440 who were trapped at the summit. And I'm the same Lieutenant Palmer who was reported dead along with the other two climbers a couple of days later after the attempted rescue failed. Please believe me. This is not a trick, and not a prank. I'm the same Lieutenant Gary Palmer.

"I am broadcasting from inside a specialized facility known as Kota Station, which is located on the Northeast Plateau approximately eighteen thousand feet up. I have learned that this facility was put here by the Army to locate and study a peculiar chemical weapon that was aboard the airplane, which killed those who survived the crash, and is still active up here...."

4

GRADY, KELLY AND FAIRFIELD arrived at the communications center to find everybody gathered around their largest radio console. The operator was twisting knobs and flipping switches, and every few seconds someone else would rush to another console to do the same thing. Whatever it was, it was not working, and as the three men entered the room, one man said to another, "Hell, that's no good either. He's walking right over us."

"What's no good?" Grady said. "What's the emergen—" Then he heard it.

"And that was why the mountain was put off limits—to keep everyone away until a way could be found to contain this deadly agent, or to destroy it. The investigation of the crash was a cover-up. The real intention was to study the effects this agent had had on human life, and to—"

Kelly and Fairfield froze where they stood. Grady said, "Who the hell is that? What's going on here?" And almost as soon as he asked, he knew both answers.

"Someone who claims to be Lieutenant Gary Palmer, sir," one of the officers answered.

"Oh, Christ!" Kelly moaned.

"Well, whoever he is," the communications officer continued, "he's broadcasting from Kota Station. He's telling all about the place, and everything that's been going on up there."

Fairfield's face was chalk-white. "Dear God, he's blabbing everything."

"Yeah, and he's blabbing it to the whole world," one of the officers said. "And there's nothing we can do."

"What are you talking about?" Grady demanded.

"That's why we called you here, sir. Palmer—or whoever he is—has Kota's transmitter locked dead on 630 mega-hertz...the frequency of KSCM Radio over in Sioux Creek. Everybody who's listening to that station right now is hearing every word of this."

"What?" Kelly yelled, almost falling over the table.

Fairfield looked as if he might faint.

"You're kidding," Grady whispered.

"No, sir, that's a fact."

"Shut 'im down!" Kelly yelled.

"We *can't* sir. We don't have the equip—"

"Goddammit, that's an order! Shut Kota Station down!"

"Sir, we can't! We don't have the equipment."

Kelly was about to scream at the lieutenant again when Grady grabbed him and pulled him aside. "Tom, for God's sake, he's—"

"There's nothing we can do, Dave. Kota's transmitter is ten times more powerful than ours, so we can't override him, or shut him off. He's locked onto a commercial frequency we can't touch, and even if we could, he could still talk right over us."

"... that this agent is still as deadly as ever, and may have killed both of the officers from the Blackstone Arsenal who were sent here to study its effects. We are protected inside this building, but to venture outside without protective gear is to risk exposure and potential lethal effects. From all we have learned about it, the gas simply remains in the local atmosphere, rising and falling with precipitation, and long-term exposure ..."

"The radio station!" Fairfield suddenly cried, coming out of his temporary shock. "Order them to shut their transmitter down!"

"No! The helicopter!" Kelly answered. "We can fly up there now!"

"No, Dave!" Grady shouted back. "Absolutely not! You heard what those men said. It's unfit to fly, so nobody goes anywhere in that thing."

"Tom," Kelly said in a lower and more desperate voice, "we have priority here. We have to use it. Don't make me pull rank on you," and he reached for the nearest telephone.

"You'll only get someone killed, and I'm not gonna stand for it, or—"

Then Fairfield stepped in between them. "I'll fly up with them," he said. "I'll go. We have to know what's happened up there."

GARY STARED AT THE RADIO. That's it. You've gone and done it now, he thought, pushed everything right up to the wall. If anyone had heard him, he had just given them enough classified military information to get himself stood before a firing squad. His only hope for protection against the Army's wrath was that if any newspeople had heard him they might storm the gates of Fort Endicott to demand answers.

The Army could always, on the other hand, deny everything he'd just said even if forced to admit that he was still alive. They had been caught in a lie, but so what? And he might have proved beyond any doubt that he really was as mad as a hatter and deserved to be locked away so he couldn't harm himself. All that remained was to climb back down, and see what had happened. The game was all but over.

By then Janey had their equipment ready. She asked if he wanted to check it, but Gary shook his head. He trusted her.

"I don't know why no one has shown up to grab us yet," he said. "But if anybody heard 'The Gary Palmer Show' just now they'll probably be in that helicopter and on their way. I think we've overstayed our welcome. Let's get the hell out of here."

He got no argument from Janey.

5

BECAUSE ITS BROADCASTING EQUIPMENT simply pushed an electronic signal through open air, Station KSCM knew that almost anything could happen to it. Their assigned frequency was protected only by aiming it away from neighboring radio and TV signals. Even then, especially during certain atmospheric conditions or sunspot cycles, the signals could overlap and produce unpredictable results. It had happened recently during a Saturday news broadcast when their signal was suddenly squelched by a nearby TV station that happened to be airing "American Bandstand." The news report had some neat lyrics, but it wasn't that good to dance to. A couple named Becky and Kevin rated it a 68.

But that morning, KSCM was on its own. Eight years of technical problems, bloopers and blackouts hadn't come within ten furlongs of what Gary Palmer and Kota Station did to it.

When Kota Station's signal suddenly came bellowing through, the engineer couldn't believe his own control panel, and he thought for a moment that some sort of wild power surge had just erupted from their transmitter. It was stronger than anything he'd ever seen, bending the meters right off their scales. The signal overrode any attempt to squelch it, even any to shut it off, because it was being aimed straight through their main transmitter tower.

Finally he knocked on the booth window, telling the deejay that he was no longer on the air.

The deejay covered his microphone. "What the hell's wrong?"

"Damned if I know," and the engineer switched on the internal audio. "Here it is. You tell me."

In under a minute the station manager stormed in, demanding an explanation, and finding both men staring in amazement like a couple of department store dummies. Then he heard it for himself: some Army guy who claimed to be broadcasting from Mount Kota, and who was talking about a plane crash, a poison gas in the local atmosphere and a whole bunch of dead people. They couldn't shut him off, and after another minute they wouldn't have dared to. It was the damnedest exclusive they were ever likely to have.

Within minutes, everything in the radio station was in high gear and shifting to overdrive. As soon as the interruption ended, the deejay stammered an apology to his estimated 3800 listeners, saying that the bizarre announcement had caught them as much off guard as everybody else and that the news department was already trying to track down and verify the source of the signal. A news bulletin was already being prepared by the station manager, and he, his secretary and the two women at the switchboard braced themselves for the barrage of calls that stormed in on them immediately. As Gary Palmer and Janey Burns were saddling up for their descent, KSCM's news crew was on its way hell-bent for Fort Endicott.

So were the news teams from four other radio and TV stations, plus reporters from five area newspapers. All of them had had their radios on; everybody had gotten the broadcast on tape. And before any of these crews ever entered the Fort Endicott military reservation, both of the national wire services had been notified and were dispatching their own people, both to Endicott and to KSCM Radio.

All of this was just for openers. Within thirty minutes, every government office in the area suddenly found itself swamped with phone calls, or nearly overrun as people pounded on the doors and stampeded the lobbies, especially those living anywhere near Mount Kota National Park. The police departments in four counties suddenly found themselves facing near-riots as hundreds of frightened, outraged citizens stormed at them demanding that they do something about a situation that they'd never even heard of. After an hour, the police in Sioux County alone counted 157 traffic accidents, were forced to make sixty-two arrests and had to ignore countless traffic violations as people began fleeing in every direction. But the worst scene of all was at Mount Kota National Park, where hundreds of campers scurried in panic. The word was out. The Army had spilled some kind of poison gas into the air, and they were all dead unless they could get out of there.

In the few moments of calm before the fire storm hit Fort Endicott, General Kelly seemed in a blank daze at what their captive, controlled subject had done. The lid to the KP Project had been blown sky-high—an iron manhole cover that was about to fall on him.

Grady watched from his office as the XM-221 took off toward Mount Kota with Dr. Fairfield aboard. He was about to ask Kelly, sagged on the couch behind him, what he wanted to do next when the question became academic. Grady's secretary entered the office. "Excuse me, but the Public Information Office is filled with yelling newspeople. Does anyone want to go talk to them before they rip the place apart?"

Grady looked at Kelly, and motioned toward the door. "Dave, after you."

TWENTY-TWO MILES WEST of Fort Endicott, Dr. Fairfield leaned forward in his seat, then sat back again. He was fighting down the sudden urge to tell the pilots to turn this clattering, rattling helicopter around and land it at the nearest flat spot they could find. But they had already begun climbing to their final altitude, and he didn't want to bother anyone who held his life in their hands.

I'll take full responsibility. We have to get to Kota Station now.

He looked out at the ground, now 12,500 feet below. The vibrations of the airframe became deeper, stronger and the engine whine was more strained.

I'll take full responsibility . . . Suddenly, that didn't mean much.

"How much farther?" he said through the intercom as he pulled his seat belt a little tighter.

"About eight miles . . . and three thousand feet or so."

"Thank you."

"I wish I could say that you're welcome."

6

THEIR EQUIPMENT WOULD have to be kept to a bare minimum, Gary said as they saddled up. The descent as he remembered it was especially dangerous from eighteen thousand to sixteen thousand feet, mostly treacherous snow and ice over a maze-like path of switchbacks. But they would need no rock-climbing gear, which would lighten the load considerably. Janey would carry the food, water, medical supplies and some of the papers Gary had hastily gathered; he would pack most of the climbing gear and shelter, and the rest of the papers and notebooks. The packing should have taken a full day. They gave themselves twenty minutes; the feeling that the hounds were closing in seemed to get stronger each minute they remained. And as they tightened straps, zipped zippers, adjusted the loads and set their caps and goggles and gloves into place they hoped to God they hadn't forgotten anything.

"All set?" Gary said at last.

Janey nodded. "I think so."

They stepped outside. The morning sun was blinding against the snow. They tied two ropes between them and tested the knots, and Gary handed her a pair of crampons. "Don't put 'em on yet. And just follow me. Do what I do, and if you get into trouble, give a yell. We'll go slow. We have time."

But Janey didn't seem to hear the last couple of statements. Her head was cocked to one side as if listening for something in the distance. And she said, "Do you hear that?"

"Hear what? Yeah . . . yeah, I do hear something." It was a minute before he could identify the noise—the strained, thudding whop-whop-whop of an approaching helicopter. "Oh, shit!" he muttered, grabbing her hand.

They couldn't see it for another minute until suddenly the noise became much louder. The twin rotors appeared over the edge of the plateau, hammering painfully as they struggled to gain the last few feet of height. Two pilots were fighting the controls in what looked to be a losing battle. Gary was frozen for a moment by the sight of the odd-looking machine, but he finally saw what was about to happen. He grabbed Janey, giving a violent jerk on the ropes tied around her waist. "Come on! Let's move!" he cried above the noise.

They turned and ran as the helicopter just cleared the edge of the mountain, rocked, swung its tail around and tried to set down. With a flying tackle, Gary wrapped both arms around Janey's waist, and they landed in the snow.

"THIS IS MELANIE RADCLIFF, Channel Nine Newswatch, at the Fort Endicott Public Information Office, where in a few minutes a news conference will be conducted by the base commander, Major General Thomas Grady. This is the second scheduled conference in as many hours this morning, the first having been canceled at the last minute because of an unexplained emergency that required General Grady's attention. Both, however, seemed to concern the incredible sequence of events this morning, involving some of the key personnel here at Endicott, and some sort of military activity at Mount Kota National Park thirty-five miles west of here.

"All the commotion began shortly before eight this morning when a local radio station, KSCM Radio of Sioux Creek, experienced an overpowering interruption of its signal during the transmission of a newscast. During the interruption, a man who identified himself as First Lieutenant Gary Palmer and said he used to be stationed here at Endicott, told listeners he was broadcasting from inside a specialized research facility located high up on Mount Kota. He went on to say that this building had been put there under orders from command personnel from both the Pentagon and Fort Stanton, Maryland, and that its purpose was not to investigate the plane crash that occurred at the summit last September, but to investigate the effects of a toxic nerve gas that was aboard the plane. This gas, he insisted, had escaped into the local atmosphere and was dangerous. At the time, KSCM Radio estimated that approximately 3800 people were tuned to the broadcast, and the interruption immediately set off a panic across the region. At this hour, police departments of four counties are just getting it under control.

"We have since learned that the radio signal did indeed come from somewhere on Mount Kota, and that it came from a transmitter far more powerful than any known to be in this part of the country. Last September 28, Air Force Flight J-440, which carried 126 passengers and crew members, crashed on Kota. An unknown number of people survived the accident, and Fort Endicott personnel sent a rescue team of three mountain climbers—Doug Gorham of Seattle, Washington; Rudi Gurdler of Bern, Switzerland; and Lieutenant Gary Palmer of Fort Endicott. The three men lost their lives at the summit the following day under circumstances still undisclosed, and only one of the bodies—that of Rudi Gurdler, who apparently fell from the summit—was recovered. At the time Army officials said the details surrounding the three deaths were unknown, and that the incident, as well as the plane crash itself, would remain under full investigation. Whether or not these investigations have led to any firm conclusions has yet to be made public.

"Since October of last year, it has been obvious to anyone visiting Mount Kota National Park that the entire mountain is under armed guard. No explanation for this security has ever been offered. Channel Nine Newswatch has also learned that effective last October 15 the Federal Aviation Administration ordered all civil air traffic away from Mount Kota. Once again, there has been no explanation why normal air traffic routes were so suddenly altered. We are asking—just one moment. I see that General Grady, the commanding officer of Fort Endicott, and another general, have entered the room, and the conference is about to begin."

Spotlights came on, and flashbulbs popped. The murmur rose quickly to stadium levels as everyone with a camera or tape recorder or microphone surged forward. Everybody called questions at once. Microphones were thrust toward Grady's face, and he backed away, squinting at the bright lights and motioning for the crowd to quiet down.

"Ladies and gentlemen...ladies and gentlemen... please..." He waved, sighing wearily. "Please sit down. Please be quiet. I'll get to your questions in a few minutes. First, I have a statement I've been directed to read." He pulled a crumpled paper from his pocket.

"At 7:57 this morning, the communications personnel here at Fort Endicott intercepted the same radio transmission that has caused all the uproar in the area and was directed at KSCM Radio in Sioux Creek. Our tracking equipment pinpointed the source as our own—a classified research facility called Kota Station that had been installed on Mount Kota.

"The purpose of Kota Station was to investigate the crash of Air Force Flight J-440, which occurred last September, and to recover all the bodies on the mountain. We also planned on using it for a number of classified high-altitude research projects in the near future, and for certain training purposes. For all of these reasons the building was equipped with a great deal of the latest and most sophisticated gear, including an extremely powerful radio transmitter. The station had been constructed and equipped only recently, and was staffed by two officers detailed specifically for the crash investigation. Such work was one of their occupational specialties. They had been working at Kota Station and on the summit for several days.

"We do not know if either of them perpetrated this radio interruption, or if so, why they would do such a foolish thing. To the best of our knowledge they were the only people on the mountain. Most of you know about our security perimeter around the base of Mount Kota, which was erected after the crash; some of you have learned about the Federal Aeronautics Administration's order to reroute all civil air traffic away from the mountain, which was put into effect at the same time. These measures were requested by both the U.S. Air Force and the Department of Defense for several reasons, the most important being that there was classified hardware aboard the transport plane, and because we did not want either the crash site or the remains disturbed until an investigation could be completed. This is the same type of order put into effect after the crash of any United States military aircraft. In this case the operation only appears mysterious or dubious because the crash site was for a long time inaccessible. But our orders still applied: keep everybody away until the crash has been investigated and the remains recovered. This does not mean that someone couldn't have penetrated the security perimeter. If that happened, we don't know who it was or what he might have been up to.

"We are able to state this: at the time of the interruption, both of the men assigned to the station had been out of contact with Fort Endicott for several hours past their normal twelve-hour check-in interval. We suspected an equipment failure, but as the period of time lengthened we became concerned that there could have been an emergency. And here we'd like to state that even though such an emergency could have been any one of many things, it could *not* have been poison gas leaking from the wreckage. Flight J-440 was a troop transport, and even if the Army had such a dangerous gas as was described by whoever caused the radio interruption, it would never have been loaded on an aircraft carrying passengers. Secondly, the person who made this broadcast was not First Lieutenant Palmer as he claimed. Unfortunately, it will be some time before we learn who it was, because at approximately nine-twenty this morning, Kota Station was destroyed by a second aircraft crash."

Gasps and murmurs filled the room. People looked at one another in astonishment; a few tried to call out questions.

Grady ignored them. He motioned for the lights to be turned out, and the curtain behind him opened. A rear projector came on, displaying a large photograph on the screen; an aerial shot of Kota Station—or what had been Kota Station until 9:20 that morning.

"All the building components, contents and personnel had been airlifted to that location by an experimental helicopter," Grady continued, and a second photo clicked onto the screen, the XM-221 parked in front of its final assembly hangar. Grady mentioned some of its history before motioning for the third and final photograph—the station and the helicopter together. Both had been reduced to burning, smoking wreckage scattered all over the Northeast Plateau. Three bodies were fully visible; part of a fourth could be seen under a heap of smoldering rubble.

The projector was turned off and the curtain closed. The lights came on, and Grady stepped back up to the podium.

"After being unable to raise Kota Station in what we deemed a reasonable length of time, we decided to dispatch the helicopter to see what was wrong up there. It was, in fact, being prepared for flight when the radio interruption occurred. We launched it immediately afterward.

"According to the last message from the pilot, the aircraft developed severe control and handling difficulties as he was attempting to land. We had experienced some of the same problems with it earlier, but thought we had them corrected. But as I understand it, this type of instability is magnified whenever the helicopter is in a takeoff or landing mode, when control is most critical. Regrettably, it happened again while the pilot tried to set it down high up on the mountain. It went completely out of control, and crashed into the building. There were no survivors.

"So we now have a second accident to investigate, and more bodies to recover. But neither of these tasks can be started or completed until we take delivery of another helicopter. And because the XM-221 was a one-of-a-kind prototype still under development, delivery of a production model could take at least six months or longer. The conclusion of both investigations may take us well into next year.

"In any case, the media now know almost as much as we do. If you have any further questions we'll try to answer them at this time."

7

ONE AT A TIME, items were removed from the desk and placed inside the cardboard box—pen and pencil set, books, desk pad, photos of his wife and daughters, coffee cup...

World's Greatest Dad.

Grady smiled as he picked up the cup. Now he needed a matching mug that said World's Greatest Goat.

General Kelly watched him from the couch across the room. The leather creaked as he shifted position. "Are you sure I can't help you with some of that, Tom?" he asked for the second time.

For the second time, Grady shook his head. He looked up at Kelly, then back down to the cardboard box. He had never seen Kelly in such a fine mood. But, then, after you've fallen into your own latrine trench and have come out fresher than the proverbial long-stemmed rose you should feel good.

"There are four reasons why you're going to deliver the press conference and answer all the questions, General Grady. Number one: I'm ordering you to. Number two: security. No way can Fort Stanton, the Blackstone Arsenal, the KP Project or any of its key personnel be compromised in this thing if it gets any further out of hand. That could still happen. We got lucky when that helicopter crashed into Kota Station and killed Palmer, so now we have to play down all he said. Deny it, or blame it on someone else. Number three: it will be easier for you to do all of this because you don't know all the details. You can't screw up what you don't know. And you already know reason number four."

Yes, sir, General Mattlock, he thought bitterly. And that quick rap on the door is probably General Martin, who will be in no mood to discuss reason number four calmly or rationally.

Martin stormed into the office, waving a piece of paper. He paused only a moment to take in the sight of Grady packing, and Kelly on the couch watching. "What the hell is this, Tom?" he demanded. "We usually have a little advance warning about the commanding general pulling up stakes for parts unknown."

Grady walked toward the closet. "Not this time. The red tape has already been gone through, and the walking papers signed...thanks to General Kelly and his boss." He nodded with a cold smile.

"But your retirement isn't up for another five months, and—"

"My retirement takes effect at 12:01 p.m. today, which is the same moment you become the new commanding general of Fort Endicott. By this time tomorrow, Martha and I will be long gone. If you find anything of mine lying around here afterward, just drop it in the mail. I'll send you a forwarding address as soon as I have one." He reached into the closet and pulled out six spare uniforms on hangers. "In the meantime, beware of generals asking for favors."

"Goddammit, Tom, do you think I like this?" Kelly shouted, coming off the couch. "Do you think I *wanted* to pull the rug out from under you? This is a rotten job. Sometimes it really stinks. But that's the business we chose a long time ago. I don't remember anybody at the Point ever saying it would be easy."

"Seven more people dead," Grady whispered, almost to himself. "All that destruction . . . waste." He laid the uniforms across the back of a chair. "As a certain young lieutenant told me one time, I think that sucks."

And now General Martin understood everything perfectly. He looked at Kelly, then at Grady, who was taking the rap for the whole damned mess. He understood. "They'll be gone . . . and you'll be retired," he said. "There won't be anyone left to blame for anything."

"The name of the game is keeping your ass covered." Grady sighed, walking to the desk and shouldering the cardboard box. "Surely you're aware of that by now. One doesn't rise to the rank of general in this army by not knowing that." He looked Kelly straight in the eyes. "Or by failing to practice the art."

Kelly shook his head sadly. "Well, you don't need me here. And I don't need this shit. I was hoping there would be no hard feelings, but . . ." He shrugged. "Well, good luck, Tom. You, too, General Martin."

Grady watched as the door closed. "If you'll give me a hand with these uniforms," he said to Martin, "I'll get the hell out of here."

8

SHELTER HALVES HAD BEEN STAKED both across the outer opening of the cave, and across the inside, where the stack of rocks had been. It was the former, its corner pulled loose and snapping in the wind, that woke Gary up.

He sat up in his sleeping bag, confused for a moment, looking around in the darkness. Cold air was whipping through the shelter, and then he saw the corner flapping in the breeze.

He relaxed a little. That was a relief. Now he knew where he was and what had happened to bring them here, and to cause the noise and cold wind.

And he remembered. Everything. That had been his biggest worry of all—that he might awaken only to find that everything had been a bad dream, that he was inside that room at Wheeler Barracks.

Janey slept peacefully next to him. He reached over and touched her hair lightly.

Sore, bruised and battered, they were lucky to be there.

As he had watched the helicopter clear the edge of the plateau, then spin one hundred eighty degrees about, he had thought it was supposed to land like that. But only for a second; he saw by then that it was in deep trouble, a machine suddenly gone berserk. Both pilots were fighting to control it. The rotors pounded the air, echoing against the rock walls like rapid cannon fire. A storm of snow and small rocks blew everywhere as the aircraft bucked and veered in a wild, gyrating dance.

That son of a bitch is gonna crash, he thought, and only then was he able to look away. He pushed Janey ahead of him, yelling at her to run for the northern edge. Behind them they heard a shrill, grinding *eeeeee* that ended with a loud bang and a *ffffwwwwoooooop-wwwoooooop-wwwoooooop*. Gary glanced back over his shoulder in time to see one of the rotor blades sheer loose and come spinning straight at them like a huge black machete. He cried to Janey, then launched himself at her in a flying tackle. Sixty feet behind them the helicopter flipped upside down and barrel-rolled into the station roof. The thunderous concussion picked them up in midair, blowing them over the edge.

Janey stirred, rolling over.

Gary thought about the past four days. He thought about guardian angels again; if he hadn't believed in them before, he thought he did now. No way could he and Janey have made all that luck on their own. They were lucky to be there, all right; they were damned lucky to be alive. Even now the past four days seemed like a dream—a dream made only partially real by the fact that they were holed up at the lower end of the cave.

But it was real.

You never told me why you ran off to the summit last night, Janey had said. That could have gotten both of us killed.

He had answered that he didn't know what he might find. He had had little more than a few disconnected ideas that were out of order and seemed to make no sense when he tried putting them together. Only one of them clicked—when he heard the crunches and footfalls in the snow, the sounds of movement coming through the motion detectors. Something was out there in the darkness, and he had to see what it was while he had the chance—sort of self-prescribed shock treatment that he hoped would jar some of his memory loose.

And it worked.

"So you remember what happened to you and Gorham and Gurdler?" Janey asked.

"Yes..."

THERE WAS REALITY, and there was stark reality. The two didn't seem related because the latter put people into places like Wheeler Barracks. It was also what he had seen at the summit.

They had found no survivors, only bodies—*"...every-where...all over the place..."* And after a while they didn't seem like so many dead strangers as much as fallen comrades—almost like friends. They wore the same uniform he wore; they came from some of the same places; their faces began to look alike. Any one of them could have been a GI back at Endicott, an acquaintance perhaps; any one group of them could have been aboard a plane like this. "It's not exactly a kinship," he said to Janey. "It's just that you're like the next guy. In the service, you're all alike."

They had kept going; someone had been photographed moving around up here. Long before they were ready for it they arrived. Just ahead lay the wreck of Flight J-440.

And still, no survivors. Doug went one way, Rudi another. Looking. "I was still at the bottom of the summit talking to the base camp, and taking pictures. Then Doug started waving to me from the wreck."

He had found them—thirteen crash survivors. They were wrapped in extra clothing and bundled in shreds of canvas or whatever they could find lying around. They had taken the time to plug most of the holes and cracks in their shelter, to string a canvas tarp across one end and to stack some of the bodies in front of the opening. Some of them had lived long enough to see that a storm was coming and to try to prepare for it. "They might even have lived through it. They might have been able to hang on until we got there. We'll never know for sure."

Nor could they be certain of much else, except that half of them looked as if they had been clubbed to death; and they had to have died long hours before the three of them ever got there.

"I just stood there in the plane...staring. I didn't know what happened, and after a while everything got kind of blurry. I don't even know how long I stood there, but Doug was gone."

WALKING AWAY FROM THE PLANE, Doug was wondering where Rudi had gone. He ain't there. And he ain't over there, either. And what the hell did he think he was doing wandering around up here by himself? Doug looked around for a minute or two, squinting at the brilliant glare against the snow, then pulled his goggles down.

"Gurdler?" he said, but the Swiss climber was nowhere to be seen—not here or there or up or down or over or out. Nope. "Damn you, Gurdler, where the hell did you go?" He took a deep breath of the sweet, cold air, finding that it was something of a rush, as he'd heard the kids say, and it was funny that he couldn't remember the air smelling that good before. But that was the right word for it, all right. The exact, perfect word. A rush. A blast from the top of the world that rattled your head. And didn't it make the sight even more spectacular? Was there any spot in the whole country more beautiful, more awesome, than the top of this mountain?

The rush...
"Gurdler? Where are you, goddammit?"

GURDLER WASN'T FAR AWAY. He heard Doug's voice clearly but ignored it. He didn't feel like answering Gorham. Whatever he wanted, it could wait.

Rudi was looking around the site, at the dead men lying everywhere, at both mangled halves of the plane, and back again to the place where he stood next to the flight deck. Such a waste, he was thinking sadly to himself. Such a terrible waste... such failure. The airplane had failed. The crew flying it had failed. And the passengers had failed, even those who had lived through the accident. Their comrades in arms had failed to help them, and so had failed themselves. Miserable. All of it. Not one thing had turned out right.

His backpack and oxygen reservoir slipped to the ground. They were not necessary, and for some reason he didn't seem to need the oxygen up here anyway. That was strange at this altitude, and in his condition. But it was not at all difficult to breathe. Not that difficulty in breathing would make any difference, because it had nothing to do with the one thing left to be done—the one thing about this ridiculous climb that could not fail.

Yes, there is only one way for an eagle to fall.

He took a deep breath and walked away from the wreck to the south edge of the summit.

WELL, NOW, THERE HE WAS, right out of the blue all of a sudden. "Hey!!" Doug shouted across the summit. "Gurdler! Where the hell have you been? You just don't go walking off on your own up here, you know."

He headed toward where Rudi was standing with his back to him. By God, there were rules about this, and Gurdler should know them better than anyone, and if he didn't, then he was about to be reminded. You do whatever the expedition leader tells you to do, goddammit, and you'd better have fifteen good reasons if you don't. "Hey, I want to talk to you! Don't you go running off again."

But Rudi didn't seem to be paying the least bit of attention. He just stood there, motionless, as if in a trance, staring at something that might be ten light-years away.

Well, by God, they would have to put the skids to that shit, too, while they were at it. In fact, it would be a good idea to round up that young Palmer pup and remind him of a few things and whys and wherefores along the way. Both of them had best listen, or he'd be kicking some ass. He'd brought both of them to where they wanted to go—and where they had no business being—and they'd damn well better listen to facts and figures and orders.

"Gurdler! Goddammit, I'm *talking* to you!" What the hell was it with people when they got up here? Why wouldn't anyone listen, or do what he said? That goddamn Karber had been like that, too... always poking his big nose into places where it didn't belong, and you didn't *do* that. Not here. Not on this mountain.

But Gurdler still wasn't paying any attention to him.

For an eagle to fall...

No failures, not this time. Not you. For you are Rudi Gurdler, the greatest mountaineer in the world... with your final climb a heroic effort to save lives. A man with accomplishments more magnificent than any other. And a man who refused to lie down and die like a barnyard animal.

Yes. An eagle... flying into the sun a final time. An eagle...

"Gurdler! Goddammit, will you pay attention! I'm talking to you! When you're up here, by God, you'll pay attention to what I'm saying or you'll pay for it! Understand? *I'm* the leader, and you'll listen to *me!*"

Gurdler looked over his shoulder, unconcerned, as Gorham stalked toward him. Doug was shouting, but the words made no sense; he could barely hear them anyway. And they certainly couldn't be important.

"You and that young pup with us—and where the hell is he? I've got something for him, too. For the both of you."

Rudi smiled. "An eagle," he said to Doug Gorham.

"Yeah, by God, I'm the eagle up here on this mountain, and it seems to me that you forgot it. So maybe this will remind you...."

"I CAN'T REMEMBER every little detail, especially while I was still inside the plane...except voices. Voices were coming from everywhere, echoing all over the interior. Like they were coming from the bottom of a well. They kept telling me to report...just report, report, over and over again. It sounded scary, but I remembered if I pressed the button on the radio, it would cut them off. So I did it, and I couldn't hear them anymore.

"But I got scared in there. Nothing was real anymore, and after a while I couldn't stand it. So I ran out. And there..."

Next to the south edge of the summit, Doug was yelling at Rudi. Screaming, shaking a fist. Rudi didn't seem to be paying any attention at all, as if he honestly couldn't hear a word. He stared off into space. Doug was furious, almost livid with rage, and it looked as if he was about to attack Gurdler.

Gary watched them. He was dumbfounded, unable to understand what was going on.

Doug stepped over a body up near the edge. He was still screaming at Rudi, who was still ignoring everything.

"You skinny son of a bitch, you *listen*!" and he gave Gurdler a hard shove.

And that was all it took.

"Report, Lieutenant! That's an order...."

"He fell," Gary whispered in shock, still staring blankly at where Gorham now stood, looking down. "Gurdler...he fell...."

"What was that, Palmer? Repeat your message! Did you say that Gurdler just fell? Over."

"Fell...fell right off..."

But even more quickly, Doug seemed to vanish for a moment, and Gary wondered if he had fallen, too. Until he looked again, seeing that the body lying near the edge wasn't there anymore. It was strange; how could a dead body have gotten up? And then he happened to see where it was, and where Doug had gone. Both of them were still there. They seemed to be rolling around together in the snow, and the man who was supposed to be dead was on top of Gorham, pounding and beating and—

"Report your situation! Immediately! Report your situation!"

"Sit...sit...chew...aaa...shunnn... Bad. Verrreee...bad... All dead. All...dead..."

The man on top of Doug Gorham bested him suddenly and swiftly with one hard blow from what looked like a curved steel bat. He stood up, panting and laughing, mumbling to himself. Planting both legs across Gorham's body, he clouted him in the head. Then again—three, four times, as if chopping furiously at a block of wood. Soft clucks echoed across the summit, and blood splattered on the snow. He looked up then, turning toward Gary, and bringing his club upright. *"Deaaathhh...!"* he whispered, grinning wildly.

Gary dropped the radio.

"You...you...you're...dead...."

"Ohhh...oh-hoooo! *Deeeathhh!*"

"...and I ran. He took off after me. He stopped to smash the radio, then came after me. I might have been thinking about the place where John Karber fell, and I know now I found it. He chased me down through that cave. I don't know how I got away from him...and I can't remember much after that." He shrugged at Janey, then gave her a smile.

Janey scooted over to him. She threw both arms around his neck and hung on to him for a long time. Tears squeezed from her eyes, and he held on to her, too.

Outside the cave, the wind and snow blew quietly.

THE SHELTER HALF FLAPPED in the wind, and Gary could see that the material was tearing. He sighed, then began fumbling for the tools, hoping that he wouldn't wake Janey. The least he could do was let her sleep while she had the chance.

He heard the nylon rip softly again.

Janey was awake from the first moment Gary stirred, because she wasn't really sleeping—not here, not while they were still on this mountain. She listened as he sat up. He stayed there for several minutes, and she remained quiet but ready to help in case he might be having another one of those nightmares. But he started moving again, turning a light on, then fidgeting around with something else. Tools clinked softly. He crawled from his sleeping bag, and she rolled over to see what he was up to. She saw him kneeling next to the cave opening, pulling against the shelter half. A moment later she could hear the whacking of metal against rock.

"Gary? What are you doing?"

"Oh, one of the corners tore loose, that's all. I'm tying it back down. Just go back to sleep."

"I wasn't sleeping . . . just resting mostly. Do you need some help?"

"No, I've got—"

Janey rolled in the opposite direction. They both heard it— a quiet ripping of nylon material that sounded as if it came from inside the cave. Gary swung the light toward the inner shelter half. A long vertical gash was torn through the center.

And as if by magic a glint of shiny metal appeared in the tear, reflecting the light.

Moving.

They heard the labored breathing from behind the nylon flap.

Janey screamed, and a dark form lunged inside.

9

MARTIN AND GRADY WALKED out the side door to the parking lot. "It must've been one hell of an invention from what I heard," Martin was saying.

Grady shrugged. "That's one way of putting it." He sighed. He had to pause as they came to the pair of newspaper coin boxes outside the door. Both papers featured front-page stories datelined Washington, D.C. One was an announcement from the Air Force that they intended to order one hundred C-181 Transport planes. The other came from the Army. Upon completion of a redesign, they were going to buy a fleet of XM-221 helicopters. They had already bestowed on it the name HM-221A Valkyrie.

"Of course," Martin continued, "I really didn't learn that much about the gas, or whatever it was. Only that it caused a lot of problems for people. Present company included," he finished in a whisper.

To say the least, Grady thought bitterly. That was the Army. They had never been in the business of solving personal problems. All they did was give you a radical new slant on the ones you already had, or else give you a whole new set.

The men stopped again at the end of the sidewalk where two colonels offered their salutes and congratulations to Grady, wishing him well on his early retirement. He would have laughed if there had been any humor in it.

"How the hell did they hear about it so soon?" Martin puzzled.

"Old command curse," Grady answered, throwing his things onto the back seat. "The CO is always the last one to hear about anything." He turned to thank Martin for all he had done as deputy commander, and wished him success. His last official act as commanding general of Fort Endicott, Montana, was to return Martin's salute.

"I'll miss you, Tom. But you know that you and Martha are always welcome here as long as I'm in command. What the hell?" They both looked up in shock as Grady's ex-secretary came flying through the door, almost knocking over one of the coin boxes. She was yelling at them, waving both arms frantically.

"What are—" Grady started to say as he leaned out the window.

"Your radio!" she cried. "Turn on your radio!" and she barely got herself stopped at the car. "AM 630! Turn it on! Hurry!"

"...REPEATING OUR TOP STORY: former U.S. Army First Lieutenant Gary S. Palmer, the man allegedly responsible for the extraordinary interruption yesterday here at KSCM Radio, which broke the story about an Army cover-up of a poison gas leak into the atmosphere around Mount Kota National Park, is indeed alive and well as he claimed. For the latest update we go to Dale McClain who is standing by at Sioux County Hospital."

"This is Dale McClain, KSCM Radio News, at Sioux County Hospital, where the strange odyssey of Lieutenant Gary Palmer continues to unfold. I have just talked briefly with him, and with Miss Janey Burns of Sioux Creek. She has been with Palmer throughout an ordeal that he says began in Kansas five days ago, and ended less than two hours ago when the pair walked away from Mount Kota and were picked up and brought here by two park rangers. Both of them were on the mountain yesterday at the Army installation that was destroyed by an aircraft crash, and Palmer did broadcast the message about the gas leak. They had left the building only minutes before the accident occurred.

"Even more incredible, however, is the fact that they brought another man down with them. According to Palmer, he was a survivor of last September's crash of Air Force Flight J-440, and somehow survived for eight long months at the summit of the mountain. Unfortunately, the man was near death by the time he arrived here, and I was handed a report only moments ago that he died while in emergency surgery. His identity is still unknown.

"Because of injuries sustained on Mount Kota that required immediate attention, neither Palmer nor Miss Burns was able to relate their entire story at this time. But Palmer insisted that not only is everything he said over the air yesterday true, but also he has evidence in his possession that will prove it. These papers, he said, will be turned over to an attorney for safe-keeping until he presents them to the press. He would elaborate no further except to say, and I quote: 'I just heard that the Army tried to declare me dead. Twice. They did it because of everything that happened on the mountain.' He added that KSCM Radio News will get his exclusive first interview about the entire story because, and I quote again: 'It was KSCM's broadcast that I screwed up. It's the least I can do for you guys.' So we at KSCM will be standing by for that interview just as soon as he and Miss Burns are released from medical care and are ready to talk.

"This is Dale McClain, KSCM Radio News, reporting from Sioux County Hospital."

"Thank you, Dale. In a closely related story coming from Yakima, Washington, Mr. and Mrs. Gordon Palmer, Lieutenant Gary Palmer's parents, were utterly shocked to learn yesterday that their son, declared dead by the Army, is still alive.

An honor guard participated in Palmer's funeral last October 2. The Palmers heard the story about their son's broadcast over KSCM yesterday and immediately got in touch with their congressman, Phillip McGee. Both McGee and U.S. Senator James W. Cray of Seattle announced that they will personally accompany Mr. and Mrs. Palmer to Fort Endicott and Sioux Creek, and afterward will investigate the Army's cover-up in the matter. Senator Cray, a junior member of the Senate Armed Services Committee, said in a short press conference that . . .''

Grady turned the radio down. There was something to laugh about after all, and a slow grin split his features. ''I'll be a son of a bitch!''

''Oh, man!'' General Martin sighed, pushing the cap back on his head. ''The shit is gonna hit the fan now.''

''Well, I'd suggest that you call the airfield and stop the plane that's about to leave for Andrews Air Force Base,'' Grady said, starting the car. ''You're the commanding general now, but if it were up to me, I sure as hell wouldn't want to try and answer all the questions on the way.''

Martin nodded.

Grady backed his car from the parking stall.

''Hey, Tom, hold on. I was sort of hoping you'd stick around. I'm not sure if I can handle all this....'' But Grady was driving from the parking lot. ''Hey! Where are you going?''

''Home to change clothes.'' Grady waved. ''Then I have to go visit somebody in the hospital.''

A historical thriller reminiscent of
The Eye of the Needle and *The Day of the Jackal*

THE MAN
ON THE
TRAIN
W.J.CHAPUT

A German spy with orders to assassinate Winston Churchill puts his
deadly plan in motion during the prime minister's historical visit to
President Roosevelt in 1941 to enlist the aid of Americans in World
War II Europe.

*"Rich wartime atmosphere, an unusual setting . . . lift this one
above the pack of Nazis-afield adventures."*

—Kirkus

Available now at your favorite retail outlet, or reserve your copy for shipping by sending your
name, address, zip or postal code, along with a check or money order for $4.70 in the U.S.
and $5.25 in Canada (includes 75¢ for postage and handling) payable to Worldwide Library
to:

In the U.S.	In Canada
Worldwide Library	Worldwide Library
901 Fuhrmann Boulevard	P.O. Box 609
Box 1325	Fort Erie, Ontario
Buffalo, NY 14269-1325	L2A 5X3

Please specify book title with your order.

 WORLDWIDE LIBRARY

MAN-1AR

**An action-packed adventure
about deception, double cross and blackmail
in the seamy underworld of Europe**

SAMUEL FULLER
QUINT'S WORLD

Quint, an aging professional bloodhound, must locate a missing tape for an international syndicate—a tape with information that could change the world.

Available now at your favorite retail outlet, or reserve your copy for shipping by sending your name, address, zip or postal code, along with a check or money order for $4.70 in the U.S. and $5.25 in Canada (includes 75¢ for postage and handling) payable to Worldwide Library to:

<u>In the U.S.</u>

Worldwide Library
901 Fuhrmann Boulevard
Box 1325
Buffalo, NY 14269-1325

<u>In Canada</u>

Worldwide Library
P.O. Box 609
Fort Erie, Ontario
L2A 5X3

Please specify book title with your order.

 ® **WORLDWIDE LIBRARY**

QUI-1AR

Author of *The Doll*

JOSH WEBSTER

QUARANTINE

The CIA paid him well.
Now he's learning the deadly price of success

A brilliant scientist becomes a pawn in a deadly plot of vengeance and greed when he builds the ultimate weapon, a microscopic organism . . . that kills.

Available now at your favorite retail outlet, or reserve your copy for shipping by sending your name, address, zip or postal code, along with a check or money order for $4.70 in the U.S. and $5.25 in Canada (includes 75¢ for postage and handling) payable to Worldwide Library to:

In the U.S.	In Canada
Worldwide Library	Worldwide Library
901 Fuhrmann Boulevard	P.O. Box 609
Box 1325	Fort Erie, Ontario
Buffalo, NY 14269-1325	L2A 5X3

Please specify book title with your order.

 ® **WORLDWIDE LIBRARY**   QUA-1AR